VANTHEA: THE RISE OF ALDUIN

Published by Spines Publishing Platform
ISBN: 979-8-89569-770-2

VANTHEA: THE RISE OF ALDUIN

TAL HADAD

CONTENTS

PROLOGUE

Tal and Mordechai were sitting in Tal's room, discussing the lore of their fictional world.

"So… show me what you came up with," Mordechai said and took a sip from his cup of tea.

"I'll read you the entire manuscript, alright?" Tal asked.

"Sure," he responded as he leaned closer to the blue lit screen, the soft clack of keystrokes from Tal's dancing fingers hum in his ears.

"But first I'll flash forward to this:

'You Dunbar[i]! You broke our deal,' a man said shakingly, tears welling in his eyes.

'Who do you think you're speaking to?! Don't dare take that tone with me! There was nothing I could do. In truth, my soldiers killed them before I could have prevented it,' the lord said.

---

[i] (Elvish) Asshole

'You... You promised to let them live! Because of you, piece of shit, I lost everyone I cared about. Everyone.'

'In Vaonie's name, continue talking to me like that and I'll reunite you with your family! Even as a vampire, you are no match for me. I am your lord. Know your place.'

'You fucking... Pfft... Fine. Fine. May I be excused?' the man ground his teeth and clenched his fists.

'Yes, get out. And you are officially relieved of your current position, taken down a rank, to teach you that I am the boss. Got it?'

'Yes, my lord,' he growled.

'Dismissed.' The lord waved the man away as if shooing a mosquito.

The angry man rushed out of the throne room.

'Shut the door behind you. Vaonie preserve us, he had already left. Imbeciles. Every last one of my subjects—a goddamn imbecile. You,' he pointed at one of the royal guards, 'yes, you, close the door. Now!'

The guard did as instructed, releasing a beastly growl of submission. The man rushed to the office of a Vaermiraiit[ii] general. The noise of a door being kicked down echoed around the halls of the castle.

'You better have an explanation for barging in like that, half-breed. Our lord may have hellishly strong patience with you, but I sure don't,' the general yelled out, sitting on the chair in his office.

'You had one job. One fucking job and you couldn't do it

[ii]   (Omnitongue) Vampire.

properly!' he hollered, his face wet from the tears he had shed.

'So, he told you.'

'And what if he did?'

'He should have waited. An important military operation is coming up,' he said coldly.

'Wha-' he exhaled heavily, 'are you kidding me? I lost my entire family,' the man cried and then laughed hysterically.

'We all lost dear ones. Get over it. You came up to us. Need I remind you? Half dead. Begging us to give you power. Don't make this about us. This was your decision. Face the consequences and get out of my face.'

'I will not!' the man punched the wall, which shook so hard it almost collapsed.

'What did you say, you little shit?'

'Fight me,' the man said, laughing and sobbing at the same time.

'Why would I waste my time fighting a wimp like you?'

'Because if you don't, I will tell all your soldiers what a coward you are. That sure would have an effect on morale.' He smirked.

'I... You will regret this, Elf.'

'I regret being alive; I have absolutely nothing to lose.' He lowered his head and stared at the floor with his fists clenched. 'So be it. Tomorrow, a duel in front of my entire garrison. Be there, or I will set a target and a sum on your head. Understood?'

'Yes.'

'Good. Leave me.'

The man nodded, picked up the huge metallic door and put it back in its place. It fell down almost immediately, and with that, the general's growl became even more menacing.

The day passed. Despite having no access to sunlight in the underground castle of the vampires, they had their own way of telling the time. Some used magic for that; some had a weird biological clock of thirst for blood with which they could tell the time. Nevertheless, the time for the duel had come. Thousands of vampires attended it, serving as an audience. After all, it was a unique occasion to bear witness to a fight between a vampire general and a mere newly turned member of their society. The fight was to take place in the underground training facility, one that looked almost exactly like a Colosseum—maybe for that exact purpose?

Sounds of beastly growls, screams and incomprehensible noises of excitement engulfed the arena from all directions.

'Blood! Blood! Blood! Blood!' the voices of the soldiers echoed in terrifying unison.

They bashed their heads in their seats, their weapons in each other, and their hands in claps of excited applause. At the highest row sat the members of the high court of vampires alongside their lord, sitting on a much bigger chair than theirs. He had an excited look on his face, saliva dripping from his mouth. This battle had awakened his primal thirst for bloodshed, or just blood altogether.

A vampire dressed in dark blue silk robes launched herself from her chair to the middle of the Colosseum. She served as one of the main advisors to the lord and, now it seemed, also as the official judge of the battle.

'Ladies and gentlemen! Are you ready for some violence?!'

The crowd went wild and shouted in unified agreement; their voices merged into one strong and scary roar.

'Are you ready for some blood?!'

The crowd roared again.

'Then let's get right down to it!'

She took out a knife and cut the veins of her left hand, causing blood to drip down. Then, she began chanting something with her fingers, making the blood at her feet accumulate into a thick red mist that allowed her to levitate above the ground. After a few meters up, she stopped and parted her lips.

'The fight we have today is going to end very fast, unfortunately, because one of them would never stand a chance. Please welcome our fighters!' she chuckled with an evil grin.

The general shot himself from his seat straight to one side of the arena, making a superhero landing.

The crowd, recognizing their high commander, was shouting even louder in excitement. Considering how powerful he was, they had no idea how strong his opponent could be. Then, after approximately four minutes, his opponent walked inside, a bit out of balance, with a bottle of red wine in his right hand.

"I mean, I love wine too, but one should know when to stop, right?"

His eyes were red like he had recently cried. Having recognized him, the audience began booing in disappointment. After all, his rank in their army was very basic; there was no way he could actually put up a fight worth watching.

The man did not let that destroy his morale; he walked slowly and confidently. When he reached his assigned position in the ring, he opened the bottle and began chugging it all in. When he finished, he threw it to the side, shattering it.

'I hate how difficult getting drunk is now that I'm a piece-of-shit vampire like you,' the man said, laughing bizarrely.

'Do you actually believe you could defeat me while intoxicated? I mean, it was clear to me that you were a fool, but not that much,' the general chuckled.

'We'll see about that,' the man smirked.

'Fighters, pick your weapons from the rack and get ready!' the judge yelled out.

The general picked out a big spear and shield, finally taking up a battle stance.

'I don't need a weapon to defeat you. Good-old magic should be enough to end your pathetic life,' the man said and pointed at his foe.

The general let out a deep, rumbling laugh and moved his spear in a way of telling him to come at him—a provocation. The man smirked again but stood in his place, not moving an inch. He began whispering something. He raised his hands in the air, performing a stance that was never seen before. Maybe that of a mage? Curious, the general began charging toward him with the spear pointing forward. While running, he pierced his fingers, letting a bit of blood drip down to the floor and then used his fingers to cast a spell. He rubbed the blade of the spear in a caressing motion, causing it to start glowing in strong crimson – the color of blood. Just about two meters from his opponent, he changed his course and began sidestepping around in a circle at an extreme speed, unleashing a wave of blood spikes every now and again, using blood that oozed out of his self-inflicted wounds.

The man reacted with a laugh that came in jagged, uncontrollable bursts, a manic, almost strangled sound. He formed a light-blue magic barrier around himself in the shape of a ball, one that none of the spikes could penetrate. Understanding this, the general stopped his little game and growled. He turned his sight toward the disappointed eyes of his lord and immediately cut off his left hand. Gazing at his wound, he made his arm grow back and chanted a spell. The blood that was splashed on the ground started glowing and levitating around him.

'Watch and learn, oaf.'

'Uh-huh.'

The blood was circling around his spear; it looked like a small tornado hinting at the upcoming doom of its target. The man remained in his place, standing and grinning like he was watching an entertaining show, tears dropping from his eyes. Having had enough of his opponent's arrogance, the general prepared the stance once used by the Spartan Peltasts. He shouted and shot it toward the man. It made a loud bang and flew at an incredible speed. The tornado of blood glowed stronger and made a screeching sound as though it was alive, flying with the power of a strong wind. The man didn't change his smug look and waited for the spear to come. The moment it entered his vicinity, he formed seals with his left hand.

'Watch and learn!'

The moment his chant was done, he moved the fingers of his right hand in a flicking motion. The crowd went nuts, anticipating the death of the man who went way ahead of his league. Or so it seemed... Until a bright circle, coloured green, enveloped the spear and disappeared alongside it with a 'whoosh' sound. Loud noises of shock were heard across the arena.

'What... What did you just do?' the general asked in confusion.

'Just a thing I picked up in my time at the Exploitation school of The Order.'

The man changed his stance, intimidating his bamboozled opponent.

'Now that everyone knows what I'm capable of, it is my turn. You have no idea who you're dealing with. I may be a young vampire, but a young Elf I am most certainly not! You and all who helped you destroy my life will pay! Jul u uli! Veridia u uli! Vetir uli, dreem din uli[iii]," the man chanted.

Immediately, the arena was engulfed by a cold breeze followed by a thick mist of ice. No one could see inside, not that they cared, considering that they were busy dealing with sudden sharp pulses of immense pain; their bodies were shutting down. Apparently, he knew of the vampires'

[iii] (Omnitongue) Sky of ice! Earth of ice! (To) call ice, (to) disappear the ice.

weakness to the cold, which was kept a secret inside the community itself. The audience began screaming for help from their lord, running around trying to escape the claws of the chilly mist that was turning more and more invisible as time went by. Despite having perfected his own resistance to the cold, the lord refused to lose his army just for a stupid conflict. He growled loudly, launched himself from his throne and stood two meters away from the mage.

He lifted his hand, formed seals of a spell with the other and grabbed the man's throat, choking him firmly. The man began gasping for air and twirling; nothing he tried had worked. He had no idea that the lord was this powerful, penetrating and nullifying all of his magical shields. After a few minutes, his face turned blue as he was reaching his limit. He formed seals with his fingers, exterminating the mist he had created.

'Good boy. I told you to know your place, didn't I?'

He released his grip from the man's throat, making him fall straight to the ground. He was choking, coughing and breathing heavily.

'I will kill you one day, you son of a bitch! I will kill all of you.' He sobbed.

'Uh-huh. Never stop believing,' the lord said, laughing. He kicked the man in the face, making blood ooze out from his nose and mouth.

'Soon, I will kill him and will find a way to get you back. Trust me... I love you...' The man whispered to himself, spitting out blood.

He stood back up and walked away. The crowd was caught in awe.

'All of you, the show is over. Dismissed.' The lord shouted to the audience.

The crowd dispersed. He walked toward the general, who was lying on the ground, tasting the earth. He helped him up. The general was wheezing and found it difficult to stand properly, exhausted and gravely injured.

'Seriously?!'

'Wha-what?' the general responded.

'How dare you embarrass me like that?! Now I have to fight that asshole. What a fucking disgrace, and you call yourself a vampire general?'

'He... He is powerful, my lord. I did... the best that I could,' he said, still trying to catch his breath.

'Hmph.'

The lord slapped the general so hard he fell back to the ground. Dirt is an acquired taste, after all.

'Don't ever disappoint me again!' the lord said, turned his back and walked away.

CHAPTER ONE

"**B**efore the chaos and betrayal there was a joyous day, the birth of a son, that is where the story truly begins. It was 13th of Ruyen, 1076 MDW on planet Syluetta."

Between heaving pants, piercing screams of, 'It hurts,' reverberated through the village of Vel Tissia Ke Aldu[i]. Sweat beaded Elys's furrowed forehead, dampening her black hair as she squeezed the hand of the white-haired man bent over her, who wore the cream-colored royal elvish attire of a clan chief.

Her white-knuckled grip was so tight, Chief Aeden struggled to soothingly say, 'Breathe, sweet Elys.' In this special moment, he recalled that her bravery and strength, even during pain, is why he chose her as his wife.

---

[i]   (Elvish) The Tree of Hope.

'You are faring well, Mother. None could do better,' their daughter, Veridia, said.

The piercing screams were cut off by a cry belonging to an entirely different entity.

Veridia, bouncing on the tip of her toes, squealed excitedly.

'It's a baby boy! May the light of Merissa shine through him.' Three gold bracelets on the man's wrist clanged together as he delivered the newborn from beneath Elys's silk skirt. 'Rejoice!' His bear claw necklaces rattled exuberantly as he cradled the babe in his bare arms for he wore nothing more than a silk loincloth and leather sandals. Like his attire, intricate ice-colored facial tattoos of a roaring bear marked him as a healer mage. 'How will you name him?'

'Gods be praised. His name is Alduin. Alduin Faëli.' Aeden's eyes gleamed as he thrust his chest out. 'May he grow to be a strong fighter and bring peace to our lands.'

'He is majestic. Isn't he?' a radiant smile spread across Elys's face.

'Indeed.' The healer coated the baby with a red ribbon and handed him to his parents.

'Hello brother.' Veridia gently caressed the baby's head. 'Mother, he is the loveliest baby I have ever seen. I already love him.'

'Brother!' Aeden called, 'Come, welcome your new nephew, Alduin.'

A tall, black-haired man, stationed outside the room to guard the family from intruders during the birth, laughed as he entered. Two long swords bearing the symbol of their clan — a pale bear baring golden fangs, were attached at the hips of his blue elvish attire, which glistened from the shards of platinum adorning it. 'I must witness what you've brought upon the world this time.'

'Are you drunk again?' Aeden asked.

'Am I ever not?' Ley chuckled. 'He has your snow-white hair, brother, so clean and pure.' He glanced up at Elys. 'I see he took your golden eyes.' Grinning with warmth and adoration at his nephew, he said, 'I will teach you great things and indulge you in my exploits when you come of age.'

'I am sure he would love that. Just don't teach him to be a drunken nomad like yourself,' Aeden said.

Elys smiled. Raising him was their task now and theirs alone.

The boy was growing up to be a powerful warrior with a greater-than-healthy sense of curiosity, courtesy of his uncle. Aeden was proud of his son yet found it increasingly difficult to express it. In his eyes, he, too, must earn the honor of wearing their clan's ice-coloured warpaint.

We leap a few years forward. Chirps and tweets of birds were heard throughout the landscape alongside other astonishing sounds of wildlife in the Euphatan region. His day began at dawn with breakfast, followed by morning practice overseen by his father. Breakfasts were the only occurrences where the entire family sat down together. Alduin learnt to cherish this special time because, unlike his friends, his family was incredibly busy, as clan reign was a difficult task to shoulder.

'As usual, you have prepared delicious food for us, my love,' Aeden said with a smile on his face.

'Thank you, my love. May Odrum bless our meal. Veridia helped me prepare it. You should thank her too.'

'Oh, right, how could I forget? You have become quite an amazing cook, sweetheart. A most marvellous woman we have raised, haven't we, Elys?'

'Absolutely. She will be a very fitting wife to a very fitting lord in the future.'

'She also ranked exceptionally in her physical examinations. Both caring and strong, yet only seventeen years of age! I am very proud of you, my daughter.'

Veridia blushed and continued eating.

'What about you, my son? Did you sleep well?' Aeden asked.

'Yes, Father,' Alduin said.

'Well enough for a few dozen kilometers run?'

'Yes, Father.'

'Good. Finish your breakfast and get dressed. We leave immediately.'

'Yes, Father,' he said and choked on his food.

'Don't speak while chewing... First, you must finish chewing and then utter your words. Don't choke needlessly... We have talked about this, Alduin... A seven-year-old should know that by now.'

Alduin finished chewing.

'Yes, Father. Sorry, Father.'

'Good. You don't have to look so frightened, dear; I only care about your wellbeing. This is not a scolding...'

'Mhm... Thank you. The food is very tasty, Mother. I love this combination of celery and dusk-lobster eggs.'

'I am glad you enjoy it, Vo Zuuviet[ii]. I know it is one of your many favorites.'

'By the way, Ley will be arriving in the village today. His latest adventure had just ended,' his father said, trying to excite him.

'Really? I must see him then!'

'I don't like Uncle Ley, father. He always reeks of Yasa[iii], and I never see the same woman exit his house in the morning. Why does he even wear that gold circlet of his? He doesn't even own any land. He is not a lord,' Veridia said.

'At least *he* is interesting and spends time with me!'

'He is only here for a few days a month!'

'You wouldn't understand, all you ever get is praise! All I've ever gotten from our father was training regimes and advice.'

'Making you way more capable than I am, so quit whining.'

'But what kind of life is that? Uncle cares for me...'

'Silence, children! Alduin, stop complaining about your father. He is doing the best he can.' Their mother shouted, eyeing her husband for aid.

'It is okay, my love. Listen, children, my brother and I are very different. You must learn to respect his way of life, Veridia. He gave up on his lordship to explore the world. It is what it is.'

'If you say so, father...' Veridia sighed.

'You never listen to me...' Alduin whispered and looked

---

ii (Elvish) My dearest.
iii (Elvish) Beer.

down at his plate in frustration, playing with what was left of his celery.

'Did you say something, honey?' his mother asked.

'Nothing.'

'Alright.'

Alduin sighed and took one last bite of his celery. The family had finished breakfast, and Aeden was already waiting outside for Alduin to get ready. He hurried to his room and donned the heavy combat armor his father insisted he wear—to grow accustomed to it should the need ever arise.

'Good. You are here. Let's go. Fast-paced running with sprints whenever I say so. Ready?'

'Yes, father.'

'Zul[iv], go!'

Aeden chanted a Cylie[v] spell and the pair started running toward the exit of the village. Alduin had no idea where they were heading but knew he was to simply follow. It was an approximately fifty-kilometers long run. Twenty-seven kilometers to the nearest frozen lake and then back through one of the polar bear habitats.

His father allowed absolutely no breaks because they allegedly give a person the mentality of giving up instead of going all-in. There must have been an ounce of truth to it as Alduin's agility had been improving wondrously. He hated how strict these workouts were yet always followed

---

[iv] (Elvish) Good.

[v] (Elvish) Time.

through, enjoying these rare moments with his father. After a few hours, they reached the village.

'Very well, Son. You have improved from last week. I am pleased.'

'Thank you... F-Father...' Alduin said, finding it hard to speak while catching his breath.

Aeden smiled, gazing at the impressive man his son was becoming.

'Father.'

'Yes?'

'Mother told me of an area in the southernmost forest where a rare phenomenon occurs once every two years. Could you take me there? She said I am old enough.'

'Sorry, Son. I must rush to the great court for a certain conflict between two noblemen. Maybe next time...' His father replied, patting his son on the head.

'You always say that.'

Aeden wore a disappointed look on his face.

'I'm sorry, Father...'

'I must go now. Have a nice day, my son.'

'Thank you. You too,' he frowned.

His uncle had overheard their conversation from behind one of the houses. He was flirting with two women but decided to leave them. Ley was considered quite the womanizer of the village, but this controversial reputation didn't seem to bother him one bit. He approached them just before they had parted ways.

'Did I hear you correctly, Alduin? You would like to go to the grand ceremony?'

'Yes!' He jumped up and down.

'Indeed, brother. Sadly, I am very busy at the moment. Could you take him instead?'

'I would love to. When would you,' he burped, 'like to leave?'

'As soon as possible, Uncle.'

'Then we shall depart right after lunch and one liter of Yasa[vi]. It is most beautiful in the evening anyways.'

'Thank you, uncle.'

'Gladly.'

Aeden patted on his brother's back in gratitude and left. Alduin and Ley began their journey south when lunchtime was over. The forest was located between a human town named 'Emerald Dawn', and a Snow Elf village named 'Vel Alis'a Resnem[vii]'. They stopped for Elvish Mer[viii] and stories of his uncle's adventures out in the wild, wild world.

'I will now tell you the story of how I met a very strange individual. At first, he looked like a regular lost child, but eventually, I discovered he was about to reign over the Merarian kingdom of the "Xierēnia" Ocean.'

'What are Merarians?'

'Long ago when the magi-' he hiccupped, '-cal races have just sprouted out of Theseus's seed, one of them was named Mitori. He fell in love with a few women in our planet, which led to the creation of a special kind of hybrid – the Merarian. It is a being that looks like a human but can also breathe underwater and communicate with sea-life.

[vi] (Elvish) Beer.
[vii] (Elvish) The Lit Horizon.
[viii] (Elvish) Coffee.

The Merarians lived in the different oceans, each one ruled by a kingdom of its own. Also, their appearances and cultures varied drastically across the kingdoms.'

'Why was he only *about* to become their king?'

'A few hundred years after my friend was born, Mitori decided to conduct an alchemy experiment using the souls of all Merarians as material. He attempted to turn himself into a god, but it didn't work, and the Merarian race was erased,' he hiccupped, 'this deed got him the nickname "The Greedy Alchemist". I met Thaxiobos before this had happened and aided him in his journey across our Tanla[ix].'

'Was he able to speak our tongue? How did you comprehend his words?'

'Yes. He was extremely intelligent. Even more than our clan's elders. I'm sure of it.'

'That is amazing.'

'It is.' He burped, 'Would you like to drink a bit of my Yasa? It seems I poured myself way too much again,' Ley let out a hearty chuckle.

'Sorry, uncle, but Father said I shouldn't be drinking yet. And Veridia says you are an irresponsible alcoholic.'

'I always liked your sister. It is a shame she has such vile thoughts about me.' He laughed.

Alduin shrugged and sipped from his cup of Mer. He was always fascinated by the stories of his uncle. 'Where did you travel together?' he asked.

'We traversed between different countries and continents in Syluetta and Earth. He taught me a thing he called

---

[ix] (Elvish) Planet.

"Science", and I taught him about Snow Elf magic and different cultures I've stumbled upon.'

'Could you teach me Snow Elf magic as well?'

'Sure. Maybe tonight... We'll see...' He burped.

Alduin smiled broadly.

'Anyways... This person's name was Thaxiobos. To tell you the truth, I have no clue regarding his whereabouts or well-being, but I hope he is fine. We went hiking in the mountains and traversed through vast landscapes of deserts, beaches, savannas and so forth. His knowledge of science allowed us to survive starvation, plagues, and even tornadoes! This one time he combined ice magic with what he called a "Gun" to unleash a tall ice wall that managed to keep away a Heelisa[x]. I could have died many times if it weren't for him.'

'This person sounds very talented.'

'He really is,' he smiled and blushed.

'Do you think I'll ever have the chance to meet him?'

'I-I don't know. I hope not...'

'Why? Didn't you like him?'

'No, it's not that. Pfft... It's more complicated than that. Let's drop the subject, please,' he sighed.

'Okay.'

'Well... Time to go now. You wanted to witness the ceremony, didn't you?' he sighed again.

'Yes! Yes! Yes!' His face glowed up.

'Let us depart then!' he said, letting out a strong exhale. Ley's exhale put out the fire.

------

[x]   Elvish) Tsunami.

'How did you do that?'

'You will learn in due time. Let's go.'

They continued running toward the forest, fighting off any hostile wildlife that stood in their way. Ley taught his nephew a simple ice ball spell that can knock out animals as big as a deer. The chant was 'Senkel u Uli[xi]'. After a few days, they finally reached their destination, and Alduin's jaw immediately dropped to the ground. They had arrived just in time to witness the beauty of the ceremony. It was performed by some of the magical reindeer that inhabit the forest. They stood in a circle and sang in a strange language resembling Elvish. Maybe a unique dialect? Every now and then strong beams of light in different colours were shot off into the sky and made an explosion sound. It was beautiful. As though an accord had been struck between them and Lune – Goddess of the night.

'Are they celebrating something?'

'Yes. They are celebrating a new year.'

'Wasn't New Year's Eve a few weeks ago?'

'Every species has their own concept of time. So yes, but also no.'

'Ah.'

'Would you like to know how I call them?'

'Absolutely.'

'I call,' he hiccupped, 'them "Rainbowers", because of the color of their antlers and hooves,' he burped.

'Ah, very original.'

'Yes!'

[xi] (Omnitongue) Ball of ice.

'They are so pretty.'

'They are,' he shed a tear.

Alduin's smile grew even larger. He was mesmerised by the lights and colours. It was a good day. When they got back to the village, his uncle gave him a long hug and went on yet another journey. He would visit them occasionally, each time wearing clothes influenced by the cultures he had explored, and with a new story to tell. Of new magic. Of new species of creatures. Of new races. Despite the vast differences in origin and appearance, all these outfits had one ongoing theme – looseness and adventure-seeking. One of Alduin's most cherished moments with his uncle happened when he was approximately ten years old.

It began at the dining table for breakfast. His mother prepared some cheese alongside tuna fish, fresh bread and a bunch of cooked algae. Wheat couldn't naturally grow in these harsh, snowy mountains, but the clan elders knew enough about magic to bypass that. Agriculture in the village was limited by its variety, but it did, in fact, exist to a satisfying extent. He finished his breakfast, kissed his sister and mother on the cheeks and departed. His father was waiting for him outside, per usual. That day's agenda was cardio, archery practice and then a bit of battle tactics.

'Are you ready, son?'

'Always.'

'Follow me. Don't fall behind.'

'Yes, father.'

It was their usual route though a bit longer, sixty kilometers instead of fifty. Fast-paced running to the nearest lake and then back through some 'Dorynie' habitats, gigantic wolf-like creatures native to their land. The purpose of going through these predator territories was to force him to learn to adapt, improvise and overcome sudden enemy attacks. Wild beasts are highly predictable which made them fitting targets for practice for a future 'Hekket' – an ancient name given for a clan lord's body-guard during the first era of the Snow Elves, thousands of years ago. They were specially trained in combat, magic and battle tactics, the 'Special Forces' if you will. On their way back, Aeden announced the beginning of the exercise. It was explained in a rather simple manner, but as these things usually go, they are easier said than done.

His task was to stealthily take down at least five Dorynies using a bow, while his father would protect them against him, acting as their beast-master. They were to begin at dawn.

He used 'Kentri Dorynie[xii]', an animal detection spell his father taught him, that was invented by the Wood Elves. Glowing red flames appeared out of the blue, signalling where every Dorynie was in the radius of half a kilometer. He climbed slowly on top of a small snowy hill and scanned his surroundings. His first target was a Dorynie guarding the entrance to a tiny fishing spot all by itself. He knelt, loaded his bow and shot seven arrows directing to the head, one after the other, at an incredible speed. Six of them hit their mark, and the seventh hit the neck. Neverthe-less, it was slain, and it was already time for him to change his position, he must not get caught.

[xii] (Omnitongue) (To) detect Dorynie.

He escaped to another hiding spot. His next kill was a pair of two sleeping Dorynies, about two hundred meters from the rest of the pack. He prepared his bow and peeked again, rendering his head vulnerable. Suddenly, he heard the whistle of arrows and took cover. His father had found him and shot fifteen arrows in his direction, as a warning perhaps.

Alduin thought hard about his next move and decided to try a useful spell that Ley had taught him, one that turns the caster invisible and leaves an ice-clone as a decoy. As he wasn't proficient in it, he focused on cloning nothing but his head, so it would appear like he was peeking again. He cast it and dashed to another hiding spot, to take down the sleeping targets. He knelt and took aim. Twelve or thirteen arrows should be enough to finish the job.

'Two left,' he thought.

While he was still fixing his sights on the last target, his father caught him. Grabbing Alduin by the jacket, he hoisted him up and delivered a firm punch to his chest. A gesture of respect and acknowledgment between men.

'Impressive, son. Well done.'

'Thank you, Father.'

'We should escape now. These beasts have an incredible sense of smell and sight.'

'Mhm.'

They sprinted back to the village and shared a few laughs.

'Your mother told me I am too strict with you. I hope you know I only do this for your own good. A man needs to be strong in this world. To protect those who are important to him. Nevertheless, I will try my best to be a little warmer.'

'It's alright, Father. I have grown used to it.'

His father nodded, unsure how to respond. They returned home in time for lunch. Aeden winked at his wife; she understood and smiled. Approaching them, she gave each a kiss before they sat down to eat.

'May Odrum bless our meal,' they chanted in unison.

Suddenly, Ley barged in. His entrance was abrupt, and something seemed off. He wore thick black robes that shrouded his entire body—oddly somber for someone who usually favoured 'fun' and 'vibrant' outfits.

'I just came back from the Interstellar Travel portal,' Ley said, his voice tinged with unease. 'I don't think I'll ever get used to the sensation. It's like someone's stirring my intestines in a pot with all their might. Oh, Elys, you've made food? Could I join you?'

'Of course.' Elys said and smiled.

'Oh, Ley. Your skin is as pale as the snow! What has happened to you?' Veridia asked.

'Yes, you look ill. Are you alright? Would you like me to fetch some herbs? Or maybe some warm soup?' Elys said.

'I'm perfectly fine, don't worry. Just tired, that's all. This adventure has taken quite a toll on me. I'd like to have what my favourite nephew is having.'

Alduin smiled and blushed, and Veridia rolled her eyes.

'Why are you dressed like that? Your outfits are usually so vibrant and full of color,' she raised an eyebrow in suspicion, 'you have never worn anything this dark before. Are you sure you're not sick, uncle?' Veridia said.

'I am just trying out something new. Is it not to your liking?' he smirked.

'If you say so...' She rolled her eyes again as her suspicion grew stronger.

The family finished their lunch and thanked Elys and Veridia for preparing it. Alduin had never fully understood what his sister did during the day; he was curious but not enough to ask. His mother would occasionally mention healing magic and sword practice, but Alduin had never thought to inquire further.

'Alduin,' Ley said.

'Yes, uncle?'

'Let's go to the market today. I'd like to buy a few things, and I'd appreciate your assistance in holding everything.'

'Ley needing help with lifting heavy things? You really are sick,' Veridia said.

'Veridia... Manners... Don't pry,' Elys said.

'Sorry, mother.'

'Apologize to your uncle, not to me.'

'I'm sorry, uncle.'

'It's quite alright, no worries. Would you like anything, Elys? Veridia?'

'No, thank you,' Elys answered.

'Get me a necklace so I can practice enchanting on it,' Veridia said.

'You got it!'

Veridia hugged her uncle and saw the pair out. Alduin seemed worried but refused to bother his uncle with further questions. He followed him to the big market in the village.

Despite being in the middle of a snowy wasteland, it was full of life. The sheer quantity of stores, enticing smells, and children's laughter was amazing. The houses were mainly made of wood and stone, which were covered by snow most of the year.

The market had stalls run by fishermen, butchers, herb collectors, blacksmiths, cooks, and bakers, among others. The primary source of light at night was candles—imagine how beautiful it must have been. Alduin loved the market. It was teeming with life and modernity—so many people to talk to, so many delightful delicacies to taste. He had a passion for food and shiny objects. He helped his uncle pick out a necklace for Veridia, choosing a leather amulet with a blue gem attached. It wasn't too expensive, only about sixteen 'Samarices[xiii]'. Ley bought a bundle of healing herbs before sitting down to share a meal with his nephew. They decided on walrus soup with greens and potatoes.

Ley ordered two servings for himself alongside a liter of Yasa[xiv] in a wooden flask. Alduin had to refuse three whole times before he would stop offering him to taste it. They reminisced about the past and finished with a quick story told by Ley. When they exited the store, Ley stopped mid-step, facing a jewelry store.

'Would you like anything?' his uncle asked.

'You already paid for my meal, it's fine.'

'Come on, it's on me.'

'Fine, fine. Let me see what they have.'

[xiii] Currency.

[xiv] (Elvish) Beer.

Alduin approached the merchant's stall.

'Everything's for sale! A bit of this and a bit of that. Jewelry for all ages!' the merchant yelled out for potential customers.

'Excuse me,' Alduin said.

The trader bowed. 'Blessings of Merissa upon ye.'

'May her light shine through you,' Alduin recited.

He smiled. 'Hello, child. How can I help you?'

'Do you sell bracelets?'

'Just the ones I have on display.'

'Ah. Hmm...'

Alduin observed the available options until he set his eyes on a silver bracelet. The sign next to it read '15S^{xv} for a custom engraving'.

Ley suddenly approached them. 'Well, Alduin, see anything you like?'

'Yes, I'd like this one, please. Could you engrave something on it for me?'

'Sure. What would you like to be written?' the seller asked.

'Uhm... "To Alduin, from the best uncle in the world!". Thank you.'

'How cute. Is *he*,' the merchant pointed at Ley, 'the mentioned uncle?'

'Guilty as charged,' Ley chuckled.

'That will be one hundred and thirty-five Samarices, please.'

[xv] S – Samarice.

Ley raised an eyebrow. 'That's too expensive. Let's call it one hundred.'

'Preposterous, the price is what I say it is.'

'One hundred and ten.'

'No.'

'One hundred and fifteen.'

'No!'

'One hundred and twenty then.'

'Fine. Hand them over.'

'Here you go.' He said, laughing.

Ley took out his wallet and paid. The merchant chanted something unfamiliar to Alduin which made his pointing finger glow in the color of red. He used it to engrave on the bracelet and then handed it to them.

'Thank you, uncle.'

'Gladly. Can we go now?'

'Yes.'

Alduin waved the merchant goodbye and followed Ley home.

CHAPTER TWO

The next winter hit hard. It was cold, very cold. He was not used to it yet despite having been born into it so many years ago. The sound of wolves howling in the distance woke him. Probably big Dorynies. His father called to him to aid the village against the attack.

'Alduin, fetch me my bow! Quickly, we haven't much time!' Aeden the Golden, they called him, befitting his status. Alduin followed his orders and quickly, running out of the house. As he glimpsed out of the door, into his line of sight immediately emerged three wolves.

'I knew those were Dorynies' howls,' he told himself quietly, smiling.

Three massive wolves, about three meters tall and one meter wide, emerged from the snow. Their dark fur, void-black eyes, and cutlass-like fangs made them a terrifying sight. Alduin tossed his father's bow to him and unsheathed his dagger, ready for the attack. Despite being one of the youngest in his village, he was the deadliest rookie. By nine, he'd mastered daggers and basic ice spells like Ice-Touch and Ice Spikes—impressive even for the Elves, who were physically stronger and more intelligent than humans. By eleven, he was a formidable opponent. But his goal wasn't just power; he sought to become a Hekket[i].

Alduin and his father moved in perfect sync, a result of years of training. Swiftly, they worked as one—while one shot an arrow, the other used it as a distraction to land a fatal blow to the wolf's vital organs with his blade. They took down one, then two, then three wolves, both eager to see Alduin's progress toward becoming a guard and following his father's footsteps.

With the raid's end came the shouts and cheers of celebration—and with them, a feast. Snow Elves, unlike the more gracious High Elves or humans, throw balls and feasts only when the occasion demands. Alduin knew today marked a great milestone; he had proven to both his father and village that he was worthy of the title of Hekket. He wondered if his uncle would attend. In Snow Elf villages, Hekkets are chosen once every decade (one hundred and ten human years) from villagers who are at least twelve and have earned the respect of their peers as both fearsome fighters and potential commanders.

'Only two more years!' he shouted to his father, grinning.

'Yes,' his father responded with a quick smile.

---

[i] Special forces (Snow Elf).

As the years passed, the villagers began to look up to Alduin, assigning him various tests to assess his resolve and virtue. One such trial involved sending him into the wilderness to survive alone for a year in the ice-cold arctic lands of Euphata. Alduin not only survived, but thrived, enduring for two years. Finally, on the 28th of Ruyen, 1220 MDW, the Hekket trials were set to take place, more than a hundred human years after the last one. Now thirteen years old, Alduin was ready to face his final test. His excitement was evident, his face adorned with a bright smile of pride. He woke early, hours before sunrise, to prepare for the important day ahead.

Tradition dictated that participation required a tribute: the bodies of two Dorynies, two snow tigers, three brown hares, one snow fox, one bear, and one snow lion. The hunt for these creatures must begin and end on the day of the trials. Alduin ate his breakfast—two slices of bread with leftover bunny stew his mother had prepared the night before—put on his hunting gear and stepped outside. He noticed three youngsters heading out to collect their own tributes. He waved to them, wishing them luck. They waved back and smiled.

'Vetir cillie, yur u cillie[ii],' he chanted.

This spell, named 'Cylie[iii]', showed the caster how much time they had left until a certain event was to occur, yet only skilled mages were able to configure it. It was mostly used by elven prophets to inform the people of upcoming

---

[ii] (Omnitongue) (To) call time, mark of time.
[iii] (Elvish) Time.

tragedies, like a natural disaster or the death of a specific person. When activated the spell coats the caster's arm with Elvish runes glowing in the color of ice, each one representing a unit of time.

His father, being the overseer of the trials, had installed magical seals on all exits, set to associate any 'virgin' Cylie with the end of the hunting phase upon detection. Alduin stepped out of the main gate. A whistling sound was heard and the runes on top of his arm began diminishing.

'Only four hours, huh? Tough, but I can do it,' he thought to himself and smiled briefly. 'Let's see... ' He tapped his fingers on his chin, 'Dorynies, bears and wolves are not active at this hour. I'll start with getting the rabbits, then the fox and then the tigers.'

Since brown hares were not native to Euphata, he had to find an artificial forest. The nearest one was the great 'Vel Anot'a Fa[iv]', created magically by the first chief of Alduin's clan many years ago. However, it was protected by a magic barrier that rendered it invisible. There was only one solution, 'Key' – the school of unsealing magic.

In Vanthea, magic was usually cast via chants spoken in the Omnitongue, requiring the utmost accuracy (including grammar) and with the risk of severe consequences. Failure in casting could result in a broad spectrum of punishment, with the best case being the spell not working, and the worst case being losing a limb (or multiple) forever. He remembered the words. They were 'Sner', 'Nor' and 'Din'. He closed his eyes and caressed his forehead.

[iv] (Elvish) The Invisible Forest.

'In which order?' he asked himself, 'come on, think.'

He opened his eyes and walked in circles, trying a few combinations in his head. Then, he decided on the one that 'rang the most bells'.

'Nor din sner[v].'

A floating ball of ice appeared out of the blue, one the size of a small city. Then, it cracked and revealed a great wonder of nature. His eyes sparkled with excitement and curiosity. He stepped inside.

'This is so bizarre. A forest inside ice?' he said, looking around. 'It is so green and colourful that it reminds me of my trips to Kontarah with my family.'

He slapped himself on the cheeks, realizing his awe was delaying him. He walked along the earthy paths, observing his surroundings. Finally, he found a few droppings that may belong to a rabbit. He knelt and proceeded to smell and examine the feces with his fingers.

'Yes, this is it.'

He climbed up a tall tree branch to gain more visibility and search for his first kill. Unlike humans, Elves have sharp hearing, keen vision and better depth perception, which grants them the ability to locate such tiny prey. Even from a few kilometers away. After about two minutes he caught a glimpse of a tail. He took out his bow and shot it instantly, he mustn't lose this opportunity. Hunting is all about precision, timing and patience.

'Less than second, I am improving.' He said, with a big

---

[v] (Omnitongue) (To) release the forest.

smile drawing from one cheek to the other. 'Two bunnies to go.'

After a few minutes he heard a noise between two bushes, about six hundred meters away. He began sprinting silently toward the location. Once in front of the bush, he drew his dagger and unleashed a powerful thrust. A sharp, high-pitched squeal echoed through the air. A small family of rabbits was hiding behind it. One mother and her two offspring.

'They said three *bunnies*, not three *adult* bunnies. I'm done here.' A soft, bubbling giggle escaped his lips. 'Now, it's time to get out of here and start looking for a fox.'

He used the same spell to reveal the exit and jumped outside, eager to carry on. The next target was a snow fox – a rare, yet majestic find. At this time of day, they were either looking for food or hiding in holes in the ice for protection and warmth. He decided to linger around their usual hunting spots – lemmings or pools in the ice where they scour for penguins, fish or other small rodents.

Suddenly, as he was walking carefully on the ice floor trying to find one, he heard the blood-curdling roar of a mighty beast. At that fierce rumble, the hair at the nape of his neck rose, his heartbeat raced, and his mind flashed to a childhood memory.

'Are you coming, son?'

'Yes.'

'Today, we will practice a specific sword-art that my father taught me when I was your age. If you impress me with your progress, I will tell your mother to prepare your favourite food today! Is that enough motivation for you?'

Alduin's grin stretched so wide his eyes sparkled. 'Yes.'

'Good.'

He followed his father, who was as usual, sprinting rather than taking his time. He must not fall behind! A five-year-old elvish fighter of his reputation and repertoire should be able to keep up. They came to a pond wolves fished in daily.

Aeden threw a sword at him, testing his reflexes. Alduin let out a moan as he flinched. He managed to catch the sword, but a little too late. It slammed hard against his chest.

'Never lose focus.'

'Yes, Father.'

'I am now going to demonstrate a move called "Whirlwind Spider". Charge at me and land a horizontal strike to my chest.'

Alduin did as was instructed. Just before it seemed like the sword would slash open his father's torso, Aeden did a backflip, landing on all fours, stretched out. Using his left arm, he spun his body around, kicking Alduin, and knocking him off his feet. Then, Aeden moving into a left handstand and curling his muscular right arm, launched into the air. A pirouette ending in a vertical strike.

Alduin used his bare arms as a shield, crossing them in an X shape. The sickening sound of a bone cracking reverberated through the air. The vibration jolted up his arm. Acute pain ripped through his body, forcing shrieking screams, silencing everything around.

'You broke my right arm,' Alduin said in a hoarse ragged voice. Hunched over, crumpled in on himself, he leaned away from his father. 'My good arm.'

'It will heal. I heard Ley taught you restoration magic. Use it.'

Tears slid down Alduin's face as the sting of hot humiliation spread through his little body. 'I only know how to cast it with my good hand.'

'Then practice. Restoration magic is crucial. A Hekket must handle their own medical care. And I made sure the sword was dull enough not to cut you, but pain is important for training to be effective. You need motivation to dodge, or this would be futile.'

'Yes, Father.' He wiped away his tears.

Aeden threw him a note of the chants for restoration spells. 'I know you tend to forget things, so I prepared this for you.'

With his head cast down, he held the paper in his trembling fingers. 'Thank you, Father.'

'Gladly. Now heal yourself and practice this move on me.'

He schooled himself to serenity, as spells are more efficient when the conjurer is calm-minded.

'Benejil ant. Benejil tvek u ant[vi].'

It did not seem to work. He repeated it five times, then

[vi] (Omnitongue) (To) heal me. (To) heal body of me.

gasped with relief as the searing pain vanished and mellow warmth spread through his body.

'Now. Let's begin,' his father said firmly.

His father executed a horizontal slash, which Alduin failed to dodge. One of his ribs broke. Screams tore from him, but the frustration was sharper than the pain in his rib. So, healed himself and got back on his feet. Over and over again he was left biting back curses. No matter how hard he tried, he ended up wounded. Two hours later, he executed a graceful backflip. But before he could puff out his chest in pride, his father struck his head with his sword.

'Again!'

A couple of hours more and he dodged, backflipped, and practiced the pirouette. With the setting of the sun, today's training ended.

'Well done. With good reflexes, agility, acrobatics and coordination, you are sure to take your place as a Hekket[vii]. Your reward is well deserved.'

'Thank you, Father,' he said between huffs, struggling to catch his breath.

'Tomorrow, we will continue practicing it if I have time.'

The vibration of the earth beneath his feet from the

[vii] Special Forces (Snow Elf).

thunderous snarling and barreling advance of a furry, bulky predicator snapped his mind back to the present.

'What in Munesa[viii] is that? A bear'' his muscles clinched.

White paws smashing packed snow. Fangs bared. Growling with fury. Jaws gnashing, ready for the kill. Charging. Fast. Furiously. Almost on top of him. No time to waste. Alduin nocked the bow. Drew back the string. Shot two sharp arrows into the bear's gleaming, black eyeballs. Strategically blinding the beast. Without a second to lose, he fired three more into the bear's forehead. Promising a kill.

The mighty polar bear staggered. Faltered. Hit the ground with a crushing thud, throwing snow into the air.

Alduin exhaled slowly, 'that was close.' He tried to catch his breath. 'At least I don't have to find a bear anymore. Now, where is this stupid fox?'

He cut off the bear's head and attached it to his belt using a small strap of leather. The sun had risen, and the beginning of the trials was closing by. He had to finish his checklist before the Cylie[ix] spell wore out, or else he would be disqualified automatically, destroying both his father's and his own reputation.

He frowned and clenched his fists. He couldn't possibly locate a fox in such a short time. It was a small creature that matched the color of the landscape. Euphata was vast, and the snow was blinding. As his spirit started wearing off, he remembered something his uncle taught him. A spell

------

[viii] (Elvish) Hell.
[ix] (Elvish) Time.

named 'Animal Call' that he had learnt from his time with the Wood Elves. Their ancestors crafted it to improve hunting efficiency. Alduin decided to try it out.

'Hmm.... So, it's "An vetir yul jerda, ternas quo". And then I need to add the name of the animal, right?' he tapped his chin. 'So, fox is "Pheolet". Okay. An vetir yul jerda, ternas quo pheolet[x].'

The high-tone howl of a fox pierced the air, followed by the thud of its stomping paws as it rushed toward him. He was not sure whether the spell had made the animal obey or whether he chanted it wrong and caused the animal to go on a violent frenzy. It didn't matter, however, since foxes, even in a magical land such as this, were not dangerous enough for him to fret. He decided he mustn't wait and used the most basic offense magic he knew.

'Serandi u uli[xi]!'

An ice spike blasted from his hand and hit the fox right in its head, killing it immediately. He smiled.

'Okay, so... Three bunnies, done. One bear, done. One snow fox, done. Now it's time to find two tigers and a lion. I'll leave the Dorynies for the end, since they are the most dangerous on this list,' he said out loud, breathing heavily.

With the help of the Animal Call spell finding snow tigers and lions was rendered easier. He chanted it multiple times but couldn't see any clear sign of it working.

He ground his teeth. 'I don't have time for this. Let's try

---

[x]   (Omnitongue) I (to) call you animal, (to) come here fox.
[xi] (Omnitongue) Spike of ice.

calling them both at once. Father taught me to take risks, right? They're just a bunch of kittens.'

Almost immediately, as though karma was pulling the threads, he heard the roars of multiple 'kittens', as he liked to call them.

"Such an arrogant boy. Right, reader?"

There was one problem, though. It had quickly become apparent that he'd forgotten to specify the quantity of animals to be summoned. Indeed, two tigers had emerged... But also, a whole pack of lions!

He launched ice spikes and multiple arrows. Some missed. Others hit their marks. Three lions went down, then five, then eight, but he also had to look out for the tigers that came from behind him! He tried to look for an offensive spell that could hit multiple targets at the same time. For some reason, the ferocious beasts kept appearing out of nowhere, as if he had been still chanting the spell. The sheer number of predators was insane. He couldn't even count them all due to their annoying decision to move constantly.

Alduin's knees buckled as fear gripped his mind like a suffocating shroud, leaving only one thought—flee before he became these kittens' breakfast.

His father always said, 'When in doubt, make the doubt perish,' to which he responded with 'Easier said than done, father!' time and time again.

This time, he knew what his father meant. Doubt is natural in dire situations. *Doubt* wasn't the problem, letting it remain in your head was. In tough situations, act fast to avoid your demise. Keep your cool and find a solution with minimal risk and a high chance of success.

Sure enough, after a few minutes of dodging their claws and killing a bunch with ice magic and his dagger, an idea popped into his head.

He remembered fishing with his uncle. Ley enjoyed showing off spells he had learnt from his journeys. This time, with an area attack. It was a sort of an ice-release spell but was rather a manifestation of the snow around him, making it gather in the shape of a circle and then muster it together into very thick ice using powerful pressure. The snow had then turned into a circular blade that expanded its radius around him. As he got in the water, the circle began expanding and shrinking in some sort of vibration, cutting everything in a radius of a few dozen meters.

'This could work. If I can figure out the words... Hmm... YES! Uli, feni to balerisa set ant[xii]!' he screamed, almost desperately.

It worked. It took almost his entire energy, but it worked! The tigers and lions were immediately slain. He stood there alone, bleeding and sweating. It was very hard for him to breathe. He went way over his head with this spell.

'I hate those things! Stupid... Fucking... Kittens... And their stupid... Fucking... Claws.'

He suddenly fell to the ground, and in his mind, he heard his father's voice shouting 'No cursing, boy!'. He pulled his head out of the snow, rolled his eyes and got back on his feet. 'What an asshole!'

[xii] (Omnitongue) Ice, (to) form a blade around me.

'I heard that,' his father responded and made him fall to the ground again.

'Are you spying on me, father?' he asked in his mind but was answered by nothing but silence.

He scrambled to his feet, brushing the snow off his clothes with swift, jerky motions. He exhaled heavily.

'So, now I just need to kill a few Dorynies, and I'm done. Right?' he sighed. 'Damn, I almost died! I thought this test would be simple, just like the previous ones...'

He slapped his cheeks, 'Never mind. Dorynies are usually found in... Yeah. They are usually found in caves surrounding water sources, because their prey is animals that hunt fish, like foxes, wolves and bears. I think I remember seeing a pack of them yesterday. I'll try there.'

Only one rune remained on his arm. His chest rose and fell with uneven breaths, the weight of the deadline pressing down on him like a heavy iron gauntlet. He sprinted toward the location.

'Yes!' he yelled, 'they're here.'

The Dorynies remained in the same spot where he'd last seen them, likely hoping some kind of snack might appear before them. Ironically, that was exactly what had happened.

These predators are weak to fire, though Alduin didn't know any fire spells. He did, however, know how to light a torch and shoot flaming arrows. Agility and accuracy were his only allies now; missing the mark was not an option against such fearsome opponents.

He sneaked into their cave, trying his best not to make a sound. He must remain undetected. He took out a small vial of oil from his pocket and coated his arrows with it. Then, he knelt and picked up two stones. With a quick, practiced motion, he struck the stones together, sending a cascade of sparks. He held the oil-soaked arrow just beneath the brief flare, waiting as the flames caught its tip, igniting in an instant. The bang caused the Dorynies to wake up. A bone-chilling howl tore through the cave, deep and guttural, reverberating off the jagged walls.

He sighed. 'Good job, Alduin. Now they're looking for you.' He rolled his eyes. 'Let's hope I'm not tasty enough for their liking.'

He climbed up a tall rock and waited for his first victim to appear, crouching with his bow drawn. The shadows were his allies. A group of three Betas approached his location, sniffing and observing their surroundings. They were looking for him. He remained hidden and found a comfortable spot for him to take aim. He put his fingers on the string of his bow and launched three arrows directly to the skull of the first one. It made an ear-deafening squeal of pain that echoed through the air. The remaining two were left confused and surprised, unable to comprehend where the arrows came from. Their eyes glowed with an unsettling luminescence, cutting through the darkness like twin beacons of death as they were scanning for any sign of him.

But they weren't fast enough. Alduin used this opportunity to ignite five more of his arrows. When he was ready, he took them out one after the other with remarkable precision.

'Is that it?' he asked himself.

He waited a few seconds and then holstered his bow.

This was a poor decision. Another Dorynie had suddenly appeared behind him, howling and roaring toward the boulder he was standing on. It was trying to alert the rest of the pack of his location. He had no time to waste, no time to strategize.

He drew his dagger and leapt onto the creature's back. It twisted violently, kicking and thrashing to throw him off, but Alduin dug his fingers into its fur, holding fast. Once his grip was secure, he drove the dagger deep into the creature's head, silencing it forever.

He backflipped off its back, avoiding the fall as the creature crumpled. Kneeling, he swiftly decapitated its head, attaching it to his belt. He crossed to the other side of the boulder, where the two remaining corpses awaited. Without hesitation, he severed the head of the next one, tying it to his belt. A smirk of victory tugged at his lips as he stood, the trophies swinging from his side.

His triumph was short-lived, however, shattered by a dark, ominous roar that came from afar, yet grew louder, closer—its power undeniable. Unlike the others, this roar was deeper, more thunderous, bone-chilling, and terrifying. It carried a presence of its own, and soon after, Alduin found its source: an Alpha Dorynie. Much larger and far more dangerous than any Beta, its crimson-red fur glistened in the dim light, its piercing blue eyes fixed on him with deadly intent. Each claw was the size of Alduin's arm, and two sinuous tails lashed behind it, moving in unison to strike.

'An Alpha? Oh no. Oh god.' He paced back and forth. 'Arrows wouldn't pierce its skin,' he thought.

His eyes darted from one shadow to the next, searching for a solution, any solution, that could keep him alive.

'Neither would my blade. I must use fire magic, but how? I don't know any flame spells, and I've never fought an Alpha before. Sneaking past it wouldn't work. Alphas are much more capable…'

Sweat clung to his forehead, mingling with dirt and grime, as a cold, shuddering breath escaped him, his chest rising and falling in shallow, desperate gasps. He didn't decide quickly enough. The Alpha had already caught his scent and was charging straight for him. Chills crept up his spine and raced down to his fingertips, his head spinning as a tingle spread through his limbs. Adrenaline surged through his veins, sharpening his senses as his body prepared for the impending threat. He turned and bolted, scrambling to find cover. As he ran, he scattered bait and pungent substances in every direction, hoping to confuse and delay the creature, but deep down, he knew it was only a matter of time before his fate caught up with him.

He recalled something his uncle had told him many times before, which he had always associated with cowardice. Now, however, it was starting to make a lot of sense.

'Today, I will tell you about the story where I was almost crucified by a unit of Roman soldiers that caught me stealing their gold. Oops, sorry... Borrowing their gold. My bad,' he laughed.

Alduin rolled his eyes. 'Roman?' he asked.

Ley took a sip from his wooden tankard. 'Yes, they were a Tri-' He burped, 'Trireme crew of the Roman Republic. I will tell you about them in greater detail next time.'

'Alright, go on.'

'I was visiting Port Piraeus in Greece. I assume you know of Greece, right?'

'It is where the ancestor of all ancestors lived.' Alduin grinned childishly.

'Yes! Can you recall which planet Greece is located on?'

'Earth?'

'Exactly. You are very knowledgeable, I see!'

'Thank you. Also, what were Roman soldiers doing in Greece?' Alduin's eyes visibly widened.

'That is a great question. Apparently, the Romans were controlling Greece at the time. Until like 189 MDW or so.'

'Ah.'

'Yes. So... This one time, a friend of mine told me about a naval unit rumored to possess such epic treasure that I just had to borrow it! Right under the deck in the ship's hold.'

'Have you fought at sea, Uncle?'

'Yes. Many times. I love the smell of salt and rum as I punch, kick, and slice up good men. And they were really good men. Tragic.'

'Yes... Very...' Alduin rolled his eyes again.

'I asked my contacts in Piraeus when the ship was deemed to arrive. I had to wait for two days before they finally came. Once they boarded, I jumped into the water and immediately began climbing onto the ship with my superb acrobatics. When an opportunity arose, I sneaked into the ship's hold and started "admiring" the biggest-looking chest I could find.'

'So, infiltrating their ship was that easy?'

'Nope,' he burped, 'They eventually caught me stea-... *Looking* at the treasure.'

'Ha!' Alduin said sarcastically.

'Unfortunately, some Dunbar[xiii] soldier decided it was time for their pre-voyage inventory assessment and caught me in the act.'

'And what happened then?'

'He started yelling for backup, and eventually, the captain had me seized. After a brief questioning, to which I responded with sheer honesty, he had decided to beat me in the head with the gold I was searching for. It was so very shiny.'

'You kind of deserved that though...'

'Right, you are. Anyways... They locked me up in a cage. I heard the captain telling his men that he was going to a tavern nearby to relax a bit. I waited for the next change in guard, which took a few hours of utter boredom. When it finally happened, I used magic to make myself appear like their captain and convinced the guard to release me.'

'Did he actually believe you?'

'Yes. I shouted, "the prisoner escaped!" And rallied up my men to try and find me. I even joined them in their search for a few hours.'

[xiii] (Elvish) Asshole.

'So stupid...'

'Yes. After it stopped being funny, I just said "I found him," and turned myself back. Their faces. You should have been there. They were so terribly confused!'

Alduin's shoulders trembled as he struggled to catch his breath between laughs.

'They circled me awfully quickly, so I just sprinted toward the captain's quarters and grabbed the shiniest thing I could find. It was a golden goblet with a bunch of diamonds attached to it. Then I immediately used that invisibility spell I taught you and escaped.'

'Why didn't you fight them? Humans are weak. You could have taken so much gold.'

'Killing soldiers of the Roman empire could get me in serious trouble,' he burped, 'Plus, I love,' he hiccupped, 'love the wine in Greece and wouldn't want to lose my access to it. See? Even mentioning it makes me all excited.'

'Uh... Uh-huh.'

'It was a time when I wasn't skilled enough in combat. A unit of that size could have easily made that day my last. I'd much rather like to keep my trousers, thank you.'

'Keep your trousers?'

'Survive, I mean. I like my trousers as much as I love life itself. Made them myself from the scales of a dragon and fur from a Dorynie Alpha. Look how astonishingly beautiful they are!'

'Right... What's your point?'

'There is no honor in death, child,' he burped, 'Life is great. There is plenty of food, booze and women to go around. Don't waste your life on futile, worthless shit.

Money isn't worth it, despite the nearly endless possibilities that it unlocks.'

Ready to put that lesson in action, he took his bow and rushed toward the exit, barely making it out without getting his hand torn off by the Alpha's claws. He made it outside and ran toward the Colosseum, which was positioned around two kilometers northeast of the village. One slip up and it could be the end for not only his chances to become a Hekket[xiv] but also to continue existing. It seemed that the Dorynie wasn't fully awake yet and found it hard to focus on one tiny Elf running away from it. It gave up eventually and headed back to the cave, to its newly pack-less life. In terms of nutrition, it should be able to survive for a few weeks since Dorynies were cannibalistic and consumed each other if the need arose.

Alduin couldn't care less about the Alpha's newly found social status in the wild. He made it to the arena when the last rune had almost faded out completely. Almost too late but also sufficiently early. A crowd at the entrance welcomed the children back from their quest with cheers and hurrahs. It had later become known that a few children didn't survive the ordeal. Some of them used to be Alduin's friends. The news hit him like a punch to the gut, the world

---

[xiv] Special Forces (Snow Elf).

around him suddenly feeling too heavy, too vast. He had always imagined he'd be able to mourn, to grieve, but now there was no time for that. His heart pounded in his chest, and his eyes blurred for a moment, but he forced himself to focus. He couldn't afford to break down, not now. Not when everything depended on him.

He decided to use his pain as fuel for the upcoming tests. After all, death was to be expected, and his goal was more important to him than depression. He vowed to mourn their death in the evening after it all ended. He carried on toward the Colosseum.

There were stalls where the candidates would place their spoils of war and get their entry ticket to the tournament. The Hekket tournaments, as they would later be known to Alduin, were brutal in every sense. It was a gladiatorial ring, but with a cruel twist. Rather than being given a weapon, each participant was forced to craft their own from the 'spoils' of the day's carnage—whatever they could salvage from the torn bodies of Dorynies, bears, tigers, and other trophies. They were given a mere hour to forge a weapon from what little remained of the slaughtered creatures. It was survival, stripped of any semblance of honor.

'How in Munesa[xv] do I do that?' he thought.

'Son. Language.'

'Right... Right... Sorry, father.'

He had never crafted weapons before, let alone from literal animal products. He took out two of the Dorynies' teeth, cut off their skin and tied them all together. Then, he

---

[xv] (Elvish) Hell

covered the improvised handle with a fox's fur. He used the tigers' teeth to make some throwing knives. Finally, the time was up. He managed to fashion a 'sword' (if you could even call it a sword) and five throwing knives in the time he was given.

The grand battle was to begin. As he stepped into the arena, his heart pounded like a war drum, the weight of the moment pressing down on his shoulders. But then, his gaze swept over the crowd, and then froze. There, amidst the sea of strangers in the audience, sat his family and his uncle Ley, still wearing his long black robes. They cheered him on.

'He... He's here!' He tried to contain himself.

His breath hitched, and for a fleeting moment, the tension in his body eased. His spine straightened, and his chin lifted slightly, as if his uncle's mere presence reminded him of who he was striving to become. His fingers, clenched tightly around the hilt of his weapon, loosened before tightening again with renewed purpose. A faint flicker of a smile ghosted across his lips, quickly replaced by a look of fierce determination.

He rolled his shoulders and took a steadying breath, his nerves now tempered by the quiet assurance that he wasn't alone in this fight, not entirely. The crowd blurred into the background as his uncle's presence sharpened his focus. If he was to survive and prove himself worthy of becoming a Hekket, he would fight not just for himself, but for the man who had always believed in him.

There were thirty-four other competitors. He saw faces he had never seen before. His father told him that the trials were very famous in Euphata, and many outsiders had come to witness the rituals and goings on. He also told him that members of all Snow Elf villages in the region were allowed to participate. Each one had its own turn in the cycle to host it and luckily for Alduin, his turn had come along with that of his village. His opponents were fearsome. Some of them were a lot more muscular than him. Some appeared a lot swifter and agile. Some looked a lot older than him. Two of them had to be at least thirty years old.

'Losers...' He chuckled.

There were bow users, sword users, spear users and many more creative ideas. Alduin couldn't fathom how one could manage to make a bow out of animal corpses, so he stood there in utter awe and childish curiosity. The match began. He saw groups of friends forming alliances in the mayhem. Only the last five survivors would be granted the title of Hekket.

Wild beasts were released from their cages by Aeden's soldiers, using their spears to lure them into the arena, adding to the chaos. On a tall pillar stood a man holding a sheet of paper, continuously announcing the number of survivors. The numbers dropped quickly because, well... Many were either exhausted, injured, or both from the entry exam, becoming easy targets for the ones the test was simple for. Some were eaten by bears. Some were first cut open by some other competitor and only then devoured whole. Utter madness engulfed the arena. Madness, agonizing screams and blood.

Alduin killed about five contestants, lost four of his fingers and had blood and sweat dripping all over him. Some of the blood was his. He hoped that not most of it. For a quick second, he turned his head toward his family, hoping to get a look of approval from his father, though strangely, he wasn't watching the battle. Alduin saw one of his father's Hekkets whispering in his ear, and he appeared concerned, nodding worriedly. Distant screams for help were ignored by the crowd as the spectacle of the Hekket trials was too enticing. Had something happened?

Eventually, it was announced that there were only ten survivors, with Alduin standing among them. He was trembling and exhausted but still very eager to win. He turned his gaze toward his father again, maybe this time he would pay attention to him, at least a quick nod, but he wasn't there. A few minutes later it was announced nine, now eight, now seven remaining. Bouncing on his feet, Alduin's excitement could not have been more apparent. But the mood turned solemn as cries of wolves, women and children arose from outside the Colosseum's gates. The sky turned crimson; a strong scent of iron pierced in the air.

'What. In the name of the gods. Is. Happening?!' Alduin thought.

'What? Where am I? What am I? Who are you?'

'I have no idea... Where are we? Why is there no one here other than us?'

'I don't know... I don't remember anything!'

The two beings were floating next to each other, facing the vast landscape.

'It is beautiful here. I don't know how to describe this with other words.'

'Yes, but why are we here?'

'I... I don't know... Who are you?'

'Again, I have no idea...'

'This place seems abandoned. It is nothing but a very large piece of land with no one on it except for us... Shall we try looking for someone to ask in case there are people residing here after all?'

'We can try...'

The two charged forward. They had no goal in mind other than trying to find another individual to question regarding their existence. It seemed helpless, however, as the land was completely and utterly empty, no creatures or buildings. Only earth, water and the sky. They kept on going for hours on end. The time it took for them to forfeit their search was immeasurable and currently unknown.

'Well... It seems we are alone here after all.'

'Yes.'

'Hmm...'

'Mmm...'

'About our names, I have an idea.'

'What is it?'

'If no one here can recall what our name is, not even us... Maybe we could name each other?'

'I like that idea. What did you have in mind?'

'For you, I thought about either Hala or Vaonie.'

'I prefer Vaonie. What about a name for you?'

'Do you have an idea?'

'I am not very creative.'

'Hmm... Lulia? Jul? Entus? Austomia? V...' They paused, 'Veridia?'

'Austomia was the one I liked the most.'

'So, Austomia it is.'

'So...'

'So...?'

'What now?'

'I think we should figure out why we are here.'

'Yes. Maybe we were put here to rule this place? After all, we are the only ones here... We could try to come up with new names for things, make them our own.'

'What a god complex you have, Vaonie... Luckily for you, I, too, possess this personality trait.'

Vaonie generated a sound that could be interpreted as a laugh, just not by any person with his right mind still intact. Vaonie and Austomia resembled orbs. Floating around and uttering words in a language not yet known to anyone. For some reason, they were able to understand each other even though this language wasn't even invented yet.

"The dialogue you, the reader, are reading right now has been directly translated via ancient sources of information and dictionaries, called 'My Imagination'."

'What would you like to name first?' Austomia asked. 'This broad thing above us. I want to name it "Jul".'

'Fine.'

'And I wish to name the thing that is below us "Veridia".'

'You can't just claim my ideas as your own.'

The same bizarre sound came out again.

'I will name this region "Heonmeyu",' Vaonie said.

'Did we just run out of things to name?'

'Unfortunately, I think so... I do hope we are mistaken... It would be very boring.'

'Hmm... What if we create new things?'

'How?'

'I don't know. What if I just think of something, and it would just appear?'

'I personally think you have officially lost it.'

'Do you have anything better to do?'

'True.'

'Let me try.'

Vaonie began thinking about a certain creature, but nothing happened.

'Maybe you need to say the word "create"?'

'That sounds way too convenient, but sure, I can give it a try. Create!'

Out of thin air, a being appeared. It bore large wings made of steel, and talons as sharp as scimitars. Hair the color of Jul[xvi]. Its eyes were the color of Veridia[xvii], and its skin had no color named after it yet. It wore no clothes and, after an unknown period of time, disappeared right back into thin air.

'That was... interesting! Now we know we can create things. Maybe we *are* meant to rule this place.'

'Maybe...'

[xvi] (Omnitongue) Sky.

[xvii] (Omnitongue) Earth.

'What do you call it?'

'I call it a "Tyrewhiin[xviii]". Now you try it.'

Austomia began the same process. The same creature appeared, though a bit different. It was no longer naked but wore something resembling knight armor in human culture. It was shiny and resembled silver. The creature had a large spear attached to its hip, which made it fall a bunch of times due to the lack of balance it had caused.

'You should have put that thing someplace else on its thing.'

'Thing on its thing?'

'The thing that is itself. I call it "Tvek[xix]". And the thing that is on it that made it fall. I call it "Platir[xx]".'

'So, you claim I should have put the platir somewhere else in its tvek?'

'Yes.'

Austomia and Vaonie began a journey of creating more and more words, creatures, concepts and beings. All of them were entirely new. They altered the appearance, abilities, strengths, weaknesses and so forth of several creatures like the Tyrewhiin whose skin color was now called 'Pol[xxi]'. Eventually, they ran out of ideas for beings to create and name. Suddenly, Austomia had yet another 'clever' idea.

'What if we create more beings like us?'

'Flying senkels[xxii]?'

[xviii] (Omnitongue) Angel.
[xix] (Omnitongue) Body.
[xx] (Omnitongue) Spear.
[xxi] (Omnitongue) White.
[xxii] (Omnitongue) Balls.

'No, you know what I mean. More gods like us.'

'Will they also be able to create things?'

'No, I think that would just invite trouble. They could be our own Qulteba[xxiii]. We will base them on us.'

'Interesting... How many did you have in mind?'

'Twelve.'

'Go on with it then. I am intrigued.'

'I need your help in this for precision.'

'Alright.'

Their thoughts intertwined, and from them immediately emerged twelve new flying orbs. Their 'parents' taught them how to speak and what the names of everything were. The children were named, in the chronological order of creation, Hanali, Jaone, Anor, Kans, Astrugiel, Lodus, Ophiin, Ayurë, Gonuiel, Pholexu, Kyyn and Fema.

The walls of the arena were smashed open like they were nothing but tea leaves, and into the arena entered a hoard of Vaermiraiits[xxiv]. Blood splashed everywhere. Most of them were wearing dark-gray battle armor made of metal, silver elegant circlets on their heads and two axes in their arms. In the middle of their torso was engraved the shape of a silver tear. A vampire general ordered his

---

[xxiii] (Omnitongue) Family.

[xxiv] (Omnitongue) Vampires.

minions to kill or kidnap everyone in sight. The women were mostly kidnapped to be used both for pleasure and the occasional thirst for blood.

Alduin was attacked by three vampire soldiers who tried to gang up on him, but they posed no real threat to his skill. They were wearing black chain-mail armor and silver helmets covering their eyes almost entirely. After all, all they needed was their sense of smell. Some fought using their claws, and some using regular weapons like halberds, axes, swords and spears. Their armor stood no chance against his ugly, improvised and deadly weapons.

In the turmoil he searched for people he knew to strategically group up and fight together. But each step across the blood-soaked ground, over corpse after corpse, dragged him into despair. His breath hitched as he stared at the face of his mother. Her eyes open but empty. Her body lifeless. Crumpled. His lips pressed tight. Trembling. Stumbling forward, arms hanging at his sides as if weighted with chains. Steps away from her lay his sister. Dead. Covered in scarlet blood. His chest squeezed tighter with every breath.

Around them lay the stiff, unmoving bodies of childhood friends, along with the corpses of hundreds of Elves. He rubbed at his eyes with shaking fingers, desperate to find out that he had only been imagining this nightmare.

'So much food in one place!' the general said and laughed loudly.

He sprinted to his mother. 'Mother, wake up, please. Mother!' he screamed and shook her torso, his hands grabbing her shoulders, sobbing but to no avail, 'please!' he shrieked again and caressed her hair with his right hand.

He tried the same with his sister.

'Veridia, please wake up! Open your eyes, I beg you. Please!' His father and uncle were all he had left now, but even their survival felt like a distant hope against the enormity of this loss.

His body refused to move, as though rooted to the ground by grief. Finally, he let out a shaky breath, his chest heaving as he tried to steady himself. The weight of everything—his failure, their deaths, his survival—bowed his shoulders, leaving him trembling and hollow. The arena stretched around him, smeared in blood and littered with the bodies of hundreds of Elves. The stench of death hung in the air, suffocating and inescapable.

Eventually, he gave up. Alduin could not beat the hoard. He'd never been taught how to fight them. He'd witnessed his father taking on three generals all by himself, but it was clear he would soon lose.

Behind Aeden, a black figure was lying on a large pool of blood in the snow. Focusing his eyes on it had made it clear that it was the body of his uncle Ley. A person Alduin had cherished and adored immensely. He was desperate. He started crying for help from the gods and got angry as he was met with no response. He blamed them for his agony and started running toward the vampire generals. Hoping he could at least die with honor. Live and die a warrior. Aeden and Alduin fought together like twins, in complete sync. One general ironically collapsed from sheer loss of blood.

They spared him no time to heal, and so he eventually perished. It was not enough, however. The two remaining generals successfully stuck their claws in Aeden's chest, who was already mortally wounded from before. Alduin started crying and lost all manner of patience and sanity. He knew he was going to die, so making foolish mistakes didn't seem as shameful to him as they once did. He tried to punch the general that stood in front of him right in his ugly little face, hoping to make him lose consciousness so he could focus on one enemy at a time. It did not work. The general caught his fist in the air, turned him around and broke his arm. Alduin screamed from shuddering pain.

'Look what we have here... Quite daring, I say. Hey, Gozo. Look at this little pipsqueak.' the general chuckled.

'He seems tasty. There's something you just can't beat when it comes to child meat. I like his eyes, let's take him with us. Don't hurt him, I want him for myself.' Gozo replied, smirking and laughing.

'Fine. Here, take him.'

'Come with me, you little insect, you're mine now.'

'Why won't you just kill me and be done with it? I am begging you, I have nothing left,' Alduin cried.

'Why do you think that I care? You're mine, and that's that. Now, be quiet and stay tasty before I take your arm instead of merely breaking it.'

A chill seeped into his veins. Alduin could not fathom the situation he was in. He woke up today to the thought of fulfilling his lifelong dream of becoming a Hekket[XXV]. Instead, his entire clan was slaughtered, his family included, and he would become a slave of a Vaermiraiit

---

[XXV] Special Forces (Snow Elf).

clan. He was all alone in the world now. He wanted to fight but he knew it would only anger the general Gozo, which would worsen his condition. He decided to act maturely and accept the situation as it was.

'Maybe if I get them to like me, they'd spare me, and I could start a new life somewhere else,' he said to himself.

He sighed.

'I know it sounds stupid, but do you actually have any better plan?' he replied to himself.

The vampires started scavenging the arena while taking all the tasty-looking corpses they could find. They also pillaged through the village's houses, taking jewelry and any other shiny-looking objects. Gozo cuffed Alduin up with some metal he had found on the ground and put him on his massive shoulder.

'Guys, let's get going! This has been fun. Let's enjoy our spoils back at base.' He commanded to his men.

As numb and useless as a statue, Alduin watched his village shrink smaller and smaller as they moved further from it. Thinking, this would be his last time seeing his home.

CHAPTER THREE

He woke up in a cell, reeking of the corpses lying beside him. The steel cell was protected by four Vaermiraiit[i] guards wearing void-black robes with silver belts. Hoods covered their heads, and each wore a bizarre steel medallion, and a silver ring adorned with a red gem.

'What? What is this? Where am I?' he tried to stand, but stabbing pulses of pain shot all the way from his head to his toes. He clasped his aching head. Nauseous, heavily dehydrated and weak, he asked, 'What have you assholes done to me?'

He suddenly noticed he was naked, his skin full of semi-healed bite marks. His waist, chest, neck, hands and legs were filled with pairs of holes surrounded by dry blood.

'Wha—?' his words broke into a piercing scream. 'What did you do to me?!' His voice cracked, rising into a frantic

---

i   (Omnitongue) Vampire.

shriek. 'I'll kill you... I'll kill all of you! You sick monsters!' A sea of tears dropped down his cheeks as he fell to his knees.

'Shut up back there!' thundered the second guard from the right.

Alduin couldn't stop. He screamed harder. He walked his fingers around the wounds and the coagulated blood. He could not fathom what he was seeing.

'I told you to shut up.' The guard bashed his spear on the metal bars, staring straight into Alduin's frightened eyes.

'Fuck you!' he yelled, his voice cracking with rage. 'You killed my parents! You killed everyone!' His fists clenched, trembling as tears streamed freely down his cheeks. 'I hate you... I hate you. I hate you!' The final words escaped in a broken whisper, his body wracked with sobs, the weight of his anguish too heavy to contain.

The leftmost guard nodded to his friend, saying 'Do it'. He unlocked the cage door and punched Alduin straight back to the ground, barely leaving him conscious. Alduin spit out blood and continued cursing.

'I told you to shut up, didn't I?!' The guard began kicking Alduin fiercely in the stomach.

He pressed his palms against the cold, filthy ground, struggling to lift his face with what little strength remained in his trembling arms. Before he could rise, the heavy boot of the prison guard slammed him back down, grinding his cheek into the dirt. The guard let out a derisive chuckle, circling him like a predator toying with its prey. Eventually, boredom won out, and with a final snort of disdain, the guard stepped out of the cage, slamming the iron door shut behind him. The lock clicked, sealing him back in his pit of despair.

Alduin was puking relentlessly, though only his digestive juices came out. He barely managed to get back on his feet, hunching forward.

'How... How much time was I out for?'

'About four days by now,' the second guard from the left chuckled.

'W-what?! Really?' his voice cracked, trembling with disbelief. 'Why did you—how could you do this to me? To us? We never did anything to you. So why? Why did we deserve this?' his chest heaved as his words grew louder, more desperate. 'You murdered everyone I loved! Why? Tell me why!' He clenched his fists, trembling as fresh tears spilled down his cheeks. 'I hope the gods smite you in your sleep, along with your children, you monsters. You'll see. I'll get justice. All of you will see.'

A few more tears escaped, tracing the lines of anguish etched into his face.

'There are only *six* gods, and believe me, they don't give a flying fuck about you. You're nothing. Food shouldn't even be talking in the first place, so shut up!' The rightmost guard's veins popped in anger.

Alduin dropped to his knees, his legs splayed out to the sides, as though his body had finally given up. 'Why did you let me live? Why me?!' he cried, his voice raw with desperation. His empty, hollow eyes stared at the dirt beneath him, searching for answers that would never come.

'Shut up!' barked the second guard from the left, his voice sharp with anger. He had finally lost his composure.

The cell became his new home. He was handed ragged clothes and 'fed' twice a day, just barely enough to survive. As for water... Well... Let's just say his survival skills were put to the test. Days blurred into one another. His routine consisted of kicking the rotten bodies in his cell, shouting, screaming, sobbing, or bothering the unlucky guards assigned to watch over him. Occasionally, he'd eavesdrop on their conversations, picking up bits of their native tongue. It might prove useful one day... Maybe... Probably... Though the faint hope felt like a distant flicker.

Optimism was a struggle, though he knew keeping his temper was the only way for him to keep his sanity intact. His cell was positioned to give him a clear view of their social gatherings, the twisted feasts and the slave trade. Humans, or 'livestock' as they called them, were consumed in every sense. Vampires ravaged and raped men, women, and children, their screams haunting him night after night. No matter how tightly he covered his ears, it was inescapable.

The horrors didn't end there. If the women weren't killed outright, they were left to suffer. The rapes often resulted in pregnancies, left to carry mutated hybrid children who appeared human, but whose bodies and minds were warped beyond recognition. The newborns, driven by an insatiable hunger, devoured their mothers, sometimes in the womb, often after birth.

His eyes grew darker with each passing day. They used to take pleasure in torturing him, but now, it seemed to no longer faze him. It was as if the mental and physical pain had become familiar, almost routine. The bites no longer stung. Their 'research' on the Snow Elves' regenerative abilities failed to break him. He didn't cry out anymore, didn't speak much at all. He had become detached, indifferent, or perhaps that was just how his mind had learned to cope with the endless trauma.

Sometimes, the guards would slip him an extra piece of bread, justifying it with the claim that thin bodies were less appetizing. In those moments, he kept his wits about him, burying the bread in the ground to save it for later. This way, they couldn't take it from him.

'I need to survive... If they wanted me dead, they'd have done it by now,' he would constantly tell himself, trying to hold onto some hope.

'Good morning,' he whispered to himself. Whether it was truly morning or not didn't matter. He was trapped in a cave, after all. The guards, however, felt the tremor in the ground and quickly realized he had awoken.

'Good morning, insect. Did you sleep well? My friend here decided to make it extra hard for you to fall asleep yesterday,' Zera laughed.

'Yes, yes, I realized. Where is my breakfast?'

'Don't speak to us like that. I'll overlook your rudeness, for now. Here,' Zera said, tossing him an apple. It was already half-eaten. 'It's less than the usual because you made me upset. Enjoy.' She flashed a mocking, open-mouthed grin, displaying her shiny white fangs.

'I am used to your mind games. Now let me eat in peace, please.'

Zera threw her spear at him. It hit the floor with a thud about one millimeter away from his foot. He didn't even try to evade it. Did not even flinch.

'You are walking on very thin ice, mortal. Mind your manners, or I will make tonight's feeding extra painful for you, do you understand?!'

'Yes.'

'Yes, what?'

'Yes, lord Zera,' he released a long, low sigh.

'Good. That's better,' she laughed and smirked.

He ate half of the remaining apple and kept the rest in his pocket for later. He preferred staying hungry in the morning over starving after lunch. During his time in the cage, he invented a few games to pass the time. One was juggling a few of the human bones lying around. Another was seeing how many sit-ups and push-ups he could do before passing out. After all, losing consciousness was like forcing sleep upon himself. It wasn't as if his waking moments were any better than the infinite, imagined worlds of dreams.

He passed the time with pointless games – holding his breath, standing on one leg, and so on. They were dull, but with nothing else to occupy him, they were the only distractions he had. Hours drifted by until the familiar sound of screaming reached his ears, a noise he had come to almost enjoy.

"I am obviously kidding, of course... Don't worry about it, reader."

'Don't you ever get bored of torturing people?' he said to Zera, pushing his luck again.

Was he trying to get himself killed?

'We love human meat. What else can I say? Would you like a slice of a woman's butt-cheek for lunch today?' she snorted.

'No, thank you.'

'Ha, as if I'd ever share my food with you. Keep dreaming.'

'Fucker...' He whispered.

'What did you say?' a guard appeared to have heard him.

'Nothing... Nothing...'

'I haven't heard you complain in ages. I've actually started missing that angry, whiny voice of yours. You know what? If you can make one of us laugh tonight, I'll give you an extra piece of meat! What do you say?' he chuckled.

'How exactly? Your sense of humour is hard to understand,' Alduin asked.

'Dance for us.' The other guard said, smirking.

More meat meant a higher chance to grow stronger, maybe even enough to break out of there someday. He chose to obey. He began mimicking his fallen sister's favourite dance, 'Shenze'. It was a traditional Snow Elvish dance often performed during matrimonial ceremonies. It involved a series of precise moves: stomps in a specific rhythm, a long-lasting pirouette, two backflips, then another pirouette while standing on one's hands. Next, the dancers would grasp each other's arms, tossing one another into the air, executing a tilted pirouette, and landing in a wide split.

This routine would be repeated several times, with

freestyle periods in between, all accompanied by traditional music. It would culminate in a display of self-chanted fireworks, conjured with Snow Elvish magic. Unfortunately, he was too weak to follow it. As he stomped, his steps grew slower until he collapsed face-first into the mud, just a few millimetres from dried feces.

'You're lucky you didn't land in your own shit, child! Fine, you've earned an extra slice. Hey, Zera, get him a piece of meat. He deserves it!' the guard said, continuing to laugh.

Zera tossed a cow's leg to Alduin, and he was barely strong enough to catch it. It was both raw and overcooked. Some parts were black as coal, others still pink.

'This is better than nothing...' He said to himself and nodded in thanks.

Many days passed, seeming to grow shorter with each one. Alduin occasionally entertained the guards for extra food. Weeks turned into months, and then a year. Suddenly, Zera opened his cage.

'Yo, wake up! Our leader wants to see you. On your feet, move. Do you want me to hit you again?'

'Fine,' Alduin sighed.

He stood up, allowing Zera to cuff him before escorting him to the clan leader's court.

'Stay quiet,' she said.

She walked him to the main hall. The lord had long brown hair, a silver tear tattooed onto his left cheek and eyes glowing in the color of roses. He was wearing dark-brown royal robes with platinum decorations. His expression was neither serious nor playful.

'Oh, finally. Hello. Did you sleep well? Oh, who am I kidding? Anyway, let me get straight to the point. Do you see that general over there, the one I'm pointing at? You two are familiar with each other, I presume?' he said, smiling.

He was pointing at a Vaermiraiit[ii] wearing a crimson mask attached to his long, black hair. His dark blue shirt had black bear fur connected to it using golden strings.

'Yes, I've met him.' Alduin sighed.

'His name is Gozo. For reasons unknown to me, he decided to put you through the ancient trial of the necklace. Have you heard of it?' he asked. 'He would never pass... It always ends the same way. With a fresh body to feast on...' He thought, grinning.

'No, what is it? I fucking hate tests.' Alduin responded.

'Understandable. Though you have heard of our lord Vaonie, right? One of "The Originals", or "The First".'

Alduin's face darkened; his jaw clenched in irritation. 'I haven't, as they aren't real. There are only four gods – Lune, Odrum, M'falnar and Merissa. They've watched over us since the dawn of time.' He looked at Lysander with a mixture of pity and frustration, unable to fathom how anyone could believe differently. 'Our gods are real. They must be. Everything else is just... stories.'

Lysander growled dismissively and scoffed. 'Your ignorance is laughable,' he spat the words like venom. 'Vaonie and Austomia forged this realm, Vanthea, from nothing. Then came their twelve children, whom we call "The Second" or "The Overseers".' Lysander leaned in, his lip

---

[ii] (Omnitongue) Vampire.

curling. 'Austomia rallied six Overseers to betray our lord. Vaonie fought to survive, defended by the remaining loyal few… until one perished.' His voice dropped, raw with fury. 'The traitors preyed on our lord's grief and took advantage of their weakness. They banished Vaonie, alongside our righteous warriors, to the realm of Tyronah[iii]. Those who betrayed our lord are known as the "Sarathiin", and the loyal six – the "Araqhaiit".'

Alduin clenched his fists, 'I refuse to believe you. These are nothing but lies… Your tongue is a dagger of heresy,' he muttered.

'You will soon enough,' he rolled his eyes, 'do you see this necklace I'm holding? It's one of Vaonie's artifacts on our planet. It sends mortals through Vaonie's trials to find a fitting successor for Lodus, the fallen Araqhaiit. Gozo believes you might be able to pass it, or at least that it will be entertaining to watch you try. Refusal isn't really an option. Take it and begin immediately.'

'May I eat first? I'll need all my strength for this,' Alduin responded, trying to sneak in an extra meal.

'I said now.' Lysander grabbed the raven-black spear that was sitting on his back and pointed it at him.

'Fine, fine. Here,' Alduin said and put it on.

Somehow, the necklace pierced his skin, and he immediately collapsed to the ground. It felt as though his consciousness was being transported to another realm. He suddenly awoke in a strange, dark place. The sky was crimson red, and he stood on a levitating circular platform.

[iii] (Omnitongue) Hell.

He couldn't see the ground beneath it. He'd better not fall off it.

'Where am I? What is this place?' he screamed.

Suddenly, an unfamiliar voice echoed through the void.

'Welcome. I'll be brief. This test consists of several seemingly infinite rounds. In each, you'll receive a weapon to fight a shadow of yourself, armed with the same one. If you die, you'll be resurrected here with a different weapon. The moment I run out of ideas for weapons, your body in Vanthea will rot and die. That's it. Good luck.'

'Wait! Who are you? What am I doing here?'

A few seconds later, a color-less black clone appeared right in front of his eyes, wielding the same weapon he had – a spear adorned with black gems. Alduin had never fought with a spear before, only with a dagger, sword and bow.

'How am I supposed to defeat myself exactly? I don't even know how to use this thing,' he said, despair in his eyes.

The shadow charged, thrusting its spear forward. Alduin dodged each strike, but he forgot he was fighting himself. The clone, mirroring his mind and technique, knew his every weakness. With a swift round kick, the shadow lifted him off the ground and impaled him with the spear through the heart. It was over. He shouted in pain, his vision fading.

This time, Alduin wielded two black daggers, each with a green gem on the handle. As he practiced slashing, strange green light beams cut through the air. Each slash sent a projectile of light, which the shadow had so rudely decided to avoid. No matter how he altered his pace, momentum, or angle, exhaustion eventually took its toll, bringing Alduin to his knees.

Suddenly, the shadow executed Alduin's signature move – a front flip into an upside-down pirouette, dagger aimed at its target. Alduin had often used this move to boost his confidence against weaker foes, and now the shadow seemed to share his arrogance. Slowing time with his supernatural vision, he lined up the perfect strike and stabbed the shadow's head. It collapsed, screeching and writhing on the floor.

Victory seemed within reach as the shadow covered its head, now seemingly harmless. But then, its hands began to glow with golden light. Alduin, fearing it might heal, moved quickly. He positioned himself behind the shadow, preparing for a final, glorious strike—one that would make the gods proud.

'We have gathered you here, children, for a very special reason.'

'What is it?'

'I will explain in just a bit, Hanali.'

'Alright.'

'Vaonie and I decided to gift you something. Activate your aura detection and tell me what you feel.'

'I feel something unfamiliar.'

'Very good, Kans. Can you try to locate it?'

'It feels like it is coming from an unknown source. Not from this realm. Did you create a new one?'

'Very good observation! We created three new realms for you to explore. The first one I named "Vanthea", the second I named "Tyronah" and the last one I have neither found a name nor a purpose for. Why did we even create it, Vaonie?'

"Reader, yes, you reading this, imagine in that fabulous brain of yours that Vaonie's orb-shaped body shrugged in response."

'What is the purpose of Vanthea and Tyronah then?' Anor asked.

'The realm of Vanthea will be inhabited by mortals. Tyronah is where bad mortals shall forever remain. "Heonmeyu", our current location, will be inhabited by the good mortals, the ones that succeeded in following our rules.'

'What are mortals?' Fema asked in her curiosity.

'Mortals are a new type of being we created, existing for a limited time specific to their species, then judged for their actions.'

'Don't forget, Austomia, we have also decided on meanings for your names.' Said Vaonie.

'Oh! What are they?' Anor asked.

'Vanthea has twelve laws, and each one is the most dominant positive trait of every one of you, children, and the significance of your name. This gift, however, comes with responsibility. You must ensure that the mortals adhere to your virtue. In essence, your names are commandments, and should you witness a mortal breaking one, you are allowed to punish them. For a serious violation, kill them so Austomia and I can judge them. For lesser offenses, you may punish as you see fit.'

'Ah, so we're their gods?' Fema said, her voice filled with excitement at the revelation.

'Yes. You, along with us, will rule and oversee the realm of Vanthea,' Vaonie said.

'I feel bad for those mortals. To have been created strictly for the purpose of being judged, especially when they are born with a shred of evil in their hearts...' Kans responded.

'I think that we should see ourselves more like guides rather than gods,' Pholexu added.

'I agree with you, sister. In general, we shouldn't look down on them. Instead, we should see them eye to eye. They may lack the power we possess, but in their struggles, they could grow stronger than us—in character, in their ability to face hardship and pain,' Fema said.

'You can count on me.' Hanali said.

'Our only goal is to make you happy, my children.' Vaonie said.

'And only that. Therefore, we grant you near complete autonomy in this matter. I hope you enjoy it!' Austomia added.

'Thank you.' They all said in unison.

'Now, go and explore. I'm not quite done creating everything, so new things will keep appearing!' Austomia declared.

Alduin focused on the shadow as it shifted its left leg, likely preparing to resume the fight. Unaware of him standing behind, weapon drawn. The dagger touched the top of its head, but instead of piercing it, Alduin froze mid-strike. A sudden shock of cold coursed through him as blood dripped from his mouth. Looking down, he saw a blade jutting from his chest. Turning his head, he saw the base of a dagger connected to a chain, piercing his back. Following it with his eyes, he saw the shadow's left leg Alduin then realized the shadow hadn't been stretching. It had delayed its attack for maximum surprise, and it worked perfectly. Choking on his blood, he lost his balance and collapsed onto his chest, dizziness quickly overtaking him.

'Oh, did I forget to mention? The shadow is a master of every fighting style that exists in Vanthea. Try to beat it.' The unfamiliar voice's laugh echoed through the void before fading away.

'Goddamn it! How can I defeat such a fighter when I'm not even a Hekket[iv] yet? This is impossible. Morale matters but being realistic matters even more!' he thought as he began losing consciousness.

He failed the task again and again. Each time it seemed as though his spirit was being sucked away from him. He'd already passed ten different weapons and was beginning to lose hope. This time he was given a black sword. It had dark-red wings attached to the handle, a silver horned skull and a little medallion hanging on it. Its sheath was crimson

---

[iv] Special Forces (Snow Elf).

red with a black Deovhaiit[V] eye in the middle. Once he tightened his grip, the white core in the middle of the handle started glowing and produced black and white flames in monochrome that engulfed it. He charged forward.

He slashed his opponent and then dodged the upcoming attack as an utter reflex. He could recognize his own moves being used by the shadow and tried to adapt to them. A swift kick there, a punch there, a twirl there and a vertical slash there. Despite this iteration being the most successful one so far, he still possessed many grave injuries, and hope was very hard to keep intact.

His opponent executed a pirouette, followed by two horizontal strikes—one aimed at Alduin's legs, the other at his heart. Simultaneously, ice spikes shot out, aiming to trap him in place and force him into a specific spot. Alduin was suddenly reminded of the Whirlwind Spider technique. Though he hadn't mastered it yet, he decided to give it a try. He managed to dodge the strike to his heart, but the one aimed at his leg landed, severing it. He attempted a backflip but ended up landing on his stomach, rather than on all fours as required by the technique. Surprisingly, the shadow, didn't take the opportunity to attack. In less than a second, Alduin advanced to the next step and launched himself into the air for a vertical strike, aiming for the shadow's head. He missed slightly but managed to slice from its right shoulder to its left leg. It screeched and faded into

------

[V] (Omnitongue) Demon.

nothingness. For the first time in a long while, Alduin felt the corners of his mouth turn up into a smile.

A surge of energy coursed through him, and his chest felt a little lighter.

'I knew I could do it!' he said.

'Very impressive mortal, follow me to my court.'

A portal appeared out of thin air and opened a pathway to a strange throne room. Entirely out of breath and terrified of the upcoming (and recent) events, he rushed inside the portal.

'What is happening?' he thought.

He found himself kneeling in a large room in front of a throne as big as a mammoth. An orb of 'light' was sitting on it and then took the shape of a man.

'Greetings mortal,' Vaonie said.

'Who are you? Where am I?' Alduin asked.

'Welcome to Tyronah[vi]. I am Vaonie, lord of this realm. To your left and right, you will find different torture chambers, military dormitories, training camps, towers and hordes of Deovhaiits. Demons, as you mortals call them.'

He blinked rapidly, his eyes darting around as his breath hitched. A cold sweat broke out across his forehead. His mouth went dry, and his voice came out in a whisper, barely audible.

'What. The. Fuck...'

'Don't you dare interrupt me!' Vaonie's eyes glowed ferociously as their voice echoed across the room, 'These five are my children. Do you know their names?'

[vi] (Omnitongue) Hell.

'You... are Vaonie? So, he spoke the truth. No, this cannot be... The village elders can't possibly be wrong. Let me go. I refuse to entertain a pretender to the divine. May M'falnar take my soul to rest.'

He suddenly fell to the ground, unable to get up. An invisible force was holding him down and choking him.

'Stop testing my patience!'

'Kill me, then.' His voice was strained, breath shallow and erratic. He met their gaze, defiance flickering in his eyes despite the laboured breaths that rattled through his chest. 'Just do it. I'm not scared of you.'

'I offer you a chance for a new life, you foolish mortal,' they weakened their grip on his body.

'What do you mean?'

'For passing my test, I can make you one of my own. Your new name will be Alduin *Lodus* Faëli, as you will serve as a replacement for my fallen child. Look at what you could become... An end to your pain....'

A big mirror appeared in front of him, showing him his new body. His white hair grew a lot longer, his eyes were shining in the color of blood. His ears were pointier. He was taller, more serious, refined and mature. His eyes had a certain shadow to them that made his depressed glare way more frightening. Menacing.

'You are now part Snow Elf, part Araqhaiit. An immortal god among men. I will give you access to the ever-burning "Ut-obliryne u Tyronah[vii]", which cannot be put out by normal means. The tattoo you have on the back

---

[vii] (Omnitongue) Flames of Hell.

of your left hand is called the "Yur u Vaonie[viii]" and it holds sacred power. All of this can become your reality if only you vow to obey me.'

He stared at Vaonie without the faintest idea of how to respond.

'And yes, there is a catch. As an Araqhaiit, your Olons[ix] are all god-activated, which means they can only be controlled by fully divine beings. Since you would only be half divine, any movement your body should wish to make, may it be walking or simply producing heartbeats, cannot happen by your own volition. Your brain would send its orders through me, as a proxy, and only then to your muscles. I control your body, not you. And if you ever dare to betray me, you will face dire consequences. That is all. You will now be transported back to Vanthea to be trained by the Vaermiraiits[x].'

'Wait, I didn't say ye—' he tried to speak, but before he could finish, he was already back in the lair.

The clan leader's jaw dropped, his eyes widening in disbelief. Alduin had expected a shout, a sneer, or some cruel, degrading remark. But what he faced instead was something far more unsettling. The entire room fell silent. One by one, the vampires, dozens of them, including the leader himself, lowered to their knees before him. The weight of their submission hung heavy in the air, suffo-

---

[viii] (Omnitongue) Mark of Vaonie.
[ix] (Omnitongue) Particles.
[x] (Omnitongue) Vampires.

cating the space with tension. Alduin's heart raced, unsure whether he should feel victorious or terrified.

'Welcome, Lodus. Welcome back!' the vampires cried out in unison.

'No… This isn't possible, they never come back alive,' the clan leader seethed inwardly, his fists clenching at his sides. 'Am I really supposed to follow *his* orders now? This… this little insect's orders? Damn it!' His thoughts were filled with frustration and disbelief.

Outwardly, he composed himself, forcing a smile as he addressed Alduin. 'Vaonie has commanded us to train you, but that can only happen after a feast. The training will be gruelling, so you need your strength. Come, come.' He gestured with false enthusiasm, masking his irritation beneath a thin veneer of politeness.

Alduin's gaze swept over the kneeling crowd, bewildered. 'What is this?' he muttered under his breath, his voice low but thick with disbelief. 'Just a few days ago, you were torturing me, and now… Now you kneel?' his eyes flicked to the clan leader, his anger barely contained. 'After everything you've put me through, you expect me to play along with this, this ridiculous game?' his tone was sharp, a challenge in his every word.

'You must. My word is the word of Vaonie. Disobeying me is disobeying them, and the day you do, that would be your last. Surely you understand that? Or are you that foolish?'

Alduin froze in place, unable to respond.

'Follow me to the feast.' The leader commanded.

'Why?'

'Because you need to eat,' he said and smirked.

'Humans? No.'

'You'll soon realise that ordinary food will make you sick to your stomach,' the leader continued, his tone a mix of warning and amusement. 'Your taste buds have been altered. Your body craves fresh meat and blood now. Trust me, you'll understand soon enough.'

'No.'

'Now!' the leader commanded, his eyes glowing with an eerie, blood-red light as he stared at him menacingly.

Alduin stood frozen, struggling to form a response. He hunched forward, his shoulders slumping in defeat, his eyes hollow and distant as he obeyed without a word. He had no other choice.

'At last, we have a successor to Lodus!' the chief bellowed, his voice echoing with a mix of triumph and anticipation. He stormed toward a grand room, with Alduin trailing behind, still numb, his every step mechanical.

He entered the room, his eyes scanning the dozens of vampires seated in royal chairs. Having recognized him they all dropped to their knees, the air thick with reverence and expectation. Then, they began feasting without hesitation, tearing into the corpses stacked in front of them, their teeth sinking into the flesh with unnerving familiarity. A large chalice filled with a blood-red liquid was passed around, its contents sloshing with each movement.

The moment Alduin sat, the room's focus shifted entirely to him, their eyes hungry not just for sustenance but for his next action. The clan leader's gaze drilled into him, a silent command to partake in the same grisly feast. Alduin's heart raced, his breath shallow. He had no choice. His eyes swept over the pile of bodies, seeking the one least damaged, the oldest, the least familiar to him. He found a man who appeared to have lived a long, quiet life—now lifeless.

His voice trembled as he whispered, 'I am sorry. Forgive me,' before lowering his head in a futile attempt to block out the cruel reality of the situation.

He took a bite, his stomach twisting as he chewed. The texture was unexpected. Juicy, almost succulent. There was no disgust, no revulsion. Instead, his body responded to the nourishment in ways he couldn't deny. He closed his eyes to block the truth, wishing for the taste of normal food, of his past life, but it was gone.

The shame pressed in on him. 'Am I even myself anymore?' he thought, the weight of the question heavy on his chest.

His body felt alien, his soul sinking as his hands shook. He couldn't recognize himself. Something had changed, something irreversible.

'What have you done to me?!' Alduin screamed, his voice raw with desperation.

He froze, his heart pounding as the weight of his actions sank in. His chest heaved, but no tears came—only a hollow, aching emptiness. He wanted to sob, to release the flood of anguish and guilt building inside him, but his body refused. His eyes burned with the desire to cry, yet they remained dry, mocking him with their inability to shed a single tear.

'Keep eating, you need to recover,' the leader said, flashing a wide grin that revealed his sharp fangs, followed by a laugh.

Alduin obeyed, each bite accompanied by a whimper. 'What the fuck is wrong with me?! Puke it out! Why am I not puking? Why... Why couldn't I die like the rest of them?!' he thought.

From a lowly slave to vampires, he had become a slave to something far worse. The strongest being he had ever heard of. Which was worse? He had no idea.

CHAPTER FOUR

The knocking at the door woke him up. It was softer, more serene than the way they banged on his cage bars a few days ago. He was sleeping in a bed, an actual bed, with sheets, a pillow and a blanket. Not only that, but his room was also fully furnished. It had a sofa, a table, a few chairs and even a few wine bottles for him to drink to his heart's content. Everything was different. The Vaermiraiits[i] were nice to him, more like servants than abductors. He was treated like royalty. This made him realize just how much he had been missing the small luxuries of his nearly forgotten home. He couldn't tell how much time had passed since then.

'Lodus, are you awake? It's time to begin your training,' a muffled voice said.

'I am getting dressed. Wait a bit,' he answered.

---

[i] (Omnitongue) Vampires.

He wore a simple outfit that they had laid out for him. Cotton white shirt with long sleeves, black pants and black shoes.

'Come in,' he muttered.

The Vaermiraiit that entered the room was a familiar face. It was Zera. The vile creature who made his life miserable several days ago was now his personal servant. Ironic. He gazed in the mirror, still unable to comprehend the drastic changes in his appearance.

'Our clan leader is waiting for you in the great dining hall to eat breakfast. Do you know his name yet?'

'Fine. And no.'

'You *should* know the name of your host. It's common etiquette,' she rolled her eyes.

'What do you vampires even know about etiquette? All you do is eat, rape, pillage and destroy everything around you, like animals. You literally live in caves.' He flexed his fingers.

'We are more connected to our wild side, that's all. Soon you will grow to like our culture.'

'I hope not... I'm going to eat, bye.' He said, 'fucking asshole,' he thought.

He entered the dining hall, greeted by a sea of candles casting eerie, bizarre flames in shades of purple, green, and blue. The clan leader sat atop his throne beside Alduin's, an even grander seat. They were meant to be at the head of the table, like nobles, but the setting felt off. The table was piled high with food, though its exact nature was unidentifiable. A bizarre mix of colours and textures that hinted at something both strange and unsettling.

'Finally, you're up. I have been waiting for you,' the clan leader said.

'I overslept. What is all this?'

'Just my regular breakfast with a few adaptations to your previous lifestyle. You see, instead of my regular morning snack, "Balagas", we have beef steak and lamb ribs. I am sure it will be to your liking. Vampires don't consume dairy products or vegetables, only meat, so unfortunately, that's your only choice of nutrition.'

'Fine.' Alduin fixed him with an unblinking glare, his eyes burning with silent fury.

'Today will be your first day in training to become an Araqhaiit. It will begin with agility training, and maybe if you show good signs of improvement, flight training too.'

'Uh-huh,' he muttered, absentmindedly playing with his food.

The memory of his father's scolding for such behaviour flashed in his mind, and a wave of frustration washed over him, turning his mood sour. He couldn't help but sulk, the weight of old reprimands lingering even now.

'After agility training, Gozo wil-' Lysander began saying but was interrupted by Alduin.

'Gozo? Fuck no,' he growled, his voice thick with anger. His fists clenched so tightly his knuckles turned white, the fury in him barely contained. His body was rigid, every muscle tight, as if he was on the verge of snapping at any moment.

'*Gozo* will teach you the fundamentals of blood magic.' He said, ignoring Alduin's interruption, 'that is all. Now, I eat.' A bone-cracking sound was heard, 'this is delicious.'

Alduin stared at his empty goblet, his eyes hollow, trying to avoid the subject. 'Can I have some wine?' he asked.

'Here,' Zera handed him a chalice and poured wine into it.

'If fruits are toxic to your bodies, how come you're able to drink wine? It baffles me,' he asked.

'Great question. We actually have no idea,' he chuckled, 'but wine is very similar in taste and texture to a baby's blood. It is what we give newly turned Vaermiraiits to drink before they move on to the real thing. This is only the case for red wine, though. White wine is toxic to us.'

'Huh.'

Alduin finished eating his breakfast. 'What now?' he asked.

'Head outside. One of my generals will conduct your agility training.'

'Okay.'

'My name is Lysander, by the way. Lysander of Thebes.'

'Okay,' he said, 'I don't remember asking for your name, you asshole,' he thought.

'Good luck,' Lysander nodded.

He stepped out of the dining hall and into the cavern's cool, damp air, leaving the underground fort he now called home behind. The fort, carved into the very rock of the cave, was dim and oppressive, but the open space outside offered a brief sense of freedom. Standing just beyond the entrance, a vampire clad in thick black armor waited, his silhouette barely visible in the low light, exuding an air of silent expectation.

'Good morning, Lodus. My name is Edward Vul. I am one of Lysander's generals, and I will be overseeing your agility training on this fine day.'

'You are awfully cheery.'

'Well, that's quite rude to say, isn't it?'

'How should I know? You guys killed my parents way before they had the chance to educate me,' he rolled his eyes.

'I used to be a human knight before I was turned by Gozo. Most of the others you've met were born as vampires.'

'I hate him,' he sulked, the mention of Gozo's name still burning in his chest. He clenched his fists again, the anger simmering just below the surface.

'I-I see... For what it's worth, I'm sorry this has happened to you... I remember how I felt when I was in your place.'

'Does... Does it get better? *Will* it get better?' he asked quietly, his voice shaky, as if the weight of the question was too heavy to carry alone. His eyes flickered with uncertainty, the rawness of his pain clear, though he tried to mask it with a glimmer of hope. He gazed at the general, awaiting reassurance.

Edward looked down, his expression softening as he sighed. 'I wish it did, kid. I really do...' He sighed again, a deeper sadness in his eyes, as if Alduin's pain weighed on him more than he cared to admit. 'Anyways, follow me to the training grounds.' He turned away, his tone shifting to something more practical, though the heaviness lingered.

Alduin nodded. After a few minutes they arrived at a

massive field, filled with weird mechanical devices for training evasion techniques. Cages full of wild beasts lined the sides of the field. In the centre stood an enormous weapon rack holding spears, swords, bows, daggers, et cetera.

'This is going to be your second home until you finally acquire the agility of an Araqhaiit. Your Elvish skills are not on par with my own, and that is unacceptable. We will begin with a simple running test. Do you see this weapon rack? Run toward it, touch it and then run back here. Do it as fast as you can! Ready? Set, go!'

Alduin was surprised by the short notice of this exam but quickly started sprinting forward. Reaching the weapons rack, he immediately turned and rushed back to Edward. It was probably about two kilometers in each direction. The clan's cave system was enormous.

'Five minutes and thirteen seconds... *I* can do this distance in a minute, and you should be able to do it even faster. Your next exam will be to dodge my attacks for at least a minute. We'll keep trying until you succeed. Ready? Go!'

Edward took out his battleaxe and started swinging it at Alduin. Despite its massive size, he wielded it like it did not weigh more than an apple. Alduin attempted to dodge the strikes, but the third landed squarely. In an instant, his head was severed, and a scream of agony tore through him. Perhaps, deep down, he didn't truly want to die just yet.

'Huh? What the hell?! Wait... why am I not dead? And why are you so tall all of a sudden? What's going on?!'

'Didn't anyone tell you? You're immortal. As for my

height, it's because you're currently just a talking head on the ground. Regrow your body, and we'll begin again. Don't take too long.'

'How?'

'What? Oh, hmm… Okay, listen carefully. Natural regeneration is an instinct you have to train. So, focus hard on regrowing your limbs, I guess? I know it is confusing. It was that way for me too many years ago.'

'Uh... Fine.'

Alduin closed his eyes, focusing on the idea of regrowing his body, but it didn't work. He switched tactics, imagining each body part in order, from head to feet, with the highest detail. Suddenly, he was staring at his feet. His body was fully restored.

'Huh. But where did my body go?' he asked.

'I knew you had it in you. You didn't actually regrow anything, just called your body back and reattached it to your head. Now get up, and let's try this again,' Edward smiled.

The process of getting beat up, torn apart and mutilated repeated itself for many long hours. Alduin could only survive for two seconds at max, which wasn't enough. At least he was getting the hang of his newly found regenerative ability.

'You've improved but it's not enough. It's time for lunch now. After that, Gozo will instruct you on blood magic. Stand up and let's go.'

'Finally,' Alduin responded.

"Lunch consisted of, you guessed it, fresh human flesh fetched straight from today's hunt."

The selection offered a variety of ages, races, and sexes. Apparently, each option had a unique taste. At least there was wine to quench his thirst. Once again, he chose meat from the oldest-looking human available. After eating, Alduin was instructed to wait outside for Gozo, who would escort him to his next training session. That afternoon, he was to unleash his blood magic for the first time. He stood outside the fort near a rock vaguely shaped like a tree, or at least it was trying hard to resemble a tree. A few benches encircled it, surrounding what appeared to be an extinguished bonfire at the centre.

'This must be a portrayal of the mortal world... It's similar, but it lacks the warmth and life of the real thing. I miss it so much,' he thought, a pang of longing hitting him. He hadn't been outside in what felt like an eternity.

At last, he heard a voice calling his name from afar. 'Lodus, I'm here. I apologize for the wait. I was dealing with a group of human bandits nosing around our cave. How was lunch?' said the Vaermiraiit[ii].

'Fine,' he said, his voice clipped. His fists curled at his sides, knuckles whitening as his shoulders stiffened. A muscle in his jaw twitched, but his eyes remained locked on Gozo.

'Follow me.'

'Okay.' He bit his lips.

'Mhm,' Gozo nodded, 'Not that you asked, but the bandits were no fun. As soon as they noticed my glowing red eyes, they just started screaming and running toward

---

[ii] (Omnitongue) Vampire.

the exit. They were literally shitting and pissing their underpants. I didn't enjoy killing them at all, so I just fed them to my hounds.'

'Okay,' he rolled his eyes.

'Let's go.' Gozo took off at remarkable speed, motioning for Alduin to follow. After a few minutes, they reached their destination. It was a strange, cave-like chamber. Four octagonal seals glowed blue, casting an eerie light around the area, and a rectangular seal marked the entrance.

'The creator of this place sealed it with magic, and only those who are familiar with the password can open it. The chant is "La Vaermiraiit, ant-ya din fennen u yul. Oniya saltu. Nor din pavette[iii]",' Gozo explained.

The entrance seal dissolved into thin air, fading like smoke. Without hesitation, he stepped forward, and Alduin followed closely behind. The room stretched out before them, vast and ominous. Pools of blood glistened across the stone floor, their dark surfaces rippling faintly as though alive. Bones bobbed within them, some half-submerged, others clinking softly as they drifted. The air was thick with the metallic scent of blood and something acrid, sharp enough to sting the nose. Shadows danced on the uneven walls.

'This place was built hundreds of years ago by our founder, whom we call "The One of Silver Blood". Because, well, his blood was silver. As simple as that. He was a

---

iii (Omnitongue) Lord vampire, me the follower of you. Blood silver. (To) release the path.

higher Vaermiraiit and the most powerful blood magic user in Euphata.'

'What had happened to him?' Alduin asked.

'He was taken down by our current clan leader.'

'Lysander? How is he still alive? How could he have killed him if he was that strong? Why would you let a traitor rule over you?' he blinked, his brow furrowing as if trying to make sense of it all. His hands hovered in the air, unsure of where to place them, and he shook his head slightly. 'I'm so confused.'

'The culture of vampires is much like that of beasts. When a Beta kills an Alpha, they take their place. If anyone has an issue with the new leader, the solution is simple: kill them and claim the role for yourself. Such is our way.'

'That's barbaric.'

'Maybe, but I'm fine with it. Also, weren't we interrupting some arena fight between you and other Elvish children? What was that about? Guess you're not as different as you think, huh?'

'That's different!' he recoiled as if the comparison itself was a personal insult. His voice grew louder, more defensive. 'It's tradition! A battle between Snow Elves at a young age for the chance to become a Hekket[iv]. You... You monsters wouldn't understand. How dare you even suggest we're the same?!' His eyes flashed with a blind certainty, as if the very idea of questioning it was incomprehensible.

'A Hekket? What is that? Also, can't you see the irony?'

'It's like a royal bodyguard,' he said, his voice filled with

---

[iv] Special Forces (Snow Elf).

pride. 'A part of an elite unit of fighters who protect nobles from the most dangerous enemies. It's an honor to become one.'

'Well, to me, that sounds like your culture *also* glorifies needless violence.' Gozo's voice remained calm, a hint of amusement underlying it. 'And as for your question, Lysander won using an artifact he stole from "The Order". It was crafted to destroy our kind, and yet he chose to use it against his own leader. Funny, isn't it?'

'The Order? The academy of magic? I didn't know they crafted weapons.'

'Yes,' Gozo said casually. 'He infiltrated one of the temples teaching curse magic and slaughtered everyone there. He took all the plunder for himself. Now, he doesn't allow us to speak our founder's name. We're only supposed to refer to him by his nickname.'

'But this entire clan, and the cave system itself, was created by *him*!' Alduin's voice was sharp, his eyes narrowing with disdain. His fists clenched at his sides, and a flicker of disgust crossed his face. 'How can you... How can any of you just forget that?'

'So? Names are meaningless and so are memories. The ones who die, die. You don't see wolves visiting their parents' graves, right? This is our culture. Now, please let's focus on the task at hand.'

'I hate your culture,' Alduin shook his head, his voice thick with disgust. 'There's no honor, no loyalty. Only this endless cycle of betrayal. You all follow whatever suits you, no matter the cost.'

'Grow up if you intend to lead us,' Gozo muttered, rolling his eyes.

Alduin scoffed in response. Gozo then escorted him to the centre of the room and, without warning, began moving his fingers in intricate patterns Alduin had never seen before. He could sense a chant, though its meaning was lost on him. Suddenly, blood surged from the nearest pool, rising unnaturally into the air.

'This is the hand-sign equivalent of chanting "Oniya, ternas nir[v]", which tells blood to float in the air. Blood magic uses your life force and blood as source material. Bear in mind that this spell and telekinesis are very alike. Meaning that if I lose focus on the spell, the blood falls back to the ground.'

'How do I do it? Same way I activated my regeneration?'

'Not quite. After chanting, try to focus your mind and imagine the blood floating up. That should be enough to make something happen. In hand-chanting, each sign represents a different rune in the Omnitongue.'

'So, they are like written incantations.'

'Yes.'

'Okay.'

Alduin concentrated, trying to recall the signs his instructor had made, his mind focused on lifting the blood from the pool. His first, second, and third attempts ended in failure, his frustration mounting with each one. But on the

---

[v] (Omnitongue) Blood, (to) come up.

fourth try, the blood shot up, slamming into the ceiling before splashing back into the pool.

'I did it,' he said, a small but proud smile tugging at his lips.

'Yes, but honestly, this wouldn't be good enough for combat. You must practice until you control it for at least ten minutes. Then, we'll move to levitation. Keep on it. I'll be off hunting in the meantime and shall return to check in on you in a few hours.'

'Okay.'

'Goodbye.'

He spent the next two hours practicing the new blood spell, but success eluded him for the most part. Frustration simmered beneath his focus as his attempts repeatedly failed. But after hours of effort, he finally managed to lift the blood, though it only lasted a minute before it shot off, crashing into the walls.

'Where... Where is Father's advice when I need it?' he muttered through gritted teeth. 'I need you.' He scuffed the front of his foot against the ground, kicking up dirt.

After another hour, he finally managed to maintain the spell for about four minutes. Then, it stretched to eight. Mentally drained from hours of practicing blood magic, Alduin felt like a candle burning down to its wick. But he did not stop. Two more hours passed, and he reached twelve minutes.

Gozo returned from hunting and immediately asked him to demonstrate what he'd learned. Thankfully, Alduin was used to performing under pressure. He lifted his fingers, forming the signs. The blood began to float, and

Gozo counted the seconds aloud. One minute passed, then three, then eight, then twelve...

'Eight hundred and ninety-six, eight hundred and ninety-seven, eight hundred and ninety-eight, eight hundred and ninety-nine, nine hundred. Well done, Lodus. Now I can teach you levitation.'

Even though Alduin's face was neutral, one could see his eyes lit up just a tiny bit. Suddenly, he collapsed onto the ground from exhaustion.

'Blood magic consumes your life force, exhausting you both mentally and physically,' Gozo explained. 'If you overuse it, you'll either fall asleep or lose your mind, whichever comes first. So, take a few minutes to rest, and then we'll continue.'

Alduin closed his eyes, exhaustion taking over, and fell asleep instantly. He woke three hours later.

'You've slept for way too long. Stand up. I want you to grasp the basics of levitation before the end of the day.'

'Alright.' He bit his lips and stretched his body.

Gozo stood before him, his fingers moving to form signs that were both familiar and entirely new. As he completed the final gesture, his body began to float, and crimson-red smoke rose from beneath his feet.

'Did you focus on the signs I made?' Gozo asked. 'Try it out. I won't test you this time. Just practice until you succeed, then get some rest. I have things to do. Farewell.' He nodded and left.

Alduin practiced the spell for hours, each attempt ending in failure. Every time, he was sent crashing into the ceiling or a wall, the impact leaving him bruised and battered.

'Being able to heal myself so quickly is useful,' Alduin thought, wincing at the pain, 'but I miss my mother's cooking... Her bunny stew, her fire-grilled caribou, or that time she made me her famous sunberry tart, drizzled in wine glaze. Was this transformation even worth it? I could have joined them in Henna[vi] by now...' He frowned, the weight of the thought lingering for a moment before he pushed it aside.

His skills had improved over time, and now he could control his levitation for fifteen minutes. He hovered in the air for a moment, eyes closed, relishing the steady lift beneath him. That was enough for now. He could feel the strength growing inside him, the power he would need to avenge his family. Satisfied, he descended and decided to take a stroll around the city.

He floated from the cave room to the bustling main square, recognized by its grand blood fountain. It was filled with noise. Dozens of children laughing and splashing the blood at each other. Atop it, a large stone statue of Lysander stood, his sword raised high, a cold reminder of his reign.

'Fucking narcissist...' He thought, eyes narrowing as he floated past the statue, the cold stone mockingly towering above him.

In between the childish mayhem, he spotted a few couples, both young and old ones, sitting on benches, talking and flirting. Some of them were eating skewers or

---

[vi] (Elvish) Heaven.

drinking wine. He also saw local street artists playing music on drums and a wind instrument he had never seen before. It was very long, and red steam was coming out of it. Some people were dancing to their tunes, though it looked more like a pagan ceremony than a dance.

'Hey, kid!'

He heard a voice and looked for its source. It came from a street food vendor operating a stall next to the fountain. Alduin pointed at himself, questioning whether he was the intended recipient.

'Yeah, you,' the seller said and laughed, 'Why are you in such shock? Come get yourself some delicious snacks,' he smiled.

'Okay,' a bit of saliva built up in his mouth.

It reminded him a bit of his 'culinary adventures' with his uncle. Ley's infectious curiosity and childlike wonder made every new dish feel like a treasure to be discovered. With a smile tugging at his lips, Alduin approached the stall, remembering how they'd laugh together over the most ridiculous of food combinations, his uncle's enthusiasm never waning.

'What do you have for sale?' Alduin asked, his voice steady but his mind elsewhere.

The vendor glanced at him briefly. 'What are you craving?'

Alduin paused, his gaze distant, before murmuring, 'To go back home...'

'What did you say? I couldn't hear you.'

'Oh, uh, nothing. Hmm... I don't know to be honest. What do you have?'

'Marinated baby fingers, skewered human intestines, Balagas…'

'Balaga? What's that?' he asked, 'I remember Lysander mentioning it,' he thought.

'Are you new here?' the merchant's widened.

'Yes.'

'Oh, well, it is a local delicious snack from our city. Crispy baby liver coated with breadcrumbs and cooked in a sauce of human breastmilk and wine. It has quite the kick!' The merchant smiled broadly, just talking about it made his eyes sparkle, and his mouth salivate.

Great uneasiness engulfed Alduin's mind. Why does that 'snack' fascinate him so? Had he finally lost his sense of mortality? His ethics? He was incredibly curious to taste it but was terrified of accidentally enjoying it. He froze in place, stuck in thought.

'Well?' the merchant pushed him for a verdict.

'I'll… Fuck. I'll have one, please… How much does it cost?'

'Fine choice! It's jus-' The merchant froze in place. He was staring at Alduin but it felt like he was looking *through* him. 'General Edward, sir!' the merchant shouted and bowed.

Suddenly, everyone in the streets stopped what they were doing. People who were sitting stood up immediately.

'General Edward!' They bowed as well.

'Hello,' Edward responded, 'Oh, Alduin, what are you doing here?' he asked.

'Hey… Uhm…' He glanced down at the ground, a hint of shyness in his voice. 'I was walking around, and this person suggested I try a local snack. I... I thought I should give it a taste...' His voice trailed off, ashamed of himself.

'Which one?'

'A Balaga, of course.' The merchant said proudly with a smile.

'Ah, those are marvellous. Yeah, you should try them. Maybe it could also help you get used to your new diet,' he said.

'Yes...' Alduin said, his voice tinged with uncertainty, still uneasy about having been caught ordering this 'food.'

'Don't worry about the price,' Edward said and smiled, 'Get two of them for me and two for my friend here.'

'Coming right up!'

'Wait, why?' Alduin said, confused.

'Because I want to make your time here more enjoyable.'

'Here you go,' the merchant said and handed Edward four skewered golden balls. They were steaming hot, 'Wait for them to cool off a bit for the best experience,' he had the bright smile of a proud chef.

'Take these,' Edward gave Alduin his pieces, 'follow me,' he said.

'General Edward!' The merchant bowed, and the people around them did the same.

'Where to?' Alduin asked.

'I know a nice spot.'

Alduin nodded and followed along. There was a huge temple carved in stone in front of the square, adorned with the symbols of Vaonie all around. Edward led him toward it and then took a sharp left, skipping it by a few 'buildings' (if you could even call them that) and then took a shortcut through a dark alley to the right. Every time they came across another vampire, they immediately bowed to Edward and did not move until he 'let' them by acknowledging their existence.

'I had no idea you held such influence around here.' Alduin looked at him, a tiny bit of admiration in his voice.

'Vampires acknowledge strength, and I am considered the best at what I do,' Edward answered, a slight awkwardness in his voice as he chuckled, looking away for a moment. The praise seemed to fluster him, though he quickly composed himself.

They went up two more flights of stairs, turned left, then left, right, up, right. They kept walking until Edward suddenly stopped in front of a platform guarded by a banister. They were high enough to see the entirety of the square, with all its wonders.

'Here we are, take a seat,' Edward smiled and pointed in the direction of a bench that oversaw everything.

They sat down. Edward sighed; his gaze distant. Alduin watched him closely. Why did he invite him here?

'Look at the floor for a second. What do you see?'

'Lines, a lot of lines that are carved on the stone. It looks like every five of them is crossed diagonally,' Alduin answered.

'Exactly. I made those back when I had just turned. I was about twenty years old. I made a promise to avenge my family, slain by this very clan. Though I knew I had to be stronger, so I vowed to keep training and stay alive until that happens. Every line you see represents a whole week. I used to come here every day to think and reminisce about my past. It is very isolated, but I loved the view. It is really quiet here...' Edward said, his lips turned downward as he reminisced about his past.

'Did you end up doing it?'

'Getting my revenge?'

Alduin nodded.

'No. As you can see, there are a lot of lines here. At some point, I just kind of forgot all about it, you know? Moved on...'

'Do you think they know you betrayed them like that?'

'Excuse me?'

'I mean,' his voice rose slightly, 'your family was murdered, and all you've done in return was befriend the ones responsible. My father would have probably disowned me for that,' he said, irritation creeping into his tone.

'Would revenge bring them back?' Edward asked, his expression hardening, the seriousness of his words hanging in the air.

'No, but...' Alduin's voice faltered for a moment, as if searching for the right words.

'Exactly. I have a new life now, and I think my parents would have wanted me to make the best of it,' Edward said, his voice steady yet tinged with resignation. 'Say I take revenge, then what? I'd be back at square one. No friends, no family, nowhere to stay, nothing to eat. And I'm not strong enough to defeat Lysander. He might just kill me, and then it would have been all for nothing.'

'That just sounds like excuses to me,' Alduin said.

'Maybe so.' Edward replied, laughing, though the sound was hollow.

'I-I'm sorry. It wasn't my place.' He looked down, afraid he might lose his only friend.

'I know. It's fine. You'll grow out of it, believe me. You're a strong kid. Plus, you're literally a god now. Maybe you might just be able to get your revenge one day,' he winked, 'feel free to make this place your own, by the way. It helped *me* so it might help *you* as well,' he smiled brightly, with warmth unaffected by the presence of his sharp fangs.

'Thank you.'

'You're welcome. Let's eat.'

They tapped their Balagas as a toast and began eating. Edward leaned forward slightly, his eyes fixed on Alduin as he took his first bite, waiting for any sign of his reaction.

'Wow, this is amazing.' Alduin smiled and said, with food still in his mouth, 'It's crispy but also soft and juicy. And creamy too!'

'I know, right?'

Alduin's smile faltered, a shadow crossing his face as he took another bite. Edward noticed immediately, his expression softening in recognition. He knew that look, that guilt.

'It will be okay, kid. The sooner you get used to your new life, the less this would trouble you. It is an acquired taste...' He patted him on the back.

'You're just in denial... You are eating your own people. How can you do that while keeping on that smile? It is sick.'

'You get used to it,' Edward sighed, his voice carrying a quiet empathy as he spoke from experience.

Alduin exhaled, the weight of his thoughts momentarily settling. They both ate their second Balaga in silence, the tension hanging between them, before their eyes wandered to the view, taking in the scene without words.

'Was it difficult? Getting used to being a vampire? To slaughter humans like cattle?' Alduin turned his head toward Edward, his eyes begging for reassurance.

'Yes, very,' he took a deep breath, 'as I've told you before, the one who turned me was Gozo. And just like in your case, he and his horde had come during a big event for my people. It was my sister's wedding, in fact. I heard people from my village call it the "Red Wedding" nowadays...'

Alduin's face fell, his heart sinking with the weight of Edward's words. He looked down, unable to meet his gaze, his thoughts heavy with the image of the pain and loss.

'Can you tell me about your past life?' Alduin asked.

'Oh, um… Okay,' Edward began telling the tale of his life as a human, as a knight, as a lover, a son and a brother. His story was cut short, though, by a sudden feeling of pressure on his shoulder. He looked to his left. Alduin had fallen asleep, resting his head on his shoulder. He sighed and decided to let it happen. After an hour, it was time for Edward to leave. He patted Alduin's head a few times, a gesture that felt almost paternal, before vanishing with a quiet flicker of teleportation. Alduin stirred, his eyes fluttering open, briefly disoriented by the sudden drop of his head.

At first, Alduin was startled, but it didn't take long for him to realise what had happened. He rubbed his eyes and stretched, his mind slowly piecing together his surroundings.

'Time to go back, I guess,' he said and practiced his levitation toward the main square.

When he finally arrived, Alduin paused for a moment, his eyes scanning the area for something new to catch his attention. The temple stood before him, its massive wooden doors wide open, welcoming worshippers inside. A wisp of orange smoke curled from the entrance.

'Let's see what's inside,' he stepped in, 'Woah, it's huge,' he muttered, his eyes widening as he took in the vastness of the temple.

It was a long hallway full of wonder. He expected there to be benches or bookshelves, but there was nothing of the sort. The floor was covered by semi-squashed red grapes, their rich color gleaming in the dim light. With each step, the squelch of crushed fruit echoed, an unsettling sound in the stillness. The walls were coated with candles and handprints in varying shades of red and orange, an eerie choice for tapestry. Orange smoke engulfed a major part of the room. There was a strong stench of iron and decay contrasted by the subtle sweetness of the burning beeswax candles, a revolting harmony between fire and blood.

'What are those for?' he wondered.

He witnessed naked vampires crawling around in circles. Each adult held a decapitated human baby in their right hand and waved it in circles above their head, making its blood splatter. Their faces were set on the floor as they were murmuring or whispering something ominous which he could not comprehend. The ones with children had them copy their movements and join their circle with lit candles in their right hand. Every couple of meters, there stood an altar filled with lit candles.

'W-What is all this?' he was shocked, his eyes wide open.

He spotted a man and a woman, holding two crying babies, stepping toward a small patch of the wall that remained untouched, its surface stark against the rest. The woman cradled one baby, her fingers stroking their hair, murmuring soft comforts. The man, in contrast, held the other by its leg with one hand, the other gripping a knife, its gleam cold in the dim light. The pair froze. The man raised his knife high, muttering something under his breath before slashing the baby's torso diagonally. Blood spilled, the cries cutting off as the child went still. The woman, eyes wide with something between excitement and reverence, pulled her own baby closer to the fresh wound, pressing it gently against the lifeless body.

'Barbaric... How could anyone do that to a helpless baby?!' he thought, his fists clenching, bile rising in his throat as disgust and fury gripped him.

'Touch it,' she said and smiled.

The man grabbed the baby's hand and pushed it against the blood. Then, the mother guided them closer to the wall. Instinctively, the curious infant gave in to its urge and pressed their palm over it, adding a vivid new handprint. The woman, watching intently, then brought her baby to a nearby altar, offering them a sip from a glass of wine as if the horrific act were a simple, sacred ritual.

'Oh, so that's what those were...' Alduin thought, his gaze shifting to the baby's face. He froze, noticing its glowing eyes. 'A newborn, huh? A bloodthirsty murder in the making... It's unfortunate that I can't rid the world of you before you turn into the monster you're destined to become.' His hatred for the creature simmered, disgust churning in his gut.

Alduin turned away, pushing his revulsion aside as he walked toward the main altar. He ignored the vampires crawling on the floor, his focus shifting to the myriad of strange decorations and ceremonies etched into the temple. Each stop was brief, a fleeting glance at yet another unsettling scene. After five minutes, he finally reached the altar. A towering stone pillar surrounded by flickering candlelight. Atop it sat a large silver chalice, filled to the brim with crimson liquid. The pillar was crowned by a colossal statue, intricately shaped like the symbol of Vaonie, looming over him. Six names were carved into the statue in seemingly random positions. 'Fema,' 'Pholexu,' 'Kans,' 'Anor,' 'Ophiin,' and 'Lodus.'

'The Araqhaiits,' he said.

Two women approached the altar, each holding a glass cup and pouring it into the chalice.

'What is inside of the cups?' he asked them.

'What do you mean? It's red wine, obviously...' The woman on the left said obnoxiously, rolled her eyes and turned back to her friend.

They bowed in front of the altar and left. He lingered for a moment longer, overwhelmed by everything he had witnessed. With a deep sigh, Alduin turned and made his way toward the temple's exit. The cold air hit him as he stepped outside, offering a brief respite from the oppressive atmosphere within. Looking to his left, he saw a row of taverns, their names carved into the same massive stone that supported the temple. 'Blood-red,' 'Taste the Iron,' 'The Dazed Human,' each one more peculiar than the last. Their signs flickered dimly in the cave's shadows, offering no comfort.

'I shall visit them another time,' he thought.

He turned his head to the right and saw an inn named 'Deathless Moonlight.'

'I wonder who sleeps there... Are there any *poor* vampires? What even *is* their money?' he asked himself.

Next to the inn stood a towering post, adorned with road signs carved from stone. One pointed toward the main square, marked 'Centre,' another directed ahead to the 'Strong Zone,' and to the right, a sign labelled 'Mediocre Zone.' Two signs pointed in the direction to the temple. One read 'Temple,' while the other bore the words 'Weak Zone.'

'Well, this confirms what they told me, that a person's place in the social hierarchy is determined by their strength. If I compare it to mortal cities, these 'Zones' must be districts. Strong vampires are allowed to live *there*, and weak ones are confined to live all the way up *there*. Interesting,' he thought, 'so maybe *poor* vampires are just *weak* vampires?' he scratched his head.

He decided it was time to head back to his dorm and rest. Another tough day awaited him tomorrow.

CHAPTER FIVE

He was getting used to the loud noises of feeding every morning. Finally, he could sleep well, relative to before, of course. Today's agenda was identical to yesterday's. Using telekinesis, he dressed and secured the scabbard of 'Vaurcarya' to his waist.

As he tightened the final knot, he froze. 'This is too uncomfortable. Let's try this,' he thought.

He unfastened it and set it on the floor.

'Why carry it when I can have it follow me instead?' he asked himself, 'it would take practice, but it *is* possible.'

He focused, lifting the sword with his powers. It fell. Again, when he opened the door. Again, when he glanced at a guard. Again, on his first step into the staircase. He had to learn to split his focus. He levitated to the dining hall for breakfast and then met Edward at the entrance to the Colosseum.

'Good morrow, Lodus. Today, we'll continue training

your dodging skills until you can maintain it for at least a minute. We will begin immediately, are you prepared?'

'Yes.'

Edward unleashed his beastly wrath, striking at every limb Alduin possessed. Alduin was already accustomed to such training and dodged many of the blows. Yet, in an unexpected shift, Edward adopted a new stance, and with one swift motion, Alduin was cleaved in twain.

'You *are* improving, but this is not good enough. Again.' The next iteration began the moment his body had regrown. This time he was able to last for eighteen seconds. Better, but not enough.

'Again.'

After a few hours Alduin was already capable of lasting forty seconds. The process was tiring and repetitive, but his determination was unwavering.

'Again.'

'Again.'

'Again.'

'Again.'

'Alright, time for lunch. Let's go, Lodus.'

'No. One more try, please,' Alduin said, his piercing gaze locked onto Edward.

'Are you sure? We can always resume this tomorrow,' Edward asked.

'Yes.'

'Ready?'

'Always.'

Edward swung to his feet. Alduin leapt above it. Then, a quick turn and a horizontal strike to the shoulder. Alduin ducked and hovered back. Edward used this opportunity to leap for a vertical strike.

Alduin responded with a swift turn to the left, and then a roll forward. Five seconds have passed. Edward pushed him with a kick, creating an opening for a swing at the chest. Alduin levitated backwards and above it. His retreat was punished by dozens of throwing knives, forcing him to practice airborne evasion. He landed and hovered further away. Fourteen seconds have passed. Edward pulled out his massive war axe, wielding it like it weighed nothing.

'How did he get Orcish steel? There are no orcs in Euphata,' Alduin asked himself, 'the orcs live in the land of the giants. Right, uncle?'

Edward swung his sword at Alduin's torso and his axe at his face. Alduin sidestepped through the strikes. Thirty-four seconds have passed. Intrigued, Edward switched approaches. He pulled out five pouches from his vest and tucked them onto his shirt. In a swift motion unseen to the naked eye, he was throwing more than fifteen knives at once with astonishing accuracy. However, none of them could hit Alduin, surprising them both. Forty-nine seconds have passed.

The deadline was closing in. A grin tugged at the corner of his lips as his chest rose with each breath, his body humming with energy. His eyes were fixed ahead, burning with resolve, and his stance was steady, feet planted firmly to the ground. Edward noticed his celebration and pressed harder. Knives blurred through the air, their numbers swelling. A dozen swords ripped free from the nearest racks with telekinesis, streaking toward Alduin. Despite standing in an open field, he felt cornered. A ground slide to the left, then a jump, then a duck, hovering away, backflip, front flip and pirouette. He nearly lost his footing.

Fifty-nine seconds have passed. A flying sword tore through Edward's left arm. Blood spattered the floor before it grew back. He used it as material for 'Rain of Blood', covering a wide area with spikes in varying shapes and sizes. Alduin wove between them, twisting, dodging, but suddenly, he felt a shock in his stomach. He was impaled by a spear.

'Bravo, Lodus, bravo! Almost sixty-one seconds. Evasion training is hereby finished.' Edward clapped.

Alduin yanked the spear from his gut, flesh knitting itself back together in seconds. Blood pooled at his feet, staining the earth deep red. He exhaled, shoulders rolling back, a slow, marvellous smile spreading across his face. They went for lunch. When he was done, he met with Gozo at the usual spot.

'Greetings, Lodus. Today I will teach you the hand signs for a strong spell called "The Blood Sun". Are you ready?'

'Yes.'

Gozo opened the seal, and they stepped inside.

'The Blood Sun spell is practically a levitating ball of blood magic that drains blood from mortals in its vicinity. Its range can be controlled. My soldiers usually use it for stealth missions.'

'Okay.'

'The hand signs go like this...' Gozo went through them one by one.

Alduin watched it carefully.

'Alright. Let me conjure up a few blood minions for you to practice on.'

From the nearest pool rose four human-shaped minions made of blood. They were glowing in red.

'Now, use it on them.'

Alduin mirrored the signs he had seen. The moment his fingers completed the motion, a deafening explosion shattered the air. A shockwave slammed into him, hurling him backwards. He crashed against the nearest wall, missing an arm.

'You are not precise in your usage of Olons[i]. Cease to be so greedy and childish! You're not accustomed to your rich Olon pool yet. It takes time to understand your limits. Start small and improve. Again.' Gozo commanded.

Alduin regrew his arm, spitting blood onto the floor. He focused on his hand and tried again—only to be blasted into the wall once more. After five attempts, a small ball of blood finally shot toward the test subjects.

'Better. I must go now. Keep practicing and show me your progress when I return. It will be right before dinner.'

'Okay.'

'Goodbye.'

Blood magic came more naturally to him, its practice far more engaging. The blood sun he conjured was small at first but grew with each attempt. Two hours in, it swelled to the size of his head; after four, his torso; and by the fifth, it matched his entire body. Yet despite its increasing size, the sun's power remained unchanged.

---

[i] (Omnitongue) Particles.

'Can it even destroy the minions?' he asked himself.

Suddenly, the sound of footsteps broke his focus.

'I'm back. Show me what you came up with.'

Alduin shot the blood sun at the minions. Upon contact, it pulsed, a deep hum filling the air. Their essence drained slowly, its glow dimming as it fed, hunger unyielding but power still weak.

'Good enough. We will keep practicing tomorrow.'

'Alright.'

Alduin's day ended, and he retreated to Edward's hidden spot, seeking peace and quiet.

'Maybe I should check out that tavern I saw yesterday. It could be interesting,' he thought.

After retracing his steps for a few minutes, Alduin finally arrived. Curiosity gnawed at him, wondering what could possibly justify such a name. He approached the entrance, but before he could step inside, a vampire guarding the door blocked his path.

'Welcome to "The Dazed Human"! I've never seen you before. Are you new in this city?' the guard asked.

'Yes, I am.'

'What is your name?'

'If I want to understand their culture, I should keep a low profile. They would act differently around me. Maybe using a false name would help, just to be safe', Alduin thought. He straightened up, meeting the guard's gaze. 'My name is Virtholdr. Virtholdr Vinyi.'

'Welcome, Virtholdr. Before you enter, there a few a rules that we must go through. Do you understand?'

Alduin nodded.

'Rule number one, absolutely no feeding or touching the humans inside. We need them to stay alive. You *are* allowed to give them food and drinks, though, if you so wish. Rule number two, absolutely no fighting inside. We have a very strict no-violence policy. Someone makes you angry? Take it outside, don't destroy the tavern. And for that reason, I'm obliged to cast a spell on you that will block your magic.'

'No violence? I thought your entire culture was based on violence. How bizarre,' he thought to himself.

'Rule number three, the most important one, no flirting with women who aren't of your own status.'

'Wait, what?' Alduin was confused.

'We are one of the only entertainment businesses in this city that allow citizens of all social statuses to enter. However, the owner of this place is disgusted with race mixing.'

'Aren't all vampires members of the same race?'

'You really *are* new here, huh?' the guard chuckled, his laugh low and mocking.

Alduin stared at him, puzzled.

'Do you agree to the terms?' the watchman asked.

'Yes, I guess so,' Alduin shrugged.

'Alright, stand still,' the guard said.

He stepped closer, placing his right hand on Alduin's forehead. His lips moved in a quiet chant; words barely audible as they swirled in the air.

'Alright, I'm done. You can step inside now,' the guard said and opened the heavy sliding door made of stone.

Alduin nodded. The tavern was coloured in red thanks to the abundance of candles that filled the room. There was a large bar area, a stage where a certain band was playing and around twenty different tables that were mostly occupied by heavily drunk customers who varied in gender and sheer size. In front of each table was a small platform with a metallic pole, onto which was chained a loosely clothed human of no specific age or sex. The humans appeared intoxicated and confused, groaning and moaning with slurred speech.

"He decided to sit by the bar on a stool of, that's right reader you guessed it correctly, stone."

A female worker wearing a black tunic and leather pants addressed him. She had a black ponytail and a pale skin tone.

'What can I get 'ya?' she asked.

'What do you have?' he responded.

She rolled her eyes and pointed upwards. The entire menu was carved in stone right above her. The menu consisted of three types of products – drinks, food and 'For the Dazed Human'. The drinks were split into two types – glasses of red wine and blood, each one with varying options and prices. He recognized some of the brands of wine, like the 'Euphatan Crimson Gold Wine' that costed fifty Samarices[ii] for a glass and two hundred for the whole bottle, or the 'Kontaran Taiquani Wine' that costed sixty-five for a glass and two hundred and thirty for the bottle. The options for blood were vaster and more sophisticated, offering different options according to the age group (zero to five, five to ten, ten to sixteen, et cetera), blood type and

---

[ii] Currency.

race of the mortal. For example, a glass of an Elvish baby's blood costed eighty Samarices on average.

'Hmm... That 'Euphatan Crimson Gold Wine' sounds good... Brings back memories of family dinners with Ley...' He thought to himself.

Available food options were different body parts of human meat, the 'Balagas' he tried last time for ten Samarices a piece, two options for soups and what they called 'Today's Special' for seventy. Options for the 'For the Dazed Human' mostly consisted of beer, human snacks like nuts and fruits, and a 'Dance' that costed twenty.

'What the fuck does 'Dance' even mean?' he wondered.

The annoying bartender's eyes narrowed, her fingers drumming impatiently on the counter. 'Well?' her voice was sharp, the edge of frustration cutting through.

"Kids these days, am I right, reader? Sheesh."

'Hmm...' He pondered loudly.

He heard someone behind him clicking his tongue and sighing.

'Fine, fine, sheesh!' he said to himself, 'I'll have a glass of that "Euphatan Crimson Gold" and three Balagas,' he said.

'Is that all?' she asked.

'Yes.'

'That would be eighty Samarices. How would you like to pay?'

'What are my options?'

The sounds of frustration coming from behind him grew louder. 'Just fucking pay already!' one of them yelled.

'I honestly don't care about your inconvenience,' he thought and ignored them.

The bartender rolled her eyes again.

'Are you some kind of alien or something?' she gave him a hard stare, eyes narrowing in disbelief. 'You can either pay on the spot, or have it written on a formal document with your personal information that we later send to the treasury offices.'

'I prefer the formal order of payment option,' he said.

She sighed and took out a piece of paper from one of the drawers.

'Under the name of?' she asked.

'Virtholdr Vinyi,' he said then added to himself, 'I will tell Lysander later that it was me using an alias.'

'Date of birth?'

'13th of Ruyen, 1076 MDW'

'How old does that make you?' she wondered, the date was old, yet Alduin looked young.

'Thirteen years old.'

'Huh. Not my problem,' she shrugged, 'identification number?'

'I don't know what that is.'

Unexpectedly, a woman got off her chair and approached them.

'I'll pay for him,' she said.

His brow furrowed deeply, eyes narrowing as he scanned the room, struggling to make sense of it. His mouth opened, then closed, as if the right words were just out of reach.

'Wait, why? Who are you? Do we know each other?' he asked.

'No, not yet anyways,' she laughed, 'Come sit next to

us.' She pointed at her table, where two other vampires were sitting.

'Hmm...' He pondered.

'Come on!'

'Fine.'

She handed the Samarices to the barkeeper.

'Alright. We will deliver everything to your table, thank you.' The bartender said.

Alduin nodded. The woman grabbed his hand and brought him to her table. They sat down. Distinct aromas of wine and iron covered the air, alongside sounds of laughter, conversation, aggressive yet 'catchy' music and loud groaning noises. The human that was detained to his table was a young girl, not older than ten. She looked at him, her eyes begging for something. She was thin, way too thin. She mumbled something, but he could not understand what it was. The vampires stared at him, waiting for him to introduce himself. Suddenly, he raised his hand and called a waiter. After about two minutes, one finally came.

'Would you like to order something?' the waiter asked.

'Yes, can I buy a cup of water and some fruit for our human? Like six fruits,' he asked.

'That would be a grand total of nine and a half Samarices. How would you like to pay?'

'I'll cover it,' said the same woman and winked.

She handed him the coins.

'Coming right up!' The waiter left, then returned after a few seconds with the food.

'You have good taste, kid. Could I use one?' she asked him, pointing at an apple.

'Okay,' he said.

She grabbed it and held it close to the mouth of the girl, but the moment she tried to take it, the vampire pulled it away, laughing loudly. The human was so hungry she practically leapt toward it, stopped violently by the length of her chain which pulled her back, choking her in the process. The vampire's friends joined her in laughter.

'What are you doing?!' His voice cracked with anger, fists slamming onto the table as he leaned forward, eyes blazing.

'What do you think I'm doing? This is what this is all about. Don't you see?' she was perplexed by his reaction.

He looked around. She was right. The items on the 'For the Dazed Human' list were used for torture. Some forced alcohol down their throats, granting the business its name – The *Dazed* Human. Some used the food to toy with them, 'feeding' on the sight of their starved, weak and thirsty faces. Chills went down his spine. He handed everything he ordered to the little girl.

'Pfft, have it your way then,' the woman said.

The poor child rushed to eat and drink as much as she could. She knew a chance like this rarely ever happened. She mumbled something to him.

'So anyways... Where were we?' the woman asked.

'Do I actually want to make friends with these people? They're nothing but violent murderers. But maybe this is the only to understand their culture? Maybe I could use this intel to plan my revenge?' he pondered, 'Yeah, so... My name is Virtholdr,' he put on a fake smile.

'I'm Tia,' she smiled. She was the one who paid for his tab.

'They call me Nexer,' he said and shook his hand.

'And I'm Ymmu,' she smiled, 'What's your last name? I heard rumors of certain Virtholdr.'

'Oh, um, it is Vinyi.'

'Ah. No, the one I've heard of is called Virtholdr Tura. Never mind.'

He sighed in relief. 'By the way, why did you pay for me?'

'Don't worry about it,' she said, avoiding the question, 'we're all friends here.'

'Yeah, it's all good.' Ymmu said, smiling.

'Okay,' he responded, puzzled by the situation he had found himself in.

'Are you a tourist? I've never seen you here before,' Tia asked.

'Uhm, no, not really. I *am* new here, though,' he responded.

'Ah, I knew it. I told you, didn't I?' she eyed her friends.

'Yeah, we never should have doubted you. You know literally everyone in this city, it's crazy.' Ymmu said, laughing.

'Is he the one you told us about?' Nexer asked.

'Nexer! Shh!' Ymmu nudged him with her shoulder.

'What?' Alduin was confused again.

'Oh, it's nothing,' Tia was nervous, staring at Nexer, 'I just told them I saw a very handsome guy yesterday in the main square,' she said, looking at him straight in the eyes.

He blushed, having no clue how to react. His chance at

flirting and romance was forcibly torn from his childhood, after all, and he had no experience with women.

'Thank you,' he muttered nervously but quickly regained his cool. He clenched his fist. 'What the fuck is wrong with you? You hate these people, remember? Compose yourself.' He thought, the voice in his head sharp and accusing.

'See? I told you he's cute.' Tia said and turned her gaze toward her friends.

'What do you do around here, Virtholdr?' Nexer asked.

'Here you go, sir,' a waiter suddenly approached their table with Alduin's order and placed it at his side of the table.

Alduin nodded and picked up his glass of wine, 'Oh, what did you ask?' he took a sip.

'I asked what you're doing here. You said you're new,' Nexer said and drank from his goblet.

'Uhm... I train here. Under Edward and Gozo,' he said.

The red liquid shot out of Nexer's mouth, splattering across the table. 'What?! Gozo and Edward?! How do you know them?' he asked.

'They're my teachers, why?' Alduin was confused by his reaction.

'Where do you live?' Tia asked.

'Uh... The castle, I think. I have a room there,' he said.

'Can you introduce me to Gozo? He is so hot!' Ymmu said.

'Here you go again with this obsession of yours. Grow up, Ymmu! You've been talking about marrying him ever since we were kids. You're twenty now. It's unbecoming...'

Nexer said, 'Plus, the two of you are scaring him, stop it. I apologize for my friends here, Virtholdr.'

'It is fine,' Alduin shrugged.

'Pfft...' Ymmu blew a raspberry.

'So... How come you're living at the castle? Are you related to Lysander?' Tia asked.

Alduin took a bite out of his first Balaga.

'Uhm, I don't know. They took me in and decided I have potential, I guess?' he shrugged.

'Yes, but you know... Not everyone gets to live in the castle... Hell, not everyone gets to live in the "Strong District" even.'

'What do you mean? Can't you just buy a house there with your money?'

'No.' Nexer burst out laughing, 'It's more difficult than that.'

'Uh-huh,' Tia said.

He looked at Ymmu and she nodded as well. 'What do you mean?' he asked.

'Do you how our society works, Virtholdr?' Tia asked.

'Not really.'

'Nexer, tell him. You're better at this than me.'

Nexer, chewing a piece of meat, finally swallowed. 'So, our society is based around our military, or rather, Lysander's military. Every one of us serves in the army from twelve until twenty. During this period, our strength is assessed. Then, according to our results, we are categorized and assigned a position. "Strong," "Mediocre," and "Weak."

We are currently in the intersection between the

districts, a zone where everyone is allowed to roam. There are few "free" zones like that around the city.' Nexer explained.

'Oh, what are your positions then?'

'All three of us were put under the "Weak" class, but it's utter and complete bullshit if you ask me!' Tia said and ground her teeth.

The other two nodded in agreement.

'Huh. Then you aren't allowed to enter the other two districts?'

'No, we'd have to pay a fine if we get caught. Absurd, right?!' Ymmu said.

'You see, the three of us believe in equality and are trying to abolish this disgraceful class system.'

'How?'

'Activism,' Nexer said and took another sip from his goblet.

Alduin ate his second Balaga and drank from his cup.

'Yes, activism. We try to convince Lysander to change this broken system.' Tia lifted her cup in the air.

'Hear! Hear!' two vampires shouted from a distant corner in the tavern.

Tia chuckled. 'See? They agree with us,' she said.

'Is it possible to move to a higher class?' he asked.

'Yes. You can enlist yourself back into the military and serve until Lysander decides that you've earned it. You see, the class you're put into reflects your rank in the army, and each class has its own acceptance threshold,' Ymmu explained.

'Can you leave the army once you rejoin it?'

'Yes, you can join and leave as many times as you please, but the only way to progress in this city is via the military.'

'And how do you earn money?'

'Either by working in a business, like that bartender, for example, or by *running* a business, like that man sitting over there in that comfy-ass chair,' he pointed toward a fat vampire with short hair, wearing a purple noble outfit that was sitting on a golden chair next to the bar, 'He is the owner of this tavern.'

'Yes, but being an employee is worth naught. Only the "Weak" class ever work these jobs, because we can't get accepted to anything else. The pay is bad. Honestly, really bad,' Ymmu said in a frustrated voice. Her friends nodded in agreement, semi-sulking.

'The only way to make good coin is via the army, or by inheriting a successful business from someone. Other than that, the game is rigged, I tell ya. Rigged!' Nexer exclaimed.

'Huh.'

'Aye,' Tia said.

'How is that advocacy going for you? Have you made any progress?'

'Quite frankly, no... Lysander's guards never let us come anywhere closer to his castle, so we can't really talk to any of the superior officers. Oh, I just thought of something!' Tia said.

'Hmm?'

'Nah, he would never help us, Tia. He's just another wealthy boy. Our problems don't concern him. It isn't even worth a try,' Nexer said.

'Yeah, he is probably just here thinking to himself "What a bunch of peasants!"' Ymmu complained.

'Shut up, everyone. You're wrong. Let me talk to him. I trust him. He has good eyes. I can see it on his face that he cares about us and our cause. You saw how he treated that filthy human. He is pure of heart.' Tia said, staring at Alduin, 'He is probably our ticket out of here, a naive do-gooder,' she thought.

'Pfft... Fine,' Nexer said, 'Have at it. Just don't complain afterwards.'

Alduin ate his last Balaga, utterly confused.

'What were they trying to do?' he thought.

'Virtholdr,' Tia said.

'Yes?'

'Can you arrange a meeting between us and Edward? Or Gozo? Or even, and tell me if I'm exaggerating here, Lysander? Please, say yes. Say yes!'

'Wh-what? How? They don't know you, why would they accept?' he said, 'Why would I even help these people?' he asked himself.

'Because you know them. Come on, say yes.' Ymmu said with excitement and fire in her eyes.

'I told you he doesn't care. He's just a rich boy, and we're poor kids. He isn't any different than the rest of them fuckers,' Nexer said.

Alduin covered his clenching fist with his other hand, staring down toward the table to try and calm himself.

'Shut up, Nexer. Virtholdr, ignore him. I know you're a good person. Please, we need you.' Tia said, full of passion.

They stared at him, waiting for an answer.

'I-I can't. I'm sorry. They would probably decline even if I tried,' he said, trying to remain polite.

'How are you so sure? Just try and let us know. Come on. You haven't even tried

yet,' Ymmu pressed him further. 'Right???'

'Pfft,' Nexer sighed.

Alduin finished his drink. He began rubbing his forehead, thinking hard about the matter.

'On the one hand, they are nice to me. On the other hand, they're fucking vampires! But on the other hand, they were just born into this, and they have a point. But on the other hand, they've slaughtered my clan, my family! Also, they were so cruel to that little girl. Okay, I've decided,' he thought, 'My answer is no,' he said.

'What a fucking asshole!' Tia barked, slamming her hand on the table, her eyes blazing with contempt.

'Excuse me?' Alduin said, surprised by the sudden shift in treatment.

'Yeah, you're just like the rest of these rich fuckers. Fuck you. Fuck you all the way to Tyronah[iii], you and all your family!' Ymmu screamed.

Those last words triggered rage in Alduin, but he tried his best to hide it. After all, violence was not allowed here. Plus, he didn't know what Vaonie or Lysander would do to him for attacking vampires.

'Aye.' Tia spat on the ground, 'Fucking entitled privileged prick. Your discomfort is nothing compared to the

---

[iii] (Omnitongue) Hell.

oppression you're supporting. If you're not actively dismantling "Strong" supremacy, you're perpetuating it.'

"The fucking irony."

'Silence is violence!' the three began chanting together.

A few other vampires in the tavern joined them in their rant, yelling at Alduin. The owner was getting visibly upset.

'Fucking loud, obnoxious, lowlife peasants,' he thought and sighed.

His hatred for their kind grew stronger. He glanced at his table's human and whispered, 'I'm sorry.' Then, he stood up and headed for the door, hearing loud curses and blasphemies on his way out.

'I'm never going back there again,' he said to himself, 'Never trust these savages again. They are all bad. Except for Edward, maybe. Is he bad? I'm not sure...'

He decided that he'd had enough for today and began his way back to his room to sleep. The following days were repetitive, consisting of tough training regimes. That spot which Edward introduced to him to had proven to be his primary solace. It calmed him. He even started etching his own lines onto the floor.

'One day...' He said to himself as he carved one more line.

After a few months, his training with Gozo had ended with a surprising twist.

'Nevertheless, I think you need actual experience in battle. Come with me to lord Lysander. He will assign you a task to test your skill and mettle.'

They walked outside and headed to the castle. The sight

of Vaermiraiits[iv] bowing to him as he walked made him smirk in evil joy.

'I can get used to this treatment.'

'You are acting like a spoiled child. I know you are mad at us, but you are a god now. Behave like one.'

'I am also only fourteen years old, so cut me some slack.'

'And so are a lot of princes and princesses that are forced to rule at a young age. You have great responsibilities now, grow up.'

'How are you allowed to talk to me this way? I am your god, aren't I?' he clenched his left fist.

'You *are* divine, in that regard, you are correct. However, you are very weak both in your mind and in your body. I may never be able to kill you, but I *could* easily seal you away forever. Vaermiraiits don't blindly respect title. We respect strength.'

'Then why do *they* bow to me every time they see me?'

'Because they are unaware of your capabilities. The details of your training are kept confidential to our society. The peasants know nothing but your title.'

'Would they have treated me the same way you do if they had known?'

'Precisely.'

'Why do vampires not respect authority?'

'Because we think it is stupid. We, *too*, are somewhat divine, a mix between mortals and wild beasts, originating from an Araqhaiit who fucked a human many years ago. Impure, inbred and full of genetic mutations that are not

---

[iv] (Omnitongue) Vampires.

entirely pleasing. Take our weakness to the cold, for example. Our bodies have changed for the better but also for the worse. Our instincts and reflexes have grown supernatural, but with it, we've lost our humanity.'

'Wait, wait. This makes no sense. If you are weak to the cold, then what are you doing in Euphata? All it has to offer is snow and ice...'

'Oh, hell, I shouldn't have told you about that...'

'Why not?'

'It is kept as a secret in our society. Only the generals and the lord know of it. We manufacture amulets that nullify this weakness to an extent, allowed by the advancement of alchemy and enchanting. These amulets are given to our babies and newly turned without explaining their purpose.'

'Huh.'

'Enough chatter. We must make haste to Lysander.'

He was waiting for them, sitting on his throne.

'Hello, Lodus.'

Alduin nodded.

'I heard from Gozo that your training is going well.'

Alduin shrugged.

'You are an ambitious boy. It will come to pass. Patience is key to that sort of thing.'

'You keep calling me a boy, yet I have lived for many years, maybe even more than you have.'

'Don't assume things you know nothing about. I have lived for hundreds of years, even in Elvish counting,' he rolled his eyes.

'What did you call me here for?'

'For a task, to test your new powers and help you acquire experience. Listen well.'

'Will the task take place outside of this cave system?'

'Yes, why?'

'I miss the outside world. The tree-shaped rocks you have here don't really do it for me. I love nature.'

'You offend me, Lodus. It was my very own research that allowed us to mimic the outside world with the rocks we had around. It took a lot of time and effort to make the shapes so realistic,' he explained, 'arrogant pipsqueak.' Lysander thought.

'Huh.'

'You will go to a cave a few hundred kilometers south-east and kill the sorcerers residing inside. It used to serve as one of our mining systems. Do with them as you see fit, but the cave must be cleared out entirely.'

'Another cave, great... ' His eyes shot across the room, 'how am I supposed to locate it? I have never strayed that far from my village by myself.'

'See that warrior sitting beside the door?' Lysander pointed his finger toward a woman.

'The one whose face is covered by a black mask?'

'Correct. Her name is Lul. She will hand you a map of the area and accompany you to assess your skills. Be aware that she is not allowed to help you.'

'Anything else?' he rolled his eyes.

'Yes. Don't dare to fail me.'

'Fine.'

The unfamiliar figure was a tall woman. Her face, apart from her mouth, was covered by a black mantis mask, her red hair running wild and free. A dagger was attached to her left hip, and a large scythe to her back. Alduin was excited to go outside for a change.

CHAPTER SIX

Alduin emerged from the cave, the sun's warmth caressing his skin as a chilly wind whipped across his torso. After years in the underground society, nature's embrace felt exquisite. Snowy peaks towered before him, surrounded by lush forests teeming with wildlife. The golden sun bathed the landscape in an ethereal glow. Alduin stood transfixed, nostalgia washing over him as he drank in the world's forgotten beauty.

He took one last long breath and parted his lips, 'so... Any idea on where we go from here?'

'Yes, but I am not going to help you. Take this map and figure it out for yourself,' she growled and handed him a piece of paper.

'Can you at least mark our current location on the map?'

Lul rolled her eyes, unsheathed her dagger, and stabbed the map to mark their location. She radiated sinister energy —violent and vulgar. He loathed her type, realizing their journey would be far from pleasant. Still, he admired her muscular physique. Despite wearing only black leather straps across her breasts, a dark-brown battle skirt, and sandals, she exuded the aura of a formidable warrior.

'"Just don't get hit,' as one legendary warrior used to say."

'Alright... So, I think we should head this way. Right past this tree there,' Alduin pointed in the direction of a small herb tree with leaves the color of bright pink.

His uncle's wisdom echoed: these leaves could cure the venom of a local water snake—deadly and common in frozen lakes. Alduin recalled the lesson, his brow furrowing at the memory. Lul nodded curtly, then, without warning, plunged her dagger into her palm. Blood pooled around her fingers as she began tracing unfamiliar symbols in the air. Her eyes gleamed with intensity. Alduin tensed, watching her movements with a mix of fascination and unease.

His eyes opened wide, 'what in Munesa[i] are you doing?!'

'Patience, annoying child.'

When she reached the last sign, the blood rose from the ground and formed the shape of a horse. The horse's eyes were shining in the color of the void. Alduin's jaw dropped so hard it metaphorically hit the floor.

'I heard from Gozo that you've already witnessed the creation of blood minions. This spell is a bit different but works the same way. You can conjure up a mount whenever

---

[i]　(Elvish) Hell.

you wish. Its speed varies with the accuracy of the signs you make with your fingers.'

'Yes, but why in the name of the Merissa did you injure yourself?'

'It's much easier to get a source of blood this way.'

'That is seriously messed up.'

'I care not for your opinion. You should use this method too, it is useful,' Lul rolled her eyes, 'my mount is called Vale. I heard you're a fast learner, copy me.'

'I will try.'

Having honed his skills, he was able to control Vaurcarya with his mind. The blade pierced his right hand and returned to its resting place – floating vertically behind him. As the blood splashed on the ground he formed the signs with his fingers, calling it to rise. It manifested into an odd creature – imagine the result of intercourse between a mule and a bunny. Its feet trembled, unable to hold its weight. Alduin scratched the back of his head, embarrassed.

'Nice one, Lodus! What a fucking abomination,' she held her stomach, laughing so hard it hurt, 'now try to mount it. I must see whether it can hold your weight. '

'My name is not Lodus,' he thought and ground his teeth.

He approached it and leapt on its back. It fell and turned back into liquid. Lul laughed even harder.

'Try again,' she said, tears of amusement dropped down her cheek.

This time, he summoned a small horse.

'Better. I was hoping you'd fail again, but eh, never mind. Let's go, we should have left already,' she said.

Alduin hesitated. Despite its size, it was able to hold his weight and walk.

'Do you have a name for it?' Lul asked.

'Not yet. When I manage to summon a proper mount, I'll think of a name.'

She nodded. The horse stared at him, and as though it had understood his words – it stopped in place. He kicked its abdomen and instructed Lul to follow him. The horses galloped in submission.

Lul's lips twisted into a smile. 'Have you ever tried to fly? It's much harder than levitation. I want to see you crash. Ooh, that sounds like fun, doesn't it?' she said.

'Later,' he rolled his eyes.

She blew a raspberry.

After a few minutes of riding, the slow speed of Alduin's horse made him question its usefulness, 'is there a way to make it any faster?' he asked.

'Yes and no. You *could* cast a spell to reduce its weight, or to increase its size – to lengthen the distance between its steps.'

'Huh... Let me try something,' he brushed his forehead with his fingertips, 'nye, sent leil-sis. Tubiri ulat-sis[ii],' he chanted.

He instructed it to resume its gallop. Lul followed from behind.

'Much better,' he sighed in relief.

'What did you do?'

'I decreased its weight. This should be enough for now.'

[ii] (Omnitongue) Mount, (to) be light (weight). (To) go fast.

Alduin pulled out the map from his pocket and with a firm tug on the reins, stopped his horse, 'alright, so... We are here,' he pointed at the map, 'and we need to get here,' he pointed again. 'I think we should go through this short forest route and then head for the mountain; it might save us time. My parents told me it's dangerous, but I'm no longer the same child I used to be...' His eyes closed and he took a deep breath. His lips tilted downwards.

'I go wherever you go, so you don't have to notify me every fucking time you make a decision, child,' she bellowed.

Alduin ground his teeth, 'why must she be so rude all the time? It's difficult enough as it is for me to team up with one of her kind, after everything they've done to me. The sheer sight of her is torture. Can't she understand that?' he thought, 'maybe that's exactly why she's doing it? Look at her twisted smile, she enjoys tormenting me... I shouldn't give in to her taunts. I mustn't let her win,' he clenched his fists to gather up courage.

They took a left turn and entered the forest. He smelled something unfamiliar but didn't give it any attention. With every step of their horses, the trees grew taller and the path thinner. Out of the blue, they heard a tree branch crack and a band of around fifteen highwaymen came out from a large bush. They blocked the road, their weapons at the ready. It was an ambush; his parents were right.

'Bandits, my favourite snack! It is such a shame that I can't kill them myself; they look so weak and soft,' Lul revealed her fangs before licking them.

'What are you babbling about, woman? Give us your

coin and we'll do you no harm. This is our territory, so you must pay the toll, as all do!' one of the men proclaimed.

Alduin's eyes scattered across the scene; he was startled and hesitant, 'I've never hurt a human before,' he thought, 'Father always told me I should be patient with them. They're quick to aggression, but it's just their way to mask their weakness, like a traumatized dog. I mustn't stoop down to their level.' He pondered what to say and then parted his lips, 'no. You do not own this road, please leave us alone.'

'Are you deaf, boy? Our leader's decision is final, what makes you think you can disrespect him, ey?! One more unnecessary remark and you'll lose much more than your coin!' shouted a man from the far-left side, wearing leather armor.

'I don't want to hurt you...' He trembled, his eyes pleading, 'just look at me, look at the color of my eyes. I am warning you, please...' He gazed at Lul, noticing the spark of excitement in her eyes and drool going down her chin, 'please, Father, I don't want to hurt them. Help me, I'm scared. I don't want to become one of them...'

The leader scoffed, 'you offend me, arseling! Go on, boys. I have grown tired of this chatter.'

With a battle-cry the bandits grouped themselves in threes.

'This is madness, stop your men before it's too late! I don't want to hurt humans for no good reason,' Alduin breathed heavily.

With an air of arrogance, the brigands marched toward him. A group of three archers stood behind and aimed directly at his head. With a sudden whistling noise six arrows were shot at him. Alduin realized he had no choice and sighed.

'I'll give them one last chance,' he thought and decided to stand still – to let the arrows hit him.

One arrow hit his forehead, two hit his shoulders and the rest hit his chest.

'Lost your desire to fight so quickly, arseling?' the bandit leader taunted him further.

Alduin stood firm and didn't move. His eyes glowed in anger and frustration, 'not really. This will be my final warning to you. If arrows can't harm me, then surely the rest can't either. Listen to reason, leave me be.'

'Yes, all because you're a fucking "Sharpie"! Men, do not be afraid. We have killed many Elves before. Keep fighting, they look rich,' the leader bellowed and smirked.

Alduin shook his head with a sigh stronger and heavier than the last.

Lul fell to the ground in laughter, her body shaking with each gasp for air. Finally, as her breathing began to steady, she opened her mouth, her voice still trembling with residual chuckles, 'see? I told you humans are stupid, so stop trying to reason with them. They aren't worth your time. You are an Araqhaiit now, for fuck's sake! Enjoy this opportunity, feast.'

The outlaws flanked Alduin from both sides. From the left rushed berserkers wielding a battle-axe in each hand, and from the right – warriors wielding scimitars. The last group charged toward him with a shield and spear.

Alduin stood still, radiating menacing confidence, 'for a

self-proclaimed commander you lack a crucial quality,'
Alduin said, summoning Vaurcarya to levitate before him.

'Oh, and what would that be?' arrogance curled at the
edges of the chieftain's chuckle. 'We have an army veteran
in front of us, boys! Let's all sit and listen to his advice,
fucking arrogant bastard,' he ground his teeth.

'Common sense!' Alduin yelled and commanded his
sword to strike.

Vaurcarya slashed horizontally with terrifying speed,
slaughtering everyone in sight except for the band chief and
his three archers.

'What the hell just happened?' he barked, his voice
cracking with urgency. His eyes darted across the battlefield, wide with disbelief. 'Men, rise! Why are you not
listening to me?!' He clenched his fists, his knuckles
whitening as he turned his head backwards, 'archers, shoot
him. Quickly!' His breath came in short, ragged gasps. 'This
is bad... This is bad...' He muttered under his breath, his
hands trembling as panic overtook him.

Arrows whistled toward Alduin, but he stood motionless. His blade flashed, cleaving the projectiles mid-flight.
Crimson eyes blazed as he surveyed the pooling blood
around him. Profane hunger consumed his mind. He licked
his lips and stalked toward the corpses, his face twisted
with menace.

The bandit leader shouted orders, cowering behind
his men.

Alduin froze and revealed his fangs, his eyes glowing
stronger, 'only a coward could hide behind his men. A

leader protects his men. You lack Lodus[iii],' he said and then looked to the sky, 'Father, I know you support my decision.'

He advanced on the archers, his blade slicing through arrows mid-flight. With a bone-chilling roar, he leapt, jaws gaping. His fangs sank into an archer's neck, draining him dry. He pounced on the next victim as the leader shrieked prayers for mercy. After dispatching his final prey, Alduin dabbed his lips with a pocket napkin. Behind him, Lul's laughter echoed.

'I... I enjoyed it. Why did I enjoy it? What the fuck have I become?! I never wanted this!' He fell to his knees and stared at the sky in mental anguish, 'Lul, is this what you people feel when you go raiding?'

'Yes, finally, you got the gist of it. I must say, watching you fight was way more fun than I had anticipated. You let out the beast, I like that.' Lul responded.

She dropped to her knees, her long, devilish tongue lapping at the blood pools. Her heavy breaths made Alduin shiver with discomfort. As she licked, her body twitched sensually. She caressed her breasts, moaning in pleasure. Nauseated, Alduin turned away, focusing on the leader who now cowered on all fours, begging forgiveness.

Alduin ground his teeth, 'why would I spare a person like you? Look at you! You have no self-respect, so why should *I* respect you?'

'Spare me, and I swear you will never hear of me again...' Tears streamed down the outlaw's face, 'I beg of you, please! Give me a chance.'

[iii] (Omnitongue) Honor.

'My name is Alduin Lodus Faëli and I am a god,' he said firmly, 'for the way you've forsaken the honor of your comrades, I sentence you to death. If you wish to die swiftly, stand up and lower your head in a bow.'

'Fine,' the mortal obliged, concealing a faint smirk. As Alduin approached, the bandit whipped out a hidden dagger, plunging it into his heart. 'Your morals are your weakness. Now you'll die, and I'll take everything!' He turned to Lul, eyes gleaming. 'You, sexy maniac, I won't just kill. I have something special planned...' He cackled, pointing at her.

Lul responded with a frightening smile, revealing sharp, white teeth.

Alduin erupted in uncontrollable laughter, lasting minutes. Finally composing himself, he pulled the dagger from his heart, fixing his gaze on the bandit, 'I haven't laughed like that in ages. Thank you,' he said, his tone shifting. 'Unfortunately, you've just squandered your only chance,' his fingers began weaving arcane signs as he spoke.

Alduin ventured into spell-crafting, conjuring a new blood spell—risky for mortals, but not for him. Blood rose from nearby pools, twirling around the bandit's body. Suddenly, it fell, forming a circle on the ground. Blood spears erupted, piercing the bandit from all directions. He screamed, his eyes twitching in agony as ragged breaths escaped him.

'I name it "Blood Impalement". Are you impressed, Lul?'

'Impressed? No. Entertained? Yes! I loved the way his

body was shaking. The fright in his eyes... Good job. Let's carry on.'

Alduin nodded. They rode on, reaching the great mountain. The atmosphere between them had softened, much to his disdain. Lul embodied everything wrong with her culture, reinforcing his belief that her kind must be eradicated. Yet, he had to maintain this facade, knowing any misstep could turn Vaonie against him. Still, he clung to hope. There had to be an exception, a way to fulfil his vengeance without jeopardizing his position. He wished to find it, somehow.

'Do you know the name of this mountain, Lul?'

'No.'

'My ancestors named it "Vel Joog Madaran Ke Zaffai" – "The Great Mountain of Deceit" in Elvish. It earned its name for its deceptive nature. Though it seems ideal for a fortress, frequent earthquakes and hostile spirits make it treacherous. My great-great-grandfather likely perished there in a collapse.'

'Sounds like fun. Let's climb it,' her eyes shone in excitement.

Alduin's brows furrowed, 'why climb, when we can fly?'

'Finally, I can see you hurt yourself!' She grinned, 'I'm not a great sorceress, so I'll just climb. See you there.'

'Alright,' he shrugged.

Lul leapt onto the mountain, her claws piercing rock as she climbed at unprecedented speed. Alduin attempted self-controlling telekinesis for flight, but struggled with accuracy, crashing or falling repeatedly. He persevered, watching Lul's swift ascent on the horizon.

'I can't loser to her. Come on, Alduin, control it. You've mastered harder things before,' he muttered.

With each attempt, his control improved. As Lul neared the peak, Alduin thought of a workaround, forged by his own shame. He launched himself upwards, crashing on his back but beating her to the summit.

'You cheated! That was not flight, you merely threw yourself here,' she growled.

'Isn't flight just controlled falling in a specific direction?' he said, 'besides, I never claimed this was a competition to begin with.'

She scoffed.

'See that black shadowy thing on the right? Near that other mountain?' he pointed toward it, 'I am certain that is our destination, follow me.'

Alduin launched himself down the mountain, crashing on his stomach. Lul followed, leaping from cliffs. They summoned their mounts and rode on, Alduin leading. They encountered Dorynies, ice spirits, bears, sabre cats, and ice trolls. Surprisingly, Alduin remained unfazed, dispatching them all with telekinetic control of Vaurcarya. After three days of relentless combat, they reached the cave. Alduin directed Lul to dismount and hide in nearby bushes to strategize. Six sorcerers guarded the entrance.

Lul smiled, her voice laced with amusement, 'given your earlier performance, I'll share some intel. These priests are formidable sorcerers, well-versed in various magical fields. Advanced sealing magic is certainly part of their repertoire. '

'So... If I don't tread carefully, I could get sealed away or paralyzed by them?'

'Do you have a plan?' she asked.

'I am thinking of one. Hmm...' Alduin stroked his chin, 'it is nearly nighttime, so blood magic could work in my favor, as it's almost invisible in the dark.'

'Experienced sorcerers use light spells. Are you that ignorant?'

'Hmm... Maybe stealth archery?'

'Again, experienced sorcerers always protect their bodies with skin-toughening spells like "Oakflesh" or "Stoneskin". Think harder.'

He looked at the palm of his left hand, 'Vaonie mentioned this tattoo has significance. Any idea what it does? It might be important.'

'No clue. Try it, you've got nothing to lose. Except your existence, of course,' she grinned.

'Very funny. Hmm... Maybe I need to treat it like an extra limb...' Alduin said closed his eyes to think.

He crouched, sneaking toward the guards. Holding his breath, he lunged, subdued a sentry, and dragged him into the bushes. Rope silenced the man's limbs and mouth.

Alduin aimed his tattooed hand—first with finger gestures, then mimicking fireball motions. Nothing. Gritting his teeth, he focused harder.

The mark pulsed with anti-light—a blackness deeper than void, swallowing all illumination. The guard's eyes bulged, mouth stretching soundlessly as his pupils darkened to obsidian. A choked gasp, then stillness.

'Hmm... So, it can kill people, or maybe it just neutralizes them. Interesting...' Alduin's eyes sparkled in childlike wonder, 'I must learn to control it. It is too slow at its current state.'

Alduin repeated the tactic on the remaining guards. Confident now, he targeted the next from the bushes, unleashing the marks's power. The guard's agonized scream alerted the last two sorcerers. Cursing his mistake, Alduin abandoned stealth and stepped into the open.

'Who are you? Where is Richard? Come to think of it, where are Luce and Lee? Tell me, or I swear your death will be extra painful!' one of the guards shouted.

'They're dead, and my name is none of your business. Let's get this over with.'

The guards roared, preparing their spells and potions. They hurled ice shards and fireballs, giving Alduin perfect dodge practice. He weaved through the barrage, then swung Vaurcarya at their necks. The sorcerers ducked smoothly—apparently versed in melee combat.

Alduin smirked. 'Interesting… Let's try that again,' he said.

Blood swirled into a shield around him as he activated Vaonie's mark. One sorcerer choked, eyes dimming to lifeless voids. His companion's anguished scream fuelled the last guard's desperation—three spirit trolls materialized alongside fiery hail.

Alduin charged, his sword slashing through his opponents in chaotic beauty. He severed his arm and regrew it immediately mid-sprint. Twin-handed signs summoned the Blood Impalement spell. Crimson fluid encircled then impaled the sorcerer, his screams dying as the battle stilled.

'This power... I wonder what Uncle would think,' he muttered, both proud and homesick.

Lul applauded by stomping a corpse's skull into pulp, cackling as she dropped to all fours. Her tongue lapped at bloody snow, moaning with perverse delight. 'I can literally taste their fear,' she said.

'Let's proceed, Lul.'

She raised her head, 'let me finish.'

'No.'

Her eyes shone in scarlet, 'excuse me?!'

'We have a mission, let's go.'

'No.'

'Lul!' he commanded, his ferocious eyes sending a direct message – 'Do not test me.'

'Fine, fine. Fucking asshole,' she said and stood up.

Alduin led the way into the cave. Suddenly, he slammed into an invisible force, hurtling about four meters backwards.

He stood up, his eyes searching for the culprit. and observed the situation. 'A magical barrier?' he mused.

'Seems like it... Why are you so surprised?'

'Well... The guards weren't that much of a fight... I wasn't expecting to face such an advanced defense system.'

Lul clicked her tongue, crossed her arms and looked away.

'Can you teach me how to dispel it, or are you just going to act like a piece of Dorynie shit?'

'Only time will tell... Alright, I thought about it. No,' she grinned.

Alduin rolled his eyes. He rocked his mind for an answer and scanned the walls. No spell seals visible – likely a regular barrier, not a trigger-activated one. Suddenly, he recalled his visit to Vaonie's dimension. They told him of a certain special flame. Curious to see what would happen, he tested his luck.

'Ut-Obliryne u Tyronah[iv].' He chanted.

Nothing happened, save for Lul's mocking laughter. Alduin's attempts to rearrange the words proved fruitless. Frustration boiled over at his master's lack of instruction.

He clenched his fists, 'why must you people be so irritating? Why couldn't Vaonie just teach me how to use this power instead of forcing me to figure it out for myself? And why do you, vampires, keep explaining my abilities in such cryptic ways that make no fucking sense?!'

'Because it is more entertaining to see you suffer. Grow some balls and stop complaining, or we'll never respect you.'

'What if I fail?'

'Vaonie has no place for pathetic losers. You would probably be replaced.'

'Then I guess you're both assholes-' Alduin was cut off by an abrupt, immense pain in his torso and collapsed.

His eyes shut down slowly, and his skin turned even paler than before.

[iv] (Omnitongue) Flames of Hell.

A familiar voice boomed from the void, 'INSOLENT MAGGOT! YOU DARE NAME ME IN DISHONOR?!'

'You've angered them, you fool!' she yelled, 'beg for mercy, or you'll die here. Hurry!'

Alduin's throat locked. His vision tunnelled.

'In your mind, you simpleton,' she said.

'Please, please, please. I am sorry. I beg you, I do not want to die yet!' he said in his head.

No response. His lungs burned as he gasped for air. The world around him spun, his skin felt as though pierced by tiny needles. Sharp pain shot from his heart.

'Please! I swear, I will never do that again.'

No response.

"By modern standard, he should die in about ten seconds. "

'What if I vow to take down a Sarathiin? Would that suffice to repent?'

A sudden gust of air filled his lungs.

'I am listening,' Vaonie responded.

'I pledge my right to live to this challenge. Kill me if I fail.'

'As you wish, you are forgiven,' Vaonie said and loosened their invisible grip on his heart and neck.

'Thank you, my lord,' Alduin responded, his body aching and his vision blurry.

He barely managed to stand up.

'You really have no control over your mouth, huh?' Lul wore a bright smile on her face.

'Shut up, Lul,' he growled, struggling to steady his ragged breaths. 'First was Father, now Vaonie?' he thought.

'Stop complaining,' Vaonie's voice echoed in his head.

'Vaonie warned me of their control over my body, but I never fathomed it so absolute…'

'They're your god, and you're their servant. Don't do that again, as their mercy is a rare gift,' Lul proclaimed and then turned toward the entrance, 'do you know what to do with the barrier yet?'

'I think so…' He stared at his tattoo for a minute, hesitant, 'I have an idea, but it could be very, very dangerous.'

Lul rolled her eyes, 'I don't really care if you live or die, to be frank.'

Alduin raised his hand and aimed at himself, the back of his palm facing forward. The arcane symbol shifted through his flesh from the back to the front, facing him. Flames erupted within. His screams echoed through the cave, body writhing. He clawed at his skin, desperate to extinguish invisible fire. Lul's laughter mocked his agony. Thirteen minutes passed. Silence fell. Alduin rose, skin obsidian-black. Naked, eyes coal-dark, he breathed in ragged gasps. Vaonie's symbol pulsed in his pupils.

She leaned closer to observe, fascinated, 'interesting-'

Alduin's jaw unhinged, revealing rows of razor fangs. A bestial roar escaped him. His gaze locked on her, pupils flaring white.

Lul convulsed, engulfed in monochrome flames. 'Wha-What are you doing?!'

Her limbs charred, body spasming like a marionette with cut strings like it was glitching. Alduin's gaze swept the area. Everything crumbled to ash, and then into nothing. The expression on his face showed no remorse, no compassion – no conscience.

The sound of pounding footsteps echoed through the cave, a thunderous drumbeat that grew louder with each passing moment. The air vibrated with the collective rush of breaths. The ground trembled beneath their feet, a seismic rumble that heralded their approach like an avalanche. They finally arrived, chanting beyond the barrier – thirty sorcerers. They came to face the intruders head-on. Alduin's head snapped toward them, like a reflex. Their screams joined Lul's cacophony as flesh melted from bone. Bodies disintegrated into nothingness.

The barrier shimmered with a whistle, then vanished. The flames refused to let go, ever-hungry – endlessly spreading and consuming everything in its path. Stone, metal, flesh, fabric, earth – they all fell prey to the fire and disappeared as though never existed, without a trace to remind of their presence. Lul, lying helpless on the floor, stared in horror as Alduin rampaged, incapable of stopping him; incapable of even standing up. Suddenly, his skin paled, markings faded. He collapsed, unconscious.

Her pupils dilated. 'What, the fuck, have you done to me?! Look at me! I have no legs, no hands, I am a fucking cripple now. I can't even heal a wound like this.' She yelled at him.

Alduin awoke and stood up, ignorant of what had happened. He noticed her on the cave floor, 'what? Lul, what happened to you? Where is the barrier?' his eyes opened widely.

Having been forcefully stripped by the flames, he could

see her face for the very first time. It was marred by a long horizontal scar.

'You don't remember, you prick? Are you fucking kidding me?!'

'I don't.'

'You started screaming and your body turned black. Then, everything you looked at began burning. You destroyed my body, fix it!' she bellowed.

'I-I don't know how to... fix you... I don't know if it is even possible.'

Mixed emotions forced their way into his mind. She was neither a friend, nor a foe. Their time together had softened his perception of her, though clearly not enough to feel guilty or saddened. He didn't know how he should feel, and it showed on his face – a faint smirk with worrying eyes, contradictions spread all over his expression.

'Must I remain this way forever? I was feared and respected. What have you done to me, you cur?!' Her eyes blazed with fury as she revealed her fangs in a roar.

'I didn't mean for it to be this way. I can't recall anything, not even telling it to cease. It probably has a time limit...' He scratched the back of his head.

'What am I to do now?' Lul sobbed, a river of tears coating her face.

Alduin walked in circles, his mind racing for a solution. He stopped and commanded Vaurcarya to shred his limbs. Blood gushed forth, shaping into arms and legs for Lul.

'This should suffice. I am certain Lysander would know what to do,' he said, 'serves her right...' He thought and smiled in his head.

Lul sprang up, her new fist slamming into Alduin's face. He crashed into the cave wall behind him.

'Okay, this is fine for now. Let's keep on going, I am tired of this mission already.'

Alduin leapt to his feet and stood in front of her. 'I see amulets and rings on the ground there. Whose are they?' he asked.

'At some point, while I was,' she raised her voice, 'burning alive, a few dozen mages arrived, and you incinerated them.'

'So, we're done here?'

'We must make sure.'

'Fine,' he said.

They sprinted through halls, reaching a vast throne room. A motionless figure sat, unresponsive.

Alduin's eyes furrowed, 'uhm... He doesn't react. Can he see us?'

'I think he's dead,' she sniffed, 'I can't smell his fear.'

Alduin approached the man. Even a foot away – he did not react. His eyes stared, vacant, as though unconscious.

Alduin parted his lips, 'dead, but why?'

'I'm equally perplexed.'

'Perhaps the flames followed the traces of the barrier, to find its source?'

'You've vaporized his brain?' Lul's jaw dropped.

'Maybe?'

'Impressive.'

'Yes.'

She scoffed, 'shut up.'

Alduin looked around, searching for oddities. Having

found nothing, he approached his companion, 'we're done, let's head home.'

She nodded. They exited the cave, summoned their mounts, and rode for the clan's base. Alduin's horse had grown larger, more agile. Vaurcarya dispatched foes effortlessly along the way. After two and a half days, they arrived. Lul dismounted.

'Cent u din oniya sal-tu,' she chanted, and the barrier dissolved.

'What incantation was that?'

'The name of my home, "Castle of The Silver Blood". Let's get in.'

They entered the cave, the barrier sealing behind them. Lul's familiarity with shortcuts led them to Lysander's throne room in three hours. Alduin, still naked, opened the massive doors telekinetically. Female servants' eyes lingered on his battle-scarred body. Mottled skin and jagged lines told tales of his complicated life.

'Lodus, you've returned.' Lysander's excitement faded to confusion as he raised his right eyebrow, 'why are you… naked?'

Lul emerged from behind Alduin, her face twisted in a scowl. 'It was utter shit!' She slammed her dagger onto the table, the clang echoing through the chamber

Lysander's brows furrowed, gaze darting between the pair. 'What? What happened to you?'

'Your so-called chosen one happened to me.'

'Can't you grow them back?'

'No. For some reason, I can't.'

'I see,' Lysander sighed, gesturing to a robed Vaermiraiit[v] at the dining table. The man's bluish-purple attire and long gray beard marked him as a sorcerer. 'Slod, tend to her. Her spirit and power are vital to my army,' he commanded.

'Yes, lord. I will take care of it,' Slod bowed and instructed her to follow him.

Lysander turned to Alduin, eyes narrowing. 'Lodus, explain yourself. Is this treason? And the base—is it dealt with? Report!' He crossed his hands, tapping his right arm with his finger, waiting with wavering patience.

Jittery with nerves, Alduin darted his gaze around the throne room. 'It wasn't intentional. My new power, Vaonie's flames, took my body hostage and scorched everything— Lul, the cave, even my clothes. I wasn't conscious,' he muttered quietly.

Lysander leaned forward, intrigued. 'These flames... I'd like to witness them someday. You've served us well, Lodus. Dismissed. I'll organize a force to reclaim the cave.'

Alduin nodded, a faint smile playing on his lips. He levitated to his room and jumped like a child onto the bed. Sleep claimed him instantly.

---

[v] (Omnitongue) Vampire.

INTERLUDE ONE

He was in the midst of writing a letter when the ear-deafening thumps of drums and blaring horns startled him. His skin prickled as adrenaline surged through his veins, heightening every sensation. It was early October of 320 BCE on planet Earth, long before the birth of our main protagonist. Instruments like these were used in wars to alert people of impending danger.

He bolted to the entrance hall, his movements sharp and urgent.

'Stay inside and protect yourself with my Dory[i]. Don't open the door for anyone but me!' Theseus commanded, grabbing his sword from the cabinet.

'Be safe,' his wife whispered, her voice trembling as he slammed the door shut and sprinted toward the village

---

[i]   Name for the standard spears that were used by the Greek Hoplites.

square. Left alone, she gripped the spear tightly, whispering a fervent prayer to Ahura Mazda[ii].

The screech of blades grinding against whetstones grew louder, mingling with the clatter of armor handed down by slaves to their masters and the distant cries of children. As Theseus approached the square, his footsteps slowed. He scanned the scene: men preparing for battle, their faces tense but resolute. At a table nearby, a group of familiar villagers sat chatting.

'Hey!' Theseus called out, his tone firm but curious. 'Have the outlaws reached the gates yet? Most of us aren't ready to fight.'

'Not yet, thank the gods,' replied Lysander of Thebes, his confident smile steadying those around him. 'But it doesn't matter. We outnumber them and have a solid defense plan.' Lysander tore into a loaf of bread and washed it down with wine before gesturing toward an empty chair. 'Sit with us while we wait. Eat while you can.'

One hundred and eighty centimeters tall, with hazel eyes and an air of authority, Lysander's appearance matched his stature as the village commander. His reputation as a skilled fighter only added to his appeal.

Nicander, a Spartan draped in a vivid red cloak, pushed back a wooden chair for Theseus. 'Yeah, join us, *Thaseus*,' he said with a grin.

Lysander locked eyes with Theseus. 'Weren't you writing a letter to Eumenes? Tell us about that,' he said.

Theseus shook his head firmly. 'I'd love to chat, but I

[ii] The god of Zoroastrianism, the ancient Persian religion.

must help the guards at the gates.' He turned to Nicander. 'Could you come with me? Let's assist them before the fun ends.'

Nicander's grin widened as he stood, his broad frame radiating strength. 'Just like old times,' he said with a chuckle. 'Let's go.'

The pair sprinted toward the gates, their steps synchronized from years of camaraderie forged under King Alexander the Great's campaigns. Theseus was thirty, and Nicander – thirty-three. They were both descendants of Meliboea's founding families who had rebuilt it from ruins.

When they reached the gates, chaos greeted them. A group of bandits had breached in Phalanx formation: ten Hoplites[iii] armed with spears and shields, five archers ready to strike from a distance, and five wielding javelins. The guards were struggling to delay their advance.

Theseus tightened his grip on his sword, assessing their opponents swiftly. 'Fuck,' he muttered. His jaw clenched, no time for hesitation. The guards ceased fire as Theseus and Nicander approached, joining them in melee combat.

An outlaw sneered, 'do you really believe you stand a chance? Fuck off, and no harm will befall you.'

Nicander's eyes glinted with mischief. 'Where's the fun in that? We're prepared to fight, are *you*?'

'These guys have a death wish,' the bandit leader chuckled, locking eyes with his men. 'Fine then.'

Nicander let out a thunderous war cry as the pair drew

[iii] Citizen-soldiers of Ancient Greek city-states who were primarily armed with spears and shields.

their weapons, standing back-to-back in fighting stances, determination etched on their faces.

'Drop your spear and shield, Nicander,' Theseus said.

'Why?'

'You wanted this battle to be fun.'

Nicander obliged, wielding only his sword. The phalanx formed a circle; the first attacker thrust his spear at Theseus's head. He dodged masterfully, losing only a few strands of dark hair to the sharp tip. The pair moved in perfect sync, incorporating the guards into their violent dance. The crack of spears against swords and shields, screams of agony, and spilling blood created a brutal symphony. Nicander felt at home.

But for every fallen enemy, two more breached the gates. As if they were fighting the legendary Hydra[iv].

Theseus panted, 'we can't hold much longer. They're too many.'

'Just hold on.' Nicander growled, his muscles burning with fatigue.

An arrow pierced the last guard's eye, and the pillagers infiltrated the village. Fifty men stood before them, far larger than previous raiding parties. Nicander and Theseus exchanged a stunned look of both fear and awe.

'We're royally fucked. Fall back!' Nicander yelled.

The bandits' leader stepped forward, smirking. 'Hoplites, Phalanx!'

'Phalanx!' The hoplites' shouts thundered through the air.

[iv] In Greek legend, a gigantic water-snake-like monster with nine heads.

'Take everything and leave no survivors. Hurry, before the militia arrives,' their chief commanded.

As the outlaws ransacked the houses, a distant rumble grew into an ear-deafening roar. Finally, the village militia arrived, armor clanking with each step. Their battle cries sent fear through the bandits' ranks. Lysander stood among them, his bronze cuirass gleaming in the sun.

The raid was quashed in an hour, with minimal friendly casualties. Their success stemmed from rigorous training during the world conquest campaign of King Alexander. That, and Lysander's exceptional command.

Minutes later, villagers regrouped in the square to assess damages. Three men had fallen: two guards at the main gates and one militia member. Their sacrifice limited the destruction to the first few houses. The atmosphere grew somber as villagers dispersed – some treating the wounded, others preparing graves, and a few consoling those who lost homes and family.

Theseus's wife, Shiraz, escorted him home, her gray eyes brimming with pride and concern. Her olive skin, just like his, and lush brown hair reflected her noble Persian descent. They met in 'Susa', the Persian capital and Shiraz's hometown, during Alexander the Great's mass wedding event. Known as the 'Susa Weddings', this gathering was Alexander's attempt to unite Greek and Persian cultures. Though Shiraz wasn't part of the official ceremony, Theseus sought Alexander's blessing for their marriage. The king, acknowledging his battlefield valor, granted his approval with a smile.

At home, Shiraz embraced him tightly, feeling his racing

heart. She noticed his dull, tired eyes filled with grief. Carefully, she removed his breastplate, unfastening straps and lifting it over his head. His clothes were stained with sweat, dirt, and blood.

While Theseus prepared the stove, herbs, and oils, Shiraz fetched water for a bath. She helped him in and scrubbed his skin meticulously, her touch gentle and loving.

'I was terrified.' Shiraz's voice quavered. 'Why do you keep risking your life? The village needs you.'

Theseus sighed. 'We had to delay the attack. If we hadn't helped, more villagers would have died.' He paused, adding softly, 'I'm just glad you're safe. I... Three died today, all because I wasn't strong enough...'

Shiraz caressed his cheek. 'You did well,' she whispered, 'it's not your fault.'

'Thank you, but I could have saved them. I used to be a great warrior, but now I fear I've become inept. And they were the ones who paid the price...' He squeezed his heart with his left hand, eyes darkening, 'it hurts... Like it's devouring me whole.'

She grasped his head firmly with both hands, turning it toward her, her eyes locking onto his with an unyielding intensity. 'Look at me,' she said, her voice a gentle yet insistent command. 'This isn't your fault.'

He took a long, deep breath. 'Maybe...'

She nodded and continued scrubbing his back.

'Shiraz,' he muttered, his face hardening.

'Yes?'

'I plan to journey north. Join me.'

'The north? Why?'

'Theron mentioned a cave near "Goldfall Lake". He said whoever entered it hasn't returned. It intrigues me.'

Shiraz frowned. 'Theron again? Don't you recall the last time you trusted him? He claimed red clothes would ward off brown bears, and you nearly lost your life.'

'Yes, but even if the cave doesn't exist, at least we'd enjoy quality time together. Village life has grown stale. You know I crave adventure. It's… how we met,' he faced her with pleading eyes.

'I understand, but I'm worried. How long would we be gone?'

'I'm still planning the route,' he grabbed a linen cloth and patted himself dry, 'but I want to leave soon.'

Shiraz's expression softened. 'I can't join you. Thesmophoria[v] is starting, and I'm preparing dough offerings. Promise to join me for breakfast tomorrow before you leave.'

Theseus nodded. 'I promise. You're not participating in the festival again?'

'No, just helping set it up.' Shiraz's face brightened. 'Now, about dinner… I'm making lamb stew. Could you get some meat?'

Theseus kissed her forehead, dressed and headed to the sheep pen. He opened the fence and picked one, leading it to a secluded spot behind the house, away from the others.

'I'm sorry,' he whispered to the unsuspecting animal

---

[v] An ancient Greek religious festival held in honor of the goddess Demeter and her daughter Persephone.

before drawing his dagger. With one motion, he decapitated it. 'Artemis, come eat!'

He tossed the head to the puppy, tied a rope around the sheep's neck, and hoisted it onto his shoulders. Back home, he announced, 'I'm back.'

'Took you long enough.' Shiraz's eyes sparkled with mischief. 'Cut the meat; I'll brew the stew in the meantime.'

He nodded and began skinning the sheep.

'By the way,' she said, 'Aristaeus stopped by. He's heard of your cave expedition. Knowing him, I think he's interested in joining you.'

Theseus's eyebrows raised. 'Really? It's been a while. I'll visit him once the stew's cooking.'

He cut the meat into small pieces and handed them to his wife, alongside a soft kiss on the cheek.

'I'll be back in a few minutes,' he said and left. At Aristaeus's house, he knocked. The exterior was lavishly adorned, reflecting his prosperity as a merchant.

'Who is it?' a voice called.

'Theseus. My wife said you were looking for me.'

Aristaeus, resplendent in a rich purple Chiton[vi] and adorned with a golden necklace, greeted him with a warm smile. Four years older and slightly shorter than Theseus, he had curly black hair and brown eyes that sparkled with enthusiasm. 'I heard about the cave. I'd like to join you,' he said.

Theseus's brows furrowed. 'Would Lyria approve?'

[vi] A form of tunic that fastens at the shoulder, worn by men and women of ancient Greece and Rome.

'She's supportive. I'm sure she'll agree.'

Theseus shook his hand. 'It's settled then. Let's meet in the square in an hour to plan our route,' he said.

Aristaeus nodded. 'Thank you,' he said and escorted him out.

Theseus waved him goodbye. Back home, the savory aroma of the stew wafted through the air, mingling with the scent of fresh herbs.

'Food is ready,' his wife announced with a smile.

A plate, a fork and a spoon were laid on the table. As they sat down to eat, the warm light of the setting sun cast a golden glow over it.

Shiraz's eyes sparkled with amusement as she smirked. 'I was right about Aristaeus, wasn't I?' she asked, her voice playful.

Theseus nodded, smiling at her intuition. 'We're meeting soon to plan. I'll likely leave tomorrow morning.'

'I'm always right after all,' she chuckled.

'I know,' his eyes gleamed with love as he looked at her.

After dinner, Theseus grabbed a map and headed to the square. Returning home, he found Shiraz asleep. He kissed her forehead gently before drifting off himself.

Dawn broke with chirping birds and crowing roosters. They rose together, preparing a breakfast of homemade bread, cheese, and olives. When they finished eating, Shiraz gestured to the backpacks by the door. 'You're done packing, right?'

'Yes,' Theseus nodded.

'Let's go over the list again. Sword and bow?'

'Yes.'

'Food?'

'Yes.'

'Medicine?'

'Yes.'

'Battle Armor?'

'I prefer fighting light, so I only brought my Linothorax[vii].'

'Warm Clothes?'

'Yes.'

'General tools and oil for a torch?'

'Right, I forgot. I will pack some now, Thank you.'

'This is everything. You are ready to go,' she beamed. 'Where will you meet?'

'At his house.'

She hugged him tightly and kissed him goodbye. Theseus reciprocated and left for Aristaeus's house.

Aristaeus and his wife Lyria were waiting. After farewells, the men set off on horseback.

'Did you know I once fished in Goldfall Lake?' Aristaeus asked.

'What did you catch?'

'Only a shoe,' he responded, and they shared a chuckle.

'Would you like to lead? I've never been there before,' Theseus asked and slowed the pace of his horse.

'Yes, thank you,' he nodded and rushed to the front.

Theseus's brows furrowed. 'Why is it called this way?' he asked.

[vii] A type of upper body armor that was used throughout the ancient Mediterranean world.

Aristaeus scratched the back of his head. 'An old legend tells of a foreigner who hid stolen Athenian treasure at the bottom of the lake. He was ambushed by Athenian soldiers when he returned for it and was killed, leaving the treasure behind.'

'Curious. I wonder if anyone ever tried to find it.'

'Perhaps... It's rumored that an evil "Naiad[viii]" resides there, preying on the greedy.'

Theseus's eyes widened. 'Then why did you go there?'

'Young and foolish,' Aristaeus shrugged. 'Saw nothing, thankfully.'

'I'd like to check it myself. Did you bring a blessed amulet and sage to burn? It could help repel it.'

'I did, and some blessed water and salt. When I told my wife about it, she got pretty worried.'

After hours of riding, their stomachs growled, and legs numbed. They dismounted to stretch, restore circulation, and eat lunch prepared by their wives. Resuming their journey, they took Aristaeus's suggested shortcuts, avoiding official roads to evade highwaymen common during this unstable era. As the sun set, they stopped to set up camp and build a fire.

'I'm famished,' Theseus said. 'Any food ideas?'

'Rabbit, perhaps? I brought a bow,' Aristaeus said.

He raised an eyebrow. 'Ever hunted?'

'Only combat training.'

He smirked. 'Well, call me if you need any help.'

[viii] In Greek mythology, a type of female spirit, or nymph, presides over fountains, wells, springs, streams and other bodies of fresh water.

'Fuck off,' he responded with a playful grin.

They crouched, bows ready, and moved silently. Theseus led, scanning for hare tracks and sounds. Suddenly, Aristaeus tapped his shoulder, signaling to stop. He dropped to all fours, examining animal droppings. He touched the feces, studying it intently.

Theseus recoiled, his face contorting in disgust. 'What the fuck are you doing?' he hissed, fighting the urge to retch.

Aristaeus pressed a finger to his lips, eyes gleaming. 'This is what skilled hunters do. Feces reveal much. Temperature indicates how close the animal is. Texture and color show diet – herbivore or carnivore. Crucial information,' he explained.

'So, what did you learn?' Theseus asked, his curiosity piqued despite his revulsion.

Aristaeus's serious expression cracked into a smile. 'That it smells like shit,' he chuckled. 'Truth is, I've never done this before. I just wanted to see your reaction.'

Theseus's face cycled through shock, disbelief, and finally, reluctant amusement as Aristaeus doubled over with laughter.

They searched, Aristaeus guiding Theseus through tracks. Suddenly, rustling in the bushes. They crouched, bows drawn, hearts racing. One question echoed in their minds: friend or foe? Silence fell. A wild brown bear emerged. They froze, breath held, praying to remain unseen. Their skin prickled with goosebumps, their hearts pounding as loud as a drum. Their terror made them realize – they had never fought together before. Thankfully, the bear, oblivious of their location, got bored and wandered off.

Aristaeus collapsed, exhaling. He spread his arms and legs on the ground. 'That was terrifying! As if Plouton[ix] himself was breathing upon me.'

'We must move. It's late, and we're still hungry,' Theseus urged.

An hour later, they'd caught three rabbits. After dinner, they planned tomorrow and slept. A blood-curdling scream jolted them awake.

'What the fuck was that?' Aristaeus grabbed his weapon.

'Help!' Another cry pierced the night.

Theseus unsheathed his sword. 'No idea. Armor up, fast.'

They followed the screams, stopping to assess. A flipped caravan, decapitated horse, and butchered corpses littered the ground. Blood's metallic scent overpowered the smell of fresh flowers in the air. Two shirtless men, broken chains dangling, attacked an elderly couple.

Theseus remembered reports of escaped prisoners nearby. He signaled Aristaeus, understanding dawning in his eyes. They charged, swords glinting in the moonlight. The attackers, caught off guard, fell swiftly.

Only the wife survived, her body trembling as she clutched her torn dress. Tears streaked her dirt-smudged

---

[ix] Referring to Hades, as uttering his true name was believed to bring misfortune.

face. 'Please, take anything,' she whispered, her voice hoarse.

Aristaeus hesitated; his brow furrowed. 'We need no reward,' he said, but his stomach growled betrayingly.

The woman's eyes softened. She pressed a bundle into his hands. 'Take this food, I insist.'

Theseus's gaze fixed on the amulet at her throat, its gemstone catching the firelight. He pointed at it. 'May I? For my wife.'

She nodded, unclasping it with shaking hands and handed it to him.

"What a dick."

The sun dipped low as they continued north, casting long shadows across the forest. They stopped to eat and rest, knowing tomorrow would bring them to the lake.

Morning arrived without incident. Sunlight filtered through the trees and birds chirping in harmony. After breakfast, they mounted their horses and resumed their journey. Four hours later, the lake came into view.

Theseus's eyes brightened with an idea. 'Let's stop here for a while and enjoy the view.'

They kicked off their sandals, dipping their feet into the cool, refreshing water. Leaning back, they took in the tranquil surroundings – the gentle ripples of the lake, the rustling of leaves in the breeze.

Aristaeus hesitated before speaking. 'Theseus... do you ever feel like running away?'

Theseus turned to him, curious. 'From your wife? I thought you loved her.'

'No. I mean with her,' Aristaeus clarified quickly. 'Village life bores me. Even with wealth and comfort, every day feels the same. I want to see new places.'

Theseus sighed. 'I understand. I've had my share of wandering – thirteen years of endless campaigns, new lands, new cultures – but no place to call home. Now that I've rebuilt the village, I've found peace in its routine.'

Aristaeus lowered his gaze. 'Maybe I just need a break… A chance to travel with Lyria. She doesn't know how I feel yet.'

'You should tell her,' Theseus said firmly. 'You said it yourself – she's supportive, and communication is crucial in a relationship.'

Aristaeus nodded. 'Thanks, I wi-' His voice cut off without a warning.

Theseus, confused by the sudden silence, looked to his left and his eyes widened in shock. Aristaeus disappeared without a trace. Heart pounding, Theseus scanned the area. Bubbles rose from the water's surface – his only clue. Without hesitation, he dove in. The salty water stung his eyes as he searched frantically. All he found was a skull and a pair of boots on the lakebed. His breath caught when he saw a familiar necklace around the skull – it was Aristaeus's.

Emerging from the water, he clutched the skull, his hands shaking. He wrapped it gently, placing it in his bag. 'For burial,' he murmured, his voice cracking.

He slumped where Aristaeus had sat moments ago. His chest constricted, each breath a struggle. Tears carved paths down his soaked face. 'Not you too, Aristaeus,' he choked out.

Theseus's shoulders sagged under an invisible weight. His fingers dug into the earth, seeking an anchor. 'I failed you. Failed them all with my incompetence.' His voice was barely audible, thick with self-loathing. He stared at his trembling hands, once steady in battle. Now they seemed foreign, useless. 'Weak,' he spat. 'Pathetic.'

The thought of facing Lyria sent a fresh wave of anguish through him. His stomach churned. 'What can I possibly tell her? I promised to protect him,' he whispered to the indifferent lake. His body curled inward, as if trying to shield himself from the crushing guilt. His days of glory turned to ashes in his mind, leaving only a shell of doubt and shame.

Theseus clasped Aristaeus's necklace around his neck, a gesture of respect. Suddenly, searing pain shot through him. The necklace transformed, its colors bleeding away to stark black and white as a pair of razor-sharp fangs erupted from its surface, sinking deep into his skin. His pupils flickered in sync with the monochromatic hues, while a searing, tingling sensation coursed through his body, radiating from the bite like a dark, electric pulse. He clawed at it, but its teeth only dug deeper into his skin.

'What the fuck?!' he exclaimed, his voice cracking with panic. 'The elders... or a priest... They must help me.' His words tumbled out in a frantic rush as he clawed at the necklace, his breath coming in ragged gasps. 'Why isn't it coming off?' he roared.

Recalling Theron's directions, he searched frantically for the cave. Hours passed, revealing nothing but Theron's deception.

'All for nothing.' Theseus roared, his voice echoing across the lake. Tears streamed down his face as he raged, fists clenched. 'Shiraz, you were right. Why must you always be right? I failed you... I failed Aristaeus.'

His laughter bordered on hysteria before he composed himself, mounting his horse for the journey home. 'I will have Theron banished. But what about this bizarre thing?' he turned his eyes to the necklace, 'what would the elders say? I hope they don't accuse me of dark magic.' As his fingers brushed against the necklace, he recoiled in horror, its texture eerily reminiscent of human skin. It hummed and twirled, as if alive.

Two days later, the reconstructed village gates loomed. Guilt gnawed at him as he contemplated breaking the news to Lyria and explaining the necklace to the elders.

At the square, Theseus dismounted, his movements heavy. He knocked urgently on the village crier's door.

'Welcome back,' the man greeted with a bright smile.

'Gather everyone immediately,' Theseus replied, his voice firm. 'This can't wait.'

'Alright. Can you help me off my chair? I am getting old these days,' the man chuckled.

Theseus pulled him from the dark wooden chair and held his hand, escorting him outside. The crier blew his bronze horn, its piercing sound echoing across the village. People flooded the square, Lyria and Shiraz among them.

Theseus stood before the crowd; his shoulders slumped under the weight of his news. The villagers waited, a mix of curiosity and concern on their faces. Lyria and Shiraz sat in the front; unaware they were the true recipients of his grim message.

He addressed the crowd, his voice barely audible. 'I-I am so sorry, Lyria...'

Lyria's brows furrowed until the realization hit her like a hammer. Her eyes widened with dread as she met his weary gaze. 'Where's my husband?' her voice quivered, tears welling up in her hazelnut eyes.

'I'm sorry... And the saddest part is that I don't even know how it happened.'

Lyria fell to her knees, sobbing. 'You promised to protect him!' she screamed.

Shiraz caught her, embracing her tightly. Rain began to fall, mirroring Lyria's grief. Shiraz looked to Theseus for reassurance, but his eyes were dark and haunted.

'I know, and I failed. It's all my fault... I'll carry this debt for life,' Theseus said, his shoulders slumping.

Aristaeus's mother's voice cut through the crowd. 'I care not for any of that. I want my son back.'

Theseus recounted their stop at Goldfall Lake, Aristaeus's disappearance, and the discovery of the skull with the necklace. He revealed the transformed necklace on his chest, its fangs piercing his skin. 'I can't remove it without tearing my flesh. I'm sorry, Lyria, I know you gave it to him the night before your wedding.'

Lyria grasped at hope. 'Could he still be alive? Is this some witch's work?'

Elder Xenophon rose, leaning on his staff. 'We're dealing with something beyond us. We must consult the oracle of Larissa, perhaps even Alexandria.'

Despite his frailty, the old man commanded respect with his majestic, long white beard. A pendant shaped like a wine cup hung from his neck, adding a touch of elegance to his presence.

Aristaeus's father stood, fists clenched. 'How was my son killed while Theseus is unharmed? We should contact every oracle in Hellas.'

The village elders exchanged glances. 'We'll discuss this with Theseus and Lysander. Prepare the funeral meanwhile.'

'Our son is missing or dead, and you expect me to sit idle?' Aristaeus's father's voice cracked with anguish and disbelief.

After hours of discussion, the family calmed and set the funeral date for two days hence. They would bury only the skull Theseus retrieved. Until then, Aristaeus's family would host meals and accept condolences at his house.

The village crier squeezed Theseus's shoulder before departing. Lysander offered a brief, 'I'm sorry, Theseus,' touching his arm before leaving with Nicander.

Shiraz embraced Theseus tightly. 'Don't blame yourself, my love. Aristaeus knew the risks,' she said, her voice soft but firm.

Theseus's shoulders sagged. 'The cave never existed. I should've listened to you. Theron lied yet again. I'll have him exiled from Hellas.'

Shiraz cupped his face, meeting his gaze. 'Let it go. It wasn't your fault.'

At home, they shared a meal of fish, rice, and olives. After bathing, they sought comfort in each other's arms, falling into a deep sleep. Theseus woke to the aroma of boiled eggs and dawn's first light. He donned a black Chiton and brown leather sandals.

'Good morning,' he kissed Shiraz, who greeted him with a bright smile.

'How did you sleep? I didn't want to disturb you, you looked so peaceful,' she said, her tone of voice higher than usual, 'I'm making breakfast.'

'Thank you, my love. Will you join me at Aristaeus's house? I need to leave an offering before meeting the elders,' Theseus asked, his voice still heavy with sleep.

Shiraz nodded. 'What will you give them?'

Theseus produced a golden amulet with a central red gem surrounded by four colored stones. 'This amulet, from a woman we saved on our journey.'

Shiraz's eyes widened in awe. 'It's beautiful. A fitting offering.'

Breakfast was served: boiled eggs, bread, olives, and grapes. Theseus and Shiraz ate in silence, except for occasionally discussing his journey. After the meal, Shiraz donned a teal Persian velvet dress, adorned with golden jewelry and a Lapis Lazuli[x] medallion.

Hand in hand, they stepped into the crisp morning air. At Aristaeus's house, mourners streamed by, a mix of nobles and merchants. Theseus, eyes downcast, offered condolences and presented the amulet.

---

[x] A deep-blue metamorphic rock used as a semi-precious stone that has been prized since antiquity for its intense color.

Lyria's face contorted with worry. 'H-How did you get this?' she stuttered.

'An elderly woman we saved gave it as a reward. Why?' Theseus replied, brow furrowing.

'I recognize the insignia,' Lyria said, her voice tight. 'It belongs to a wealthy family of slave traders in a nearby village.'

Theseus's eyes widened in shock as realization dawned. 'Wait, what? Oh, no…'

His voice weighed down by sorrow, Theseus recounted the tale, then bid farewell and left for his meeting. Shiraz stayed behind, offering solace to the bereaved family.

INTERLUDE TWO

Theseus knocked on the thick oak door and entered the room, finding the three village elders and Lysander sharing wine around a weathered wooden table.

'Theseus. Join us,' Lysander gestured to an empty chair on his left.

'You're late,' Hesperos grumbled, his tone sharp.

'Cut him some slack. He visited the deceased's family,' Lysander countered.

'A friend he killed through foolishness,' Hesperos sneered.

'The same man who gave you your title. Know your place,' Lysander retorted, his eyes narrowing.

Xenophon, wearing a simple white Himation[i], intervened. 'We're not here to discuss blame. Theseus, I'll meet

---

[i] An outer garment worn by the ancient Greeks over the left shoulder and under the right.

with Larissa's oracle while you and Lysander consult Alexandria's in Egypt.' He was the youngest of the elders.

Theseus raised an eyebrow. 'Wait, is that all? I expected more discussion.'

'We needed your agreement first. It's a two-week journey, minimum,' Xenophon explained, sipping his wine.

'I'll need a ship,' Theseus proclaimed.

Lysander interjected, 'or borrow Aristaeus's family's vessel.'

'I'll convince Lyria to lend you the ship,' Xenophon assured. 'Can you travel to Alexandria?'

Theseus nodded firmly. 'Yes, I'll go.'

'Excellent. We'll arrange everything. Alexandria's scholars might help with your necklace too.'

They agreed to depart the day after Aristaeus's funeral. As the meeting concluded, they shook hands and dispersed.

Later, Theseus recounted the meeting to his wife. 'We leave for Alexandria after the funeral. It's a two-week journey, possibly longer. We'll consult the oracle about Aristaeus and perhaps this necklace,' he explained.

Shiraz's gaze dropped momentarily. 'I understand. It's important. Just... promise you'll return to me. And bring a souvenir.' She winked, masking her concern.

Theseus wrapped his arms around her, pulling her close as he breathed in the familiar scent of her hair, a mix of lavender and honey that always brought him peace. His voice was filled with emotion as he whispered, 'I promise, my love. This will be my final adventure. We've earned our rest, and I long to spend the rest of my days by your side.'

'And to start a family,' Shiraz added with a soft chuckle.

'And start a family,' Theseus echoed, his eyes twinkling.

Aristaeus's funeral was a somber affair, filled with mournful songs and tears. A small coffin containing his skull was buried, followed by a commemorative feast known as the 'Perideipnon'. It was held at Aristaeus's home

Relatives and friends assembled, wearing garlands and offering eulogies in honor of the deceased. The table was laden with traditional offerings such as milk, honey, water, wine, and 'Koliva[ii]'.

As the guests partook in the meal, they shared memories of Aristaeus, their voices a mix of sorrow and fond recollection. The feast served not only as a time of mourning but also as a gesture of gratitude towards those who had participated in the burial rites. This gathering marked the transition of Aristaeus from the world of the living to the realm of the dead, a final farewell before his spirit's journey to the underworld.

At dawn the next day, Xenophon secured Lyria's boat for the journey. Theseus and Lysander set sail for Alexandria, stopping at key ports: replenishing supplies at Piraeus, waiting for a storm to pass at Rhodes, and pausing at the grand Phoenician port of Byblos. As they approached Alexandria, the emerging new capital came into view. It was founded by Alexander less than a decade ago. They docked on the eastern side, greeted by a magnificent array of ships unloading goods and passengers from across the world.

[ii] A mixture of dried fruits and the first fruits of the crops.

Lysander's stomach growled. 'Theseus, could we eat before we begin our search? I'm fucking famished.'

'Sure. I could use a meal myself.'

They entered the market, immediately engulfed by a cacophony of sights, sounds, and smells. Vendors shouted in various languages, offering exotic fruits, spices, meats, fish, and treasures from distant lands. Grain, ivory and gemstones from Africa. Spices and incense from the Middle East. Wine and oil from Greece. Silk and jade from the Far East.

Lysander's eyes widened, drawn to a stall of sizzling lamb skewers. The aroma mingled tantalizingly with nearby dates and apricots, creating an intoxicating blend. He inhaled deeply, his mouth watering. 'What a feast for the senses.'

They navigated through the bustling crowd, dodging persistent beggars and zealous vendors.

"The secret is to ignore them."

The air was thick with the scent of roasting meat, sweet fruits, and pungent spices.

Theseus placed a hand on Lysander's shoulder, guiding him through the throng. 'Let's find a place to eat,' he suggested, his own stomach beginning to rumble in response to the enticing aromas.

Lysander put both hands on his head, overwhelmed. 'There's so much variety. I don't even know where to begin,' he said.

An unfamiliar voice interrupted their bewilderment. 'If you're looking for something to eat, I know just the place.

I'm actually on my way there, care to join me?' a warm smile accompanied his words.

The pair nodded with eyes full of wonder.

"I fucking love it when locals show me around when I travel."

'Do you like Egyptian "Hummus[iii]"?' the stranger asked, 'oh, who am I kidding? Who in their right mind doesn't?'

Theseus and Lysander burst into laughter, adoring his enthusiasm.

Lysander extended a firm hand, his face lighting up with a bright smile. 'I'm Lysander, and this is Theseus,' he pointed at his friend, 'nice to meet you.'

'I'm Nethanel, but call me Nati,' he replied, shaking their hands. 'Hellenic[iv] names, I see. You're tourists, aren't you? I'd be delighted to introduce you to my country.'

'Yes, we're seeking a scholar or an oracle. We believe they could help us with something,' Theseus explained.

'Sounds like an incredible adventure. I wish you both good fortune,' Nethanel said and gestured for them to follow.

He led them to a nearby restaurant, telling them about his culture with stars in his eyes.

As they entered, the owner greeted him with a firm handshake and a smile. 'Herete[v], Nati. How are you today? And who are these fine gentlemen?'

[iii] A Middle Eastern dip, spread, or savory dish made from cooked, mashed chickpeas blended with tahini, lemon juice, and garlic.

[iv] Of or relating to Greece, its people, or its language.

[v] (Greek) A formal way of saying hello.

Nethanel extended a warm hand to his new friends. 'Two travelers I met. They're quite hungry,' he chuckled.

The owner shook their hands, welcoming them. 'Please, take a seat.'

As they perused the menu, Theseus asked, 'Nati, what do you recommend? There are so many options.'

Nethanel smiled. 'Honestly? You can't go wrong with a Pita[vi], Hummus, and lamb meat.'

Theseus and Lysander nodded in agreement.

'Khufu[vii], we're ready to order,' their new friend called out.

The owner presented flatbread with a dish of Hummus, crowned by an island of perfectly cooked lamb meat and drizzled with olive oil. As eclectic music played, they dipped bread into the hummus, sharing laughter and stories. Nethanel revealed his work as a security guard and volunteer with the terminally ill.

After finishing their meals, they sought out the owner, paid, and thanked him, not forgetting to request the recipe.

Nethanel extended his hand, his smile warm with gratitude. 'It's been a pleasure. Perhaps we'll meet again.'

They shook hands firmly before parting.

'He's great, isn't he? And that Hummus… best I've ever tasted,' Lysander's eyes sparkled. He gestured for Theseus to move aside, making way for a woman carrying apples. 'The meat added so much flavor, though I struggled to

---

[vi] A family of yeast-leavened round flatbreads baked from wheat flour, common in the Mediterranean, Levant, and neighboring areas.
[vii] An Egyptian name derived from the second Pharaoh of the Fourth dynasty, in the Old Kingdom period.

scoop both hummus and meat at once. It kept slipping off,' he chortled.

Theseus grinned. 'Absolutely. I can't wait to share the recipe with Shiraz.'

'Invite me over then,' Lysander said. 'This city has everything. And the ladies... I might just bring one of them home with me,' he winked.

They shared a chuckle.

Suddenly, an elderly woman's voice cut through the air. 'Jewelry from all corners of the world! Sparkling diamonds, radiant rubies, and royal Lapis Lazuli. Buy them for your wives, your mothers, your sisters, hell, buy some for your-selves. Perfect gifts to embellish beauty.'

Theseus's gaze was drawn to the glistening stones on her stall. 'Give me a minute,' he said to his companion, approaching the display of emerald necklaces and diamond rings. 'I promised Shiraz a souvenir.'

Lysander nodded.

'What would you have?' the vendor greeted him, 'we have this ring with sapphires as blue as the Mediterranean Sea, or this bracelet with lush green emeralds. Or what about this ring with a beautiful diamond? It looks like a star in a cage.' She handed him the diamond ring, its surface polished to a mirror-like sheen.

Theseus admired the ring, turning it in his fingers. 'It is beautiful, but I seek something with a deeper meaning... to showcase my love.'

'I have just the thing, dear,' the merchant said, retrieving a decorated wooden box. She extracted two necklaces, 'these are adorned with "Prostasia" stones. Have you heard of them?'

Theseus began to respond, but the merchant continued, 'it's a Hellenic stone that emits light when broken. Legend says two can be uniquely bonded. Cracking one causes the other to glow. It is a symbol of unity, protection, and care. All you need is an oracle's blessing for this to work.'

'Interesting. I'll take them,' Theseus nodded, his lips twisting into a bright smile.

'300 Drachmas[viii] each, but 500 total for you, handsome,' the woman winked.

Theseus laughed, handing over the coins. Returning to Lysander, his face lit up with excitement. 'Look at this,' he said, revealing one necklace.

Lysander examined it closely. 'Is that... a Prostasia stone?'

'Yes! Shiraz loves special jewelry. Could you hold onto this one? It might be useful in case we ever get lost in the dark.'

'Fine choice,' Lysander smiled and put it in his pocket.

'Thank you,' he beamed with pride.

They decided to linger in the market, strolling leisurely through the bustling streets. The vibrant fabrics and enticing perfumes captivated them as they browsed every stall selling exotic clothing, trying on anything that caught their eye. After two and a half hours, they finally resolved to end their tour and begin their quest.

[viii] A former monetary unit of Greece, was replaced in 2002 by the Euro.

'This city is magnificent. Honestly, I don't want to leave,' Lysander said, laughing.

'Neither do I. I thin-' Theseus began but stopped abruptly.

Across the street, a desperate voice cried out. 'Please, let us go! We've done nothing wrong. *They* attacked *us*,' an elderly peasant woman pleaded.

'Quit your blabbering, woman,' a soldier barked, striking her with the back of his hand.

"A bitch-slap."

Nine armored soldiers stood around her, sneering and laughing. Another soldier jabbed his sword at the bloodied back of a young man, forcing him into a caged wagon filled with eight other prisoners. Their hollow eyes stared blankly at one another; despair etched into their faces. Among them was Nethanel, their new friend from earlier, bruised and beaten. The soldier slammed the metal door shut with a resounding bang of authority.

'What is he doing there?!' Lysander growled, fists clenched and teeth grinding in anger. 'He doesn't seem like the type to do what they're accusing him of... Something's off. Look at how they're laughing at her, it's disgusting.'

'And what exactly do you plan on doing?' Theseus snapped, his voice tense. 'We're unarmed in enemy territory. Are you suggesting we follow them?' he paused, noticing a sudden spark in Lysander's eyes. 'Oh, Malaka[ix]... Seriously?! This is suicide.'

Two soldiers climbed onto the wagon while the others

[ix] (Greek slang) Stupid, idiot, without common sense, jerk, and dumbass.

dispersed. Lysander's eyes tracked the wagon as it jolted down the stone street. 'Quick! Make a decision, they're leaving.' He urged, his voice sharp with urgency.

Theseus hesitated, sweat forming on his palms as he watched it sway further away, its wheels creaking against the cobblestones. The cries of the prisoners grew faint.

'It's almost out of view!' Lysander pressed harder.

'Alright, let's go.' He finally relented, his voice tinged with uncertainty.

They pursued the cart, matching its pace from three meters behind. The prisoners' pleas faded as the limestone roads gave way to hot sand. Housing density decreased, and the sounds of civilization dimmed. The wagon entered isolation, with only sand and occasional trees stretching to the hazed horizon.

After an hour, a lone fortress emerged, its pale limestone walls standing proud amidst the barren landscape. Towers reinforced its formidable structure, heavy iron gates barred entry, and countless archers perched atop stone platforms. Two spear-wielding guards checked the cart before allowing it through a briefly opened gate.

Theseus's brow furrowed, his voice low and laced with unease. 'What could warrant such defenses?' his eyes scanned the perimeter, searching for any weakness. 'Let's circle around for a breach or a weak spot. We must act quickly.'

Crouching low, they trudged around the fortress as the sun descended toward the dunes. In the fading light, their fingers traced the smooth stone walls until Lysander felt a crevice.

'Theseus,' Lysander whispered, his eyes wide with wonder. 'I found something.'

Theseus's face lit up with a spark of hope. 'Alright,' he replied, his voice barely audible. The tension in his body eased slightly, replaced by a sense of determination.

They expanded the fissure with a small knife until they could slip inside. They froze, struck by the sight of people moving normally in utter darkness, save for a hint of fading sunlight. To their left stood two metal doors where the wagon had entered – its current location unknown. Theseus, eyes wide, identified the main building's entrance, guarded by four heavily armored sentinels.

'What's behind there? We must take these guys out,' Lysander whispered, brow furrowed.

Theseus nodded, pointing to a nearby weapon rack. They crouched low, each 'borrowing' a dagger.

'How do they see anything?' Lysander hissed.

'No idea, but we can take advantage of it. Do you still have that necklace?'

Lysander nodded.

'We'll sneak closer. When I signal, crack the stone and throw it. The light should blind them temporarily,' Theseus explained.

They crept forward, hearts pounding, until they reached a wooden box three meters from the left-most guard.

Theseus signaled to stop, then ripped a strip from his sleeve, fashioning a makeshift blindfold. 'Copy me. It's not perfect, but it'll help,' he said.

Lysander mirrored the action. Theseus raised his hand,

then dropped it swiftly. Lysander pierced the stone and hurled it toward the guards.

'Now, we wait,' Theseus whispered.

'What's that noise?' a guard's voice cut through the darkness.

'I think something fell next to us,' another watchman said, 'I can't see a fucking thing. What's the point of posting us here without giving us torches? We're useless in this darkness,' he grumbled.

'Forget it. If it were important, the masters would'v -' The third sentinel's words cut into a sudden cry of pain, 'my eyes!' he shouted, his voice laced with agony.

'What the fuck is this?!' the first guard bellowed, hands flying to his face.

But it was too late, their vision had already been stolen by the DIY[X] flash-bang. The pair waited four seconds, letting their semi-covered eyes adjust before springing into action, daggers drawn. There was no time for a prolonged fight; they slit the warders' throats from behind, the blades slicing cleanly as hot blood spilled onto their hands. Dragging the bodies by their coats, they concealed them behind the wooden box. Stripping two of the guards of their armor, they donned it as a precaution.

With a final nod exchanged between them, they approached the metal doors. Theseus pushed them open silently, revealing an interior even darker than before. Disappointment flickered across their faces, but determination drove them forward. Picking up the broken necklace to

---

[X] Acronym for Do-It-Yourself.

use as a makeshift torch, they stepped inside. The sound of their footsteps echoed ominously through the oppressive darkness, their minds heavy with worry. They wandered through endless halls, searching for Nethanel and hoping to free the other prisoners.

Eventually, they entered a vast, empty room. Its metal doors stood wide open, and an eerie silence hung in the air. On the wall in the center was an unfamiliar crest: an inverted silver 'V' intersected by a symbol resembling a goat's head. Unease crept into their expressions as they approached. Theseus held up the glowing necklace to inspect the emblem for any hidden clues but found nothing. He placed the pendant in the center of the room as a light source.

'Look at this,' Lysander murmured, pointing to faint outlines on the floor.

The markings resembled a hatch or a cellar door, camouflaged to blend with its surroundings. Theseus retrieved the amulet and held it close to the floor, tracing his fingers along its surface until he found a latch. Exchanging steady breaths, they pulled together in one powerful motion. The hatch groaned open with a metallic creak that sent shivers down their spines.

Theseus shot his comrade a nervous look that spoke volumes: 'We must move before someone hears.'

Lysander nodded sharply as they slipped inside and closed the hatch behind them with painstaking care.

Turning around, they were met with a long staircase plunging into darkness. Theseus glanced at Lysander for confirmation; his companion nodded and gestured for him to lead. With Lysander following closely behind for protection, they descended step by step into the endless void. With each passing second, the air grew colder, and the necklace's light waned.

Their grip on their daggers tightened as anxiety clawed at them. The silence was suffocating; all they had were their weapons, each other, and a fading light guiding them deeper into uncertainty.

Theseus mumbled, 'I have a bad feeling about this place.' Suddenly, he yelped, 'fuck!'

Lysander tensed, gripping his dagger. 'What happened? Are you okay?'

'I'm fine, but the amulet that's on my chest just bit me. It used to be weak, but now I really felt it.'

Lysander snickered nervously, 'oh, phew. I thought you were hurt.'

'Let's continue,' Theseus commanded, rolling his eyes.

Strange noises echoed from below – singing, blaring horns, drums, and guffaw. The necklace's light diminished. At the staircase's end, they faced a semi-cliff overlooking an enormous cave. The lower floor was strewn with corpses and rivers of blood; an ominous aura and metallic smell permeated the air. Chilling screams of chained victims filled the center as they were brutalized. Lysander and Theseus stood paralyzed with shock, their eyes wide, their jaw hitting the floor.

A woman's screams from the far-left corner drew their attention. Two vampires were raping her. One, annoyed by her cries, revealed his sharp fangs and bit off her vocal cords. She died instantly, blood oozing from her neck as she choked.

In the center of the cave, a muscular, bare-chested vampire grabbed a pregnant woman, throwing her against a large cauldron filled with blazing fluid. The liquid cast an eerie light, one of the few sources in the darkened cave. He viciously cut her open from the abdomen to the uterus, ripping out the fetus and tossing it inside. Her screams faded with her life, blood painting the ground crimson.

A loud bang silenced the crypt.

A large vampire stood, flanked by two handcuffed men – Nethanel and an unknown muscular man. 'Silence!' he roared as he slammed his fist on the table, 'before we celebrate, we must welcome our new guests. Nothing's more important than tradition, right, boys?!' His gnarly chuckle echoed through the undercroft, met with shouts of agreement.

He flung open a door, unveiling a procession of prisoners, their faces twisted in agony as they choked against the cold, metallic chains that bound them. They were of varying ages; the crowd's reaction shifted from boos for the older ones to excited cheers for the younger.

Lysander clutched Theseus's shoulder, his eyes vacant. 'We're in hell. This... must be hell,' his grip tightened. 'W-We have to get out and call for help, fast!' His pupils darted across the cave walls in panic.

'Wait,' the vampire leader's grin widened. 'We have a pleasant surprise. Two new guests. Oh, where are my manners? Welcome,' he tilted his head toward the entrance, scarlet eyes locking onto Lysander's. 'Come closer and introduce yourselves. Let's have some fun,' he cackled menacingly.

Their hearts stopped, frozen in place. Nethanel's eyes widened, recognizing his friends. The music's abrupt halt gave way to bone-chilling silence – the eerie music of death.

'I don't appreciate being ignored,' the chief snarled, vanishing into thin air.

Suddenly, they were shoved onto the lower platform, crashing into the hard-stone floor. They scrambled up, facing their bloodthirsty foes. Theseus gripped his dagger while Lysander's face darkened in acceptance of death.

'I don't think we'll survive this,' Lysander whispered with ragged breath.

The lord reappeared on his throne, clapping with a broad smile. 'Get them!' he commanded, raising a clenched fist.

A horde of vampires roared, charging toward the pair, claws extended. They grinned, licking blood-stained lips. Our protagonists were forced back, their spines pressed against the cliff wall. More vampires emerged, saliva dripping from gore-smeared mouths. Lysander locked eyes with Theseus, seeking comfort, but found only mirrored desperation.

'Theseus, on your left!' Lysander shouted, yanking his friend aside and swiftly stabbing an attacking vampire in the forehead. It collapsed with a piercing screech.

'Kill them already!' the master bellowed.

Lysander and Theseus fought valiantly, dodging and counterattacking. Claws versus daggers. Animalistic brutality versus human technique. More vampires joined the fray, refusing to share. They felled a few, but fatigue set in. Their breaths shortened, muscles ached, responses slowed.

'We'll never beat them. We must climb up and run,' Lysander shouted. 'Use the other necklace.'

Theseus hesitated, then nodded. He pulled it from his pocket, positioning the stone in his left palm. 'Get ready,' he yelled. 'Three, two, one!' He plunged his dagger into the stone.

An explosion of blinding light erupted, fracturing shadows and blinding the surrounding vampires. The creatures screamed in high tones, hissing and shielding their eyes as light engulfed the enormous lair. The leader saved his sight with a plate held before his face.

'Now!' Lysander thundered, crouching by the cliff wall. 'Jump on my shoulder and climb up.'

Theseus's muscles bulged as he hauled himself up, nails splintering against the rock's unforgiving crevices. He reached down for Lysander.

Nethanel, regaining vision, rushed to the table with another captive, each grabbing a sword to fight back. 'Lysander, start climbing. We'll stall them!' he commanded with a warm smile.

With his hands still cuffed, he roared an ancient prayer while hacking down the monsters. Lysander climbed frantically, his muscles burning. Halfway up, he glanced back, witnessing Nethanel's body being ripped apart. The blinded vampires altered their course, ascending the wall with relentless ferocity as they tracked the pungent scent of blood and sweat that clung to Lysander.

Theseus's hand appeared above, urging his companion faster, pelting vampires with rocks. Their hands connected, and Lysander pulled with all his might. Suddenly, his foot slipped. Time slowed as he desperately sought a foothold, clinging to his friend's palm.

Lysander's voice cracked with desperation as he screamed, 'pull me up!' Panic clawed at his throat, his words tumbling out in a frantic plea.

Vampires advanced below, claws piercing the wall as they climbed with terrifying speed.

'I'm trying.' Theseus responded through gritted teeth, straining with both hands to pull him up.

The vampires advanced, driven by ancient bloodlust. Theseus struggled, muscles screaming, but Lysander was too heavy.

Lysander's voice cut through the chaos, eerily monotone. 'Theseus, let me go. Save yourself, run. I'll hold them off,' his eyes betrayed utter fear despite his authoritative tone.

'No, I won't lose you too!' Theseus screamed, agonized. Visions of Aristaeus's smile flashed in his mind. 'You're coming back with me. I won't leave you.' Tears streamed down his cheeks as he pulled with all his might, muscles on the verge of tearing.

'This is your only hope. Please, respect my decision,' Lysander's words were firm. 'It's not a bad day to die,' his lips twisted into a bright smile, though his eyes remained dark and empty. He released his grasp, but Theseus held tight, refusing to let go.

'I can't do this to you,' Theseus pleaded, face wet with

tears. 'We're here because of me. I can't bear the guilt of another death. Gods, please take me instead…' He lifted his gaze heavenward, his voice trembling in a silent plea.

Lysander smiled again. 'Forgive me,' he said, drawing his dagger. 'I'm sorry, my friend.' He sliced off his palm and plummeted into the horde, eyes locked on Theseus.

Vampires swarmed him, draining him.

With his last breath, he gasped, 'I love you, my friend. Run! I want you to... surv-vive, this…' His eyes fluttered shut.

But Theseus didn't run. He stared into the growing pool of blood, his friend's corpse engulfed by starving vampires. The chaos faded, silenced in his ears. His mind wandered, flooding with memories of shared laughter and battles.

'Why am I so fucking weak?!' he screamed internally. 'Why must my friends keep dying because of me?!'

He punched his face, his stomach, clawed at his skin until blood flowed. Then he froze, face contorted with despair, watching the monsters feed on Nethanel and Lysander's remains.

His wife's image suddenly pierced his thoughts. 'I can't leave her,' he realized. 'She shouldn't pay for my incompetence. I won't make her a victim too.'

He clenched his fists and slapped himself hard three times, snapping out of shock. He sprinted, determined to honor his friends' sacrifice.

With blurred vision, he stumbled up the stairs, heart pounding. Time warped as adrenaline surged through him. His legs faltered near the top, each step a battle. He collapsed at the summit, then forced himself up, driven by desperation to survive.

He burst outside, cold wind stinging his sweaty face. Rushing to nearby weapon racks, he barricaded the gates with spears, trapping the vampires inside. He knew it was only temporary.

With the doors secured, Theseus leaned against them, gasping for breath. After a brief rest, he stumbled toward the stables, his legs trembling and heavy from exhaustion. The faint light inside illuminated the smell of hay and manure. Spotting several horses, he took a deep breath and limped to the nearest one. Summoning the last of his strength, he hoisted himself onto its back. With trembling limbs and a sharp inhale, he kicked the horse into a gallop, disappearing into the dark horizon toward the harbor. Through the haze of numbness, he noticed the strange amulet's bite had weakened.

Nine months later, the moon hung high in the sky as the night air carried whispers of anticipation The ambiance resonated with the familiar sounds of labor. Shiraz lay on her bed, her contractions intensifying with every passing moment. Theseus stood beside her, holding her hand tightly and brushing sweat from her forehead. His eyes were filled with worry and determination as he whispered reassurances.

Lyria lifted Shiraz's dress to allow the elder to examine her swollen belly.

His eyes widened in surprise. 'By the gods,' he murmured with a smile. 'This can't be just one baby...

Judging by the sheer size of her belly, I'd say twins, or perhaps even triplets.'

Lyria gasped in delight. 'Those are marvelous news. Did you hear that, Shiraz?'

Shiraz's face paled as she looked up at her husband with wide, frightened eyes. 'How are we going to handle three? We don't even know how to take care of one!'

Theseus squeezed her hand gently, his voice steady despite his own nerves. 'We'll figure it out together. Lyria will help us, and your parents too. We'll manage this, I promise.'

Lyria stroked her friend's hair, 'I will. Don't worry,' she whispered with a bright smile.

The elder nodded firmly. 'Let's focus now. Lyria, fetch clean towels, water, and herbs immediately. Theseus, stay here and support her.' He turned to Shiraz with calm authority, 'listen to your body, Shiraz. Push when it urges you to push.'

She nodded weakly, panting through clenched teeth as sweat dripped down her face.

Lyria rushed out of the room, her heart pounding as she gathered supplies. She returned quickly, hands shaking but determined to help. Shiraz's screams grew louder with each push, echoing through the room like thunderclaps. Her face contorted in pain as she fought through each contraction. Theseus whispered encouragements and prayers to the gods, his grip on her hand unwavering.

Finally, after an agonizing effort, Shiraz let out one last guttural scream and the first baby emerged into the world.

Lyria's eyes widened in horror as she beheld the newborn. 'What... is this?!' she shrieked and fainted.

The elder's hands trembled, holding an abomination – a creature with a bushy tail, pointed cat ears, and piercing feline eyes; its human-like body covered in thick fur. He passed it to Theseus, then delivered two more infants: one wolf-like, the other human with butterfly wings, sharp long ears and golden eyes.

'In all my years...' the elder whispered, jaw slack with disbelief.

Shiraz's wails intensified, the sheets twisting around her body as she struggled to endure the pain. A fourth child burst forth, abnormally large – towering over boys at the age of four. Then came a rapid succession of bizarre offspring: a furry monkey-tailed infant with monkey-like ears, one with bat wings and fangs, another with dragon scales and majestic wings, followed by bear-like, spider-like, bird-like, and horse-like humanoid hybrids. The last emerged with gills and razor-sharp teeth.

Twelve unnatural beings filled the room with their otherworldly cries. Howls, screeches and high-pitched whistling noises echoing relentlessly. Lyria jolted awake, her breath hitching as her eyes fell upon the grotesque sight before her. A strangled gasp escaped her lips before her body gave out, collapsing back into unconsciousness.

Theseus and the elder remained rooted in place, their faces ashen, eyes struck by disbelief. The room seemed to close in around them, the air heavy with the weight of horror. Neither could speak, their silence screaming louder than words as they stared at these glitches of nature.

'I must call a council,' the elder mumbled, fear evident in his voice.

Shiraz unleashed a final, bone-chilling shriek that shattered the air, her body convulsing in agony before collapsing limp and silent. The sudden stillness was deafening.

'Shiraz!' Theseus cried out, his voice raw with desperation. He clutched her motionless form, terror clawing at his chest. 'My love, please. Come back to me!' His trembling hands cupped her ashen face as panic consumed him, each second of silence an eternity of dread.

The elder checked her pulse. 'Weak, but she lives. Let her rest,' he said, relief washing over him.

Theseus's voice trembled, barely audible as he whispered, 'Thank the gods,' his eyes brimming with tears of relief. His chest heaved with a deep, shuddering breath as he clutched his wife's hand, the weight of his fear slowly lifting. For a moment, he just held her, his gaze locked on her face, his heart overflowing with gratitude.

Villagers, awakened by piercing screams, gathered around Theseus's house.

One barged in, witnessing the horrifying sight. 'What is the meaning of this?' she demanded, her jaw dropping.

'Relax,' the elder responded, 'These are Theseus's and Shiraz's babies. They pose no threat. Tomorrow, we'll discuss this matter.'

'How can they be harmless? They're monsters!' another villager yelled, eyes wide with deep, primal terror.

'Theseus and I will take full responsibility,' the elder assured.

'If anything happens, you and this... family will be banished,' he glared at Theseus with pleading eyes, 'you brought this village to life. Don't bring it to its death.'

Theseus took a deep breath and nodded solemnly. 'I bet this amulet is at fault,' he looked down, 'this is all my fault. Again,' he sighed.

At first light, the elders announced their decision in the town square. 'The babies will sta-' One elder began, cut off by the angry mob.

'They're cursed!'

'They're monsters!'

The elders raised their hands, demanding silence. The crowd hushed.

'Ten families will adopt one child each. In return, the grown babies will protect our village. Theseus will keep two: the one with the butterfly wings and the one resembling a shark. The rest of you can choose from the other ten,' the elder explained.

'Before we continue, I'd like to name the-' Theseus started but was interrupted.

Suddenly, the babies' eyes and mouths glowed bright red. One by one, they announced their names in the order of their birth: 'Ji', 'Ave', 'Rui', 'Yaruv', 'Luya', 'Narui', 'Sakui', 'Sever', 'Madur', 'Kabui', 'Ino', and 'Mitori'.

The crowd stood in stunned silence as the chosen families stepped forward to claim their extraordinary new charges.

Theseus rushed back to his unconscious wife. Neither water, noise, smell, nor touch could undo it. For eleven days, she remained unresponsive. When she finally awoke, weak and famished, he explained the situation while preparing her food. Healers from Alexandria concluded her uterus was irreparably damaged; they marveled at her survival.

The children grew rapidly. At six, the giant matched Theseus's size. They spoke an odd language Rui named 'Omnitongue'. Rui, the most intelligent, mastered magic and taught the village elders. News of these magical humanoids spread throughout Hellas, drawing curious onlookers.

Rui led a campaign teaching humans magic while his siblings aided in battles, construction, exploration, trade, and scientific advancement. He developed the 'All-Seeing Eye' spell, revealing other planets.

Witnessing the incredible powers of the children, later known as 'The Ancestors', village elders approached Rui with a momentous request. The Ancestors were to embark on a monumental journey to a distant planet they christened 'Syluetta'. This alien planet teemed with intelligent beasts but lacked humanoid life. Each of the twelve children, accompanied by a cadre of brave human volunteers, set forth to establish new civilizations across Syluetta's varied landscapes.

As they arrived, The Ancestors and their human companions faced the daunting task of adapting to an unfamiliar and often hostile environment. They encountered bizarre flora and fauna, navigating treacherous terrains from vast oceans to dense forests. The intelligent beasts of Syluetta posed both challenges and opportunities, as the colonists sought to coexist and potentially form alliances with them.

The colonization effort became a testament to human resilience and The Ancestors' unique powers. Each group carved out their own niche on the planet. They established settlements, developed new technologies suited to their surroundings, and began the delicate process of building a new society from the ground up.

This interstellar colonization marked a pivotal moment in human history, as the species took its first steps towards becoming a multi-planet civilization. The story of Syluetta's settlement would become legend, a tale of courage, innovation, and the indomitable human spirit in the face of the unknown.

Mitori oversaw the oceans, including 'Xierēnia'. These became home to the Merarians, with each ocean developing its own kingdom and sub-species. Some found the children of Theseus impressive, others irresistibly attractive. They married and bore children, some with corresponding beast races, others with the human volunteers.

Thus, the Elven race descended from Rui, and the Merarian race from Mitori, marking the dawn of new humanoid species.

Rui's campaign evolved into 'The Order' – an organization dedicated to unraveling the mysteries of magic while shielding mortals from supernatural threats. In the wake of the devastating Mortal Demon War, its mission expanded: establish magical academies across Syluetta and construct interstellar portals powered by arcane energy throughout the solar system. Magic was explained like so:

Each spell consumes Olons[xi] from the casting limb, for which the mage must change the nature and 'Activations' – runes commanding the particle. Every individual possesses a unique 'Olon Recovery Rate' for each specific body part, determined by their race, genetic makeup, and other factors. This rate dictates how quickly a person can replenish the Olons expended during spellcasting.

Overuse leads to irreversible decay – a mage might lose a finger from casting too many Finger-Activated Blast spells. This was the essence of equivalent exchange, a cosmic balance sheet where power always demanded payment.

Magic can be performed using chants and written sigils in the Omnitongue. Written magic does not require the use of Olons, and as such, it is much easier to handle in combat. But once activated, if only one mistake is made in the runes, the user would immediately lose as many Olons as the spell itself should require.

Written magic bypasses Olon costs, making it easier to handle in combat. However, a single misplaced stroke would immediately unleash catastrophic backlash, draining the caster of as many Olons as required by the spell.

Only certain beings could wield it: descendants of The Ancestors, gifted humans, and 'Awakened' humans. Humans grappled with limitations, restricted to three sub-schools of magic – two assigned automatically (according to genetics and personality), and one chosen. The 'Magical

____

[xi] (Omnitongue) Particles.

Races', however, commanded the full spectrum of arcane arts.

At The Order's Syluettan headquarters, obsidian altars hummed with latent energy. There, humans underwent the ceremony of awakening. They stood atop glyph-carved stones as elders chanted, their bodies trembling as ancient power coursed through them. Success granted access to Olon reserves and assigned schools. Failure meant a fifteen-year wait before another attempt.

Shiraz, the 'All-Mother' of magic, devoted her twilight years to spreading The Order's philosophy. Even in death, her presence lingered – her ashes interred beneath the central altar, whispering guidance to those deemed worthy.

CHAPTER SEVEN

At seventeen, Alduin had grown more adept with his newfound abilities. Yet captivity still chafed – a gilded prison, but a prison, nonetheless. He sulked as he recalled Vaonie's dominion over him – over his actions, his body, and his very thoughts – violating what should have been his basic sanctuary. The presence of this invisible leash grew ever clearer, making sure he knew not to stray from the path of his lord. Although his contempt for both jailer and captor deepened, he made sure not to show it.

He measured his breaths, clinging to survival until vengeance became possible. His lips twitched against forbidden laughter. The irony burned – his captors themselves, the vampires, armed him with their tools: Regeneration, evasion, telekinesis – weapons he'd later turn against them. Each hard-won mastery sparked his anticipation further.

The Araqhaiit traits now marked him – raw power

coiled beneath inexperience. Time would temper both skill and schemes. Days followed rigid patterns – combat drills and shared meals with Lysander punctuated by stolen moments studying Vaonical texts.

Unanswerable questions haunted him: 'Do gods face judgment for breaking their own commandment? Another's?'

He completed his nightly ritual – refining his control of telekinesis by rearranging books – when sharp knuckles rapped the door.

'Who is it?' he asked.

'Lord Lodus, report to Lysander's court immediately,' a familiar voice commanded.

'Fine, I'll be right out,' he sighed.

Alduin dressed quickly, his movements sharp with urgency. He opened the door.

'Isn't it a bit late for a meeting?' he asked and yawned.

'Good evening. It is,' Gozo responded flatly, 'but you don't have a choice. Follow me.'

They walked in silence until they reached Lysander's chambers. Gozo graced his lord with a deep bow, while Alduin stood rigid, his jaw tight.

'Apologies for summoning you at this late hour,' Lysander began, his tone grave, 'but the matter is urgent.'

'What happened?' Alduin raised an eyebrow.

'Your first task as an Araqhaiit has been issued.'

'What?' his eyes widened, darting across the room, 'but I'm not ready!' Anxiety clawed at him, as his promise to Vaonie loomed in his mind.

'That's not for you to decide,' Lysaner said.

Gozo ground his teeth at the audacity of his student.

A violent flash of memory appeared in his mind, recalling the consequences of defying his lord. His freewill had long been gone. 'How do I get there?' he slumped forward, surrendering.

'With the help of this ring,' Lysander explained, holding it out, 'it gives a person entry to Tyronah[i].'

'How do I use it?'

'You simply say "Los ant di Tyronah[ii]",' he noticed Alduin's brows furrowing and resumed, 'and before you ask – no, not just *any* wizard can travel to Tyronah. This ring is vital for protection against its hostile defenses. Without it, you'd be vaporized, or worse.'

Alduin nodded.

Lysander handed him the ring. 'Take it. I wish you luck. This will be our last meeting. My duty as your supervisor is now complete,' he said.

He noticed Gozo's excited gaze and with nothing but a look he reassured him he was right. Without words, they communicated – 'Fucking finally, we will never see his ugly, rude face again.'

Alduin hesitated before replying quietly, 'I'd like to say goodbye to my teachers before I leave.'

'As you wish,' Lysander nodded.

Alduin turned to Gozo and offered a curt goodbye before rushing off to find Edward and Lul. Lul barely concealed her satisfaction at his departure, but Edward

---

[i] (Omnitongue) Hell.
[ii] (Omnitongue) (To) take me to Hell.

looked crestfallen. He clasped Alduin's shoulder firmly. Alduin, the only mortal he had met since the day he was turned, had been the only reminder of his childhood—a rare connection in this strange world.

Edward unclasped the dangly earring bearing Vaonie's symbol from his earlobe. 'Take this,' he said, offering it to Alduin with a solemn smile. 'Farewell. Wreak havoc on those who wish you harm. Be strong. Be brave.'

Alduin's fingers closed around it, his jaw tightening. 'I'll take those words to heart,' he responded softly, 'thank you. Goodbye...'

Slipping on Lysander's ring, Alduin intoned, 'los ant di Tyronah.'

He materialized in Vaonie's throne room.

'Welcome to your new home,' Vaonie proclaimed, voice echoing off stone walls.

Alduin's eyes darted around the chamber, 'am I to live here?'

'Indeed. Any objections?'

'None. I've always wondered about the castle's exterior.'

'Soon enough. First, a task. Listen carefully, as I won't repeat myself.'

Alduin's spine stiffened, 'yes, my lord.'

'My son has long been dead, and that has weakened my army, delaying my vengeance on Austomia. Now, we strike Heonmeyu[iii]. Join your kin and invade it. Kill all but the spirits, they're uninvolved. Understood?'

The word vengeance rang in his head, he knew it all too

[iii] (Omnitongue) Heaven.

well. He smiled and bore his fangs – the sound of it excited him, despite not being his own. 'Perfectly, my lord,' he said.

'Very well. It's time for introductions. Araqhaiits, assemble.'

As they walked toward him, five beings materialized, their forms sharpening with each step. They radiated authority, power, godhood.

Kans, hooded in drab gray, his arm adorned with jangling gold bands, spoke first. His tanned face bore a French-style mustache, reddish-purple eyes glowing beneath his cowl.

'I am Fema,' announced a beautiful brunette in gleaming silver armor. A golden circlet graced her brow, a matching spear strapped to her back. An olive cape draped from her pauldron, shaped like the head of a mighty mammoth.

'My name... is Ophiin,' growled a beast-like figure, crouching low. His bright red eyes bore into Alduin, sizing him up. Long, black and silky hair framed his bare chest, matching his pants and sandals. That was all he wore.

A man clad in royal gold armor, bowed slightly. 'Anor,' he said, his short red hair contrasting with the crimson cape fastened to lion-shaped pauldrons. A longsword hung at his hip, his eyes the palest red of the group.

'Pholexu,' whispered a thin, short woman in peasant leather attire. A black hat obscured her white hair, no visible weapon in sight.

Vaonie's firm voice cut through the air, 'now go. Lodus, do not fail me. And do not forget that which you have promised.'

'Yes, lord,' Alduin replied, jaw clenching.

Kans wove his fingers, the rings on his arm pulsing in emerald. A portal shimmered into existence.

Alduin's brows furrowed, 'how come you didn't chant anything?' he asked.

Kans's eyes narrowed as he shifted his gaze from Alduin, disappointment etched in his features. 'This is how gods do magic, Vanthealing. You are not mortal, act accordingly,' he said.

The portal swallowed them whole, depositing the group into a realm of ethereal beauty. A white-tinted sky arched over snow-white grass and blue trees. Light-blue crystal rivers and lakes sparkled, all beneath a sunless, cloudless expanse.

Alduin gawked at the beauty of Heonmeyu. Then, tipped his head back, inhaled slowly, drawing in the wonder of the place, and exhaled in a soft, awestruck sigh. Alduin's eyes widened, drinking in the realm's splendor.

He inhaled slowly, savouring the otherworldly air. 'What are those?' he gestured at distant flying figures.

"I bet you wanna look at your shoes right now."

'Tyrewhiins[iv]. Austomia's celestial army,' Kans replied, his voice taut. 'Numerous and formidable. Prepare for battle.'

Alduin's gaze swept the horizon, teeming with uncountable beings. He swallowed hard. 'I've only ever faced mortals. Are you sure I'm ready for celestials?' he asked softly, hesitant.

Anor's eyes flashed in scarlet red. 'We fight alongside

[iv] (Omnitongue) Angels.

you. Doubting Vaonie's wisdom is blasphemy. Tread carefully, lest it lead to your demise.'

Alduin looked away from Anor's strong stare. 'Okay,' he muttered. Now, it was clearer than ever – he was no longer formidable, no longer respected.

Fema cracked her knuckles and summoned her mount. The others followed suit, each calling forth a unique beast. A silver-brown griffin materialized for Fema, a massive black lion with cream fur for Anor, a winged blue-white panda for Kans, an oddly regular dark brown horse for Pholexu, and a colossal dark-purple serpent with void-black eyes for Ophiin. Their gazes bore into Alduin, expectant.

'We must make haste, Lodus,' Fema urged firmly.

Alduin lowered his head in shame. 'I... I haven't thought of a mount yet,' he said.

Kans placed his hand on his hip, 'then come up with one. Now.'

'Don't be harsh,' Pholexu interjected softly, 'he's new.'

Alduin sat on the ground, brow furrowed in concentration. A fox – his favourite animal. But not just any fox. He recalled an ancient myth of a nine-tailed demon fox, its image crystallizing in his mind. Mammoth-sized, to match his companions' mounts. The vibrant red of snow foxes from his homeland, with blood the color of silver – influenced by the story of the Vaermiraiit[v] clan that had taken him.

---

[v] (Omnitongue) Vampires.

His eyes snapped open, the majestic beast fully formed in his imagination, ready to be called forth.

'How do you cast without verbal chants?' Alduin asked Kans.

'Gods need only think the chants in the Omnitongue,' he explained, 'No words are required.'

Alduin focused, using Vaurcarya to spill his blood. After five failed attempts, a nine-tailed fox materialized on the sixth try. It was horse-sized, with crimson eyes and Vaonie's mark on its forehead. The fox's back and head were a fiery red, while its lower body was snow-white.

Alduin mounted the beast, addressing Kans. 'This is what I envisioned. I tried to make it larger, but it didn't work. Do you know why?'

Kans shrugged, 'Perhaps your control of conjuration magic isn't sufficient yet. Practice will improve your skills. We must go now, follow our lead.'

'Evisi[vi],' Alduin responded with a light bow.

'Well done, Lodus. I am proud of you,' Pholexu said.

The words echoed in his brain as he blushed intensely. He hadn't heard these words in such a long time. 'Evisi,' he said and smiled brightly, with the pride of a child eager to show their parents a drawing he had made.

'What do you call it?' she asked.

'Acaroth[vii].'

'Interesting name. Against whom?'

The spark in Alduin's eyes diminished as memories of

[vi] (Elvish) Thanks.
[vii] (Elvish) Revenge.

his past flashed in his brain. 'It's personal,' he muttered softly.

She nodded, 'Mhmm... Alright.'

The group rode toward the swirling Tyrewhiins, Alduin lingering behind to observe their tactics. Fema signaled Kans—a sharp nod—and they split off. She vaulted skyward, spear glinting as it severed feathered wings in clean arcs. Kans hovered beside her, emerald projectiles erupting from his rings to blast remaining feathers into ash. Celestial screams pierced the air as angels fell, their silver blood misting the battlefield.

But the Tyrewhiins fought viciously. A coordinated strike severed Fema's left hand mid-swing, another volley sheared Kans' legs below the knees. They crashed earthward, regeneration already knitting flesh—slower than Alduin's own, he noticed with grim fascination.

Anor roared, his lion pouncing on grounded angels. Ophiin's serpent coiled around clusters, arrows herding prey into its gaping maw. Pholexu dismounted with a mocking bow, then erupted into motion—fists a blur, bones crunching under her divine strength. Her technique resembled that of the martial artists from planet Earth. His uncle loved sharing tales of their glory.

Alduin leapt from his fox, levitating on a platform of crystallized blood. He danced through the fray: telekinetic slashes bisected wings, blood-spikes impaled stragglers, life drained from foes to fuel his magic. Elvish grace fused with Araqhaiit brutality. Finally, he had his own unique fighting style.

When the last angel fell, Anor wiped gore from his blade. 'More will come. Prepare yourself, Lodus.'

Fema flexed her half-formed hand, tendons squelching. 'We will soon reach the territory of the Sarathiins. They will pose a much greater threat.'

Alduin stared at the carnage, blood magic humming in his veins. 'Let them try,' he said as his eyes glowed in crimson red. His lips turned into a subtle smirk.

Pholexu clicked her tongue and shook her head. 'Arrogance is the downfall of your kind,' she said, her voice low and measured.

His smile faltered, replaced by a frown as the weight of her words settled within him. He felt a surge of determination, his mind echoing with a silent vow: 'I mustn't let them down.' He turned his gaze to the sky. 'How could they fight their own siblings?' he thought, 'sure, Veridia and I have had our own share of arguments, but we've never shed each other's blood...' A relentless question forced its way into his mind: 'What sparked this discord? How could Vaonie hate their family so?'

'Our children seem to enjoy their gift, Vaonie. We had such a great idea,' Austomia said.

'We?'

Awkward silence lingered.

"I am sorry, reader, but it is incredibly hard to describe

body language when they're literally just floating, talking orbs... You'll have to make do."

'I am joking, of course. Have you created anything new?' Vaonie asked.

'Ah, yes. I made something called "Insects" – species like "Spiders", "Ants", "Flies" and "Bees". Each one has its own purpose.'

'Which is?'

'You'll see. I'm sure they'll be to your liking.'

'Fine, now about my request...'

'Which one? Oh, natural disasters? My answer is no. Mortals shouldn't face dangers beyond their capabilities.'

The silence returned, heavier than before.

'Don't look at me like that. Suggest something to progress mortalkind,' Austomia said.

'What if I proposed something I call "Diseases"? Tiny beings that kill if ignored. It'd push them to study their bodies.'

'Why must your ideas always come with a destructive aspect?'

'Perfect lives breed no sin. True adherence to our laws must be tested in adversity, not comfort.'

'The answer is no.'

'But-' Vaonie began saying, not left a chance to finish.

'Torturing them isn't necessary to reveal their true selves. A good human isn't only good because life is easy.'

'You're naive! Without hardship, what reason do they have to complain? Without lack, what reason do they have to sin? It's foolish, delusional.'

'I have made my decision.'

"Imagine a visual representation of the '...' meme appeared on Vaonie's face. See? I have my ways."

Vaonie seethed at Austomia's dismissal of their shared authority over Vanthea. As co-creators and parents, their voice deserved equal weight. In secret, Vaonie began crafting disasters: land-ravaging tornadoes and sea-swallowing tsunamis that struck without warning.

Their arsenal grew—predators like bears, venomous spiders and snakes, carnivorous white mammoths, magical green koalas, and Vaonie's own personal favourite – the 'Flying Cockroach'. Such mighty creature left any mortal fool who dared stand against its utter fright and disgust.

Diseases followed: malaria coiled in mosquito bites, cancers blooming silently, diabetes, sexually transmitted diseases, herpes, and plagues unleashed through innocuous acts like eating a camel or a cute bat.

Austomia remained oblivious until mortal deaths spiked. They interrogated their children first, then analysed average mortal morality—both dead ends. The truth struck during their investigation of a particularly warped mortal: a swarm of massive bee-vulture hybrids, eviscerated the man with their sting – capable of even killing an elephant.

They stormed into Vaonie's sanctum as they sculpted a new horror—a disease freezing human bodies in perpetual infancy.

'Austomia... Hello.'

'I don't know how to handle this, Vaonie.'

Vaonie manifested a humanoid body and sat on an enormous black throne, their voice sharp. 'Handle what? Me having a backbone?'

'Destroying everything we built!'

'*We*? How is it a "we" when you never let me intervene?'

'Because your ideas were terrible.'

'And who are you to decide what's a good idea?'

Austomia fell silent.

Vaonie scoffed. 'Exactly,' they bellowed.

They glared at each other, neither willing to back down.

Vaonie hesitated and parted their lips. 'I... I'm sorry for betraying you,' they said softly, 'but I stand by my choices. I don't regret what I've created. They're my mark on Vanthea.'

'I can't let them exist...'

'Why not?'

'Your creations will break them – turn good humans bitter and angry at life and the divine. They'll cause needless death and war. I refuse to accept your ways.'

'Then fight me for it, we have no other choice.'

'What?' Austomia's voice wavered.

'You heard me. Fight me. The winner gives the final say.'

'I don't want to...'

'Does it look like I care?'

They both went silent and stared at each other.

A heavy silence fell between them before Austomia finally whispered, 'right now?'

Vaonie nodded. 'Mhmm.'

'I-I... Alright.'

Vaonie summoned their battle armor, designed for magical protection. Austomia manifested their own humanoid form, already well-equipped, wielded a staff controlling Talismirit—the primordial material of Heon-meyu[viii]. Its color shifted based on the wielder's position on the 'Great Dilemma': Austomia's blue, Vaonie's red.

As Austomia shot enormous spears of Talismirit, Vaonie spoke, unfazed, halting their advancement mid-air. 'Not here,' they commanded, 'our children mustn't witness our conflict.'

'Then where?'

'That unnamed dimension you created.'

'Agreed.'

'I hereby name it "Olana[ix]", realm of justice.'

They teleported instantly. Olana was chaos incarnate — neither light nor dark, neither sound nor silence.

"Nothing had been invented yet, so it was simply nothing yet also everything at the same time – a 42 joke if you will."

Austomia and Vaonie forged sound and light into the realm, their clash now underscored by thunderous harmonics. Floating platforms materialized for ground combat, shimmering with unstable energy.

'Ready, Austomia?' Vaonie's voice crackled like static.

Austomia levitated, staff humming. Blue Talismirit coalesced around them, fracturing into elemental projectiles: jagged stone, balls of fire, glacial shards, rays of energy and spectral jaws snapping at their foe.

Vaonie countered with crimson Talismirit, weaving a shield that dissolved attacks into ash. 'Predictable,' they

---

[viii] (Omnitongue) Heaven.
[ix] (Omnitongue) Justice.

growled, retaliating with a molten spear of red energy. Austomia teleported, the strike cratering the platform behind them.

The battle unfolded in timeless fury—a storm of creation and negation. Millennia blurred as neither gained ground: Austomia's light-spears met Vaonie's void-shields; Vaonie's banishment magic evaded by Austomia's celestial agility. Their parity felt cosmic, inevitable—two halves of a fractured whole.

Suspicion and worry grew in their children's hearts, as they noticed their parents' unannounced disappearance. They sensed the void where divine presence once hummed.

'Where are they? Austomia demanded an update on a task, but they're nowhere to be found,' Lodus asked.

Hanali bit the side of her lower lip, 'I don't know... Ask Kyyn, maybe he knows.'

Having later confirmed Kyyn's ignorance of their parents' whereabouts, Lodus called a family meeting in Heona's[X] main throne room.

'Our parents are missing,' Lodus began, his brow furrowed. 'I fear not for their safety against outsiders, but against each other. Their ambition might be their downfall. Has anyone noticed changes in their auras? Any unusual movements?'

Pholexu's eyes narrowed. 'Why are you acting like their guardian? *They* created *us*, not the other way around.'

'They cared for us,' Lodus countered, his voice firm. 'We owe them the same courtesy if they're in danger.'

[X] Heaven's capital city.

Fema nodded in agreement.

Ayurë's eyes widened suddenly. 'I remember feeling a shift a while back... They might have gone to the nameless realm.'

'We should investigate,' Anor said, leaning forward.

Kans summoned a portal, and the twelve deities stepped through. They froze, awestruck by the sight of their parents locked in fierce combat.

Pholexu's jaw dropped. 'What are they doing?!'

'This is bad...' Hanali muttered, pacing frantically, 'this is bad...'

'Why are you panicking, Hanali?' Jaone asked, his arms crossed. 'We just need to stop them. It'll be easy.'

Hanali froze, her hands trembling. 'Because conflicts have sides. If we can't stop them, we'll have to choose one. Choosing means betraying the other... and breaking my own commandment.'

Jaone's confidence faltered. 'Oh. That is bad. What happens if you break it? How does that even work? They never told us!'

'Calm down,' Fema interjected, placing a steadying hand on Hanali's shoulder. 'We'll figure this out. You're our eldest sister. You'll be fine.'

'Calm down. We will get through this, don't worry. You are our eldest sister. You will be fine,' Fema tried to cheer them up.

Bolstered by Fema's words, the children flew up to intervene. Their voices were drowned out by their parents' furious shouts.

'AUSTOMIA NEGLECTED ME. THEY PUSHED ME

ASIDE LIKE I WAS NOTHING. I AM THEIR EQUAL, YET THEY MADE ME INFERIOR. THEY DESERVE TO BE PUT DOWN!' Vaonie roared, crimson Talismirit[xi] crackling around them.

'VAONIE BROKE MY TRUST. THEY BETRAYED US ALL AND KILLED MILLIONS OF MORTALS FOR THEIR TWISTED IDEOLOGY!' Austomia countered, their staff glowing with searing blue light.

The siblings hovered in the chaos, torn between their warring parents. Eleven chose sides – bringing Hanali's fear to life – seven for Austomia, four for Vaonie. Hanali stood paralyzed, fists clenched, her breath shallow.

Jaone, Astrugiel, Ayurë, Gonuiel, Kyyn, Kans and Fema took the side of Austomia. Lodus, Pholexu, Ophiin, and Anor picked the side of Vaonie.

'How could you betray me so? My own children... I trusted you,' Vaonie screamed in anguish, the sound of their heartbreak violently taking over the static atmosphere.

Fema watched her eldest sister's trembling hands and reconsidered her decision. The numbers were in favor of Austomia, putting the others at a great disadvantage. Out of fear for breaking her own tenet, she drifted to Vaonie's side with a reluctant sigh. Kans followed, guilt and empathy tightening his jaw.

Six to five. Hanali's gaze locked on Lodus, her favourite brother, now glowing red with Vaonie's Talismirit. 'I must protect them all,' she thought, her inner voice cracking with

---

[xi] (Omnitongue) Name of the first element.

the duty of an elder sibling. 'Austomia's side,' she announced with a soft tone, ached by great anguish.

The battlefield erupted in chaos as Talismirit energy tore through the void. Austomia's blue light clashed with Vaonie's crimson fury, the sheer force of their attacks shaking the floating platforms beneath them. The siblings hesitated, caught between loyalty and fear, before reluctantly joining the fray.

Fema darted forward, her rose red Talismirit shimmering as she neutralized Austomia's attacks mid-air. Sparks burst around her like dying stars. Lodus, his Talismirit coloured in the strongest of reds, unleashed a barrage of monochrome flames. The fire preyed on Austomia's shields, erasing them from existence. His movements were sharp and calculated, his face twisted with determination.

Hanali hovered above the chaos, her bluish-purple Talismirit swirling around her like a storm. She clenched her fists, her heart pounding as she watched her siblings fight each other. 'This isn't right...' She thought, but there was no time to think – Austomia was under attack from all sides.

With a cry of desperation, Hanali surged forward, her Talismirit flaring in the color of violet. She focused on Fema's projectiles and tried to change their course, sending a wave of red darts toward Lodus. She meant to stop his assault on Austomia.

But something went wrong. Lodus froze mid-attack, his form flickering like a fading star as his own black flames fed upon him. His eyes widened in shock as his body began to dissolve into nothingness.

'No, Lodus!' Hanali screamed, reaching out toward him,

but it was too late. His form disintegrated into particles of light and shadow, scattering into the void.

The battlefield fell silent. The siblings stopped fighting, their eyes fixed on the empty space where Lodus had stood just moments ago.

Hanali dropped to her knees on a floating platform, her hands trembling. 'I didn't mean to...' She whispered, her voice breaking, 'I didn't mean to...'

Kans landed beside her and placed a hand on her shoulder, though his own expression was stricken with guilt and fear. 'It was an accident. We all know it wasn't your intention,' he murmured.

The rest of them nodded in agreement. They watched in stunned silence as Hanali, always the composed one, shattered before their eyes. She clawed at her own face, leaving angry scarlet marks. 'I killed him,' she wailed, her voice breaking, 'my brother...'

Hanali's siblings exchanged helpless glances, unsure how to console her. She alone bore the weight of 'mortal' emotions, though it was never known why.

Suddenly, her grief twisted into rage. She vanished in a flash, reappearing before Vaonie. Her eyes, usually soft, now blazed with a ferocity that made even the divine step back. 'THIS IS ALL YOUR FAULT!' Spectral tears streaming down her face. 'Your ambition, your betrayal... This is all because you.'

Hanali's body trembled, caught between the urge to attack and the crushing weight of her guilt. She fell to her knees again, her cries echoing through the realm. Her siblings exchanged helpless glances, never having witnessed such raw, mortal-like anguish from one of their own.

Austomia stood frozen, their staff quivering.

'What happened?' Vaonie demanded.

'Lodus... he's gone,' Hanali choked out.

Vaonie's face contorted in anguish and rage, he was their favourite child. 'Austomia, we must end this madness!' they roared.

Austomia materialized before them, their voice low and strained. 'Vaonie... I mourn him too. But you're outmatched now. I offer you this: exile to Tyronah[xii] with your supporters. You'll rule there. No more bloodshed, I can't bear to see more of it. Agreed?'

Vaonie's shoulders slumped in defeat. 'I... have no choice. Fine.'

In a flash of light, Vaonie and their five loyal children vanished, banished to their new home.

The scene shimmers, reality rippling as our perspective shifts. We're thrust back to the aftermath of the divine conflict, its echoes still reverberating through the pursuit of Vaonie's vengeance.

Hoofbeats punctuate the eerie silence of Heonmeyu's landscape. Alduin's hand wove a subtle gesture, and a

---

[xii] (Omnitongue) Hell.

whisper of ice magic danced along his blade. The ethereal blue blood of fallen angels crystallized, then shattered, leaving his sword clean and gleaming. His eyes, sharp yet haunted, scanned the horizon.

'If Austomia's so powerful,' he muttered, knuckles white on the reins, 'why not just obliterate us and be done with it?'

Anor rode beside him, face etched with the weight of eons. 'Family ties shackle their wrath,' he said, his voice low, 'banishment was Austomia's mercy for Vaonie. They can't bring themselves to kill us. We mean too much to them.'

Alduin's throat tightened. The Sarathiins loomed in his mind, a threat beyond death. His immortality felt like a curse – defeat could mean an eternity sealed away, consciousness trapped in an immobile prison.

He straightened in the saddle, steeling himself. A true warrior faces their fate, no matter how grim. The path ahead stretched into uncertainty, each step bringing them closer to a battle that would reshape realms.

The air itself held its breath, waiting for the clash that was to come.

CHAPTER EIGHT

The Araqhaiits traversed the gardens of Heonmeyu[i], a tapestry of fragrant blooms and tall grass fields – designed to resemble the mortals' vision of paradise. Fruit trees and flowers painted the landscape in vibrant hues. Wild animals, predator and prey alike, frolicked by crystal lakes that cooled the air.

Angels darted through fields, playing with joyful spirits of the deceased. Alduin's chest tightened with bittersweet nostalgia. Innocent happiness, a fleeting luxury in his immortal existence.

After each angelic slaughter, Alduin paused, inhaling the realm's crisp air. His mount's flanks heaved beneath him, a stark reminder of the carnage they left in their wake. Hours bled into one another as divine brethren cut down tens of thousands of angels.

---

[i] (Omnitongue) Heaven.

A castle loomed on the horizon, a gleaming beacon of their final target. Alduin's jaw clenched, steeling himself for the battle to come.

'This is Austomia's palace,' Kans announced, gripping his weapon tightly. 'Inside, we'll face our siblings. To the death. It will be brutal, and the cost will be high. Brace yourselves, brothers!' his voice rang out like a battle horn.

Without hesitation, they charged toward it, ignoring the swarm of guardian angels descending from the skies. The sound of wings and war cries filled the air, but their focus remained on the gates ahead. At last, they reached them.

Fema turned to address the group. 'This is Heona, the capital of Heonmeyu. Austomia resides here, along with the Sarathiins and the spirits of Vanthea's greatest mortals. Do not harm the spirits. Our goal is to seek justice for Vaonie, not punish the innocent. Is that clear, Lodus? Ophiin?'

Both nodded sharply. 'As you command,' they answered in unison.

Kans stepped forward, whispering a chant under his breath. The gates trembled before shattering into rubble with a deafening crash. 'Charge!' he roared.

They dismounted, each Araqhaiit splitting off to carve their own path through Heona's streets. Alduin darted between houses, his blade drawn and blood magic thrumming at his fingertips. The scent of crushed flowers and burning wood mingled in the air as angels descended upon him.

His moves were methodical. He was calm, precise – his earlier uneasiness replaced by grim efficiency. He had learned their tactics well: their sweeping dives, their predictable strikes. His blade found its mark again and again as he cut through their ranks like a seasoned predator.

The city was beautiful even in chaos: golden spires rising above fields of radiant flowers, shimmering lakes reflecting the carnage below. But Alduin barely noticed it. He focused on his mission – find and destroy any angel or Sarathiin in his path.

The front door creaked as Alduin pushed it open, his hand trembling slightly. He stepped inside cautiously, Vaurcarya swirling around him like a coiled predator, ready to strike. Sudden shock rushed through his spine as he recognized a few decorations that adorned the wall to his right.

His brows furrowed in confusion. 'A painting of Merissa? I should go, surely angels don't live here...' He said.

A voice, soft and familiar, floated from the living room. His breath caught. He crept forward and peeked inside. His heart stopped.

'F-Father?' he stuttered, the word barely escaped his lips.

Aeden turned sharply, his eyes widening in disbelief. 'Alduin? Is it really you?'

Before Alduin could respond, his mother rushed to him, tears streaming down her face. 'What kept you so long? We thought... we thought you'd been sent to Munesa[ii]. We were so worried!' She threw her arms around him, holding him as if afraid he'd vanish again.

[ii] (Elvish) Hell.

Alduin stood frozen for a moment before wrapping his arms around her tightly. 'It... it's hard to explain,' he murmured, his voice cracking. 'I'm just... glad you're here. That you made it to heaven.'

A sharp, searing pain tore through his arms, as if countless needles pierced him at once. Vaonie's voice thundered in his mind, 'what are you doing? Get back to your mission!'

His veins felt ready to burst, but he refused to yield. The warmth of his mother's embrace anchored him, giving him strength. He clung tighter instead of recoiling, defying the agony. 'Please,' he pleaded, 'let me have this. I haven't seen them in so long.'

A tense pause followed before Vaonie relented. 'You have a few minutes.'

'Thank you, my lord,' he responded.

He struggled to conceal his terror of Vaonie, his fear of dying for the simple act of spending time with his family. He mustn't worry them, not now, not ever.

Elys pulled back slightly, her hands gripping his shoulders as she searched his face. 'And what of our village?' she asked with worry in her tone, 'do you know what became of it?'

His throat tightened. 'Probably destroyed... abandoned,' he hesitated, then forced the words out. 'The Vaermiraiits[iii] killed everyone.'

Elys's gasp was sharp and pained, but before she could respond, a blur of motion came from the stairs. Veridia

---

[iii] (Omnitongue) Vampires.

sprinted down, her face lighting up with joy. 'Alduin!' she cried, throwing her arms around him.

He held her close, his chest aching with overflowing, unyielding emotions. 'I've missed you too,' he whispered.

For a moment, he allowed himself to bask in their warmth, their love, but guilt clawed at him like a starving beast. 'Why them and not me? I should have died with them…' He thought. 'Where's Uncle Ley?' he asked suddenly, pulling back from Veridia's embrace. 'Is he here too?'

Aeden's smile faltered. 'We haven't seen him yet,' he said softly, 'we thought he was with you.'

Alduin's jaw tightened as the memory surfaced unbidden: his uncle lying lifeless beside his father in the ruins of their village.

'He's probably in hell,' Veridia giggled. 'For all that needless shit that he did,' she said.

Alduin glanced at her sharply but said nothing. His shrug conveyed what words couldn't: 'I loved him all the same.'

Veridia caught the gesture and realized her brother had changed, that he wasn't the same childish brat she once knew. She noticed his dark, gloomy aura – one even her parents couldn't pick up on, that of deep trauma. She anticipated a fiery retort to her jabs – just like old times – but instead, he met her with an unsettling silence. 'What had happened to him?' she asked herself. 'I'm just kidding,' she reassured him with a quick smile.

'Are you leaving already?' Aeden asked suddenly, noticing Alduin's gaze lingering on the door.

'I must…' Alduin whispered.

'What? But you just got here!' Veridia protested. She turned to her mother with despair in his gleaming eyes. 'Mother, tell him!'

Elys raised an eyebrow and stepped forward, her voice trembling with emotion. 'Where could you possibly go that's more important than being here with us?'

Alduin clenched his fists until his knuckles turned white. The weight of his duty pressed heavily on his chest, an unbearable burden he couldn't share with them. The words hovered on his tongue: 'I must avenge you all. I must make them pay.' But he swallowed them back; they wouldn't understand. 'I'm sorry…' He said instead, quietly.

'When will you be back?' Aeden asked.

'I... I don't know.' His voice broke as he spoke the truth. He wasn't sure he'd survive that which lay ahead.

He reached out and shook his father's hand firmly, meeting his gaze one last time. 'I'll make sure they pay, he thought silently. Then I'll return,' he thought.

Aeden turned his eyes to his wife, he noticed her sharp, disappointed stare. She said nothing, though her eyes communed one clear message: 'Stop being such a fool. Hug him.' He obliged.

'I'm proud of you,' her eyes said as her lips twisted into a bright smile.

Astonished, Alduin's eyes opened as widely as physically possible. This had never happened to him. Has his father gone soft?

He let it play out, cherishing every passing second. His arms slowly crawled upwards, finishing in a mutual embrace – a deep one. One of love, appreciation, fatherly pride, compassion.

Veridia's face soaked with tears as she joined them, squeezing them both, hard.

His father smiled and returned the favor with a sharp stare. 'You too?' he asked his wife in a soft tone.

She nodded and joined the group hug, tears dripping down her cheeks.

Sudden pain raced down his spine, jolting him back to reality. His mission. Vaonie's wrath loomed if he lingered. For a moment, he wavered. 'Dying in their embrace... it wouldn't be so bad,' he pondered in his mind, 'much better than dying in a battle that isn't mine.' But resolve hardened his features. 'No. Not before I avenge them. Forgive me, lord, for this blasphemy.'

Time's up,' the voice of Vaonie popped into his head.

His body tensed, a silent signal. Elys, sensing the shift, loosened her hold. The others followed, the warmth of their embrace fading as they stepped back. It lasted for seven whole minutes – the best seven minutes of his teenage years. Alduin, his heart taken hostage by anguish, gave them one long reassuring smile before stepping away and walking toward the door.

'We'll be waiting for you here, my son. May the light of Merissa shine through you,' his father said.

Alduin's lips moved, as though willing to respond, but he stopped himself. He mustn't grow false hope in their hearts. He looked down, nodded and stepped out.

Heaven's fresh air blew in his face, as if trying to console him. The ache in his chest grew unbearable as he glanced backwards. His heart felt heavier than ever before, hollowed by overbearing weight that no vengeance could fill.

'I needed that,' he muttered under his breath as tears threatened to spill but never came. He clenched his jaw and punched the wall of a nearby house in frustration. The impact left a massive crack and echoed loudly through the air. Too loud.

They heard him. The thunderous sound of huge, flapping wings echoed in his ears. A band of angels descended – a blur of ivory feathers and celestial screeches. Alduin's back hit the cracked wall, talons raking the stone inches from his face. Claws like blades. Breath like frost. Their attacks came not in turns, but in a storm: a wing slammed his ribs, a spear grazed his thigh, a gauntleted fist cracked his jaw.

Pain. Not the mortal kind. It burned deeper, hotter – fruit of celestial wrath. He choked on his blood. 'I can't die like this... Not after everything I've been through,' he thought.

Vaonie's voice slithered through the agony and into his mind, 'you will be a god, or you will be carrion,' they said.

Alduin ducked to dodge the thrust of a spear, and it finally hit him – 'Surely, they're ignorant of Snow Elf tactics,' the words popped in his mind.

He let his knees buckle, feigning collapse. Feathers rustled as the circle tightened. 'Now,' he shouted in his head. Arcane words hissed between his teeth, 'nor din feni u uli. Dreem te uli[iv].'

It was a technique his uncle had taught him. An ice clone materialized in his place, perfect mimicry down to the blood on its lips. Alduin vanished, invisible, as the angels swarmed the decoy. Claws tore into ice. Wings beat frozen shrapnel into the air.

He ran away. Burning lungs. Hammering heart. He used every spare Olon[v] to increase its lifespan – to buy him time. He didn't stop until a great fountain entered his sight, its waters shimmering with stolen emeralds.

Encircled by vibrant flowers and berry-laden bushes, it radiated an almost sacred tranquillity. Alduin felt an inexplicable pull toward it, but his steps faltered as his gaze locked onto a figure seated by the water. He froze. A stranger.

Heart pounding, he dove into the cover of the bushes, his breath shallow as he peeked through the leaves. His eyes narrowed, assessing the potential threat. It was a woman.

She was stunning, otherworldly. Long scarlet hair cascaded down her back like fire. She wore a flowing light-green dress adorned with golden markings and red buttons, a snow-white scarf draped elegantly around her shoulders. Rings, bracelets, and necklaces of pure gold gleamed in the sunlight, and her knight's boots shone with the same brilliance. But what struck him most were her eyes – glowing

---

[iv] (Omnitongue) (To) release the (to) form of ice. (To) disappear in ice.
[v] (Omnitongue) Particles.

pupils in the color of blue violet, piercing the water like knives. Her ears tapered to fine points, resembling his own.

Alduin's mind raced. 'No wings, so she can't be an angel. But is that even a requirement?' he wondered, 'and spirits' eyes don't glow. Could she be a Sarathiin? If so, why hasn't she attacked me? And how hasn't she noticed my aura?'

He stared at her longer than intended, his curiosity warring with caution. Then it happened – their eyes met.

His chest tightened as fear surged through him like ice water. Her gaze held his for a heartbeat, sharp and knowing, before she vanished into thin air without a sound.

Alduin's breath hitched. 'How could she see me? I'm invisible,' he thought.

Before he could react, she materialized in front of him, her hand clamped down on his neck, firm and unyielding. He was yanked upright as though he weighed nothing at all. The scent of vanilla and clove filled the air around him, a soft contrast to his pain.

A violent flash of memory forced its way into his brain, reminding him of the vow to his lord.

As Austomia's banishment loomed, Vaonie executed a desperate plan. They severed their physical essence from their Olons, transforming it into artifacts scattered across Vanthea. These relics were hidden in ancient crypts, forgotten ruins, and other secret places, waiting to be discovered by unsuspecting mortals. The power within them was a double-edged sword—capable of unleashing chaos and 'glitches' in reality, but also holding the key to Vaonie's eventual return.

In the depths of Tyronah[vi], Vaonie forged a new order. They decreed so: The Araqhaiits would continue their divine duties, and the Deovhaiits[vii], serving as natives to the land, would torment the evil souls of the damned.

After eons, Vaonie suddenly gave the signal, tearing open portals to unleash the demons into Vanthea. Their mission was clear: retrieve the artifacts and pave the way for Vaonie's return.

The demons descended upon the mortal realm like a plague, slaughtering innocents who dared resist. Some revelled in cruelty, burning cities and defiling temples, while others hunted the relics with relentless determination. The war that ensued would be remembered as the 'Mortal Demon War' – a conflict that lasted 1023 long years and reshaped the world.

In the 56th year of this war, the 'Vaermiraiit Plague' erupted, turning mortals into predators of the night that roamed the land, spreading terror and despair. Despite these horrors, some people found the strength to rally, determined to survive the frightening ordeal.

The war's end marked the beginning of a new era – the

[vi] (Omnitongue) Hell.
[vii] (Omnitongue) Demons.

'Renaissance'. The mortals began counting their years from the day it unfolded – 0 MDW.

"For all you history nerds out there, this war took place just a few years after the failed assassination attempt on the Roman Emperor Commodus."

The Sarathiins, in their ignorance, mistook the infiltrators for yet another of Vaonie's foul creations. Their inaction proved catastrophic. The demons tore through Vanthea, leaving a trail of carnage in their wake. Billions perished, their screams echoing across ravaged landscapes. Yet despite the bloodshed, a handful of artifacts remained elusive.

Frustrated, the items were nowhere to be found, the demons retreated home under their lord's approval, their mission unfulfilled. Vaonie's grand scheme crumbled, leaving them trapped with no path back. Hope kept to its fragile nature – withered and died.

In a final act of spite, Vaonie cast the artifacts back into Vanthea. They sought out the most conflicted souls – mortals so corrupt they embraced demonic worship and Vaonie's twisted ideals. The common folk spat the name 'Vaonical worshippers' like a curse, hunting these fanatics with righteous fury. Among their ranks, the Vaermiraiits stood proud, revelling in their infamy.

The artifacts' purpose shifted. No longer tools of resurrection, they became instruments of pure chaos. Each relic pulsed with the power to shatter Austomia's creation, a childish message born of Vaonie's bitter heartbreak: 'If *I* can't play with it, no one else can.'

From the tale of the artifacts, our perspective turns to their living legacy – our protagonist – now choking in the grip of a goddess.

Her grip tightened around Alduin's throat. 'Who are you? Speak!' she demanded, her eyes blazing in lavender blue.

Alduin's mind raced. No right answer existed. She radiated power far beyond his own. 'Please... p-put me down,' he stuttered in ragged breath.

She sighed and released him.

Alduin steadied himself mid-air. 'My name is Alduin Lodus Fa-' He wasn't allowed to finish.

'Lodus?!' A fierce gleam flashed in her eyes. 'My brother died long ago. Lie again, and I'll feed you to my Nasyryl[viii]!'

'I swear it's true,' his voice cracked. 'Vaonie appointed me as his successor.'

'Prove it,' she snarled, seizing his left hand. Her eyes widened at the mark of her parent, her body going rigid.

'Who... are you?' Alduin whispered.

'Hanali, of the Sarathiin.' Her voice trembled, 'that makes me your... enemy. But I never wanted this. I never intended to kill my brother!' A river of tears streamed down her cheeks.

Alduin's jaw dropped to the floor, 'you... killed Lodus?'

[viii] Magical bear species native to Heaven.

'Yes,' she choked out. 'Vaonie's uprising forced us to choose sides. I betrayed everything I stood for. Austomia insists I did nothing wrong, but...' She shook her head, unable to continue.

'I know of loss,' Alduin said softly.

'Is... that so?' Hanali wiped the tears from her cheeks. Her posture suddenly stiffened, her grief giving way to steel. 'Why are you here, Araqhaiit?'

'V-Vaonie's orders,' he tried to hide his fear, 'we're to kill every celestial in Heonmeyu[ix]. Vengeance marks our paths.' His words hung heavy in the air, 'we've already slaughtered thousands of angels, and I'm not allowed to leave before killing at least one of the Sarathiin. I'm sorry...'

'No. This... This can't be,' horror struck her eyes as they lost their mesmerising spark, 'no more!" She hissed. 'This ends now. Follow me or die where you stand.'

Alduin nodded, knowing he had no choice.

Hanali shot into the air, her movements sharp and deliberate. Her scarlet hair whipped around her face as she scanned the battlefield, her glowing eyes cutting through the chaos.

Spotting her siblings amidst the carnage, she cried out, her voice trembling with desperation. 'Brothers! Sisters! It's me, Hanali, your elder sister. Stop this madness. This battle is not your cause!'

Her plea rang out like thunder, silencing the clash of weapons below. Alduin watched in awe as the fighting

---

[ix] (Omnitongue) Heaven.

ceased. One by one, Sarathiins and Araqhaiits abandoned their battles and ascended toward her.

The Sarathiins gathered beside her, their presence commanding yet distinct. Alduin recalled their names: Astrugiel, Ayurë, Gonuiel, Kyyn, and Jaone. Opposite them stood the Araqhaiits, their eyes fixed on Alduin as he stood between the two factions. Kans glared at him with disappointment etched across his face.

'Hello, sister,' Ophiin sneered, his grin twisted with malice. 'Did you miss me?'

Hanali met his provocation with calm resolve. 'Yes. Deeply.'

'Always so serious,' he mocked, leaning forward like a predator sizing up prey.

Ayurë cut in sharply. 'What do you want? We were ridding Heonmeyu of these pests.'

Hanali's voice hardened. 'This man told me of the reason they're here. This isn't just an attack, it's a genocide. Of angels. Of our family."

Gonuiel's gaze sharpened as he turned to Alduin. 'And who is he?' he pointed at him.

'M-My name is Alduin Lodus Faëli,' he stuttered in fear. 'Vaonie chose me t-to continue your fallen brother's legacy.'

'Is that so?' Ayurë asked, his tone dripping with scepticism.

Hanali's voice cracked as she spoke again. 'It is true... and blasphemous. Vaonie has turned us against each other once more!'

Ophiin smirked and revealed his sharp, long tongue.

'You find this amusing?' Hanali snapped, her composure breaking for a moment. 'Fighting among ourselves is foolish. We need not kill each other for a cause that isn't even ours!'

Kans stepped forward, his voice steady but cold. 'What else would you have us do? Disobey our lord? You know as well as we do that Austomia and Vaonie are not to be defied.'

Astrugiel nodded grimly. 'He speaks the truth.'

Jaone and Fema murmured their agreement.

Hanali clenched her fists, her glowing eyes dimming as sorrow overtook her features. 'I know... And it pains me deeply. But I have found a solution, a way to satisfy your lord without further bloodshed.' She straightened herself, her voice resolute but heavy with grief. 'I will relinquish my title as Sarathiin and leave Heonmeyu forever.'

Astrugiel stepped forward in shock. 'Are you insane? Banishing yourself? You've done nothing wrong!'

Ophiin laughed. 'You're even dumber than I remembered,' he taunted.

Alduin's eyes opened widely before losing their light to the hands of anguish. 'Why... punish yourself for crimes that aren't yours?'

Hanali turned to him sharply but softened as she spoke. 'Because I am the eldest. I must protect them at all costs. This is my decision alone.' Her gaze swept over the Araqhaiits and Sarathiins alike. 'Now ask your master if this plan satisfies them,' she commanded.

'Could this work in my favor?' Alduin wondered, 'I don't want to kill them.'

Kans met his sister's gaze, her eyes radiating determination and authoritative resolve. He hesitated before nodding curtly. 'As you wish, sister.'

Kans raised his hands, chanting a portal to Tyronah. Vaonie's initial fury at seeing the Sarathiins alive melted into curiosity. Scepticism gave way to reluctant agreement.

Hanali's voice rang out, clear and resolute. 'It is settled. I pay the price for Lodus's fall. I relinquish my Sarathiin title, now finally neutral. At last, I find peace!'

"Impeccably balanced, as everything is meant to be."

Her eyes flashed, the color in them deepening to a rich, equilibrated purple. A smile, genuine and almost forgotten, graced her face. She looked both gentle and commanding, both soft and formidable.

Kans opened the portal back home. This time seven were to enter, instead of six. Hanali strode forward, her siblings' faces a mix of awe and respect at her sacrifice for harmony.

Alduin stood transfixed. Each glance at Hanali sent warmth flooding his neck, his heart hammering like a forge. Her bravery, her fierce loyalty to family, it stirred something long dormant within him.

He saw in her a mirror of his shattered past: his mother's warmth, a treasure once taken for granted, now forever beyond his grasp. The realization crashed over him like a tidal wave – he will never see his family again. As the light in his eyes dimmed, a void threatened to consume him. Yet her presence, her gaze, acted as a lifeline, a balm to his raw wounds. She drew him in, an irresistible force promising solace with the mystical scent of vanilla and clove. Like an addict to his fix, his brain told him to never leave her side.

Hanali caught his lingering stare. She held it for a heartbeat, then looked away. But not before an unbidden smile curved her lips, a flicker of possibility in the midst of cosmic change.

CHAPTER NINE

The group emerged from the portal into Tyronah[i].

Vaonie stood before them, chin raised, a grin spreading across their face. 'Welcome back, my children.'

They bowed, their movements synchronized.

Vaonie's gaze fixed on a figure partially hidden behind the others. 'Oh, and what do we have here? Step forward, my daughter.'

Hanali emerged, her posture rigid. 'Hello.'

Vaonie's eyes narrowed. 'Is that all you have to say after your betrayal?'

Hanali's beauty struck Alduin anew, but her unwavering stance impressed him more. His muscles tensed, his right hand instinctively jumped to the scabbard of his sword – ready to defend her. 'Lord,' Alduin interjected, his voice steady despite his racing heart, 'Her actions

---

[i]   (Omnitongue) Hell.

prevented further bloodshed. You agreed to her terms. Why this hostility?'

'SILENCE!' Vaonie's roar reverberated through the chamber. Candles and torches flickered as if sharing the anger.

Alduin collapsed, his limbs suddenly useless. He writhed on the ground, struggling to regain control.

Ophiin's laughter echoed off the walls. 'Always the fool, huh?'

Alduin strained to lift his head, focusing on the unfolding scene.

Vaonie's attention returned to Hanali, their eyes glowing in intense red. 'Well?'

Hanali's chin lifted, her eyes meeting her maker's. She stood firm, full of resolve. 'I won't apologize. My only regret is my brother's death. I chose neutrality, not sides.'

Vaonie's lips curled into a snarl. With a wave of their hand, the throne room's walls shimmered, becoming transparent. 'Look outside. See what my life has become, courtesy of your beloved Austomia.'

Hanali's eyes widened as she witnessed the horrors, her face draining of color. She recoiled and shut her eyes.

Vaonie forced them open with telekinesis and grabbed her neck, choking her. 'Take it all in,' they hissed.

Alduin's muscles screamed as he fought against the invisible force pinning him down. The Araqhaiits stood motionless, their expressions unreadable.

'You're hurting me,' Hanali gasped, her voice barely audible.

Vaonie's telekinetic grip tightened. 'Good. As you've hurt me. You'll witness it all.'

Hanali's resistance crumbled. Her eyes, wide and unblinking, absorbed the landscape. Alduin, curiosity overcoming his paralysis, craned his neck to glimpse the world beyond.

Shock rippled through him. Tyronah bore no resemblance to Heonmeyu[ii]. A monochromatic tapestry of reds stretched as far as the eye could see. Dark gray earth sprouted scarlet trees and blood-red bushes, all engulfed in eerily static crimson flames. The fires, unnaturally still, seemed more atmospheric than destructive.

A pitch-black sky loomed overhead, punctuated by countless stars and moons that cast an otherworldly glow. The land teemed with life – primarily Deovhaiits[iii], but also unfamiliar creatures.

The demons defied categorization. Giants towered over diminutive figures shorter than Alduin himself. Skin tones ranged from ashen gray to vibrant red. Wings of varying sizes adorned some, while others sported horns in myriad shapes. All were armed, their brutal weapons a stark contrast to their unabashed nakedness.

One group captivated Alduin's attention: pink Deovhaiits, roughly his height, with dragon-like horns and three monkey-like tails. Four-armed and two-legged, they moved

---

[ii] (Omnitongue) Heaven.
[iii] (Omnitongue) Demons.

with feline grace on razor-sharp claws. Their snake-like pupils glowed crimson, their beautiful faces framed by long, intricately braided black hair.

Despite their grotesque appearance, Alduin found himself attracted to them, as if pulled by an invisible force of seduction. He stared at them, mesmerised.

Ophiin's laughter cut through the tension. 'Admiring the "Succubus", are we, Lodus? They prey on mortal lust and greed, destroying lives. My personal favourites.'

Alduin's grin vanished as Hanali's disappointed glare met his eyes.

Vaonie released Hanali, their voice low. 'Now you understand the consequences of your betrayal?'

Hanali's voice trembled. 'This... this is horrific. From gods to prisoners in this abomination. I'm speechless.'

Her siblings murmured in unison, 'will you apologize now?'

'No,' she said firmly.

Alduin's lips twitched into a half-smile, his body still aching.

'What?' Anor raised his voice, his eyes shining fiercely.

Hanali stood straighter. 'I won't apologize. I stand by my decision to support the Sarathiin, just as you stood against Austomia. Now, I choose to join you and my remaining siblings. That's all.'

'I see,' Vaonie said.

Hanali and the Araqhaiits stared at their lord, awaiting the verdict.

'I'm proud, daughter. You certainly inherited your stubbornness from me. Welcome to our ranks,' Vaonie proclaimed.

Kans nodded. 'If our lord welcomes you, so do we, sister.'

'I *did* miss you, actually,' Ophiin added, a hint of warmth in their voice.

Hanali's grin widened as she caught Alduin's eye. His smile mirrored hers, a silent exchange of support.

Vaonie's voice rang out. 'I hereby grant you the title "Hanali the Peacemaker". Serve me well.'

'Thank you,' Hanali bowed her head.

'One more thing,' Vaonie turned to Alduin, 'stand.'

Alduin mumbled, struggling. His breaths were hollow and desperate.

'Oh, right,' they released their constraints on his body.

His body finally obeyed him. He rose, bowing deeply.

'Your debt is repaid. I have a new task for you,' Vaonie said.

'I am yours to command,' Alduin said through ragged breaths.

"What an ass-kisser. Though, I'd have done the same if I were in his shoes."

'You should explore Tyronah together. I want my daughter to settle in, and you must aid her. As former mortal and Sarathiin, you're both ignorant of our ways.'

Alduin nodded. 'I'll do my best.'

'Hanali, watch Lodus. Ensure his loyalty.'

'Yes, maker,' Hanali affirmed.

'Araqhaiits, dismissed,' Vaonie announced.

The others departed with a deep bow, leaving Alduin and Hanali bewildered in the throne room.

'How…' Alduin cleared his throat. 'How do we exit?'

Hanali stifled a giggle as Alduin's cheeks flushed.

'W-What? It's a legitimate question,' he stuttered.

Vaonie sighed, 'explore. There are no restrictions. Walk wherever you please.'

They approached the leftmost door near the throne.

'Lodus,' Hanali began.

'Please, my name is Alduin,' he said, his voice softening, 'though no one seems to fucking understand that…' He muttered in angry gibberish.

'Alduin,' she corrected, 'what did Vaonie mean about you being a former mortal?'

He blushed at the sight of her lips uttering his name. 'I was born a Snow Elf in Vanthea,' he explained.

Hanali's eyes widened, her jaw nearly hit the floor. 'Why would…' She murmured.

'Am I your first mortal?'

'Y-Yes,' she stuttered, 'I never spoke or even met one before.'

He grinned. 'Then I better make a good impression.'

A faint color rose to her cheeks.

'Let's go here,' he pointed to the left.

The echo of their footsteps grew louder as they descended the staircase. A heavy door blocked their way. Alduin struggled to open it.

'Need help?' she asked.

'Yes,' he looked to the floor, embarrassed.

'Move aside,' she said. Her eyes glowed purple as she effortlessly pushed it open.

'How did you do that?' Alduin marvelled.

'Aren't you an Araqhaiit?'

Alduin clenched his fists, 'Vaonie left me part mortal. I'm their puppet, I can't even raise a finger against their will…' He ground his teeth, ashamed of his helplessness, 'the last time I defied them, I lost my breath and nearly died.'

Hanali's expression softened. 'That's… unfortunate.'

'Thanks,' he murmured.

'I'm not used to mortals. I'll improve,' Hanali promised, a gentle smile forming.

Alduin returned the smile. 'In any case, Vaonie's refusal to teach me of my parents is what truly bothers me.'

'Don't worry,' Hanali reassured. 'I'll teach you.'

'Really?' his eyes sparkled with renewed hope. Perhaps one day he'd grow powerful enough to avenge his family.

'Of course. I owe you that. Plus, you could teach me about your culture.'

Alduin smiled and extended his hand. 'In my country, we seal deals this way,' he said.

They shook hands awkwardly. He couldn't help but notice how warm and smooth her skin was. How easily her fingers rested in his. His pulse raced.

Hanali's eyes locked with his, a mix of confusion and intrigue in her gaze. His friendliness perplexed her.

'You'll get used to it,' he said softly, 'have you ever met Deovhaiits?'

'No, you?'

'Same here. Shall we?'

'Certainly,' she said.

'Ah, curious like me. Good to hear.'

Hanali smiled, her earlier hesitation fading. 'Do you know where we're going?' she asked, having followed his lead for the past fifteen minutes.

'Absolutely not,' he scratched the back of his head, 'I just go with whichever door looks prettiest,' he chuckled.

'Foolproof,' she giggled.

'I know, right?'

Vaonie's castle resembled a maze – each door led to more doors, as if they were being tested.

'Three identical doors... Let's go with the one in the middle,' she said.

'You just can't pick a side, huh?' he winked at her and followed her inside.

Hanali blew a raspberry in response.

'What languages do you speak?' he asked.

'All of them, I guess?'

'Wow,' his jaw dropped to the floor, 'how old are you?'

'Hasn't your mother told you never to ask a woman that?'

'I... No, I apologize,' his eyes grew darker.

'I'm kidding. Gods aren't that insecure,' she giggled, 'you should have seen the look on your face.'

A tint of pink caressed his cheeks.

'It's a difficult question, since time works differently in Heonmeyu. I don't know, what about you?' she asked.

'I spent many years underground, so I am not sure. But I

should be around seventeen years old. Perhaps a bit closer to eighteen.'

'Young.'

'Y-Yes…' He shrugged, 'why did your eyes change color back in Heonmeyu?'

'No one explained this to you?'

'No. Let's take that door,' he gestured.

'Our eyes and tattoos change color according to our alignment in the dilemma of "Austomia vs Vaonie". Blue for Austomia, and red for Vaonie.'

'Then why are yours purple?'

Hanali raised an eyebrow, 'isn't it clear?'

'Oh, right,' he smirked, 'you suck at picking sides.'

'I prefer the term "celestial abstention".'

Alduin snorted, 'sure, sure.'

'Is that doubt I'm hearing?'

'Me? Doubting you? Pfft… never.'

They shared a laugh. After a few minutes, they reached a towering gate.

strained against it, muscles trembling. 'Why can't I…?'

'This… this is Talismirit[iv],' her eyes widened, 'your mortal part prevents you from opening it.'

'What do you mean?'

'My siblings have taught you nothing, huh?'

'Something like that,' he rolled his eyes.

'Munesa[v],' she cursed in the tongue of his people, trying to impress him. 'Long ago, Heonmeyu was nothing but an

---

[iv] Name of the first element.
[v] (Elvish) Hell.

enormous flat surface made of Talismirit. It is the primordial substance, the first material to ever exist.'

Alduin's eyes furrowed in confusion.

'Only pure divines can interact with it,' she explained, 'and its color matches our eyes. When unattended, it turns black.'

'So, your Talismirit is purple?'

'Exactly,' she smiled, 'Let me open the gate, stand back.'

She levitated, eyes blazing violet. The gate glowed and slid open in sync with her hand. 'Here you go,' she grinned.

Four Deovhaiit guards greeted them with a bow. Alduin mirrored them, but she pulled him by the collar of his shirt.

'They mustn't think of you as an equal,' she whispered in his ear, 'it could spark rebellion.'

As the pair turned to leave, one of the guards uttered something in an unfamiliar language. 'What?' Hanali asked.

'So there *is* a language you can't speak. I knew it,' Alduin chuckled.

'Not for long,' she blushed, 'I will ask Fema to teach me.'

'May I join?'

Hanali's lips curved into a smile. 'Gladly.'

The sentinels gestured with their spears, indicating a direction. Her eyes narrowed. 'You want us to go that way? What's there?'

They mimed, but their attempts at communication fell flat.

She shrugged. 'We'll find out ourselves. Let's go, Alduin.'

The sentries nodded, their faces expressionless.

They ventured in the indicated direction, soon encountering a vibrant village. Towering structures in every shade of red and orange imaginable lined the streets, with the occasional pink or deep crimson edifice breaking the pattern. A solitary yellow house stood out amidst the warm hues.

The streets teemed with 'life'. Merchants haggled, blacksmiths hammered, and children darted between adults' legs. Hanali's eyes lit up at the sight of the young ones, her smile infectious. Alduin caught her expression and mirrored it.

Their eyes locked. 'W-What? Children are adorable,' Hanali said, her tone defensive.

Alduin raised his hands in mock surrender. 'I said nothing,' he chuckled.

A gray-skinned woman caught their attention, her brush dancing across a canvas. As they approached, she added a white smile to two circles on a black background. Alduin recoiled, unnerved. He found it creepy. His reaction sent Hanali into peals of laughter.

Misinterpreting Hanali's mirth, the artist clutched her painting and fled inside her orange-hued dwelling.

Hanali's laughter died abruptly. 'No, don't go!' she shouted.

But the door was already closed shut.

'Did I offend her?' she asked him.

He shrugged.

They approached the artist's door, knocking tentatively. Silence greeted them. They tried again. A towering, bull-horned man answered, his lighter skin a stark contrast to the artist's. An axe gleamed in his left hand, his stance radiating hostility. Guttural Deovhaiitish spilled from his lips, incomprehensible yet clearly threatening.

'Uh...' Alduin turned to his companion. 'Help me, Hanali.'

She stepped forward, her movements deliberate. 'I,' she pointed at herself, 'don't,' she made an X with her hands, 'speak,' her right hand mimicked a tweeting bird, 'Deovhaiitish,' she pointed at the man.

The demon sighed, then addressed her in the Omni-tongue. After a brief exchange, he called for the lady. Hanali's posture relaxed as she conveyed her apology through the translator. The conversation concluded, and the door closed with a soft thud.

Alduin's brow furrowed. 'What transpired? My Omni-tongue is rusty.'

'The lady is his daughter. We frightened her. I apologized, he thanked us, and that was it,' Hanali summarized, her tone firm.

'Ah.' Alduin's gaze swept the street. 'Why are they all unclothed? It's... bizarre.'

Hanali shrugged. 'Perhaps they deem clothing unnecessary.'

'Would you do it?' Alduin asked, his curiosity piqued.

She paused, considering. 'I've never tried it, but maybe...'

Alduin's cheeks warmed, a faint color suddenly rising to his face.

She noticed it and looked to the side. 'I'm just thinking aloud.'

'Your curiosity is... refreshing,' he admitted, a playful smile on his lips.

'Thank you,' she rolled her eyes and turned around, hiding a tiny smile.

They strolled through the town, marvelling at its rich culture. Merchants hawked peculiar wares, from exotic foods to bizarre services. One vendor, noticing their powerful aura, claimed her husband had been cheating on her with their neighbour. She offered them her house, if Hanali agreed to beat up the bastard.

Alduin's brow furrowed. 'They're oddly... human.'

Hanali nodded, her eyes wide. 'Right? I expected savagery, not... civilization.'

'What if,' Alduin mused, 'Vaonie created them as their own "mortals" to design?'

Hanali's eyes lit up. 'Brilliant. It fits their nature.'

'Thank you.' A sign caught Alduin's eye, 'what is that?'

'It's written in the Omnitongue. There're a lot of mistakes but I think it's a clothing shop.'

Alduin's head tilted slightly, 'a... tailor? In a nude society?'

'I don't know. Let's find out,' her eyes lit up.

They entered, greeted by a pink, goat-horned demon with twin cat tails. The irony of his nakedness wasn't lost on them.

'Welcome, Araqhaiits,' the merchant beamed, 'to the best tailor in Tyronah!'

Hanali put her lips close to Alduin's ear and whispered, 'he's speaking in the Omnitongue, but he's making so many grammatical errors that it's impressive by itself.'

Alduin tried his best to hide his laugh. 'Ask him why he sells clothes in a land where people wear none,' he told her.

Hanali translated his query.

'Ah, I don't serve my kind,' the tailor explained. 'My shop, "Din La u Pol", is for you, my lords. Every Araqhaiit wears my brand.'

Hanali's eyes sparkled. 'Intriguing. But do you earn enough? We're only six.'

'I own many businesses, don't worry,' the shopkeeper smiled. 'Are you interested?' he asked.

Alduin scratched his ear. 'What is he saying?' he asked.

'This shop is called "The Lord of White", and he designs outfits for Araqhaiits,' Hanali explained. 'I have a proposition,' she turned her head to the seller. She gestured to Alduin, 'special armor for him.'

Alduin tensed. 'W-What? What's wrong with my current attire?'

'It's, uh… Your pants don't even fit you properly!' Hanali's gaze softened, 'just trust me, okay? You must wear something that befits your status.'

Alduin's shoulders slumped, then he nodded reluctantly.

'I'll translate,' Hanali offered, leading him to follow the eager tailor.

They followed the merchant into a private room. His flamboyant design suggestions were met with immediate rejection from both Alduin and Hanali. Finally, they agreed on a concept.

'He needs your measurements,' Hanali translated. 'You'll have to undress.'

Alduin's eyes darted across the room. 'I've never... in front of a woman...'

Hanali burst into laughter.

Alduin tensed, his eyes glowed red, 'don't laugh at me! I spent most of my teenage years in a cage...' The ferocious glow diminished, replaced by a sulk.

Hanali's laughter died as she caught Alduin's pained expression. 'My apologies.'

Alduin stayed silent and glared at her.

'Forgive me,' she insisted.

Alduin sighed, his expression softening into a gentle smile, acknowledging her apology. She smiled back.

The clothier raised an eyebrow. 'What is happening?'

'He's shy,' she explained.

'An Araqhaiit, shy?'

'He'll manage,' Hanali assured him. 'Come on, I won't look,' she addressed Alduin.

He hesitated, his fingers trembling as he slowly disrobed. His cheeks flushed pink, and he shifted his weight from foot to foot, nervously darting his gaze around the room.

Hanali made a show of averting her gaze, but kept shifting it back to Alduin. While suppressing a smile, she stole quick, discreet glances at his form. Her heart raced, a mix of guilt and excitement coursing through her.

'What is happening to me? Why am I doing this?' she asked herself. 'It's okay,' she murmured to him, her tone gentle yet tinged with amusement.

Alduin's ears burned at her words. He crossed his arms over his chest, then uncrossed them, unsure where to place his hands. 'R-Right,' he stammered, his voice cracking slightly.

The tailor approached with his measuring tape, and Alduin flinched at the first touch. He held his breath, trying his best to stand rigidly as the man's hands moved with practiced precision. Through separate frames, Hanali watched the scene unfold, her eyes twinkling with a mixture of sympathy and intrigue.

As the measurements continued, Alduin's body began twirling and jumping at the clothier's touch. He closed his eyes tightly, as if hoping to disappear

The demon sighed. 'Calm him down, please.'

If you keep making this poor man's job harder, I'll have to hold you down myself,' she said playfully, her eyes averted.

'D-Don't,' Alduin shouted. 'Fine, I'll calm down.'

Alduin's eyes snapped open, a mix of surprise and curiosity momentarily overriding his embarrassment. He finally managed to stay still.

After about twelve minutes, the clothier stopped and approached Hanali. 'All done,' he announced, and she translated.

'How much time would it take?' Hanali relayed Alduin's query.

'Magic speeds the process,' the demon explained. 'I'll return shortly. He can dress in the meantime.'

Hanali translated, but seemed to 'forget' the last part. She suppressed a smirk, trying to maintain a straight face.

The garment maker bowed, entered another room and closed the door.

'Y-You don't have to look away...' Alduin said, 'just keep your eyes on my face, okay?' he covered his groin with his hands.

Hanali's cheeks turned into ripe tomatoes. 'Okay,' she muttered and turned around to face him.

Alduin exhaled in relief. 'Glad we found a design you approved.'

Hanali grinned. 'Your taste needed refinement,' she said, her gaze drifting casually over him, as if merely glancing at the air, before quickly returning to his face with an air of nonchalance.

He still hadn't noticed it.

"What a virgin."

'It's *my* outfit,' Alduin protested.

'And I want it perfect,' Hanali countered, her eyes softening.

'Fine... And what of the color scheme you *insisted* on picking for me?' Alduin pressed.

Hanali's eyes twinkled. 'A surprise.'

Alduin let out a long, playful sigh.

'I'm almost done,' the merchant shouted from across the wall.

Hanali translated and took another discreet peek.

'Oh, good,' he muttered, his fingers drumming a hesitant rhythm on his hips as he struggled to reconcile himself with his nakedness, his eyes darting away in a mix of embarrassment and discomfort.

The demon burst through the door, arms laden with fabric. 'It's ready!'

The outfit lay in carefully arranged layers. He rushed back to the other room, to give them some privacy. Hanali guided Alduin through each piece:

Black underpants. White fabric pants. Silver knight's boots with red accents. Off-white cotton shirt.

'Now,' Hanali instructed, 'vest, belt, amulet, jacket.'

Alduin wore the black leather vest adorned with silver, followed by a silver belt with a red gem centrepiece. A silver necklace bearing Vaonie's symbol came next. Finally, he slipped on a long white jacket, its fabric cascading to his feet, adorned with silver buttons and red ornaments. He left it unbuttoned, giving it a robe-like quality. Hanali conjured a mirror.

Alduin's eyes widened. 'It's stunning! How did you know?'

She smiled, explaining her color choices – white for his heritage, red for his eyes, silver for contrast. 'We're not done yet,' she added, gesturing to the remaining pieces.

A white cape and a silver fox-shaped pauldron awaited. Alduin used telekinesis to secure the pauldron, attaching the cape in one fluid motion.

As he admired his reflection, Alduin's voice softened. 'It's perfect.'

Drawn by her radiant smile, Alduin leaned in. His heart raced as he brushed his lips across Hanali's cheek, the chaste kiss lingering.

Hanali's breath caught. 'What... What was that?'

'I'm sorry,' Alduin stammered. 'Was it wrong of me?'

'No, just... unusual,' she replied, her voice a mix of surprise and intrigue.

'Good unusual?' Alduin asked, hope tinging his words.

Hanali's lips curved into a shy smile, 'perhaps.'

'May I make it regular?' he asked, his eyes searching hers.

'If you wish,' she whispered.

'I do,' he affirmed, their smiles mirroring each other's growing affection.

Hanali shouted to the merchant. 'We'd like to pay for your work. We love it.'

The tailor emerged with a smile on his face. 'I knew you'd adore it. I'm the best, after all.'

Alduin whispered to Hanali, 'and also the only one,' prompting them both to chuckle.

'What did he say?' the merchant raised a curious eyebrow.

'He said you're truly the best,' Hanali replied, making Alduin grin.

'With pleasure,' the tailor bowed.

Hanali parted her lips, 'How much does it cost? And what currency do you use here?'

The merchant explained, 'In Tyronah, we don't use traditional money. We trade in tokens – essentially, entry passes to Vanthea. Vaonie wanted us to build a thriving economy here.'

Hanali translated.

Alduin's brow furrowed. 'I don't understand.'

The clothier shrugged. 'It's complex. You might want to

ask scholars in the big city. This village, "Qil Binor", meaning "The Red Tree" in my tongue, doesn't have any.'

Alduin asked, 'How can we pay? We don't have any tokens.'

The merchant hesitated. 'I could put it on your tab.'

'Would my word suffice?' Alduin offered.

Just then, Vaonie's voice intervened, 'Let them have it. I'll ensure you're granted free passage a few times.'

The merchant bowed. 'As you command, my lord.'

Alduin whispered, 'No place is safe from Vaonie's eavesdropping, huh?'

Vaonie's voice replied, 'I heard that. Don't push your luck.'

Hanali reassured him, 'You'll get used to it. I lived under Austomia's jurisdiction once.'

Alduin nodded, his eyes locking onto hers. 'I sure hope so.'

Hanali smiled. 'Good. Let's find a place to train. I have a few things to teach you.'

'Alright. Uh…' Alduin addressed the garment seller, 'ke'ev[vi].'

'It was my pleasure,' he bowed.

They exited the store with bright smiles on their faces.

[vi] (Omnitongue) Thanks.

CHAPTER TEN

"Let's keep exploring," Alduin said.

"Sure. Now that you're finally dressed properly, people won't be staring at you anymore," Hanali teased, flashing a grin.

Alduin's lips twisted into a subtle smile. They strolled through the village pathways until they reached an intersection. At its centre stood a signpost inscribed in the demons' language – a script neither Hanali nor Alduin could read.

Hanali scanned the area and spotted a pedestrian. "Excuse me! Could you help us?" she called out.

A crimson-skinned demon paused mid-step and pointed at herself in surprise.

"Yes, you," Hanali confirmed, approaching her confidently. The demon had an athletic build that caught Alduin's eye. He fought to keep his gaze steady, for Hanali's sake, but the demon's lack of clothing made it nearly impossible. Surprisingly, Hanali was equally captivated by the figure before them: bull-like horns, flowing black hair tied in a ponytail, and a striking gold necklace that gleamed against her skin.

"Oh, you have a necklace," Hanali exclaimed, curiosity lighting up her face. "I thought demons never wore anything."

The Deovhaiit touched her necklace lightly. 'I thought demons didn't wear anything. 'It's... special. My father gave it to me. His father passed it down after returning from the war in Vanthea.'

'I like it,' Hanali said, leaning forward slightly. 'Anyway, we need help reading this sign. Could you translate it for us?'

The demon nodded and approached the post. 'The left path leads to the "Chapel", and the right one goes to "Tyl Heona", our capital city.'

'Thank you. Did you say "Chapel"?' Hanali's brows furrowed, 'demons have chapels?' she asked.

'It's not exactly a chapel,' the demon replied with a small shrug. 'It's more of a prayer site dedicated to Vaonie. I translated it into something familiar for you.'

'Ah, I see. Thank you so much,' Hanali said with a bright smile.

'You're welcome,' the Deovhaiit offered a light bow before continuing on her way.

Hanali turned to Alduin and relayed the translation. 'She said the capital is called "Tyl Heona", which means "New Heona" in my language.'

Alduin scratched the back of his head, 'Vaonie recreated their home in Tyronah[i]... Interesting.'

Hanali's expression softened as she wiped away an unexpected tear. 'They must miss our home deeply...'

Alduin noticed the sudden darkness in her eyes. 'I-I'm sorry. I didn't mean to remind you of that,' he said softly.

'It's okay,' she smiled faintly. 'Thank you for being kind. My siblings are always so stoic, my emotions confuse them.' She looked away, trying to hide her face, 'I will miss them...'

Without thinking, Alduin stepped closer, his heart swelling with a sudden urge to comfort her. He wrapped his arms around her gently, feeling a deep sense of warmth and connection as she leaned into him. The softness of her body against his was a gentle reminder of her vulnerability, and he held her a little tighter, wanting to shield her from the pain of her memories. As she relaxed into his embrace, her smile grew warmer, and he could feel her tension easing, replaced by a sense of peace that seemed to spread through both of them.

'Let's go,' Hanali said, wiping the last of her tears from her cheeks.

They began their journey toward Tyl Heona on a dirt road, the soft crunch of their footsteps filling the quiet. Suddenly, Alduin stopped in his tracks.

'Hey, look.' He pointed to a nearby lake, 'It's water, or at least I think it is. Why is it red?'

---

[i] (Omnitongue) Hell.

Hanali squinted at the shimmering surface. 'I don't know. Let's check it out.'

They veered off-road and approached the lake cautiously. Alduin crouched by the edge, cupping his hands into the water.

He brought some to his lips and took a sip. 'Hmm...' His brows furrowed as he swirled the liquid in his mouth.

'What? Does it taste weird? Are you going to puke?' Hanali teased with a laugh.

'No,' Alduin said slowly, swallowing, 'it's... good. It tastes like red wine.'

Hanali blinked in disbelief. 'Red wine? Why would a lake be filled with an alcoholic drink from Vanthea?'

'I have no idea,' Alduin muttered, staring his scarlet reflection.

Hanali tilted her head.

His lips parted slowly as he gathered the words in his head, 'Wait... I remember something. Someone told me that vampires and Araqhaiits can only drink blood and red wine. Maybe it's tied to Tyronah somehow? Could it be the same for Deovhaiits?'

Before Hanali could respond, Vaonie's voice resonated around them like a soft echo on the wind. 'This is indeed red wine,' they said. 'For demons, it serves as water does for mortals. Lysander spoke the truth; red wine *is* the only mortal drink vampires can consume.'

Alduin straightened, looking toward the unseen deity. 'Why red wine, though?'

'Because it is the original alcohol,' Vaonie replied simply.

'What do you mean by that?' he asked.

Vaonie's tone grew wistful as they explained, 'Long ago, when I was fiddling with Vanthea, I created a crimson fruit. When consumed, it induces dizziness, confidence, bravery... and foolishness – the effects mortals now associate with alcohol. They decided to call it the "red grape".'

Hanali crossed her arms and raised an eyebrow. 'You mean you invented alcohol?'

'Yes,' Vaonie answered with a firm voice, 'to test their moral competence, to see if they could resist being faithful, violent, reckless. Many deaths have resulted from its influence.'

Alduin glanced at the lake uneasily. 'So that's why this water is red wine?'

'Precisely,' Vaonie confirmed.

'And that's why vampires can drink it? Because it's alcoholic?' Hanali asked.

"No, not all alcoholic beverages are safe for them to consume," Vaonie said firmly, 'white wine and mead are imitations. During an experiment by "The Order", they extracted the euphoric component from red grapes and mixed it with other juices to create similar effects without true alcohol's properties. Vampires and demons cannot consume these imitations because they lack my aura.'

'Huh...' Alduin murmured.

Vaonie's voice faded. Hanali and Alduin returned to the path, passing towering statues of a demon wielding twin halberds. One horn was severed, the other curved like a bison's.

The earth trembled. Screams pierced the air. A carriage

thundered into view, but instead of horses, naked humans of all ages strained against ropes, their backs bloodied by the driver's lash. Mud and blisters caked their legs as they stumbled forward, wailing. Before they could react, it took a sharp turn and left their line of sight.

Alduin's face paled, his eyes widened. 'What in Munesa[ii] was that? Is that what happens to mortals in Tyronah?'

Hanali's hands trembled as she raised them to her mouth, her fingers covering her lips as if to stifle a cry. Her eyes, wide with horror, darted back to the spot where the carriage had vanished, her gaze lingering on the empty space as if she expected the scene to reappear. She took a deep, shuddering breath, her chest heaving beneath her clothes.

'They're as cruel as the vampires...' Alduin muttered quietly, his mind flashing memories of his time in captivity. His shoulders slumped as he gazed at the gloomy horizon.

She struggled to part her lips, wishing to console him. The silence between them grew thick.

More gruesome sights assaulted them as they pressed on without saying a word. Predators stalked bizarre creatures in the distance. A tower loomed on the horizon, promising civilization.

Suddenly, hoofbeats approached from behind, an ambush orchestrated by a band of demons. They wore black leather battle skirts and white gold arm bracelets.

[ii] (Elvish) Hell.

'Well, well, well… Mortal fugitives wandering unattended?' a gruff voice called out. 'Baffling, isn't it, Druk?'

'Indeed. Elves, too. I love Elvish meat,' Druk replied, licking his lips.

Alduin stepped forward. 'We're headed to Tyl Heona. Move aside, please.'

The first demon's eyes narrowed. 'Who gave you permission to speak, filth? We're the ones deciding your fate,' he stroked his chin, 'hmm… should we sell them, or keep them to ourselves?'

'Let's cut out his tongue first,' Druk sneered, unsheathing a blade.

Hanali's eyes flashed. 'We are not mortals. I'm a Sarathiin, he's an Araqhaiit. Believe us, or it will cost you dearly.'

The demons laughed, circling with weapons drawn. 'Vaonie's children look nothing like Elves, and there are no Sarathiins here. Try harder, woman,' Druk said.

Alduin noticed Hanali's fists clenching, ready to attack. 'Wait, Hanali… Are we allowed to hurt them? I…' He paused, hesitant, 'I don't want Vaonie to kill me.'

'If they fail to believe you, that's on them. You have permission,' the sharp voice of Vaonie echoed in their heads.

'Thank you, my lord,' Alduin said, facing the sky.

'What are you babbling about, you cur?' Druk said and slapped him hard.

Hanali's patience finally snapped. A blinding beam of purple light erupted from her hands, leaving nothing but ash where the attackers once stood. Her eyes glowed in rageful purple.

Alduin touched his bruised cheek and healed it. 'Why are they so cruel?' he asked.

Hanali shrugged, 'they brought it upon themselves.'

After more encounters with highwaymen and night-mare-ish carriages, they finally reached the towering gates of Tyl Heona. The massive gates creaked open at Vaonie's command. Hanali and Alduin stepped into a bustling metropolis, their senses overwhelmed by the sights and sounds.

Demons of all shapes and sizes hurried past, their voices a cacophony of shouts and laughter. Children darted between legs, playing games of tag. Shop owners bellowed their wares, competing for attention. Signs in both demonic script and Omnitongue advertised 'Hospital', 'Chapel', 'Brothel', 'Tavern', and 'Colosseum'.

Drawn by the crowd, they entered a packed pub. An Elvish hostess, her face a map of scars, led them to a table. Alduin fumbled with the menu until Hanali ordered two cups of red wine. As they sipped, they noticed the staff – all mortals bearing fresh bruises and haunted expressions. One waiter's ear was a ragged stump.

Alduin reached out to a passing waitress and tapped her on the shoulder. 'Excuse me, why does everyone look so-'

She flinched, 'I'm n-not allowed to talk,' she stuttered and ran off.

'This feels familiar...' He ground his teeth, his eyes shining wrathful red.

Hanali caressed his trembling right hand. 'Are you okay?' she asked softly.

'Let's go, Hanali. I can't stay here,' he said.

She nodded and stood up. They stepped toward the entrance, only to be confronted by three leering demons.

'Well, well, well. Unattended mortals, huh?' the leader's eyes gleamed. 'That Elf will surely fetch a beautiful price,' he smirked, revealing sharp yellow fangs.

As they approached with their fists raised, a towering female demon burst from a nearby shop. She flashed her great sword toward them, radiating the intent to kill, and they scurried off in but a mere second.

She rounded on Hanali and Alduin, nostrils flaring. 'Are you mad? Wandering alone here? You could've been killed, or worse!'

Hanali's head tilted a bit, 'are you saying this treatment is… normal?'

The demon's stern expression softened, her eyes widening in surprise. 'Newly deceased, huh? I see. Well, in Tyronah, mortals serve as slaves. No rights, no privileges. It's Vaonie's decree.'

Alduin's brow furrowed. 'Divine punishment is enslavement by demons?'

The demon nodded solemnly, her shoulders slumping slightly. Her somber face reflected a hint of sympathy.

Hanali straightened, her voice firm. 'In any case, we're not mortals. He's an Araqhaiit, and I'm a Sarathiin.'

The demon's eyes narrowed, scanning Alduin. 'That Elf is… an Araqhaiit? How is that possible?'

'He was once mortal,' Hanali explained.

'Intriguing…' She turned her sceptical glare at Hanali, 'but Sarathiins reside in Heonmeyu. Why are *you* here?'

'I've joined forces with Vaonie,' Hanali said, her tone guarded.

"Vaonie and Austomia are like divorced parents. It's just Vaonie's turn this week, don't worry about it."

The demon's eyes sparkled in childish excitement. 'You know nothing of our culture then? What a rare opportunity! To think I'd someday teach the gods about my people,' she restrained her desire to jump and down, though it was apparent.

'Well… We know you don't wear clothes," Alduin chuckled.

'There is neither heat nor cold here, so why should we?' the demon shrugged, a hint of a smile on her lips.

'Fair point,' Alduin conceded, 'what is your name?'

'Ysmet, you?' the Deovhaiit smiled.

'Hanali, and he's Alduin,' she pointed at him, 'pleased to meet you.'

'It is an honor to meet you,' she lowered her head in subtle bow. 'I have an idea. Follow me,' she said with gleaming eyes, 'I'll take you to the national museum.'

They navigated the bustling streets, Ysmet deflecting hostile glances from passersby. At the museum entrance, she purchased tickets and ushered them inside.

They joined a group of young demons gathered around a stern-looking instructor. Hanali served as both a tourist and an interpreter between Alduin and the tour-guide. The air was thick with the scent of old parchment and dust, and the flickering torches cast shadows on the walls, adding to the sense of ancient knowledge. An incredible quantity of exhibits told the story of Tyronah's rich history.

'Our journey begins here,' the instructor gestured grandly toward six imposing statues. 'Behold, the Araqhaiits who built Tyl Heona, mirroring their original home.'

Alduin's eyes narrowed as he studied the figures. Five bore striking resemblances to the Araqhaiits he'd met, but the second from the left was a faceless stone mannequin.

'Hanali,' he murmured, 'why is that one blank?'

After Hanali translated, the instructor's eyes lit up. 'Ah, excellent observation. That represents Lodus, the sixth Araqhaiit we never met. Legend says he perished long before Vaonie and the others arrived.'

As they continued, the instructor's voice swelled with pride before a towering statue. 'Behold Ugal Zun, first and current head of our military.'

Alduin's brow furrowed. 'Military? Tyronah has an official army?'

"In order to avoid repeating myself, assume that everything Alduin asks or is told – is translated by Hanali."

'How stupid can you be?' a kid snorted, giggling with his friends.

'Shh, that's mean.' A girl said and revealed her fangs, 'ignore him, sir,' she looked at Alduin with eyes full of wonder.

He smiled and nodded, 'it's okay,' he pat her head.

'Yeni's got a boyfriend, Yeni's got a boyfriend!' the arrogant group chanted.

Her eyes shone angry red, 'SHUT UP.'

And fortunately, they did. Hanali laughed from behind at the grotesque scene.

The instructor put his hands together and addressed Alduin. 'So… back to your question. Indeed. Tyronah is a militaristic state. The army enforces law, protects civilians, and prepares for war. Ugal and his commanders lead, with the Araqhaiits and Vaonie above them. We call it "Sav'ul u Tyronah" in the Omnitongue.'

'I thought there'd be anarchy,' Alduin said.

'No. Laws are essential for our civilization to flourish. It was Vaonie's will. To name a few: murder, rape, and thievery between demons are prohibited. Cannibalism too.'

'So raping humans is allowed?'

'Obviously,' the tour guide raised an eyebrow of suspicion, 'mortals are slaves, nothing more and nothing less.'

'I see…' Alduin's voice softened with grief, 'you mentioned cannibalism. Is that a common thing here?' his brow's furrowed.

'If we're starving, sure.'

'Why are they so stupid, asking all these questions?' silently murmured the annoying child from before.

'Uh-huh,' Alduin said as he walked toward Hanali.

She was unbothered by the story, her face relaxed. 'How do you distinguish soldiers from civilians if no one wears clothes?'

'All soldiers wear black battle skirts and white gold arm bracelets,' the instructor explained, 'they live in barracks scattered around the region, and the military provides them with food, drink and other needs.'

Alduin's eyes widened, 'curious…' he whispered, his

eyes locking into Hanali's in a moment of awkward realization.

The instructor walked toward a series of four colourful monoliths, his eyes sparkling with pride. 'These represent our callings. Oops, I can't recall… ' He raised his hand and slapped his forehead in a playful gesture, 'children, can you help me remember?' he said, smiling.

The students were excited to show off their knowledge. A few of them even gave Hanali and Alduin a private lesson.

'Well done!' The instructor's black lips tilted into a bright smile, 'but you forgot one thing.'

'What is it?' asked the irritating child as he kicked his friend's leg just for the fun of it.

The tour guide rolled his eyes. Clearly, this wasn't his first rodeo. 'Indeed: pink for "Succubus", green for "Terrorizer", red for "Butcher", and gray for…?' he asked, looking at the children with anticipation.

'"Bio-chaos"!' a gray child in the back called out, earning glares from his classmates.

The instructor beamed, 'excellent. Can you tell us about it?'

The child straightened, chest puffing with pride. 'Bio-chaos demons alter animal species. Like the Vaermiraiits, born when a demon forced himself on a human woman. Their child became Vanthea's first vampire.'

A chorus of jeers erupted from the other children. 'Prick! Jerk! Nerd!'

The instructor's voice cut through the chaos, 'enough. Show her some respect.' He turned to the teary-eyed student, 'they're just jealous. It will pass. Let's continue, okay?'

The girl smiled and wiped her tears, 'mhm...' She nodded.

The instructor halted before a towering monument, its face etched with a date and two staggering numbers.

'Our final stop,' he announced, gesturing dramatically. 'A monument dedicated to the "Great Plummet", or as the mortals call it – the "Mortal Demon War".'

Hanali's brow furrowed. 'Why is it called that?'

The instructor's eyes gleamed. 'It's tied to our currency – entry tickets to Vanthea. Each token suppresses our aura for an hour, hiding us from the Sarathiins.'

Alduin leaned in, his eyes sparkling with childlike curiosity.

'During the war,' the instructor continued, voice lowering, 'Vaonie flooded the market with tokens. Before, one token bought a week in Vanthea. After...' He trailed off, letting the implications sink in.

Hanali's eyes widened. 'Inflation,' she said.

'Precisely,' The instructor nodded, 'the numbers represent the deaths of demons who starved from the economic collapse, and of those who fell on duty.'

A child's whine cut through the air. 'Can we go? I'm bored.'

Hanali's eyes flashed. The child's smug expression crumpled, replaced by wide-eyed fear. Alduin caught Hanali's subtle smirk, a glimmer of mischief in her eyes.

'Tragic,' Hanali murmured, her tone carefully neutral.

Alduin's face betrayed a flicker of conflict. Empathy

warred with the memory of mortal casualties, his own kind. He schooled his features, nodding solemnly for the instructor's benefit.

As the group dispersed, Alduin turned to Hanali, eyes bright with excitement. 'Fascinating, wasn't it?'

Hanali nodded, her eyes gleaming with wonder. 'I had no idea about any of this.'

The pair lingered, gazing at the exhibits, the weight of Deovhaiit history manifesting around them.

Exiting the museum, their eyes sparkled with newfound knowledge. Their demon friend, Ysmet, pleased by their enthusiasm, led them to a marvellous structure – Tyronah's most prestigious elementary school.

With a mix of charm and veiled threats, she persuaded the chairman to grant the pair access to classes. 'Consider it... cultural exchange, ' she purred, her smile sharp.

"Speech 100."

Ysmet showed them the way from her house and back, allowing them to stay over. For a week, Hanali and Alduin immersed themselves in demon education with a perfect attendance score. Alduin's grasp of the Deovhaiitish language grew, though Hanali's translations remained crucial. They learned of demons' paradoxical immortality – a lifespan without limit, yet requiring constant extension. At every given moment, a demon was both immortal *and* of a fixed lifespan.

"Confused? Imagine the looks on their faces when they first heard that."

The answer was simple: despite having a fixed lifespan, demons could extend it an infinite number of times.

In hushed tones, their teacher explained the Callings: Butcher – genocide of mortals, Succubus – inciting mortals to sin and wreak havoc, Terrorizer – causing mass hysteria through nightmares, myths, and so forth, Bio-chaos – biologically changing the nature of creatures to cause mayhem. 'Each one of you must fulfil their role in Vanthea,' she intoned. 'After which you must pray in a temple of Vaonie to have your lifespan reassessed, it is the only way. But bear in mind that your lifespan is merely potential – not absolute. You must also tend to your injuries, eat, and drink.'

The economy of Tyronah unfolded before them – an intricate dance of duty and survival. Demons could outsource their callings, paying others to venture into Vanthea on their behalf. 'The rich play by different rules,' a classmate whispered, eyes darting.

Biology lessons brought gruesome revelations. Demon births, violent and traumatic, often included cannibalism as the babies ate their way out of the womb. 'Our young know nothing of our laws,' the instructor sighed, tracing a large unhealed scar across her abdomen.

They learned how eating plants reduced a demon's lifespan, but its usage in potions and ointments could treat wounds and diseases (of which Tyronah bore a plethora of options). In general, wounds led to a decrease in one's lifespan – even if they were caused by a fetus.

"Ironic, isn't it?"

Similarly to their descendants, Deovhaiits could only consume meat – animals, mortals and even each other. They also possessed basic regenerative abilities, telekinesis, and telepathy.

Survival lessons introduced the many disasters native to Tyronah – fruits of Vaonie's infinite imagination and creativity. Tornadoes, typhoons, unique diseases, enormous predators – including insects and worms, landscape-swallowing sinkholes, volcanic eruptions, earthquakes et cetera. Oh, and cockroaches too.

As the week drew to a close, Alduin observed his peers. Their laughter, tears, and fleeting moments of compassion challenged his preconceptions. These beings, capable of atrocities, also harboured deeply mortal emotions.

Bidding farewell to their host, Hanali and Alduin set out for Vaonie's castle, their minds brimming with the complexities of Vaonie's pet project – like a homemade ant farm teeming with death and destruction.

A civilization forged in the crucible of jealousy, born from the ashes of resentment, nurtured by the tears of heartbreak, and baptized in the fires of controversy.

"All because Austomia chose to be a stubborn cunt, instead of sharing their toys."

CHAPTER ELEVEN

A familiar voice echoed through the chamber. 'Lodus, report to my throne room. I have a surprise for you,' Vaonie called.

'Yes, lord,' Alduin replied, his voice tinged with curiosity.

He glided through the air, the door swinging open with a thought. Inside, Vaonie and Hanali stood waiting.

'Good. You're here,' Vaonie stated, their voice resonating with power.

Alduin took his place beside Hanali, dropping to one knee in reverence.

'Stand,' Vaonie commanded.

He rose, his eyes fixed forward.

'I've made a decision you may find... intriguing,' Vaonie began, their gaze piercing.

Alduin's breath caught. 'Oh?'

Vaonie's eyes narrowed slightly as they spoke, their

voice firm and commanding. 'My daughter has been pestering me about your longing for Vanthea. Is it true?' the air seemed to thicken with their unspoken frustration, their aura flickering with a hint of annoyance.

Panic gripped Alduin like a vice, his eyes bulging in terror as he stumbled over his words. His voice trembled, barely audible. 'Y-Yes, my lord. B-But I never meant any offence. Forgive me.'

Hanali stepped forward, but Vaonie raised a hand, silencing her. 'Calm yourself. Your mortal heart yearns for the familiar. Tyronah[i], beautiful as it is, failed to replace Euphata in your soul,' Vaonie said, their tone softening.

Alduin bowed his head, shame colouring his cheeks.

'I grant you passage to Vanthea,' Vaonie declared. 'You may travel freely between realms, residing where you choose.'

Alduin's eyes widened, hope blooming in his chest. 'Thank you, lord. I've dreamed of rebuilding my village for so long!'

'Don't celebrate yet. There's a condition,' Vaonie cautioned, a hint of amusement in their voice.

Alduin stiffened. 'What is it?'

'Your affection for my daughter hasn't gone unnoticed.'

Hanali's face flushed pink. Alduin, mortified, bowed so violently his head smashed into the floor, cracking it.

Vaonie's laughter filled the room as they motioned for Alduin to rise. 'Fear not, I meant no harm. She shall accompany you. Show her the mortal realm through your eyes.'

---

[i] (Omnitongue) Hell.

Alduin's heart raced. 'I... would be honoured. But shouldn't we ask her first?'

'She has already agreed.'

Alduin turned to Hanali, his voice barely a whisper. 'Is this true?'

'Yes,' Hanali breathed, her eyes meeting his in an electric gaze.

A moment passed between them, unspoken yet palpable. Their fingers twitched, yearning to intertwine as matching blushes painted their cheeks.

'It's settled then,' Vaonie declared. 'You'll be my envoy in the mortal realm, with my daughter at your side. Now, go.'

'H-How?' his brows furrowed, 'I've never travelled between the realms.'

Hanali nodded. 'For now, take my hand. I'll guide you. Farewell, maker.'

Alduin lowered his head in a bow and approached her. As their hands intertwined, he closed his eyes, and a surge of energy pulsed through them. In a flash of violet light, they vanished, leaving Vaonie alone in the throne room, a knowing smile playing on their lips.

Alduin's eyes fluttered open, assaulted by the sun's glare. A gentle breeze caressed his skin as the symphony of wildlife filled his ears. They stood amidst a vast field, nature's canvas stretching in every direction.

'Where are we?' he asked, his voice tinged with wonder.

Hanali shrugged, a mischievous glint in her eye. 'No clue. I didn't pick a destination. But rest assured, we're in Vanthea.'

Alduin nodded, his gaze sweeping the horizon. 'I'll scout the area.'

He ascended, the ground shrinking beneath him. His eyes scanned the landscape, drinking in the details. An immense forest sprawled before him, their clearing a tiny oasis in a sea of green. Kilometers away, a cluster of cottages nestled among fenced pastures. Noises of cattle and hens echoed in his ears. Narrowing his eyes, he spotted another clearing and slivers of white land in the distance.

Descending, Alduin landed softly beside Hanali. 'We're in the heart of an enormous forest. It can't be Euphata.'

Hanali's eyes sparkled with excitement. 'Shall we explore? Time is on our side.'

Before Alduin could respond, a gruff voice shattered the tranquillity. 'Hey, what are you doing on my land? Piss off!'

A man emerged from one of the houses, face contorted with anger. Alduin's muscles tensed, ready to retaliate, but Hanali's hand clamped over his mouth.

'Divines mustn't interfere in mortal life,' she whispered urgently. 'It's Austomia's decree.'

Alduin's brow furrowed in confusion. 'But I've already done that with some bandits a few yea-'

'Identify yourselves!' the man bellowed, cutting him off.

'One moment,' Alduin gestured with a finger and leaned toward Hanali, 'well?' he whispered in her ear.

'We *are* allowed to intervene, but only to punish. Remember, the right of free will diminish once they know of us. When it's only belief, a mortal may desire to be better or choose to sin. The problem arises once a mortal *knows* of us – could it truly be said that they *chose* not to sin? When a murderer holds a knife to your throat, do you *decide* to give up your coin purse, or do you simply *comply* out of fear of the *known* consequences? In essence, mortals must never know about our identity,' she explained.

Alduin nodded, understanding dawning in his eyes.

The man ground his teeth, 'Evan, get up. Intruders!'

Their whispered conference was interrupted by the arrival of a second man, brandishing a pitchfork. His keen gaze raked over them, his face stiffening with revulsion. He spat on the ground. 'Rudolf, they're Elves!' he exclaimed, nudging his companion. 'Look at their ears, their strange attire.'

Rudolf's anger morphed into predatory glee. 'Let's spill some elvish blood, brother.'

'I want the girl,' Evan leered, his eyes fixed on Hanali.

'You never told me you liked Elvish girls,' Rudolf said.

Evan's lips twisted into a smirk, 'you never asked.'

Alduin's body tensed, torn between restraint and the urge to protect. He scanned for escape routes, his voice low and urgent. 'What now?'

Hanali's eyes darted between him and the approaching men, her mind racing for a solution as the distance between them rapidly closed.

Rudolf ran down the stairs toward a haystack. When he reached it, he took out the pitchfork that was piercing it and regrouped with his comrade. They started walking slowly toward them, side by side.

'Hanali, come on. Think,' Alduin said.

'I am trying to.'

The men's laughter echoed as they closed in, Rudolf's excitement palpable at the prospect of Elvish blood.

Alduin groaned, 'So much responsibility... I thought godhood meant freedom.'

Hanali's eyes flashed purple with irritation. 'You're tasked with keeping mortals at bay, Alduin. This isn't a vacation, grow up.'

Suddenly, Rudolf circled behind them, creating an improvised ambush. Hanali spun to face him, leaving Alduin to confront Evan.

'I'll savor this, brother,' Evan let out a feral grin.

'Not as much as me,' Rudolf's eyes gleamed with anticipation.

A woman's voice pierced the air. 'Dear, be careful! I can't raise Viola by myself. They look dangerous,' she screamed, but locked her gaze on Evan.

Rudolf scoffed, 'quiet, woman. I know what I'm doing,' he rolled his eyes, 'brother, you were right about marriage. They never cease their yapping.'

The woman slammed the door shut with a loud sigh.

Evan chuckled, 'I could always take her off your hands.'

A stone whistled through the air, striking Evan in the forehead. 'She may be difficult, but she's my wife!' Rudolf growled.

'That hurt, you bastard.'

'Grow a pair, will you?'

Alduin and Hanali were on the verge of collapsing into laughter, their bodies trembling with suppressed mirth.

"It's like a Sitcom."

Rudolf clenched his fists. 'Oy, what are you laughing about, little Sharpie? I'll have your head, Elf.'

Alduin and Hanali shared a glance, a plan forming. 'Oh, it wasn't that funny,' he said firmly. 'Shall we continue?'

The men raised their pitchforks, but Alduin's words froze them mid-strike.

'Such a beauty, your wife,' he taunted Evan. 'Shame she'll be a widow soon.'

Confusion twisted Rudolf's features. 'What are you blabbering about? She's *my* wife.'

'Oh? Surprising, given how she looked at him,' Alduin's voice dripped with insinuation.

Doubt crept into Rudolf's eyes as Evan's poorly concealed smile betrayed him.

'It's true,' Hanali added, her voice honey-sweet. 'Your wife's affair is clear as day.'

'It-It can't be...' Rudolf's gaze snapped to his brother. 'Is this true?!'

'Why would I steal your woman?' Evan's protest rang hollow.

Rudolf turned his head to Alduin, 'see?'

'Since when do thieves confess?' Alduin pressed, 'wasn't she the one who told you to check out the noises outside? She probably wanted us to kill you so she can move in with Evan,' he said with a straight face.

Rudolf's face contorted with rage. 'RAGRRR. Brother, I'll kill you!' He charged, pitchfork raised.

Evan's brows furrowed. 'What? They're lying, brother. Please, you're scaring me.'

'Don't lie to me, it all makes sense now,' Rudolf bellowed with wrath in his eyes.

Metal met flesh with a sickening thud.

As Evan crumpled, Rudolf's wife burst from the house, her scream shattering the air. 'WHAT HAVE YOU DONE, YOU FOOL?! What the fuck. What the fuck.'

Hanali kicked Alduin's leg – a signal. They flew to the clouds, high enough to be unseen.

'Why?' the woman's anguish echoed behind them. She stroked Evan's hair as the light in his eyes gradually diminished.

'Because you cheated with him, you whore.' Rudolf's voice broke.

'What? I've been faithful since our wedding day.'

'Then why do I keep waking to an empty bed? Why do you look at him the way you used to look at me?'

A river of tears ran down her cheeks. 'We were working on a birthday gift for you, a carriage. You kept saying you wanted one, so we thought we'd surprise you. What have you done...'

'Y-You... what?' Rudolf's hands trembled, his voice unsteady.

Evan's dying words were barely audible. 'I always loved you, brother. I'd never betray you. Farewell.'

'How could you believe them?' she asked.

'I don't know...' He sobbed with ragged breath, 'these filthy Sharpies must have cast a spell on me.'

'Kill them, please,' she wailed.

'I'll avenge you brother. Forgive me,' Rudolf kissed her

on the cheek and turned around, pitchfork in hand. 'Oh?' he scratched the back of his head, 'where are they?'

'They must have ran off. Find them, I will be waiting for you here,' she said.

He nodded and sprinted into the woods. When his figure vanished into the shadows, she began caressing Evan's cheeks. 'I'm sorry, my love. I'm so sorry,' she whispered.

Her final scream of anguish pierced the air, echoing through the forest and reaching Hanali and Alduin as they soared above, its raw emotion lingering in their ears.

Hanali bit her lips, hesitant. 'How could you… do that to them? It was awfully cruel,' her eyes flashed purple with disappointment.

'Didn't you hear them? They called us Sharpies, it's a racial slur against my kind.'

'So?'

'So fuck them and their racism.'

'You're a god, couldn't you just ignore it?'

'I refuse to. You're exactly right – I *am* a god, so now I can finally take matters into my own hands.'

She stopped in front of him, 'what made you think your plan would work? Tell me.'

'I saw how his wife looked at his brother. I peered into his mind, found his deepest fears. He suspected an affair, so I used it.'

Hanali's eyes widened, a mix of surprise and anger. 'That's brutal.'

Alduin scoffed, 'why do you care so much for mortals?'

'I'm just baffled by your indifference. Playing with

mortal emotions this way, without batting an eye. You were once a mortal yourself.'

'Because I have been through so fucking much,' Alduin's voice trembled, 'even before was my life was taken from me. Before the death of my family, or the vampires' torture. I have witnessed the cruelty of humans, and I can no longer let it slide.'

'Why not show compassion, or forgiveness? I know your kind is capable of that,' she put her hand on his right shoulder.

'Because I refuse to do that. To let bullies bully, to let evil win. Evil is evil. It doesn't matter if it's lesser or greater. I will personally tear it off this world, and my role as a god only fuels my thirst for justice.'

Hanali's jaw clenched, her eyes narrowing as she turned to the horizon. Disappointment etched deep lines across her face, her shoulders tensing with each passing moment. This vigilante mentality of Alduin's – it was a revelation, and not a welcome one. Her lips pressed into a thin line, swallowing the words she longed to say. With a sharp exhale, she rose into the air, her body rigid as she followed Alduin. The silence between them grew heavy as they soared through the sky, the weight of unspoken judgments hanging in the air.

After a few minutes, Alduin turned his head backwards. 'Why are you so quiet?' he asked with darkness in his eyes.

She sighed, 'It's not my place to judge. I've never been mortal, never felt that pain.'

'I want your opinion,' Alduin insisted, his eyes searching hers.

'Maybe one day,' she whispered.

He nodded and resumed his course.

They flew in silence until he spotted a white strand in the distance. 'That could be my homeland,' he announced and pointed at it.

'Let's go,' she said. She took a deep breath, 'forgive me for seeming hostile, Alduin. I simply realized that my opinion is irrelevant. I've always observed mortals from afar, never truly experiencing their lives.'

'It's alright,' he flashed a smile, 'and I apologize for ranting. I haven't had a person to share my pain with for…' His shoulders sagged as he looked down, 'years, actually.'

Hanali's eyes gleamed with sympathy and curiosity. 'I-I could listen… if you'd like. Kick, scream, complain. My time as a Sarathiin taught me that it helps.'

Alduin's eyes widened, his lips shaky. 'Are you sure?'

'Yes,' she smiled.

'Then, can we stop there?' he pointed at hill covered by trees, 'my uncle told me that heart-to-heart conversations should always be held while seated.'

'Whatever you wish.'

They landed under one of the trees and sat in front of each other, leaning on its trunk.

They settled beneath a tree, Alduin's breath unsteady. 'Are you sure? This might take a while,' he said.

She nodded, her beautiful eyes encouraging.

Alduin's voice cracked as he began. 'It started at birth. My father, the clan chief, had no time for me. Only endless training. He never attended my birthdays, my graduations, my bad days. My mother and uncle Ley were my sole joy, and sister Veridia too sometimes. Mother used to make me my favourite dishes, even when she was busy. And Uncle taught me about the world and all its wonders. I owe my curiosity to him, only him.'

Hanali's brow furrowed, unsure how to respond.

Alduin continued, his eyes distant. 'I pushed myself to become a Hekket[ii], following through with my father's training regime, all to win his approval. To make him appreciate me. But the day of my final examination, Vaermi-raiits[iii] attacked. They slaughtered everyone – my parents, sister, uncle, the whole clan… '

Hanali's eyes glistened, a foreign moisture threatening to form. Her brow furrowed deeply, lips parting in a silent gasp. Her hands trembled slightly as she reached out, stopping just short of touching Alduin. 'I'm so sorry,' she whispered softly. Her posture softened, shoulders dropping as if bearing the weight of his pain. Though her divine nature fought against it, her body seemed to yearn to comfort him, to share in his grief.

Alduin's eyes finally betrayed him. A group of six tears escaped, tracing a solitary path down his cheek before he hastily wiped it away. His jaw clenched, fighting the tremble that threatened to consume him. He took a deep, shuddering breath, the sound barely audible. His gaze dropped, his voice barely above a whisper as he struggled to regain control, the façade of toughness beginning to

---

[ii]   Special Forces (Snow Elf).
[iii] (Omnitongue) Vampires.

crack. 'There's more, but... I'm overwhelmed,' his voice faltered, 'I don't want you to see me like this.'

Hanali reached out, her hand hovering near his. 'Take your time. I'm here,' she said as her lips twisted into a warm smile of sympathy.

Alduin managed a weak smile as they stood, the weight of his past hanging between them. They stared into each other's eyes for a few moments and continued their journey in the sky.

They soared over oceans and lands, finally reaching a snowy continent. Alduin's eyes lit up with excitement as he scanned for his village. Despite passing numerous Snow Elvish settlements, his homeland eluded him. Suddenly, a familiar establishment caught his eye, prompting them to land.

They approached the village's main gate as twilight descended. Four well-armed guards stood vigilant.

'Who goes there? State your identity and business!' a guard barked.

Hanali placed a gentle hand on Alduin's arm, whispering, 'let me handle this.'

Alduin nodded, his jaw tightening.

'We're travellers seeking a place to stay for the night," Hanali replied calmly.

'Names?' the guard demanded.

"I'm Hanali. My companion is Alduin.'

The guards huddled, whispering. Alduin's enhanced hearing caught their words. 'Look at his eyes... Elvish ears, but those red, glowing eyes...'

'Prepare the men,' his companion muttered quietly.

Alduin's muscles tensed, but Hanali's steady gaze kept him grounded.

The commanding guard approached. 'You,' he pointed at Alduin, 'step forward.'

Alduin complied, forcing a smile.

'I recognize that tattoo, the one you have around your left eye. Only Snow Elf warriors wear it. Who are you?"

'My name is Alduin Faëli,' he said, omitting his title as requested by his companion.

The guard's eyes narrowed. 'Explain the strangeness in your eyes. There's a bad hunger to them.'

'I-' Alduin began saying.

'It's a mild genetic discoloration,' Hanali interjected with a polite smile.

'Silence, wench.' The guard snarled. 'Speak, boy, or my men will kill you where you stand.'

A dozen archers appeared atop the gate.

Alduin inhaled deeply, his fists clenching. 'It's as Hanali said. May we pass?'

'I don't believe you. Men, cuff them. The lord will decide their fate.'

'No.' Alduin's voice thundered, his hand instinctively reaching for Vaurcarya.

"Weapons down, and hands up. Now!' the leftmost guard commanded.

Hanali's gaze pierced Alduin, silently pleading. He growled, reluctantly placing Vaurcarya on the ground. His shoulders slumped in submission, and he raised his arms high. She knelt, bowing her head and raised her own.

The officer smirked. 'Your wife's smarter than you. Take them to the dungeon for interrogation.'

Hanali's eyes flickered in the color of violet as the word 'wife' echoed in her ears. Her cheeks turned pink as she looked away, avoiding Alduin's gaze.

'Aye!' the guards chorused, moving to restrain the pair.

Alduin's jaw clenched, his eyes flashing with rage as he surrendered to the guards. They were shackled and dragged like slaves, their weapons confiscated. Despite the humiliation, Alduin's anger softened as he gazed upon the familiar sights of his kin, the Snow Elves.

In the throne room, they were forced to bow before the clan leader. Alduin's muscles tensed, his divine status a stark contrast to this mortal subjugation. The lord sat on his throne, surrounded by fur-clad warriors wearing a Dorynie's head as a helmet. After about three minutes of looking at their warpaints, Alduin realized they were Hekkets.

Finally, the chief addressed them. 'I don't have time for this nonsense. You, Snow Elf. What is your name?'

'Alduin. Alduin Faëli.'

'That's impossible…' The headman's face twisted, his eyes bulging as if the very air had been knocked from his lungs. His mouth hung open, the word 'Faëli' lingering on his lips like a whispered secret. His gaze locked onto Alduin, a mixture of disbelief and anguish etched across his features. For a moment, he seemed frozen, unable to form another word.

'My lord, what is the problem? What ails you?' a Hekket approached.

'I'm alright, leave me be,' the chief said and turned his face to Alduin, 'where are you from, boy?' he asked with shaky breath.

'What's it to you?' Alduin scoffed and locked eyes with Hanali.

'Please trust me…' Her eyes said calmly.

The Hekkets readied their weapons. 'You can't speak that way to the chief!' One of them bellowed.

'Let him speak,' the chief said and shoo-ed them away with his left hand.

After a tense exchange of glares, Alduin parted his lips. 'I was born in "Vel Tissia Ke Aldu[iv]",' he responded.

The lord's composure shattered like fragile glass. His shoulders sagged, his chest heaving with a deep, shuddering breath. His hands, once clasped together in a gesture of authority, now trembled as they fell to his sides. 'I am Virtholdr Vinyi, lord of this clan and… your grandfather,' he announced with a large, bright smile on his face.

Alduin's world tilted. A storm of emotions surged through him – recognition, grief, excitement. His body trembled, goosebumps rippling across his skin. He opened his mouth, but words failed him.

Virtholdr's eyes glistened. 'Guards, remove his cuffs! My grandson lives.'

'What about his companion?' a Hekket consulted his lord, 'she looks even stranger than he is.'

'Do you trust her, grandson?' Virtholdr asked.

[iv] (Elvish) The Village of Hope.

'More than I trust myself,' a genuine smile spread across his face as he looked at her.

'Free her too,' the lord commanded.

As Hanali was freed at Alduin's vouching, she whispered, 'I told you to trust me,' a smug smile playing on her lips.

His face softened. 'Evisi[v],' he whispered back. Reunited with Vaurcarya, Alduin's posture relaxed slightly.

Virtholdr, noting his grandson's unease, said gently, 'Rest now. We'll feast and talk tomorrow.'

'Th-Thank you, grandfather,' Alduin stammered, his voice thick with emotion.

Virtholdr dismissed them with a wave of his hand, his expression softening into a rare smile. The pair were escorted to their room, where the sight of a single, massive bed immediately drew their attention. Alduin shifted awkwardly, scratching the back of his neck, while Hanali's cheeks flushed a delicate pink. Their eyes met briefly, both caught in a moment of shared embarrassment before they quickly looked away and shrugged it off. He took the right side of the bed and she the left.

'Did... Did you know where we were and who he was? Is that why you told me to stay calm?' Alduin asked, his voice low and tentative.

Hanali hesitated, her fingers lightly brushing the edge of her necklace as she glanced down. 'Yes. I wanted you to see it through. To finally have a moment of peace,' she admitted, her voice soft as a faint blush crept across her face.

---

[v]   (Elvish) Thanks.

Without warning, Alduin stepped forward and wrapped his arms around her in a firm embrace. The scent of vanilla and clove wafted from her. It enveloped him, calming his nerves and drawing him closer, a reminder of her presence and warmth. Hanali stiffened at first, her breath catching in surprise. But as his warmth enveloped her and she felt the steady rhythm of his heartbeat against her chest, her body relaxed. She let herself lean into him, closing her eyes as the tension melted away.

'Thank you,' Alduin whispered into her ear, his voice thick with sincerity.

Hanali smiled faintly, her blush deepening as she murmured back, 'You're welcome.'

The two eventually drifted into sleep, the quiet stillness of the room broken only by their slow, even breaths.

With dawn came the gentle hum of life outside – the distant clatter of carts, the chirping of birds, and the muffled voices of villagers beginning their day. A knock at the door startled them awake.

'Lord and Lady Faëli,' came a voice from outside. 'The Lord is expecting you at the grand hall for the feast.'

Hanali sat up abruptly, her fingers instinctively reaching for her necklace again. 'Lady Faëli...' She whispered to herself, her cheeks flushing as she toyed with the pendant.

Alduin stretched and replied loudly, 'we'll be ready in a few minutes. Thank you.'

'There are proper clothes for you on the nightstand,' the voice added before footsteps faded down the hallway.

Once dressed in elegant garments befitting honoured guests, they opened the door to find their escort waiting.

The walk to the hall was brief but filled with anticipation. When they entered, Alduin froze in place, his breath catching at the sight before him.

The grand table stretched endlessly, laden with an overwhelming spread of food -vibrant fruits glistening like jewels, freshly baked bread still steaming from the oven, fragrant cheeses stacked high among colourful vegetables and decadent desserts. The rich aroma filled the air, stirring something deep within Alduin. His chest tightened as nostalgia washed over him like a wave – memories of feasts long past in his childhood village mingling with bittersweet longing. His mouth watered involuntarily as he stood there, awestruck by both the abundance, familiarity, and sheer aroma.

Hanali nudged him gently with her elbow and smiled. 'Come on,' she said softly. 'Let's not keep them waiting.'

Alduin nodded slowly, his lips curving into a small smile as he stepped forward toward the table. Where Virtholdr saw a mere meal, Alduin saw a tapestry of memories – fragments of a life he thought lost forever, now vividly alive before him.

The pair sat beside Virtholdr, their proximity a silent testament to their status. As the last morsels were consumed, Virtholdr's hand swept through the air, dismissing all but Alduin and Hanali.

Virtholdr's eyes bore into his grandson. 'Is what I've heard true?'

Alduin's shoulders slumped. 'Sadly, yes...'

'Tell me yourself. Rumors are poor substitutes for the truth.'

Alduin's gaze dropped to his hands. 'Vaermiraiits[vi] raided during the final fight. They... slaughtered everyone.'

Virtholdr's face paled. 'Is… Is my daughter dead?'

Alduin took a long deep breath. 'Yes,' Alduin whispered, his voice thick, 'I miss her.'

A single tear traced Virtholdr's cheek before he straightened, jaw clenching. 'How did you survive?'

'A vampire general enslaved me. Years in a cage, then a cult ceremony... changed me,' Alduin gestured to his altered form.

Virtholdr's hand flew to his weapon. 'Do you serve them now?!'

'Never!' Alduin's fist slammed the table. 'I'll never serve my family's murderers!'

Virtholdr's grip on his weapon loosened, but wariness lingered in his eyes.

Weeks passed. Alduin's smile grew wider, his laughter more frequent. He immersed himself in Snow Elf culture – the food, the chatter, the smells. Hanali watched from afar, her own lips curving upward at his joy.

On New Year's Eve, Alduin's eyes sparkled as he led her to the folk dance. Dancers dressed as wolves and bears moved on all fours, growling and howling. Hanali's eyes widened, a mix of confusion and delight playing across her face.

Alduin threw himself into Elvish writing lessons, his quill flying across parchment with growing confidence. But one night, fate intervened.

[vi] (Omnitongue) Vampires.

Months into their stay, Alduin and Hanali left the dining hall. At their door, Alduin's brows furrowed. 'Wait here,' he murmured to Hanali. She nodded, slipping inside.

Alduin retraced his steps, the Hekkets granting him passage with a silent nod. As he approached his grandfather's room, raised voices pierced the air. Alduin froze, his hand hovering inches from the door. His uncle's lessons in curiosity won out, and he leaned closer, straining to hear.

'Lord, we should battle in daylight. Attacking in their sleep might hinder our fighter's morale, taint their conscienc-' An unfamiliar man said.

'No.' Virtholdr's fist slammed the table. 'Who cares if it's cowardly? We must win!'

'A warrior is nothing without their honor, lord,' the man's voice softened

'Even if you're right, it may be our only path to victory.'

Alduin burst in, finding his grandfather in bed, and an armoured man standing close. Wine glasses and an empty bottle sat nearby.

'Grandson. Are you lost?' Virtholdr's brow furrowed.

'I overheard... What's the argument about?'

Virtholdr sighed. 'Battle tactics. Did your father teach you?'

'A bit. I'd love to help,' Alduin smiled.

Virtholdr pointed at the man next to him. 'This is my advisor, Ladriel.'

'We're facing skilled bandits that raid our farms. We must send soldiers, but how?' Ladriel explained.

Alduin stroked his chin. 'I see.'

'I say we declare formal war, fight with grace,' his chest puffed.

'But we risk good men,' Virtholdr countered. 'I propose a night assassination in their camp.'

Alduin's eyes darted between them. 'It's... complex. His plan is risky, but a warrior's honor is vital. Your fighters must feel proud after each mission.'

Ladriel nodded, a smile tugging at his lips. Virtholdr ground his teeth.

'Honor is crucial, grandfather,' Alduin leaned forward. 'Please consider my view. The consequences could be dire.'

Virtholdr's eyes closed briefly. 'I'll... think on it. Goodnight, both of you.'

'Goodnight, lord,' Ladriel bowed slightly.

'Goodnight, grandfather,' Alduin's voice wavered with concern as he backed out of the room.

Alduin smiled faintly as he left the room, his mind churning with frustration and doubt. When he returned to his quarters, Hanali greeted him with a soft smile, her eyes searching his face. He relayed the dilemma he had overheard, his voice tinged with anger and disappointment.

Hanali listened intently, her expression thoughtful before she hugged him tightly, her arms a quiet reassurance. 'You've grown into someone I respect,' she said softly.

Alduin's shoulders relaxed as he held her for a moment longer before they both settled into bed. Hours later, he was startled awake by the muffled sounds of cheering outside. Frowning, he rose quietly and stepped out into the cool night air. The village square was alive with celebration – men laughing and embracing their wives, women crying tears of joy. Yet amidst the revelry, his sharp eyes caught glimpses of somber faces among the soldiers.

Curious, Alduin approached one of the men who stood apart from the crowd, his shoulders slumped and his gaze distant. 'Hey,' Alduin said gently. 'What happened? Why aren't you celebrating like the others?'

The soldier turned slowly, his face lined with frustration and guilt. 'Haven't you heard? Last night, we were woken by the general. The Lord ordered us to take out a group of highwaymen... in their sleep.' His voice cracked as he continued, 'How can I celebrate that? How can I feel proud?
'

Alduin's stomach twisted. 'What? No... that's not possible. He told me he'd decide today,' His voice grew louder, disbelief etched into every word.

'It's true,' another soldier interjected quietly, holding his wife's hand. His face mirrored the same guilt as his comrade's.

Before Alduin could respond, another soldier shouted from across the square, grinning as he embraced his wife. 'Who cares? We won. Those bastards won't pillage us anymore. Orders are orders. deal with it.'

Alduin clenched his fists, his jaw tightening as anger surged through him. Without another word, he turned and strode toward Virtholdr's office, his mind racing with questions and betrayal.

He barged into the room without hesitation, interrupting a conversation between Virtholdr and two generals. The clan chief flinched at the sudden intrusion.

'Alduin!' Virtholdr exclaimed, placing a hand over his

chest. 'Must you always barge in like this? You scare me half to death.'

'Did you really do it?' Alduin demanded, his voice trembling with anger.

'Do what?' Virtholdr asked sharply.

'You told me you'd decide today. But I just spoke to your men, they said you ordered them to kill the bandits last night. Why did you lie to me? Why did you go against your word?' Alduin's voice rose with each word until it echoed through the room.

Virtholdr's expression hardened as he straightened in his chair. 'Lower your voice, boy. I am you grandfather. Has your father taught you no respect?'

Alduin hesitated for a moment before muttering, 'I'm sorry... but why? Why did you do it?'

Virtholdr sighed heavily and leaned back in his chair. 'I considered your opinion and fell asleep shortly after our conversation. But I woke up with clarity in the middle of the night and summoned Ladriel to give the order. You're too young to understand matters of war, too naive. I did what I believed was necessary.'

'But it wasn't right!' Alduin shot back, stepping closer to the desk. 'It's dishonorable. An utter disgrace.'

Virtholdr waved a hand dismissively. 'I don't care about your opinion on this matter. It was my decision to make as clan leader, and I stand by it.'

'You know what must be done,' Vaonie urged him in his thoughts.

Alduin's hands trembled at his sides as tears welled in his eyes. His voice cracked as he whispered, 'Why... why did you have to do this? Why are you making me do this?' he turned his head to the ceiling, 'Vaonie, please. Let me spare him, I beg you, my lord.'

Vaonie's voice thundered in his mind. 'No, you are a god. Judge the sinner. I will not tolerate anything else.'

Sharp pain ran through Alduin's body, all the way from his toes to the skull. Violent and unyielding. His hands.

'Do not test me, Lodus,' Vaonie commanded.

Virtholdr tilted his head in confusion. 'What are you talking about? Who are you talking to?'

'Why are you making me do this?!' Alduin shouted, three tears slipping down his cheek before he quickly wiped them away.

'Do what?'

The room fell silent except for Alduin's ragged breathing as Virtholdr stared at him with a mixture of surprise and discomfort.

Alduin's world shattered. Shock coursed through him like ice, followed by a wave of terror that left him breathless. Anger and fury churned in his chest, but it was the shock that consumed him, repeating itself like a mantra in his mind. He stumbled, his legs giving way beneath him as if the very ground had betrayed him. He fell to the floor, his hands clamping over his ears as if to block out the reality that had just been thrust upon him. A raw, primal scream tore from his throat, echoing through the room like a cry of despair. His body shook, his eyes wide with a horror that seemed to have no end. For a moment, he was a child again, cowering from a monster that lurked in every shadow, his mind unable to grasp what he must do.

Virtholdr's voice cracked with fear. 'Alduin, what in Munesa[vii] is happening to you?!'

Minutes passed. Alduin rose slowly, his eyes blazing red, predatory. Virtholdr's hand flew to his sword hilt.

'HOW. DARE. YOU. DO. THIS!!!' Alduin roared, Vaurcarya unsheathing itself with a metallic hiss.

Virtholdr froze, eyes wide. 'Wh-What? Put that back!'

His men's blades flashed out, forming a protective ring.

Alduin's voice trembled, tears streaming down his face. 'You monster. You lunatic. You left me no choice…'

'N-No choice to do what?' Virtholdr stammered, backing away.

'I am Alduin Lodus Faëli. And I judge you… ' Alduin's voice broke, '…to death.'

'Have you gone mad? I'm your grandfather. Men, seize him!'

Vaurcarya arced through the air. A sickening thud. Virtholdr's head rolled, blood spraying the floor.

Alduin stood motionless, his gaze locked on his grandfather's lifeless eyes. Tears flowed freely, yet his expression remained stone-like.

A blade pressed against Alduin's throat. 'What have you done, lunatic?' a Hekket bellowed.

'Farewell, grandfather,' Alduin whispered.

'Good job, Lodus,' Vaonie praised him in his mind.

'But at what cost…' He muttered.

'This is treason. Murder of the clan chief.' The general snarled. 'Any final words?'

[vii] (Elvish) Hell.

Silence. Alduin's gaze never wavered from Virtholdr's soulless eyes.

The general's blade slashed across Alduin's neck. Minutes passed. Sobbing and nervous murmurs echoed through the room. They sheathed their weapons and rushed to their lord's corpse.

Suddenly, they heard Alduin sobbing. Confused, one of them turned his head to check it. It was a grave mistake which shook him to his core, his eyes widening in terror.

Alduin stood still in a pool of his own blood, keeping his eyes locked on his grandfather. His pupils glowed in the color of blood. Ferocious. Menacing. Otherworldly.

'How are you not dead?' the Hekket gasped. 'Your eyes… you're a vampire. Girlor, prepare for battle. And call the guards, hurry!'

Alduin blinked, snapping back to reality. The Hekkets charged, weapons raised.

He collapsed to his knees, anguish twisting his features. 'What have I done? Grandfather, why did you make me do this to you? Why, Grandfather? Why?!'

'Quick, Celefaris. Guards, come quick.' Girlor bellowed, seizing the moment of vulnerability.

Clarity struck Alduin like lightning. He lunged for the window, glass shattering around him as he took flight. The village erupted in chaos, horns wailing with a mournful cry. He burst into his room, his eyes wild and desperate. 'We must leave,' he gasped to Hanali. She nodded, trust overriding confusion.

They soared into the night, arrows whistling past them. As the village faded behind them, Alduin halted abruptly, his body rigid with anguish. He turned to Hanali, tears streaming down his face, his voice raw with pain.

'I killed him. My grandfather. I judged him... executed him. I had to…' His words came in broken sobs. 'Why must I bear this burden? This... mortal heart?' his hands clutched at his chest as if trying to tear out the source of his agony. 'He was my blood, Hanali. My last family.'

Hanali's face crumpled with empathy, her voice barely a whisper. 'I am sorry...' She knew he had no choice, the burdens of a god must be heavy on a mortal's shoulders.

Alduin's body shook, his hands trembling with each ragged breath. 'What if... what if my children...?' he couldn't finish the thought, horror etched across his features. 'I'm not cold like your siblings. This pain... it's unbearable.' His voice broke, despair threatening to overwhelm him. 'I'm not ready. I'll never be ready for this.'

They pressed on toward Euphata, Alduin's anguished cries echoing in the vast, uncaring sky.

CHAPTER TWELVE

Weeks dragged by as Alduin refused to speak, to even utter a word. He kept quiet. Kept his thoughts to himself. Feeling like a massive serpent coiled around him. Its weight crushing his head. He never imagined a day such as this would come. A day where he would have to judge his own blood. Without any bias or discrimination. His motivation to exist had become rather flaky and unstable. The invisible serpent squeezed Alduin's chest.

During the nights, he would ask to stop for a bit in order to reminisce. To rethink past decisions. To wonder about how he would find the strength to keep going with the duty he had been entrusted with. The snake's fangs pierced deep into Alduin's skull, though as painful as it was – it wasn't real. The one who wrestled with Alduin, was Alduin himself. Maybe death was better than this inner struggle? Death comes to us all anyway.

Eventually, after a couple of weeks, he had regained the strength to speak.

'Hanali.'

'Yes?'

'I-I think I'm ready to tell you the rest of my story. Would you like to hear it? Before we reach Euphata...'

'Sure.'

They lowered down and sat on a big snowy rock in front of each other.

'What I told you back then... It-It didn't stop there...' His face turned somber.

She nodded and looked him right in the eyes.

'The vampires abducted and caged me on the orders of a twisted man named Gozo. The guards tortured, starved, and fed on me... They tried their best to kill my sanity. And they did... Slowly but surely, they did... Until I could no longer feel anything. Until I was no longer sad nor happy, neither angry nor calm. I have gone into a state of simply existing. Torture had become my reality, and I have grown accustomed to it. Then, one day, I was summoned to the clan leader's courtroom. His name was Lysander. He forced me to go through Vaonie's trials of the necklace,' he stopped for a second to exhale, to calm himself.

'I am glad you survived it...' She tried to smile.

'Thank you.'

They went quiet for a few seconds and stared into each other's eyes. Then, he continued.

'After I beat the trials, I was transformed into an

Araqhaiit and returned to Vanthea. The Vaermiraiits[i] that abducted me were tasked with my training. When I proved worthy of my title, Vaonie sent me to Heonmeyu[ii]. To slaughter everyone there...'

'When we first met...'

'Yes,' he blushed.

Noticing his blush, she blushed too.

'Sorry for bothering you with this. My sister always said that I whine too much... Let's just keep on going...'

'No, no... Don't apologize! I want to listen.'

'You did. I feel a lot better now, like a huge burden was taken off my shoulders.'

She smiled and hugged him awkwardly, like a robot learning about affection. Was it her first time embracing someone? He was surprised but his body did not let him escape her grasp, it was comfortable, safe, warm. His hands jumped up to hug her back, out of instinct. Suddenly, the only thing he could feel was her body and her chest going up and down, the only thing he could hear was her breath. His eyes lost focus, resting. He slowly closed them. Nothing else mattered. Nothing felt more serene or important than this moment.

Uncertain when she was supposed to let go, she waited for him to end the hug. It took about ten minutes, maybe a bit more. He took a deep breath, looked at her, blushed, and then turned his gaze to the sky.

'Thank you for that,' he said.

---

[i]   (Omnitongue) Vampires.
[ii] (Omnitongue) Heaven.

She smiled, nodded, and they flew away. Back to their journey.

'Hey, um...' He said after about half an hour.

'Yes?'

'How do-... How do you judge people? What helps you decide which level of punishment is required?' he asked.

'Oh, well... Hmm... I just follow the way I feel about the crime. I believe I was given the right to decide for a reason. I follow my intuition.'

'I see.'

'It is *your* job now, too. If you find it difficult then maybe you should sit down and think about it.'

'I mean, I already have an idea. But I think you'll hate it.'

'Tell me.'

'No... It is too dark...'

'Please?'

'Well... I don't believe there is a lesser evil or a greater one, just evil, and I believe in equal punishment for all of it. Liars, thieves, murderers, backstabbers and racists all deserve the same fate.' He hesitated and then said quietly, staring at Hanali's eyes to see her reaction.

'If they are all equal, then how would you pass judgement? Would you punish everyone the same way?' she raised an eyebrow.

'Exactly.'

'How?'

'Well... Death.'

'Huh?'

'Death. Of course, I don't mean that lying to someone is

as vile as rape, but since there will be no greater or lesser punishments than death, those two are put into the same "box," so to speak... It sounds like I am contradicting myself, but if you think hard about it, you will understand my point.' He said.

'You may take a life only if someone violates your tenet in a severe way. Vaonie and Austomia decreed it so, and their word is law.'

'I am aware. But... Bear in mind that all they did was say *severe*. Meaning that I am entitled to decide what deserves the death sentence and what doesn't.'

'Hmm, I did not think about it that way... I see... Well, I ask you not to abuse it. It is *their* realm and their *lives*. They have the right of free will. Don't take that away from them.'

'*Do* they, though?'

'What do you mean?' she tried her best not to roll her eyes.

'I don't think we have free will, it doesn't exist.'

'Explain, please.'

They reached the Arctic continent and continued flying above it.

'I started noticing animal-like behavioural patterns in mortals. We seek dominance. We seek to be above and put others at bay. We seek agreeability and acceptance. We are social creatures, craving validation.'

'Validation? From whom?'

'Everyone. Our friends, family, lovers, society. Even that of the people who bully us. We crave to be understood and listened to. Despite our futile attempts to hide our true selfish nature, it all comes out the moment we are put to the test. Our bodies crave to sin, but we simply restrain ourselves.'

'What is your point?' Hanali asked.

'I believe Austomia first created the animals, then us— shaped in their image. Women are often submissive, men dominant, like in the animal kingdom. We value physical strength and appearance over purity of heart or intellect, like in the animal kingdom. No matter how far we stray, we return to our instincts—to run, freeze, or fight. Once you accept this, mortals no longer seem random. They become predictable. You know exactly how they will act, what drives them, what breaks them. There is no free will. We are all programmed the same, merely shaped by different experiences, people, and stories. No one is special.'

'I disagree.'

'Why?'

'Because it is nothing but pessimistic. Our makers gave you life, not out of boredom but out of decision.'

"'If only you knew...' I bet you want to say that to her. Right, reader?"

She resumed, 'yes, they also gave you pain, but so what? I believe pain exists to force growth and strengthen character. I believe it was created to make you, mortals, better.'

'It is a valid point, but they could have made us flawless from the beginning. Also, the sheer quantity of mortals along with the fact that Vanthea was created to be *your* "plaything," only strengthens my belief about the meaning of our life.'

'Which is?'

'That there is none.' He said.

'Excuse me?'

'There are far too many mortals, making a single life, or even an entire city, utterly insignificant, expendable, meaningless. In the grand scheme of things our lives hold no weight. People are born and then they die.'

'So why live in the first place if that's what you believe to be true? Why not just kill yourself?'

'Well, currently, I can't die... I am immortal,' he said.

'You are wrong, and in denial. You *can* die, you just have to disobey Vaonie in order to do that... So why not do it and be done with this realm you call a hoax?'

'That's a good question. I-I don't know... Maybe... Hmm...' He scratched his forehead.

'Yes?'

'Maybe... Maybe because our lives mean so little that they amount to nothing, there is no meaning to them. And precisely because there is no meaning, that by itself gives it meaning? Something along those lines, perhaps.'

'And what would that be?'

'To make your own meaning.'

'I don't quite follow.'

'Maybe it is a matter of "if it already is like this, then why the fuck not?"'

She blinked, her head tilting slightly as she replayed his words in her mind, her brow knitting in confusion.

'Now that I stopped to think about it, it makes much more sense. A mortal's purpose is to find, or rather *create*, their own purpose. And that must be why I am still here, in a quest to give value to my existence...' Alduin said.

'This is interesting. I like that idea.'

'What is *your* theory about this? I just noticed I was the only one talki-. Oh, wait! Stop!' He suddenly stopped in midair.

'What? What happened?'

'I recognize this place,' his eyes glowed flame red with the rage of a wildfire.

'Really? Why? Where are we?'

He pointed at a cave. 'See that?'

'Yes, what about it?'

'That is where I was held as a child. The fucking Vaermiraiits' lair. I must go there. Oh, how long have I waited for this moment!' he said and began flying fast toward it.

She quickly passed him and 'stood' (or rather levitated) in his way.

'What? Let me pass, Hanali. I beg of you.'

'Show compassion. Forgive. Move on! Pain is necessary.'

'Bullies don't stop bullying. Murderers never stop murdering. Evil is only beaten by necessary evil.'

'Necessary evil? Are you hearing yourself talking?'

'Yes, and I stand by it. Let me through!'

'You are your own person, so I will let you do as you wish. But please think about it.'

'About what?'

'Sparing them. For me.'

'I-I don't know if I can do that.'

'Try to.'

'We will see.'

He blasted his way toward the entrance to the cave and landed. It was guarded by five vampire guards. They recognized him.

'Welcome back, Lodus.'

'Yes. Greetings, my lord.'

His fists clenched at his sides, his face flushed with fury as he stepped forward. The invisible force of Vaonie pressed on his chest, warning him against reckless actions, but he chose to ignore the pain. 'Fuck obeying, fuck the gods, fuck everything! If Vaonie kills me, at least it will be on my own terms,' he thought. His voice rose in a forceful, trembling shout. 'My name. Is not. Lodus!'

'Wha-' A guard began speaking but Alduin cut him off.

Vaurcarya slashed through them, reducing them to tiny pieces.

Alduin froze in place. 'I'm... not dead? How?' he pondered, his eyes opened widely, 'perhaps Vaonie agrees with me? Surely, that must be the case...' His eyes blazed with a ferocious red light, as if ignited by an inner fire. His lips curled into a twisted, menacing smirk, 'good,' he said.

He turned and strode inside. He knew the underground system like the back of his hand—the tunnels, the pathways, every twist and turn. Stealth wasn't on his mind. Only slaughter. His resolve was clear: no one would be spared. Vaermiraiit soldiers who crossed his path met their end without hesitation. He moved deeper into the inner caves, each passageway opening into another section of the labyrinth.

His tactic was simple: butcher everyone, then retrace his steps to try another route. When he reached the barracks, he hesitated. Instead of entering, he chanted the runes of the Blood Sun spell, a massive one. It began draining the life force of the entire unit within. Screams of agony echoed through the cave as they perished, one by one.

'There is no honor in killing children. In raping children. In taking a child from their parents. So, you don't deserve my honor!' he screamed and turned back around.

After killing a few, then a dozen, then a few dozen and then finally a few hundred, he reached the main cave.

'Hmm... Houses... Good.' He began laughing hysterically.

He finally understood why they called it a 'Cave City.' It was quite breathtaking. An incredible number of houses were carved into the cave itself, made of stone. Candle-lit pathways and torches every now and again. Some houses were lit in the color of red, strengthening the dark ambience.

'I never realized how different each house is from the rest.' He muttered.

"Vampires? Having a sense of taste in architecture? Who would have thunk?!"

Cold air wrapped around him, brushing his ears and carrying the aroma of iron to his nostrils. The streets were busy with children, parents and guards. It reminded him of the market back in the village. He stopped to reminisce a bit but, after about five minutes, set his mind right back on track. He opened each house's door, delved inside and butchered everyone. Everyone except for the children.

'No child deserves death. Not before they do something truly deserving of it...'

As if it were the gods' wish, he came across the house of Zera. He kicked the door open.

'Oh, Lodus. Do you need somethi-' She began, but had no chance to finish.

Using telekinesis, he slammed Zera and her husband against a wall. With blood magic he cuffed their legs and hands. Restrained, they yelled for help.

He smiled. 'No one is coming for you, Zera,' he said.

He approached her husband and thrusted Vaurcarya into his throat. Blood gurgled out of his mouth as he coughed until he perished. Alduin turned to Zera with a twisted sneer on his face.

'You traitor!' she screamed, her voice breaking as tears welled in her eyes, her chest heaving with the immense weight of her agony.

He bid his time, killing her slowly, painfully. Using his sword and blood magic together. Spilling a bit of her blood with each strike. Not too much. It was too soon for her to die. He would keep healing her whenever an injury seemed too grave.

'I have an idea,' he said.

She stared at him, her face wet from blood and tears as her eyes begged for mercy. He released her legs from the wall and chained her right hand to another one, forcing somewhat of a crucifixion in midair.

'Dance for me!' he shouted and shot dozens of blood spikes toward her lower body, forcing her to move her legs in order to dodge.

The floor was soaked with blood, and his scarlet eyes glowed ever fierce. When he grew bored, he shot a sharp spike directly at her forehead, ending her miserable life. He let go of his magic and the chains returned to their original crimson form. She fell straight to the puddle of blood, life-less. He exited the house, his eyes set dead ahead.

Screams of women, men, and children echoed through the cave, clawing at his mind. The sound brought him back to the Hekket[iii] arena. The same tortured cries, the same sense of helplessness. His pulse raced, blood pounding in his ears as his grip tightened. A dry throat burned from his rushed breathing, the anger surging like a wildfire, choking out all reason. His vision narrowed, focusing only on the source of his fury, a force driving him forward.

He could feel the heat of revenge rising in him, stronger than ever. The massacre of his family and friends played like a broken record, and with each scream, the desire to hurt, to destroy, grew. He smiled. A twisted, feral grin. His face was smeared with vampire blood, but it was the fire of vengeance that consumed him now, blinding him to every-thing but the need to make them pay.

Suddenly, he came across a familiar sight – the tavern he visited a long while ago, 'The Dazed Human.' He remem-bered what he hated about it and burst inside, killing the guard with the sharp tip of Vaurcarya. Immediately, his eyes located the chained human slaves that were the whole gimmick of the business. He slayed everyone inside and used his sword to break the humans' shackles.

'You are free now!' he roared, 'Run away from here. Escape and don't look back!'

They bolted out the door, trying their best to escape, considering the shape their bodies were in. He heard heavy

---

iii Special Forces (Snow Elf).

breathing and crying from behind the bar. It was that irritating bartender who treated him badly when he visited four years ago. Their eyes locked, and she recognized him.

'You! Why are you doing this? Please, Spare me. Please,' tears ran down her cheeks.

He grabbed her head, smashed it into the wall and then into the bar's stone table. She died instantly. The tavern was finally empty of people. Dead silent and painted in dark red. He breathed in the sweet aroma. It got him excited.

'Off to the next one, I guess.' He yelled out and smiled.

He stepped out of the tavern and kept on walking, killing everyone he came across. After a few hours, he was interrupted by the first actual challenge. It was Lul, standing directly at the entrance and blocking his path.

'Move, Lul. My business is with Lysander first. Your time will come later on.'

'I refuse. I heard the screams. The cries for help. Are you insane? We practically raised you, you scum!'

'You took my family from me! You forced me into this twisted life. I never wished for it.'

'Those are fine words, but can you back them up? Do you honestly think you could defeat me?'

'I see you're still amputated,' he laughed, his voice laced with mockery.

Lul growled in anger.

'And to answer your question, of course I can,' he added.

'Then try, you pipsqueak. I hate you. This is for everything you have done!'

As Alduin lifted Vaurcarya, Lul disappeared into a

cloud of red mist. Still, he felt her presence. He throbbed with stabbing pain. She'd thrust her sword into him. Pierced from behind. The blade cut all the way through. The tip poked out of his chest. She leapt onto his shoulders. Grabbed his head. Ripped it off with her bare hands. Threw it down. His head rolled on the ground. Not sparing a moment, she began chanting. The words of a sealing spell—to lock him in place—for eternity.

He'd never fought anyone as powerful. before. The other vampires were small fry compared to her. Strategizing, he had to unleash a crushing blow before she finished chanting.

It finally struck him. He needed a distraction. Raising the fresh blood on the ground, he summoned his mount, Acaroth.

'I see you finally got the gist of mounts. This is a rather sad attempt to keep me at bay, however. Simply pathetic,' she said, laughing.

'I was not trying to protect myself.'

'Huh?'

'I was trying to distract you. And it worked.'

'Huh?'

Runes of blood magic surrounded her, forming a triangle. He activated a spell. Trapped her in a triangular cage of blood. At her screams of, 'let me go,' blood spikes, from all directions, flew into her. Impaling her. Wailing in agony. Gushing blood. She dropped dead.

'I call this "The Iron Maiden,"' he said and recovered his body, 'off I go.'

He walked further into the castle, seeking Lysander's

throne room. When he reached the main gate, he was interrupted by guards who were no longer friendly. He killed them with ease and kicked down the gate. He walked inside. In front of him stood two familiar faces. Edward and Gozo.

'Why are you doing this, Lodus? We took you in quite nicely. We trained, dined and treated you like a king!' Gozo shouted with a disappointed face.

'Why? Are you seriously asking me why? You took everything from me. My home. My family. My destiny!'

'There is no such thing as destiny, Lodus,' Edward said.

'I am here to avenge my clan and nothing, no one, will stand in my way. Destiny is all!' Alduin shouted.

'How foolish you are,' Gozo clicked his tongue.

'Oh, and by the way.'

'Oh, please do share your final words with us,' Gozo rolled his eyes, 'you bastard.'

'My name. It's not Lodus, you fucking asshole.'

Blood smeared his face as a twisted smile spread across it. He floated, thick red mist swirling around his feet. Vaurcarya fought Gozo while Alduin unleashed the fury of his blood magic on Edward. Edward, preferring physical combat, blocked blood spikes with his enchanted axes and hurled knives in retaliation.

Gozo struck back with his own blood magic, a warrior's ferocity behind every move. Blood spikes, suns, saws, knives, and minions rained down. Streams of blood surged from the city nearby. Gozo used the remains of the deceased to his advantage. Pools of blood formed on the ground, rising into figures, their colours shifting until they gained life.

Giants and man-eating gargoyles emerged, controlled by Gozo. They roared, shaking the ground to intimidate their opponent. Alduin used Vaurcarya to distract Edward and deflect the projectiles targeting him. Turning to face Gozo and his minions, he saw a giant swing its club in a vertical strike. Alduin sidestepped and leapt onto it, scrambling up its body to the head. With a swift slash of his claws, he tore the head from the spine and threw it aside.

He quickly jumped onto the next giant, dodging Gozo's magic and evading banishment seals spread across the battlefield. Large seals, both circular and triangular, activated around him—on the cave floor, walls, and ceiling. Fortunately for Alduin, Gozo had never sealed anyone away and wasn't familiar with the tactics involved.

Edward struggled to breach Vaurcarya's protection, despite throwing axes and knives to distract it. He sidestepped, but Vaurcarya tracked his every movement with precision, preventing him from joining Gozo. Alduin used blood spikes to take down the gargoyles, ensuring they wouldn't interfere with his fight against the next giant. He kept Gozo busy with impalement spells.

Standing on the giant's shoulders, Alduin taunted it by punching its neck. Enraged, the giant swung its massive sword. Alduin dodged, stepping to the other shoulder, causing the giant to slash its own arm off. It screamed in agony.

Alduin backflipped off its shoulders, landing with a high kick that sent the giant crashing into a wall lined with blood spikes. Only one giant and four gargoyles remained. A sudden realization hit him. He slapped his forehead in frustration, then turned to face Gozo.

Alduin sank his teeth into his right arm, ripping through flesh until blood poured freely, painting the floor. He regenerated quickly, repeating the process three more times. Chanting in his mind, he shaped the blood into minotaur forms. Their right hands twisted into spears, left into massive shields like those of the Spartan soldiers his uncle had told him about. The bulls took up defensive positions, keeping Gozo's minions at bay and blocking the flying gargoyles. Alduin smirked.

'Why are you smiling?' Gozo asked.

'I just remembered something,' he cracked his knuckles.

'What is it?'

'Do you remember telling me about the biggest weakness of vampires?'

'FUCK!'

Alduin chose to embrace Gozo's blood magic, moving his hands and whispering as he bowed his head.

'What are you doing? At least try to fight. I don't remember you being so pathetic,' Gozo shouted, his brow furrowed as he tilted his head, eyes narrowing in disbelief.

Alduin raised his voice in the middle of his chant. The temperature plummeted as snow and raindrops swirled around him, forming a spinning mist like a small tornado. The only word that registered in Gozo's mind was 'Uli[iv].'

Suddenly, the mist shot toward him, enveloping him. As

[iv] (Omnitongue) Ice.

Gozo screamed, frostbite spread over his body, freezing him in place like an ice statue. His face was no longer recognizable.

'No!' Edward shouted, adrenaline surging as he broke through Vaurcarya's defenses.

The cries of battle rumbled through the realms, echoing even into the depths of hell.

'Oh. Greetings. What are you doing here?'

Hanali opened a door and entered Vaonie's courtroom. 'Greetings, maker.'

'Actually, this is quite good timing. I wanted to ask you why Alduin is massacring my followers. Explain yourself. You were tasked to keep him at bay.'

'Yes, that is exactly what I came here for.'

'Speak then.'

'I hereby request you ignore Alduin's rampage.'

'What?' Vaonie snorted. 'Why would I do that?'

Hanali rubbed her arms. 'Uhm... because it would benefit you.'

'I expected more from my first child.' Vaonie's eyes glowed in strong red. 'Letting a traitor kill my subjects? You make no sense. How could that benefit me?' they balked.

'Alduin told me his story. I know every detail of it.' Her voice choked with sadness, close to breaking. 'Including the way that pain, anger, guilt, and desperation dig into him and explode at any reminder of his past.'

'What's your point?'

'Alduin's whole mind is set on revenge. He will never be able to be a loyal servant that way. Also, his mind will never be focused on the task at hand. It will always wander off to thoughts of revenge. He was deeply wounded… Damaged by his past. Mortals are like that.'

'Why shouldn't I just get rid of him? Attain an entirely new replacement for Lodus? One that lacks such drastic symptoms of post-trauma?'

'Because.'

'Because what?' Vaonie scoffed.

'Because it would make me sad. Here, I said it! It would depress to lose my time with him. I… I enjoy his company.'

'You? Fell for a mortal? How revolting.'

'I have no idea how it happened either, but it did. Without him, I'd be far less loyal and focused. Make your choice.'

'Is that an ultimatum I'm hearing?' their voice rose, strained and furious.

'Call it whatever you like, maker. In the end, I'm simply offering you something unique.'

'Unique? How exactly?' Vaonie leaned toward her.

'A chance to keep me at peace. To make me happy. I have lived in pain for endless millennia, ever since Lodus died.' Hanali looked up at them, her eyes wide and glassy. 'Please, just give me this, ' her voice cracked.

'Alright.'

'What?' she held her breath.

'I said alright! I will spare him. For you. But only this once.'

'Thank you, maker. Thank you!' Bouncing on her feet, Hanali smiled brightly, broadly.

Ignorant of Vaonie's surprising show of empathy, Alduin dodged all the attacks aimed at him with such precision that even his tutor, Edward, smiled.

'I taught you well.'

'You did,' he smiled back.

Alduin felt a pang of nostalgia. Edward was the only vampire he knew that was turned and he felt great empathy for him. He unleashed a larger wave of blood spikes, targeting his teacher. A few found their mark, pinning Edward to the wall.

'I do not wish to fight you, my friend. I'm giving you a chance to relive your life, maybe even find a cure for your vampirism. You are free to go once I am done here.'

'I-... Why?'

'Like me, you didn't choose this life. It chose you. Mortals should have the right to make their own destiny.'

'What makes you think I wouldn't try to hunt you down once I'm freed from these restraints?'

'You can try. I won't give you a second chance, howe-' Alduin was slammed from behind by Gozo's enormous blood hammer, launching him into another wall, which cracked widely.

The sudden loss of focus turned the spikes back into liquid.

'Understood,' Edward said and ran off.

'You coward! Traitor. I will take this to the chief directly, you fucking traitor. How dare you leave me here?!' Gozo yelled out.

Gozo advanced menacingly, placing banishment seals around Alduin, trapping him. He circled him with seals on the walls and in the air, cutting off all escape. Reaching Alduin, he pressed his hand to his forehead and chanted. Alduin vanished into thin air. Gozo let out a victorious roar. He won.

"Or did he?"

'Hey, Dunbar[v], behind you!' Alduin shouted and flew directly toward him.

'What?'

Vaurcarya flew at Alduin's side as he commanded the bulls to merge into a humanoid titan, wielding a massive hammer. It charged at Gozo's minions, smashing two gargoyles into oblivion. Gozo's face turned blue with fear. Just as Alduin was closing in, he stopped in midair and levitated, rising slowly while chanting. The volume of his chants grew deafening, and his eyes glowed blue.

He wasted no time. Using Vaurcarya, he severed his own limbs—arms, legs, and head. The head continued to float while the rest of his body crashed to the ground, melting into pools of blood. The temperature dropped rapidly. Gozo's left hand froze off, followed by his right leg.

---

[v] (Elvish) Asshole.

A thick snow mist surrounded them, engulfing Alduin as he summoned the blood to rise and mix with the snow. He hurled the swirling red and white mass at Gozo, forming a tornado of pain. The snow burned with frostbite, while blood-sculpted swords pierced Gozo from every angle. His screams faded, and the tornado died. Alduin's severed head dropped to the ground. He regenerated his body and stood over Gozo's now unrecognizable corpse, laughing.

'Fuck him. Fuck him. Fuck him!' Alduin bellowed.

He sprinted to Lysander's courtroom. At the door, he hesitated, then unleashed his other form. Vaonie's mark flared on him, and he screamed as the pain seared his body. Though, surprisingly, his consciousness didn't leave him this time. Kicking the door open, he found Lysander facing a painting of a naked woman and drinking from a blood chalice.

CHAPTER THIRTEEN

Decaying corpses, of humanoids and terrifying abominations, covered the floor. It looked like a lab of a failed necromancer.

'I heard the ruckus outside and wondered when you were going to show up. Did it please you to massacre my people?' Lysander held a glass of wine and twirled it around with his wrist.

Alduin was breathing heavily, like a feral beast.

'No response, huh? Very well then,' Lysander said and turned around.

Alduin screamed at the top of his lungs, then lost consciousness. It wasn't Lysander he faced, but his uncle, Ley. The shock and emotional toll had shattered his berserk form, returning him to normal. Before rising, he conjured his clothing back into place.

'Uncle?'

'Who?'

'What the fuck are you doing here?! I thought you died!'

'Who the hell are you?'

'A-Alduin. Your nephew!'

'What in Munesa[i] are you talking about? My nephew died a long time ago... Don't play with me. It would only anger me further.'

'I speak the truth. Gozo spared me and I was enslaved here. I took on the trials of Vaonie and became the new Lodus, an Araqhaiit...'

'What is this nonsense? Why should I believe you?'

'Do you remember teaching me to fish using ice magic? How you helped me sneak out at night to meet your human friends in "The Festival of The Eight Trees?"'

'I-Yes, I remember. But... But how... I was told you were dead!'

'Now it's your turn to answer my question. How are you alive?! I saw your corpse in the Colosseum. And why are you here, in Lysander's throne room? Answer me.' Alduin's eyes shot across the room, panicking, seeking to make sense of it all.

'Indeed, I died in the village but was resurrected a few days later as a vampire.'

'Why are you here?' he asked while huffing as if having an anxiety attack.

'What do you mean *why*? I am their leader, couldn't you tell? Why else would I be here, in the throne room?'

'What? What happened to Lysander?!'

'I-' Ley burped, 'I killed him.'

---

[i] (Elvish) Hell.

'Why?'

'You have known me for how long now, Alduin?'

'About ten years.'

'Yeah, exactly. Don't you know how much I despise taking orders from people?'

'I guess that's true.'

'Mhm.'

'Well, what now?'

'What do you mean?'

'I don't want to fight you… You're my uncle! Let's just get out of here and rebuild our clan.'

'I am one of them now, so I must stay here and rebuild… Also, do you really think I'd just let you go after killing everyone?'

'Since when do you care about vampires?!'

'Since I joined them seven years ago.'

'But you were turned. Why would you be on their side?!'

'You don't get it, do you? I was turned voluntarily.'

'What? Why the fuck would you do that?'

'I sought power, more power than I had before. I reached my peak at too young an age. What use is there to being an adventurer if I lack the lifespan to see it all?'

'You are insane. They killed everyone! Your brother. My mother. The women you slept with. Even your friends!'

'I'll let you in on a little secret.'

'What is it?'

'I am the reason it happened,' Ley smirked.

"Shock emoji."

'What? What the fuck are you talking about?!' He stumbled back, hands flailing in disbelief.

'I was promised a reward in exchange for information.'

'A reward? Since when do you care about Samarices[ii]?'

'I didn't do it for money, but for Royal Vaermiraiit[iii] blood. They claimed mortals who drank it would evolve instantly, jumping straight to a high-tier rank. Turns out they were lying, but by then it was already too late. Meh,' he shrugged.

'What kind of information did you give them?'

'I don't remember you being this slow.'

'It is just incredibly hard for me to process all of this, you monster.'

'The information I gave them was the specific date, location and details of the Hekket[iv] trials. Simple. I thought you guessed it by now... Disappointing...'

'YOU DID WHAT?!!!' he screamed, chest heaving, fists clenched so tight his knuckles went white. His body trembled, eyes wide and frantic, like he was struggling to hold himself together. His breath came in ragged bursts, panic clawing at him. Every muscle in him coiled, ready to lash out, yet he was frozen in place, fighting an explosion of rage and disbelief.

'Exactly what I just said.'

'I-I can't believe this!' He shook, fists clenched. 'You're the reason this happened! The reason I'm orphaned! Alone!

[ii] Currency.
[iii] (Omnitongue) Vampire.
[iv] Special Forces (Snow Elf).

You're why I was tortured!' He stepped forward, voice rising. 'You ruined my life! For what? Power?!' His chest heaved with every word, his breath ragged.

'What else is there to life, huh? There will always be predators and prey. I decided to never become prey. Simple.'

'What happened to your sense of adventure? Your love of booze, women and the wonders of the world?' he began coughing loudly, 'Was it all a ruse?' it was hard for him to breathe.

'Do you think there aren't women here? Or-' He burped, 'or booze? I *am* drunk now, after all. My life remains the same. I still explore the world, and I still get drunk daily. I'm just much more powerful than I used to be, that's all.'

'Have you no value for our family?'

'What makes you think I had such a peculiar thing?'

'You... You taught me so much about the world! Was it all fake? Your love for me? Was... Was it fake too?'

'I simply found it fascinating to raise a child.'

'I-I don't know how to respond to that,' he stuttered.

'You don't need to. Just accept your death.'

'You fucking maniac!'

'Good. Use this anger to make this more entertaining. I haven't had a good fight in such a long time!' He burst into laughter and held his fists in the air.

Alduin lost control and charged, sword drawn, pointing it at Ley as he ran. Ley didn't flinch. Alduin unleashed a flurry of strikes, each swift and calculated. Ley dodged them all effortlessly. On the fifth, he sidestepped right.

'Didn't your father teach you how to fight?' Ley said.

He swung his sword, smacking Alduin into the wall. Mid-flight, Alduin levitated Vaurcarya and sent it at Ley with telekinesis. He crashed into the wall, losing focus, and the sword dropped before hitting its mark. He hit the ground, pushed himself up like a push-up, and regained his stance. Alduin called his sword back.

'Pathetic,' Ley sneered.

Alduin charged, severing his left arm to unleash fifteen blood spikes in rapid intervals. They flew toward Ley. Alduin's battle cry roared.

Ley pivoted, dodging seven spikes. He spun, avoiding another by performing a pirouette, then faced Alduin again. The remaining eight came at him in a cluster, closing in. Just as they neared, Ley vanished. The spikes slammed into the wall, turning back into liquid blood. Alduin kept charging, expecting Ley to be invisible.

Without warning, Ley reappeared behind Alduin, decapitating him. Alduin's head dropped, his body still standing. Ley grabbed his cape, wiping the blood from his blade.

In an instant, Alduin's body spun, his left hand seizing Ley's neck while Vaurcarya pierced his stomach. Blood dripped from Ley's mouth. With a swift strike, Ley severed Alduin's left hand, breaking his grip. As Alduin's hand regenerated, Ley gripped his right shoulder and left hip, pulling with force. Alduin's body tilted, his sword still lodged into Ley.

Ley completed the spin, turning Alduin's body upside down. With both hands on Alduin's waist, Ley lifted him, yanking the sword free and smashing him into the ground.

Levelling a few meters back, Ley watched as Alduin quickly recovered, levitating back to his feet.

'Interesting...' Ley said.

Alduin regained his composure, floating toward Ley. Noticing the shift in Alduin's eyes, Ley took a defensive stance, ready for the strike. The battle had begun.

Alduin reached him, slashing vertically. Ley dodged right and kicked him hard in the chest. Alduin blocked with both hands, then countered with a push kick. Ley grabbed his leg mid-air, floating back, forcing Alduin into a split. In a fluid motion, Ley moved to Alduin's side, seized his leg, and elbowed it from above, shattering the bones.

Without hesitation, Alduin grabbed Ley by the shoulders and headbutted him, making Ley flinch. Alduin quickly healed his leg and unleashed a series of kicks while Ley recovered from the blow.

Ley blocked most, but the last three caught him. He coughed blood, crashing into another wall.

'I always thought this place needed a bit of renovation,' Alduin smirked.

He walked slowly toward Ley, his blade floating at his side. Ley coughed up blood and spat on the ground, pushing himself off the wall and back to his feet. He waited. Alduin stopped, facing him, four and a half meters apart.

Ley raised his sword in defense. Vaurcarya floated in front of Alduin, a shield against any attack. Alduin focused, silently chanting in his mind, blocking Ley from reading his spell. The temperature plummeted.

'Ice magic, against me, are you serious? You're nothing

but an amateur, I taught you everything you know,' Ley said.

Alduin smirked as the temperature dropped. Ley rolled his eyes and lunged forward. An enormous ice spike descended from the ceiling, but Ley didn't hesitate. Spitting, he turned his saliva into a ball of ice which collided with the spike, shattering it mid-air. He landed, only to leap again as the floor beneath him turned slick with ice, trying to trip him.

'Cheap tricks aren't enough to take me down, you Dunbar[v].' Ley bellowed mid-air, his voice echoing.

As his feet hit the ground, Ley charged again. Thick mist filled the room, but he boiled his blood to counter it. Three mini tornadoes formed around him, whipping at him with blasts of frostbite.

Instead of dodging, he lifted the palms of his hands toward them and chanted. 'Yorda u Ut-oblryine[vi].' Humongous flames sprouted out from his hands, voiding the cold. 'Here's a trick I learned a few years ago. Bear witness!'

He chanted, his fingers weaving through the air. Suddenly, his sword blazed with flames, its red glow pulsing.

Ley leapt to a chair and drove his sword through it. 'Nor[vii],' he chanted.

The chair vanished. Ley laughed, then turned back to Alduin, pointing his sword as he charged. Alduin stomped,

---

[v]   (Elvish) Asshole.
[vi] (Omnitongue) Wave of flames.
[vii] (Omnitongue) (To) release.

sending a splash of water into the air, then froze it into a large block. He punched it at Ley, launching it multiple times to try and knock him off balance. Ley sliced through the ice with ease, undeterred.

Alduin fired flames, forcing Ley to dodge, uncertain of the spell's nature. Alduin zigzagged backward, avoiding the flames, as Ley advanced. Despite Alduin's slashes, Ley expertly deflected each one. He slid across the wet floor using 'Ice Step.'

Whenever Alduin dropped the temperature, Ley countered with Pyromancy[viii], igniting the air. Alduin retreated, but with nowhere to go—he hit a wall. Ley smirked and leapt forward with a vertical slash. Alduin spun to the side, throwing a hook punch. Ley caught it mid-swing, throwing Alduin into the ceiling.

Alduin rebounded off the ceiling and landed, forming an ice cloak around him.

'So futile...' Ley said.

Alduin clashed Vaurcarya against Ley, their swords ringing with each strike. While Ley defended and countered, Alduin fired large ice balls. Ley dodged them effortlessly, keeping up the clash. Alduin took the chance to launch an enormous flame from his mouth.

Alduin leapt aside but was bombarded by fireballs. He zigzagged backward to avoid them, until suddenly, two hands grabbed him from behind. Ley stood in front of him, flashing his blade. Alduin turned and realised a clone held him in place. He elbowed it, but it was futile.

[viii] Fire Magic.

Ley approached slowly, twirling his sword, a grin spreading across his face. Alduin realised Ley was toying with him. Finally, Ley reached him and pressed the sword to his body.

'Lay this foolish ambition to rest. You are not worthy of my time,' Ley said.

The flaming blade inched closer, its tip pressing against Alduin's chest. Ley aimed for the heart, bracing his left hand against his right to drive it in. Suddenly, the sword clattered to the floor—along with his arm. Ley screamed in agony. He turned to his right, eyes wide with terror. Another Alduin stood there. Blood sprayed, staining the floor beneath him.

'You… W-what? How? I never saw you summoning a clone.'

'You are not fighting a mere mortal. Do not dare to underestimate me.'

Alduin struck with a vertical slash, aiming for Ley's right eye. Ley snatched up his sword with his remaining hand, barely deflecting the blow. But the clone had never intended to land the strike. It grabbed Ley's wrist, ice creeping over his flesh until it turned solid. With a swift elbow and knee combo, the frozen limb shattered.

Ley shrieked, now defenseless. Alduin's next strike landed, slashing through his eye. He carved an X across Ley's chest, then stabbed his hips—shallow thrusts, designed for pain, not death. His blade drove deep into Ley's stomach before raking downward in a long, brutal slash from waist to feet. Blood gushed, soaking his clothes.

Ley convulsed, spewing blood in ragged, choking gasps.

Alduin methodically severed one leg, then the other, sending him crashing to the floor, howling for mercy. He ignored the pleas. Releasing his sword, he placed both hands on Ley's head—and squeezed.

Ley thrashed, cursed, and screamed, desperate to break free. He exhaled a blast of ice in a last, futile attempt to freeze Alduin's grip. It failed. Alduin's fingers crushed deeper, bone cracking, flesh rupturing—until Ley's skull exploded in a geyser of blood and shattered bone. His corpse collapsed, lifeless.

The clone dissolved into a pool of blood. Vaurcarya clattered into the puddle with a metallic ring. Alduin expected to be released from the clone's grasp. He waited. Seconds stretched into minutes. The grip didn't loosen.

Frowning, he turned to face the clone—only to freeze in place. It was staring back at him. It smirked. Ley's corpse melted into blood. The clone laughed.

'You fool. Did you really think you could defeat me that easily?'

Ley summoned a new clone and made it stand in front of them.

'I'm assuming you don't feel pain, so there's no use in torturing you. What should I do with you instead? Hmm... Oh, yes. I have an idea.' Ley's eyes glistened in excitement.

Ley caught Alduin eyeing his sword, likely ready to summon it back and strike. Before he could, Ley ordered his clone to drive a knife into his eyes—again and again. Each time they healed, only for the blade to return.

As Alduin suffered, Ley pulled the spilled blood into seven vast pools. From three, more clones emerged. From another trio, something else took shape—minions. But not just any minions…

'W-What? What are you doing?! Stop!' Alduin's breath hitched, his voice trembling, raw with desperation.

The minions took the form of Alduin's family – Aeden, Elys, Veridia, and even a younger Ley. Hollow-eyed, shambling like the dead, they lurched forward and stopped in a line, two metres from him. Ley laughed, then his three clones drew Elvish hunting knives and began stabbing the minions—throat, chest, limbs—methodical, relentless. Alduin's breath came in short, ragged gasps, his chest heaving as if he were drowning.

'WHAT ARE YOU DOING?! STOP! FATHER. MOTHER. STOP THIS, LEY. STOP!' Alduin screamed, his voice cracking. His chest heaved, breaths sharp and erratic. His hands clutched at his head, fingers digging into his scalp as if trying to ground himself. His legs trembled, barely holding him upright. A choked sob tore from his throat as his vision blurred, dizziness threatening to pull him under.

'Not good enough,' Ley said.

The clone gripped Alduin's chin, forcing him to face the scene. Another clone appeared, holding his eyelids open. Ley commanded the minions to scream in agony, their voices mimicking those of the people they resembled. Each stab was followed by a shriek, identical to Aeden's, Elys's, Veridia's.

Alduin thrashed, kicking and spinning in a desperate attempt to break free, but Ley's grip held firm. His screams grew louder, more frantic, tearing from his lungs in a raw, primal howl.

'Stop!' his bone-chilling scream echoed through the castle.

Ley didn't stop. He summoned more clones, the minions' screams growing louder, more agonising. Alduin felt tears welling up, but they wouldn't come. Sobbing could relieve the crushing weight of anger, grief, and trauma—but it was beyond him.

Hours stretched on, and Alduin, who once believed he could no longer feel mental pain after his time with the Vaermiraiits[ix], was proven wrong. His past, his family, his home—all flashed before him. Ley laughed when he saw the last traces of hope leave Alduin's eyes.

Alduin began to fade, but his uncle kept him conscious with a brutal punch to the face each time he slipped. Hours passed. Ley summoned more clones, torturing Alduin's soul with relentless precision, aiming to shatter his mind.

Desperate, Alduin used blood magic to try to blind himself. He tore out his eyes, but they healed immediately. Ley, sensing Alduin's attempt to escape, grinned. He summoned a massive pool of blood from the city, shaping it into a vision of Alduin as a child, trapped in his cell.

More blood summoned Zera, his tormentors, the vampires who starved and raped him, who drained him of everything. The last of the blood formed scenes of mortals being slaughtered by vampires, each scene a reminder of his trauma.

The weight of it all crashed down. The progress Alduin had made toward inner peace with Hanali crumbled to ash

---

[ix] (Omnitongue) Vampires.

in his subconscious. His sanity, his peace, his happiness—everything was slipping away.

Alduin's pupils vanished, his eyes flickering between pure white and pitch black, glowing with an unholy light. A trance of rage, despair, and misery consumed him. Suddenly, everything around him ignited in the flames of Tyronah[x].

The minions and clones were consumed by Vaonie's fire, vanishing into nothing. Ley, terrified, had never seen the Obliryne u Tyronah[xi] before. Desperate, he locked eyes with Alduin, but the gaze he met was both conscious and empty —pure PTSD[xii].

Ley gathered his strength, but it was clear: nothing would stop Alduin now.

'Alduin, wake up!' He slapped him. It did not work. 'WAKE UP! WAKE UP. YOU MUST WAKE UP, YOU FUCKING BASTARD, PIECE OF SHIT NEPHEW! WAKE UP.' He slapped him, again and again, with the wrath of a god.

Alduin regained consciousness, still trapped in Ley's grasp, who at that point was nothing but a floating torso, arms and head.

He chuckled, 'at least I've removed most of your body. You can't heal these wounds. You'll be crippled forever!'

Ley's face twisted with fury as he spat, 'Fuck you!' His

---

[x] (Omnitongue) Hell.
[xi] (Omnitongue) Flame of Hell.
[xii] Post-Traumatic Stress Disorder.

fists clenched, and his body tensed as if ready to strike, his eyes burning with rage. 'I have had enough of this.'

Ley released Alduin and fell on his back. The last pool of blood surged toward him like a swift current, twisting and reshaping into legs. Alduin leapt back, assessing the situation. Ley had only been toying with him and this fight must end. Alduin grew impatient.

Pressing both hands to the ground, he chanted, willing the sanguine essence to rise. Nothing happened. Then, a tingling sensation shot through his body. The blood glowed orange. He fell to the floor.

'Ha! You fell right into my trap.' Ley said.

The blood vibrated around Alduin, then shifted, forming a triangle. Nearby candles and torches flared violently. His vision blurred, his consciousness slipping away again.

'Did you honestly think I didn't know what you are, my stupid nephew? All this time you avoided my attacks like I was trying to kill you, even though we both know that isn't possible. You are hereby banished. This is my farewell, Alduin. A-' he hiccupped, '-au revoir[xiii], srynaia[xiv]!'

Ley turned back to the painting, wiping sweat from his forehead and sipping his wine.

Alduin drifted, torn from his body as all five of his senses diminished. He lay motionless, breathless. Dead, in technicality. His presence vanished from Vanthea, and every realm known to man.

[xiii] (French) Goodbye.
[xiv] (Elvish) Goodbye.

Hanali felt the sudden shift, his aura gone. Panic surged through her as she teleported to his last known location. Her eyes fixated on the gruesome sight. Alduin's body lay atop a massive banishment seal. A stranger stood a few meters away, unaware of her presence.

'Are you the one who did this to him?!' She yelled.

'Who the fuck are you? What are you doing here?' he turned his face toward her.

'Answer me!'

'Yes. Why? Do you know him?'

She let out a guttural growl before unleashing her wrath, giving him no chance to react. She impaled him with spears made of purple Talismirit[xv], their numbers beyond counting.

'Thank you,' he murmured, barely a whisper, as he coughed up blood.

He died one second later. As his body slumped, a small, book-like object slipped from his pocket, landing beside him in the pooling blood. Hanali dropped to her knees, experiencing a frightening sensation in her chest – total emptiness and intense heaviness at the same time. She felt like an empty cast iron cauldron.

'What is this? What is happening to me?' she whispered, her voice unsteady. Her posture crumbled—shoulders caving in, back hunched, as if the weight of the moment had physically diminished her. She covered her face with trembling hands, curling inward as if trying to disappear. 'Why does it hurt so fucking much?!' she screamed.

[xv] Name of the first element.

CHAPTER FOURTEEN

He woke up in a peculiar monochrome world, stripped of all color—only black, white, and gray remained. He heard nothing but blood curdling shouts, screams, and screeches. Only sounds of panic.

'Where in Munesa[i] am I? Who are these people?' he asked while getting up.

All around him stood panicked individuals. They were sobbing—severely stricken by anxiety. This world was terrifying, as though unfinished. The ground was gray but had an earthish texture.

There were no trees or mountains, it was just one plain surface. The sky was coloured as if someone had drawn it in pastel, like it had never actually existed. Like someone couldn't be arsed to add the concept of color to it.

The moment he got himself up, he heard a voice in his

---

i   (Elvish) Hell.

head. 'Welcome to the shadow realm. Don't try to figure out where I am because this is a prerecorded message prepared for new arrivals,' an unfamiliar voice said. 'Just like you, we found ourselves here with no explanation. Most of us committed suicide, though some chose to stay, to research. Unfortunately, despite our many efforts this realm remains an enigma.

Let me introduce myself. I am Yang Xiong and I was once the head of the school of Alteration in China, of "The Order". As the first mage who arrived here, I took charge of the research department. We have come up with several theories.

The first and most popular one is that people who are caught in banishment magic get sent here. The second is that this realm serves no purpose and that the gods send random mortals here for fun. The third is that this is hell. Optimists would rather tell themselves it is heaven, but I believe that to be nonsense.

During our long time here, we have made a few conclusions. I will share the most important ones. Firstly, you don't age here, and your body will forever look the same.

Secondly, this realm seems to have no end. The horizon just leads to more and more "horizons". I have yet to reach neither a dead-end nor a full circle.

Thirdly, in this seemingly infinite realm you can find an endless number of holes in the ground. Those are probably meant for people who wish to end their lives, as it is quite boring here. There is no wildlife, no nature, neither a sun nor a moon or stars. Just one big flat surface.

Fourthly, all newcomers are summoned exactly at the

same spot you're standing right now. It is probably config-
ured as the spawn point and is about the size of an acre.

The last thing I'd like to say is that if you consider yourself a scholar or knowledgeable, please consider joining our
team. We are stationed in that big castle-looking building on
the horizon.

This message was delivered to you on behalf of the
"Void Research Society."' The voice diminished.

Alduin launched himself up in the air to observe his.
The man in the recording was right. All he could see was
one endless flat surface, full of strange holes every now and
then.

One would think that a hole in the ground would lack
symmetry and be shaped like an imperfect circle or some
other random shape, though these ones were perfect cubes
and all of them were of identical size. He flew toward one
of them to look inside it. Suddenly, he heard voices getting
closer and closer.

'I can't do this anymore, Lilly. I can't! I have had enough
of this place. We can't do anything. I have no job, our children aren't here with us, and we can't even make new ones
for some odd fucking reason. I have had enough,' a man
yelled.

'Please, don't leave me! Without you, I have nothing
here. I have no one. Please don't leave me,' his spouse
replied.

'Join me then.'

'I do not wish to die yet.'

'What life have we here? There is nothing in this place.
We were cast aside by our god. Well fuck them and fuck

their plans. I will not let them play around with my life. Join me, my love,' the man replied.

'I-But... What if... I... I don't know... What if there is an option to start a family here? And even if there isn't a way, why not just start a new one entirely? Why not have hope? I do not want to lose my life at such a young age.'

'Lilly, my love... I have set my mind to it. You've known me for how long exactly?'

'Around thirty years...'

'Yes. Then you know me well enough to understand that once I decide something, it's final... I am sorry to lay out this ultimatum against you, darling, but you leave me no choice. It is either you join me or stay here by yourself. No matter what you pick, remember that I loved, love and will continue loving you.'

'Do you remember what I said in my vows when we got married?' the wife asked.

'Till death do us part?'

'Together till the end.'

A group of approximately fifteen frantic men sprinted toward them and joined in, all so eager to end their own lives. Alduin wanted to stop them but decided he should respect their right to choose. All he could do was witness the tragedy. They jumped in together.

He looked at them, falling into the abyss. The hole looked infinite, like it led to nowhere.

"Imagine an enormous cube-shaped hole that has a pitch-black surface-seeming pit to it."

Their screams grew further and further away but never actually faded completely. Peculiar. He decided to leave and approached a group of people conversing a few kilometers away.

'Hello,' Alduin said.

'Hey,' a woman responded.

'Hello there,' a man responded.

'I just arrived here. Could you explain where we are?'

'No clue, mate. I know nothing more than you already do – what Xiong Yang tells every new person.'

'I see...' Alduin's shoulders sagged slightly, and his gaze dropped to the ground. His lips pressed into a thin line, and the faintest furrow appeared between his brows.

'Where did you come from?' the woman asked.

'Planet Syluetta, Euphata. I am a Snow Elf. What about you?'

'Huh... Never met one of your kind before,' she scratched her head, 'we're from planet Earth, Iran. Pleased to meet you,' she smiled brightly.

'I think you should visit the academy of Xiong Yang. He knows way more than we do,' the man said.

'Alright, I'll do that. Sorry for bothering you.'

'It's all fine. Farewell,' the man responded.

Alduin nodded and turned around.

'Wait. You never introduced yourself,' the woman said.

'Oh yeah, sorry. I am Alduin,' he chuckled.

'Goodbye, Alduin,' she waved her right hand.

He smiled back. He recognized the enormous castle-looking structure on the horizon and flew toward it, waving goodbye to her and the others.

'What a strange man,' a man said.

'Handsome though.'

After an indistinguishable amount of time, he finally reached his destination. A few scholars who were heading inside greeted him at the main gate.

'Excuse me, could you help me out with something?' Alduin asked them.

'Certainly, with what?'

'Could you give me directions to the office of a person named "Xiong Yang"? I wish to speak with him.'

'Oh, the chief. It will be my pleasure. Our paths intertwine for a bit, so just follow us, and I'll tell you when we come closer to it.'

'Thank you,' he nodded.

He followed them inside and through the halls. The walls were filled with paintings of Vanthea, in black and white, of course, yet still letting out a sense of familiarity and peace. Students were seen practicing their magic or reading books in the library. It was like an entirely new school of The Order. A hidden one. Unknown to the outside world, the *real* world.

'Could you tell me a bit about this place?'

'Sure, what would you like to know?' a female scholar asked.

'Everything you could would be great.'

'Hmm... Alright. This is the main headquarters of our research organization.'

'Meaning there are more branches?'

'Yes, and they are well spread out. We aim to find an end to this realm or some answers, at least. That's why we put each branch quite far away from the previous one.'

'I see.'

'This is the first branch and was built long ago by Xiong Yang. When did you arrive here?'

'Not long ago.'

'Were you greeted by our automatic introduction at the spawn point?'

'You mean the telepathically delivered message of Xiong?'

'Yes.'

'Then yes.'

'So that about sums up the basics of what there is to know about where we are right now. Through the years, many mages and scholars arrived and some of them decided to join our organization to further understand the meaning and characteristics of this world.'

'When were you put here?'

'Honestly, we couldn't tell. There is no sun here to tell the time so we can't count days. All I know is that my friend here,' he pointed at the woman, 'came before me, and I came here a lot of time ago.'

'I see.'

The scholars continued explaining about the history of the society. They told him about that which was known, and that which was only assumed. The more popular theories and those that were considered unfounded and irrational. Finally, they stopped in their steps.

'This is us. I wish you good fortune in your journey.'

'Thank you, you too. Where do I proceed from here?'

'See that bald man over there, to your left?'

'Yes, what about him?'

'He is one of the professors and knows the way better than we do. Ask him for assistance.'

'Very well. Thank you.'

'Gladly.'

He raced up the stairs and approached the man. He explained the situation to him and was met with exceptional friendliness. The teacher agreed to escort him to the leader's quarters. While following, Alduin had asked the man many questions, most of which were answered. To some of the questions he had no answer, like what was the real name of this realm, or its initial purpose.

Eventually, they reached their destination. The man shook the hands of Alduin and told him to knock on the door and wait for approval to come inside. Alduin obliged.

'Why is everyone so friendly?' he pondered and then knocked on the door.

'Come in,' a voice said.

He opened the door and saw two people talking. One of them was a bearded man with long hair wearing glasses, sitting in front of his desk and observing a map. He was wearing long white robes with flowers on them, a ring on each finger and his hair fixed by hairbands. It reminded him of his culture's attire. Alduin had never seen a human that looked like him before.

The other was a tall young man with short hair standing on the left and pointed at the map, explaining something. He was wearing a sleeveless leather shirt with a few decorations, a metallic-ish belt, leather pants that started out slim with wide ends, sandals and several metallic arm bracelets.

His aura felt absurdly familiar to Alduin, though he could not comprehend why.

The bearded man raised his head toward Alduin. 'Welcome. Who might you be?'

The tall man stared at Alduin as if analysing him.

'Greetings. I am Alduin Lodus Faëli. Are you Xiong Yang?'

'Yes, I am. What a peculiar middle name you have. Do you know what it means?'

'Yes, it means honor, sir.'

'Fascinating, did your parents give it to you?'

'Not exactly, sir.'

The tall man smiled and approached Alduin. He shook his hand firmly. 'I am Han. Pleased to meet you.'

'The feeling is mutual,' Alduin smiled back, revealing his sharp teeth unintentionally.

Han's brows arched as he observed him but then relaxed and his lips turned up into and easy smile.

Xiong tilted his head toward Alduin. 'Anyway. What are you here for? Do you need anything, boy?'

'Yes, actually. I just arrived here and would like a bit more information than what was provided.'

'Ah, a curious one, I see. Unfortunately, I have not enough time for this right now.'

'Oh?' Alduin frowned.

'Fear not. My deputy here will assist you. Won't you, Han?'

'Yes, sir. I will gladly do so.'

'Very well then. You have your answer. Would that be all?' Xiong said in a pleasant yet dismissive tone.

'Uhm. Yes. Wait, actually, no. I am quite curious as to how you got here. You look powerful.'

'Ah, a fine question indeed. However, I have no valid explanation. All I can recall is going to sleep in my bedchambers and waking up here.'

'Oh. Do you think someone sneaked in your room while you were sleeping and cast a spell on you?'

'That is a possibility, yes.'

Alduin's brow furrowed, and his head tilted slightly to one side. His piercing eyes darted over the scene, narrowing for a moment before widening with a glimmer of curiosity.

'Wait outside for a few minutes until I finish my conversation with Han. He will lead you to his study and explain everything that he knows.'

'Understood. Thank you.'

'Bù kèqì[ii].'

'Hmm?' Alduin asked.

'It means "You're welcome" in my mother tongue,' Xiong said.

Alduin stepped out, closed the door and floated in the air in a sitting position, waiting for their conversation to end. Eventually, it was over. He followed him to his study, a rather marvellous room filled with maps, photo-realistic pictures hung on walls, rugs, books and basically everything you would imagine from a mage's office. Smells of incense and pencil shavings pushed their way into his nose, as though screaming 'This person is interesting.' There were

---

[ii] (Chinese) You're welcome.

two desks, one at the end of the room, probably serving Han, and a long one in the middle of the office, maybe for dinners or debates with other scholars.

Han noticed Alduin's awe and laughed hard. 'Have you never been to a wizard's study before?'

'Well, I've been to Xiong's one, but it looked nothing like yours. I would expect a deputy to have a smaller office than his superior.'

'He believes in minimalism, whereas I believe in pragmatism.'

Alduin approached a bookshelf to the right, his eyes scanning the spines of the books with a mix of curiosity and intent. He reached out, fingers grazing the titles, pausing as he read each one. Some titles sparked recognition, while others were completely foreign to him. The musty scent of aged paper filled the air as he pulled a volume free, its cover worn but still intact.

'May I?' he asked.

'Sure. How long have you been here for?' Han responded.

'I don't know,' he said and flipped through the pages.

'I see. Do you have any questions before we begin?' the smooth, hard wooden floor creaked as Han walked over to sit in a cushy chair and invited Alduin to do the same.

Alduin put the book back and took a swift gander at every painting that adorned the walls. Then, he sat down in front of him. 'Yes, I have a few questions I'd like to begin with.'

'Go on,' Han said, smiling.

'How was this place built? Or any other branch, for that

matter. There are no building materials here, and the ground seems purely cosmetic from what I could tell by its Olon[iii] structure.'

'You know of Olons? That's impressive.'

'A bit, yes. I read about it in the book "Physics of Our Solar System: The Olon".'

Han's eyes glowed in sudden excitement, 'you know, I was the one who wrote that book! Well, Rui and I did, a lot of time ago.'

'What? Really?' Alduin's eyes opened widely in shock.

'Yes. Actually, I am pretty sure I arrived here just when I was trying to uncover something new about them. You see, Rui sent me on an expedition to planet Memrin to research Olons further. We reckoned foreign materials, from a new planet, might help us unravel their mysteries. When I was there, I found a bizarre piece of jewelry,' Han showed Alduin his index finger, it was adorned with a ring.

Alduin's jaw dropped as he observed it. The aura radiating from it reeked of Vaonie's presence. His lips parted slowly, 'where did you find this?' he muttered.

'I don't remember... It gave off this energy that just demanded my attention. It felt otherworldly, cunning, begging me to put it on. It was as though it was speaking to me. Eventually, I gave up and listened to it. That's when everything changed. Suddenly, it seized control of my finger, its metal edge biting deep into my skin as it secured itself. No matter how hard I tried, it refused to be removed. And ever since then...' Han paused and tapped his fingers

---

[iii] (Omnitongue) Particle.

on the table, 'never mind, this isn't what you came here for. Before I answer your question, I have to explain something.'

'I'm listening,' Alduin nodded.

'Do you know of "The Division"?'

'I don't. A division of what?'

'Of people. Of belief. You see, there are two running philosophies in this place. One side states that this realm is just a step in the process toward divine judgement and that to progress, one must die. The other side believes that once you come here you are stuck forever without any chance for peace. Meaning that you're screwed and whether you live or die means nothing.'

'Hmm...' Alduin's fingers stroked his chin gently, 'which side do *you* stand by?'

'To be honest I haven't decided yet, though I lean more toward the first one.'

'Alright,' he said as his eyes scanned the room even further.

'Now, to answer your question. The ones that identify themselves among the latter, decided to dedicate their very existence to our cause. Instead of killing themselves, they give their life to transmutation mages who convert their Olons into resources.'

'That's tragic,' Alduin said, his voice low and resonant. He paused, a shadow crossing his features as he lowered his gaze to the table. After a moment, he lifted his head, his piercing crimson eyes glinting with a mixture of sorrow and respect. 'Though very noble of them,' he continued and straightened his posture.

'I agree. Any other questions?'

'Yes. Sorry for being blunt, but you seem extremely young, maybe even my age. I almost couldn't believe it when he said you were the deputy leader of this organization. How old are you?'

'I'll take that as a compliment!' Han chuckled, 'I am eighteen years of age. You?'

'Almost eighteen.'

'Then you were right in your assumption. However, I've been here for quite a long time, so I am probably much older than you.'

'Can you recall the date on which you found yourself here?' Alduin asked.

'Hmm... Probably somewhere around 344? Maybe?'

'344? We haven't reached that year yet. Maybe you meant 344 BMDW[iv]?' Alduin's brows knitted together as he tilted his head slightly, his pointed ears twitching ever so faintly.

'BMDW? What the hell does that mean?'

'Hmm... The grand war between mortals and demons? A total war in our solar system? Does any of that ring a bell?'

'I truly have no idea what you're talking about,' Han said.

'Huh. How do you count years, then? From what occurrence?'

'Why, The Allfather's birth, of course.'

'The Allfather? You mean the ancestor of all ancestors?'

'Theseus.'

[iv] Before Mortal Demon War.

'Hmm... Yes. I never heard someone call him that though, fascinating. Wait, so, if it's 344 from Theseus's birth... And he was birthed at around 505 BMDW... That means you were put here at around 161 BMDW. That is 1237 human years before I was born!'

'Wow.'

'How old were you when it happened?'

'Well, I was born in 184.'

'Which is 321 BMDW... Wow. You are one hundred and twelve years older than me.'

'Hmm? One hundred and twelve? How did you calculate that? I would say I am almost one hundred and thirty-seven years older than you.'

'Huh? Oh, right! I am a Snow Elf. We count every eleven human years as one year.'

'Oh? Back where I'm from, it's every nine years.'

'Wait, aren't you human?' Alduin exclaimed, his eyes widening with excitement. He leaned forward, his posture shifting as he rested his hands on the table, fingertips pressing into the surface.

'No, I am not.'

'What are you then?'

'I'd rather not talk about it.'

'Ah, well… alright,' he frowned.

'Thank you. So, you're saying that people begin counting their years from this "Mortal Demon War"?'

'Yes.'

'Hmm…' Han's gaze turned toward his bookshelves as he stroked his beard. 'Any more questions?'

'Yes. What is the name of this place?'

'We don't know yet. For now, we simply called it "The Void" or "The Shadow Realm".'

'I see. This will be all, thank you.'

Alduin stood up and headed for the door. Then, he stopped mid-step and turned around. 'Let me try something,' he said.

'Like what?'

Alduin pulled out a ring from his pocket. It was the one Lysander had given him many years ago. 'Los ant di Tyronah[v],' he chanted.

It did not work. He tried three more times, then gave up.

"You should have seen Han's face when he witnessed that. It was incredible, such entertaining confusion!"

'What are you trying to do? Los ant di…' Han repeated the words, 'teleportation magic? What is this Tyronah you mentioned? I never heard of that place.'

Alduin's jaw clenched as the harsh reality sank in. He was trapped, perhaps for eternity. Doubts gnawed at him. Had Hanali forsaken him? Vaonie surely had; his defeat by a mere vampire was unforgivable. His throat tightened, choking back words that wouldn't come. His shoulders slumped, and a dull ache spread through his chest. He clenched his fists, nails digging into his palms as rage bubbled up. His uncle's triumph mocked him, a testament to evil's victory. Alduin's eyes burned, not with tears, but with the bitter sting of failure.

Han decided to change his question as he noticed

---

[v]   (Omnitongue) (To) take me to Hell.

Alduin's odd hand tattoo, 'who are you exactly? What are you?'

'My name is Alduin Lodus Faëli. I told you that already!' he snapped.

'Easy, easy, I was only asking. You did not answer my other question, though. What are you? Don't think that I didn't notice your fangs. Or that weird fashion choice of yours. I have met many Elves in my lifetime, but none of them looked quite like you!'

'Pfft...' Alduin exhaled sharply, his lips curling in a dismissive scoff. He crossed his arms tightly over his chest, shifting his weight from one foot to the other as he glared at him. His brow furrowed, and he tapped his fingers impatiently against his arm.

'Please?' Han's head tilted a bit.

Alduin shrugged dismissively.

'Pretty please?' Han smiled sweetly.

'Alright, alright! I am an Araqhaiit, a divine race that serves Vaonie in their realm. Tyronah[vi]. You probably know it by its mortal nickname – 'Hell'.'

Han raised an eyebrow as though this answer had awoken something in him. 'Who is Vaonie? Are you a god? Is that why you look like a Vaermiraiit[vii]?'

Alduin's eyes glowed in fierce red as his fists clenched, trying to control his rage. 'Don't ever call me that again! I am nothing like those filthy abominations.'

'Alright, alright, I apologize. I am just curious, that's all.'

[vi] (Omnitongue) Hell.

[vii] (Omnitongue) Vampire.

The ferocity of Alduin's eyes diminished as he managed to calm himself down, 'no, no, don't apologize. *I* should be the one to apologize for treating you this way. You have been nothing but friendly. Forgive me.'

'Then all is forgiven,' Han winked, 'now, explain what your divinity means.'

'There are two three types of gods. One is the "First" divinity, also called "The Originals." Those are Vaonie and Austomia, the first gods. Then there is the "Second" divinity, their children, which are split into two groups. Araqhaiits and Sarathiins. I am one of the Araqhaiits, the children that serve Vaonie.'

'Is that why your middle name is a word in the Omnitongue?'

'Yes, how did you know?'

'Just a generic assumption. I know its definition, but what does it mean in your case?'

'Each child was entrusted with a commandment to enforce among mortals. Mine is honor, and I must punish those who forsake it. The gods we follow in Vanthea are nothing but myths.'

Han shrugged. 'I never quite cared for religion. I prefer science,' he said, 'and what is this Vanthea you speak of?'

'The realm in which you and I used to live in, the one of mortals. There are three more: Tyronah – serving as hell, Heonmeyu – the original realm and currently serving as heaven and finally Olana[viii] – the one currently without a purpose.'

[viii] (Omnitongue) Justice.

'Without a purpose? Hmm... Well, we *are* in a realm right now, aren't we? And I take it you've been to the other realms. You obviously don't recognize this place... Doesn't that mean that we are in Olana right now?'

'H-How did I not realize this sooner?' he stuttered in frustration, 'what a fool I am.'

'Woah, take it easy, pal. You just got here, I bet you're still overwhelmed from the shock.'

'Yes, you're right. Thank you.'

Han looked Alduin up and down. 'I have a question I've been quite curious about.'

'What is it?' Alduin asked.

'What happened to you? How did you get here?'

'I...' Alduin's face shot downwards in embarrassment and regret as he exhaled strongly. He paused for a few seconds, sighed and then turned his eyes back to Han. 'I fought a strong Vaermiraiit that managed to seal me away from Vanthea...'

'What? You? How? That's pathetic,' Han appeared disappointed.

'Excuse me?' Alduin uncontrollably revealed his fangs.

'You heard what I said. A god losing to a "filthy abomination", as you called them. It's laughable.'

'You take that back!' he shouted.

'No.'

'Take that back now!' Alduin's eyes glowed again, even stronger this time.

'I will not. And another thing... It's good your parents aren't here. They would have been greatly disappointed... Shameful is what it is,' Han grinned like a proud child.

Alduin roared, unsheathing his blade, poised to strike the jester. But before he could act, his surroundings shifted. He found himself standing alone on the grounds of this realm, stranded and disoriented.

CHAPTER FIFTEEN

Alduin scanned the area, his jaw tight.

'Where are you, coward?' his voice cut through the silence like a blade.

Han appeared a few feet in front of him, a faint smirk tugging at his lips. Before Alduin could react, Han vanished. A light tap on Alduin's shoulder made him spin around, his hand darting to the hilt of his sword. No one was there. Again, and again, Han's presence teased him—always out of reach.

Alduin's fists clenched at his sides, his knuckles whitening. His breaths grew heavier, each one sharper than the last. A vein pulsed at his temple. His patience was fraying.

Then, Han reappeared five meters away, as if nothing had happened. He set down a chair with deliberate ease, sat back, and opened a book. Without sparing Alduin a glance, he began to read, unbothered. was nowhere to be seen and Alduin was oblivious.

'Stop playing games!' Alduin shouted.

'It's not my fault you're so incompetent,' Han replied.

Fury blazed in Alduin's eyes. Enough games. He summoned Vaurcarya, the blade humming with power. Han remained seated, unfazed. Alduin lunged. Slash. Thrust. Swipe. Han's movements were fluid, effortless. A slight tilt of the head. A lean to the left. A subtle shift of the shoulders. Each dodge precise, minimal. His eyes never left the page. The elf's attacks grew wilder, more desperate. Vaurcarya whistled through the air. Han's chair teetered on two legs, avoiding the blade by a hair's breadth.

Alduin roared in frustration. Sweat beaded on his brow. His chest heaved. Han turned a page, nonchalant. The absurdity peaked. Han, still reading, leapt into the air. Cross-legged. Floating. Untouchable. Alduin's sword arm trembled. Disbelief etched across his face.

The book hurtled through the air, arrow-swift. Alduin snatched it mid-flight, inches from his face. 'How to Befriend an Elf,' the title mocked. He flung it aside, eyes snapping back to his opponent.

Han sprang from his chair, fists raised. 'It's time to duel.'

Alduin's brow furrowed. 'What the fuck are you doing?'

'Taking this incredibly seriously.' Han shifted stances, each more bizarre than the last. 'I learned these from my master, Xiong Yang.' Kicks. Punches. Monkey screeches. 'Hyah! Hwooa! Hai-ya!'

Alduin's chest heaved, frustration boiling over. A deep sigh escaped him as he lowered his gaze, struggling to contain his rage.

Han's antics continued. Flailing limbs. Exaggerated poses. Then, abruptly, his demeanour shifted.

'Can you fucking sto-?' Alduin began but was suddenly silenced.

Han shifted his stance. Right leg back. Fist ready. He launched forward like a bolt, closing the gap in an instant. His punch connected, and he flipped back effortlessly.

Alduin's body exploded. Flesh and organs splattered across the ground. Only his head remained intact.

'You say I don't take this seriously,' Han said, brushing off his hands. 'Yet look how quickly I took you down.'

Alduin sighed, slow and measured. His body began to reform, muscle and bone knitting together in seconds. When he stood again, his expression was cold, serious.

Han raised an eyebrow, intrigued. 'Impressive. Alright, I'll give you a chance to make this fun. Come at me. I won't move until you strike.'

Alduin's glare deepened as he stepped forward, blade floating at his side. His movements were slow, deliberate, each step radiating menace. When he stopped a meter away, Han struck another exaggerated stance and waved him forward with a smirk.

'No weapon?' Alduin asked.

'None,' Han said, kissing his fists.

'Then I won't use mine either.'

'Why?'

'I fight fair.'

'Fine,' Han muttered. 'Do you mind if I take it?'

'Huh?' Alduin turned his eyes at Vaurcarya.

It was gone. Han held the sword now, grinning—until it

burned into his palm. He dropped it instantly. 'What the fuck?! This thing is eating my hand!'

He held up his scorched hand, blood dripping from the imprint of the handle. Muttering an unfamiliar chant, Han pressed his hands together. When he opened them again, the wound was gone.

Without missing a beat, Han stomped on Vaurcarya's hilt, launching it into the air before kicking it far into the distance. He turned back to Alduin with a cocky grin.

Both assumed their stances again. The air between them crackled with tension. The fight was far from over.

'Let's go,' Han said.

Alduin nodded. Both fighters assumed their stances, right legs back. They charged, fists ready.

Alduin leapt, front-flipping for a heel kick. Han dodged left, countering with a right hook. Alduin's guard absorbed the blow, but he skidded back meters. Undeterred, he sprinted forward. Jab, cross, jab, cross. Han weaved through each punch effortlessly.

Han vanished, grinning. Alduin soared upward, scanning for his opponent. Nothing. Han's aura was everywhere and nowhere.

Alduin descended, baiting a reaction. It worked. Han materialized, unleashing a flurry of kicks from all angles. Alduin dodged, landing a solid punch to Han's face. Blood trickled from Han's nose as he retreated. He smirked and disappeared, reappearing instantly in front of Alduin. A barrage of strikes followed. Hooks, uppercuts, spinning kicks. Alduin, overwhelmed, raised his guard. A swift kick exploded Alduin's hands. Han capitalized with an upper-cut, launching Alduin skyward.

Han built momentum, leaping for a bicycle kick. Alduin crashed to the ground. He regenerated, calling Vaurcarya. He severed his hands, summoning blood clones. Han went berserk, demolishing each clone with boulder-shattering punches. His speed was unmatched.

Alduin, buying time, began casting. 'Death of the Ice Giant, I call you!' he shouted, airborne.

Snowy mist swirled. Blood rose from the ground, alive. Han retreated and ran in circles, aiming to use the immense kinetic energy as a shield. A storm of snow and blood erupted. Ferocious, raging, terrifying. Han outran it, reappearing before Alduin in an instant. Alduin sighed.

Han unleashed a dizzying array of attacks. Backflips, twenty-punch combos, spinning kicks. Alduin's body shattered and reformed repeatedly.

Desperate, Alduin activated his tattoo. His flesh melted, skin turning pitch black. He collapsed, transforming into a monstrous form radiating killer intent.

Han froze momentarily, then resumed evasive manoeuvres. He dodged relentlessly, avoiding contact with Alduin's eyes.

The fight dragged on until Alduin, exhausted, reverted to normal. He regained consciousness and his eyes glowed in monstrous fierceness. He called his sword back.

'Stop!' Han thundered, his hand raised high.

Alduin halted, honor-bound. 'Why are we stopping?'

Han sighed, shoulders slumping. 'This fight is endless. You're immortal, I'm too fast. It's pointless.'

Alduin's brow furrowed. *You* provoked this fight. Explain.'

'I'm tired of this realm,' Han said, his eyes distant. 'I hoped you could end my misery.'

Alduin's face contorted in disbelief. Munesa[i]! A fight against a god for that?! Why not end yourself?'

'I can't,' Han's voice was low. 'Not mentally. I come from a race of warriors. Suicide is disgraceful in our culture.'

Alduin's expression softened slightly. 'Where are you from?'

'I'm a Merarian from the ocean of Xierēnia.'

Alduin's eyes widened. 'A Merarian? How curious, I've never met any of your people.'

'Yes, becau—' Han began, but Alduin cut him off.

'Yes, I just remembered "The Great Alchemical Slaughter". I apologize for bringing it up. This must trouble you greatly...'

Han's brow furrowed. 'Wait, what? I was about to say my race rarely leaves Xierēnia. Explain!'

Alduin's eyes widened. 'Oh no... It happened in 109 BDMW, about seventy years after you arrived here.'

'Go on,' Han pressed, his jaw tightening.

Alduin exhaled heavily. 'Your ancestor Mitori conducted large-scale alchemy, sacrificing all Merarians as materials.'

Han's face crumpled, his shoulders sagging as if bearing an immense weight. 'But... Everyone...' His voice cracked, barely above a whisper.

------

i   (Elvish) Hell.

'I'm truly sorry,' Alduin said softly, his own voice thick with empathy.

Han's knees buckled, and he collapsed to the floor. His body shook with violent sobs, each one tearing from his throat like a primal scream of loss. Tears streamed down his face, dripping onto the ground beneath him. His fingers clawed at the earth, as if trying to grasp onto something, anything, to anchor him in this moment of overwhelming grief.

Alduin knelt beside him, placing a gentle hand on Han's trembling back. His eyes softened, a flicker of shared pain crossing his features. He understood Han's anguish all too well.

'Han,' Alduin said gently, his voice thick with empathy, 'I know the pain you're feeling. My clan, my family... they were all slaughtered too.'

Han looked up, his tear-stained face a mixture of surprise and sorrow. 'W-What?'

Alduin continued, 'The grief... it's overwhelming. Like a void that threatens to consume you. But you're not alone in this.' He placed a hand on Han's shoulder, a gesture of solidarity. 'Our people may be gone, but their memory lives on through us. We carry their legacy, their stories. It's a heavy burden, but it's also a gift.'

Han's breathing steadied slightly, his eyes fixed on Alduin.

'In time,' Alduin said softly, 'the pain will dull. It never truly leaves, but you learn to live with it. To honor them by living.'

Han nodded slowly, a glimmer of understanding in his

eyes. 'Continue,' he said, his voice hoarse and barely audible, 'you were saying something.'

'Are you sure?'

'Please...' Han whispered.

I was saying I've never met a Merarian before, though my uncle had once met one of your kind, an adventurer that was supposed to be king.'

Han's eyes narrowed. 'Wait... You're a Snow Elf, right? Was your uncle named Lial?'

'No, his name is Ley.'

Han's eyes sparkled from excitement and nostalgia, as if he had forgotten about the tragedy that had befallen his people. 'Ley... oh, that's right! I remember travelling with a talented, drunken Snow Elf named Ley. He was a great friend of mine.'

'But this cannot be... My uncle said he travelled with a man named *Thaxiobos*, not *Han*.'

'Oh, right. My given name is Thaxiobos, but I go by Han now.'

Alduin's jaw dropped.

'How is he? He was family to me.'

Alduin's posture sagged, his expression falling. The silence spoke volumes.

'Has he... passed away?' Han asked softly.

'No, it's... complicated. I'd rather not share.'

'You don't have to,' Han said, his smile understanding.

Alduin's shoulders tensed. 'He hurt me deeply.'

'I see. It's your story to tell. I'll wait,' Han reassured.

'Thank you,' Alduin's focus scattered, getting lost in

thought. Then, his eyes turned back to Han, 'could you share some stories about your time together? '

'A few. Do you have the time?' Han's eyes twinkled.

Alduin rolled his eyes childishly.

'Kidding! Let me tell you about the time Ley and I joined the giants' civil war.'

'Go on.'

Han leaned forward, his eyes bright with nostalgia. 'During my time on Earth, I heard of a grand arena in the land of giants. It housed the strongest fighters on the planet. I couldn't resist.'

Alduin's brow furrowed. 'But weren't you meant to reign over your race? Why seek money?'

'Ah,' Han's smile turned wistful. 'It was because of the "Battle of Kings".'

'What's that?'

Han's posture straightened, his voice taking on a reverent tone. 'Our most important event. Every decade, Xierēnia's nobility gathered for a clash of swords and wits. The winner became the new king. Despite my intellect, my strength was lacking. My parents urged me to gain power quickly.'

Alduin nodded, understanding dawning on his face. 'So, you left home to train.'

'Exactly,' Han continued, his gaze distant. 'I journeyed to the Ice Giants' region, following rumors of the arena. As night fell, I sought refuge in a tavern.'

Alduin's eyes narrowed. 'Strange. I've never heard of this allegedly famous arena in giant territory.'

'Huh... ' Han shrugged, 'well, in my time, it went by the

name of "The Crystal Arena". Although, it wasn't very "crystally" when I think about it.'

'Oh, I *have* heard of it! My father loved telling me of the epic battles that ensued in the ring. I was always so curious about the glory of the gladiators.'

'Entering the inn, I was greeted by old giants shouting, "Welcome to the Drunken Giant, friend!" They raised massive mugs, gulping and slamming them on an enormous table. The innkeeper approached. I ordered their finest drink – a strong blend of wine and blueberries. "Here for the grand finale?" he asked. I shook my head, explaining I was there to fight. He laughed, eyeing me sceptically. "See this?" he said, tapping his wooden arm engraved with "Wolf." His voice turned gruff, "I, too, was an adventurer until a bandit's sword found my arm!" I smiled politely, retreating to a table my size, grateful for the rest.'

Alduin leaned forward, intrigued. 'How do you recall such detail?'

Han tapped his temple, grinning. 'Childhood memory training. I remember the essence and recreate it. It's not verbatim, but close enough.'

Alduin's brow furrowed. 'What do you mean by "a table that matched my size" or "massive" table?'

Han's eyes lit up, his hands gesturing enthusiastically. 'The inn had furniture for both humans and giants. Just meters away, a giant sat at a table twice my height. His fork was as big as my leg!'

Alduin's jaw dropped, his eyes widening as he imagined the scene. A wistful smile tugged at his lips, memories of adventures with his uncle flooding back, before they turned sour.

Han leaned forward, 'as I sipped my drink, an Elf approached. "Hello there! You seem foreign. Rather tiny by their standards," he chuckled. "I'm Ley." I invited him to join me. He described himself as an adventurer, driven from his dull homeland in search of new experiences.'

Alduin's jaw clenched, muttering angrily under his breath, 'dull, huh?'

Han continued, 'I shared my plans to join the arena. Ley's eyes lit up, "The strongest foes, coin, women, and mead!"'

'Sounds like him...' Alduin frowned.

'Ley advised me on local cuisine, warning that Giants were sensitive about meat consumption. He recommended me to order "Ktema" – a local specialty made from locally grown vegetables and potatoes of different varieties. We talked for hours before parting.

At sunrise, we set off for the arena, swapping stories along the way. When we finally arrived, we heard a giant shouting, "tickets! Tickets for the grand finale, buy them before they run out!" Ley asked him for directions to register ourselves as fighters. We passed the entry exams with ease and got accepted. Fighting in the ring was an experience of no other. We fought fighters ranging from giants, to humans, to beasts! I have never witnessed such an incredible array of powerful foes. Ley and I quickly stacked up on wins and earned a new nickname, "The Cold-Blooded Champions."

Months later, Ley approached me, excitement radiating

from him. He thrust a poster in my hands: "Mercenary? Join us in the civil war for freedom!" His eyes gleamed as he said, "what do you say? This opportunity is *new* and *exciting*. I love both of those things!"'

'Fucking Dunbar[ii]...' Alduin murmured in angry gibberish.

'Dunbar?'

'Forget it. Continue please.'

'I told him to give me a day to think about it, and then I joined him.'

'Why?'

'Curiosity, I guess?' Han shrugged, 'Ley was a fascinating individual, and we've become close friends by then.'

'What caused the civil war? Giants are known for their friendliness and pacifism. That's what my father told me, at least.'

Han's expression darkened as he spoke, his voice low and somber. 'The civil war erupted over succession. Two twin princes, equally liked but with opposing views, vied for the throne. The main conflict? Meat consumption.'

Alduin's brow furrowed. 'All this over food?'

'It was their culture,' Han sighed, his eyes distant. 'Giants living in harsh conditions, like the Ice Giants for example, wanted to allow animal consumption. Forest Giants vehemently opposed. The debate escalated beyond reason.' Han's hands clenched as he continued, 'Borders filled with rotting bodies. Childhood friends murdered each other in streets. Families slaughtered kin. Famine drove

---

[ii] (Elvish) Asshole.

some to cannibalism. The only animals I've seen were the worms that fed on the corpses.'

Alduin leaned back, his face a mix of disgust and disbelief. 'Wait. No fauna at all?'

'All animals died mysteriously long ago,' Han explained, his tone grim. 'Giants, being vegan, didn't intervene. Now, no trace remains.'

Alduin shook his head, a wry smile on his lips.

Han's eyes grew distant, 'and just when you thought it couldn't get any worse, a plague spread like wildfire. Hospitals overflowed, forcing operations onto the streets. Villages vanished. Cities crumbled. Orphans, skin and bones, scavenged for scraps. The suffering seemed endless, all for naught.'

Alduin's head tilted slightly, his brows furrowed. 'For nothing? Surely one side prevailed?'

'Both brothers perished – battle or plague, no one knows,' Han sighed, shoulders slumping. 'I deeply regret my part. It shrouded my dreams in darkness.'

Alduin's fists clenched, his voice rising and his eyes piercing like scarlet blades. 'So fucking stupid! Such carnage for a mere throne. I despise politics. I never asked to be a clan leader's son. A simpler life would've sufficed.'

'As the son of Xierēnia's king, I understand,' Han said softly, meeting Alduin's gaze.

'I... I suppose you do,' Alduin murmured, tension easing from his shoulders. His eyes calmed.

Han shared more tales of his adventures with Ley – treasure-filled caves, exotic cultures, and linguistic discoveries.

Mid-story, Alduin's consciousness faded. He awoke to a warm embrace, the air fragrant with vanilla and clove.

CHAPTER SIXTEEN

Alduin found himself lying on the floor, his head resting on someone's lap. They were caressing his hair. His vision was blurry at first, but he quickly regained his senses.

'Wha-What? H-Hanali?' his eyes were wide open, staring directly into her own.

'Oh, you're back!' Tears dropped down her cheeks.

'You… didn't give up on me?' he asked softly.

'I would never do that. I've been sitting here all this time, waiting for you to return from Olana[i],' she smiled.

'So, Han *was* right…' He muttered.

'Who?'

'Never mind… I am thrilled to see you again,' his eyes sparkled.

'M-Me too…'

---

[i] (Omnitongue) Justice.

He slowly propped himself up to embrace her.

Suddenly, his jaw dropped, 'what happened to you? Who did this to you?!'

'Oh... It was me...' She turned her gaze to the side, embarrassed.

'What do you mean?' his head titled a bit.

'Vaonie was infuriated by your genocide against the vampires, especially since you ended up losing. I sacrificed my right arm and leg to persuade them to overlook it as a personal favor.'

'What?! You did that... for me? I am so sorry. I am so, so sorry,' his eyes shone with moisture as his face turned sour, 'I beg you to forgive me, I never intended for you to take the blame.'

'It is alright, I've already found an alternative,' she giggled.

Prosthetics replaced her right arm and leg, perfectly mimicking the original limbs. They glowed purple, semi-transparent, with a texture resembling a star-lit night sky. Made of pure Talismirit, they inherited the hue of her position on the 'Cosmic-Purity Scale'.

'I-I see...' He stuttered, his head overflown with feelings of guilt. Then, his eyes glowed ferociously, 'this means I get a second chance to kill that bastard. Where is he?!'

'Where is who?'

'The vampire that was here.'

'Oh, him? I killed him.'

'What? What the hell did you do that for?!' His fists clenched in anger and regret, guilt and relief. His mind was overwhelmed by contradicting emotions.

Her brows furrowed, 'I-I thought it would make you happy... It's finally over, now your life can continue.'

He sighed, 'that's not how it works, Hanali!'

'What do you mean?'

'Forget it...'

'Come on, tell me.'

'What's the point? You would never understand it.'

Her voice turned serious and sharp, 'you're being rude and ungrateful. I did it for you.'

His gaze went downwards, 'it's... You made it impossible to avenge my parents, to come full circle. The burden of regret will continue haunting for eternity. This must be the price of immortality...' He breathed heavily.

'I didn't know... I'm sorry.'

'Don't apologize, I will be fine. me for the way I acted,' his voice lowered, 'can we go, please? This place makes me uncomfortable.'

She nodded, 'yes, let's head out.'

On their way out, Alduin noticed a small book that lay on the floor next to his uncle's corpse. It was begging to be opened. He crouched to grab it. It read:

'

...

4th of Inoren, 348

Dire news today. Encountered Juvel, the town crier, on my morning walk. Usually, I ignore him or toss coins to silence him. Today was different. He refused my coin, insisting on an announcement of grave import. I listened. Blessed are the ignorant...

Juvel spoke of rumors from planet Memrin: a black sphere engulfed a city, then vanished with it. For you, my imaginary confidant, this may seem trivial. For me, it's devastating. The man I loved journeyed there for research. The first and last to stir my heart. None other than Thaxiobos.

In my culture, love between men is shameful. Meaningless liaisons are merely discouraged, not forbidden. Families require both a mother and a father, after all. Perhaps I was simply craven.

My deepest regret: lacking the courage to discover if he reciprocated. I am despondent, feeling wretched. Ask anyone of Ley Faëli, they'll speak of a forthright, blunt soul. Why couldn't I confess? Now it's too late for love to grace the doorstep of this notorious rake.

Perhaps it would be wiser for me to indulge in fleeting dalliances. Indeed, women are easier to beguile – status and honeyed words suffice. And coin, coin works well in that regard (as with all regards, to be honest).

Oh, who am I kidding? I loved you, Thaxiobos. More than you could fathom.

...

1st of Jien, 350

I have decided to take matters into my own hands. Part of my New Year's resolution, I guess... A man of my prestige and glory cannot give up this easily. I shall devote my life to mastering every aspect of magic that I know of. This will take some time but so be it. Mark my words. I. WILL. GET. THAXIO-BOS. BACK.

...

12th of Mitoren, 2 MDW

I finally mastered the last spell known to me, "Refraction". An Illusion spell I learned during my travels with my beloved Thaxiobos, may M'falnar rest his soul. In short, it turns me invisible. There is nothing more for me to practice, though my skill in the art of Conjuration is severely lacking.

...

14th of Mitoren, 2 MDW

I decided to set off on a quest to the nearest altar of the Order. I shall ask them for further knowledge. Wish me good fortune. I will set sail at dawn tomorrow. I wonder what they have in store for me. I heard The Order was established by my ancestors. Would they have a higher motivation to aid Elves?

...

15th of Mitoren, 2 MDW

I began my journey today. The waters are diffi-cult yet manageable. I hope to arrive soon. This trip is supposed to take a few days, approximately nine. I decided to sail alone this time, my crew shan't bear witness to my desperation. I will see to this matter myself. I am heading for a region named "Kontarah". It is supposed to be occupied by humans and Wood Elves.

Peculiar people those are. Cannibalistic, more barbaric than we are. They live on top of trees and possess ancient knowledge of nature magic. They can bend plants to their will. Not via telekinesis, however. No, they simply order the trees to grow and move in a certain direction.

Like they have a special connection, or a proxy of sorts—an envoy. I once stayed with a tribe of them a few years back, in the land of "Brasid" – the land of the Dwarves. The ones in Kontarah are considered even wilder, though. Time will tell.

...

17th of Mitoren, 2 MDW

A tempest assailed my vessel today. I live, though I know not why. Rain pounded, wind lashed, waves thrashed. Myriad typhoons churned the sea, vortexes threatening to devour my ship whole. I steered fran-tically, port and starboard, narrowly evading doom.

One colossal cyclone, brimming with fury, forced a drastic course change. My journey shall be delayed.

As I navigated these perils, a monstrous tiger octopus emerged. Vast as five houses, tall as two, its gray fur, striped, black like its namesake. Green eyes glowed with menace. Terror gripped me as its tentacles lashed out, splintering my ship's hull. One mighty limb seized my leg, tearing it asunder.

I summoned my courage and unleashed a deafening blast of sound magic. The beast recoiled, releasing me from its grasp. As it retreated, I swiftly employed restoration magic to reattach my severed limb.

Though battered and shaken, I endure. The sea's dangers are many, but my resolve remains unbroken.

...

21st of Mitoren, 2 MDW

Navigation magic guided me true, returning me to my charted course. Perhaps this twist of fate shall hasten my journey.

...

22nd of Mitoren, 2 MDW

A wondrous creature graced my voyage today — a dolphin with three powerful tails and a unicorn's horn. I hereby name it a "Uniphin". Yes, I am quite aware of the artistic genius that I am. For some reason, it spoke our tongue and shared knowledge of a swifter route to my destination. I expect to make landfall in two days hence. May the lights of Merissa and Lune guide me true.

...

24th of Mitoren, 2 MDW

It is nearing nighttime, but I bear exciting news: I see land, finally. I will certainly arrive tomorrow. Once I do, I will purchase a steed from one of the stables and ride north—one last trip of a day or two.

...

25th of Mitoren, 2 MDW

I am here, Kontarah awaits. I got myself a beautiful black horse. I was told it's quite quick on its feet; we'll see about that. In the worst case, I'll improve its velocity with gravity magic. I have high hopes for this one.

...

I decided to delay my trip a bit because I met quite an interesting woman in the harbour. Her name is Lul. She's quite fierce, and her glowing eyes only add to my point. I will spend the night with her, and then we'll see how she turns out.

...

Lul was excited to learn I was a powerful mage. She told me about her love for Destruction magic. I promised to teach her a bit. She also holds a fascination for Vaonical magic and the Vaonical races. She claimed they are the only ones capable of wielding it with without repercussions. I personally believe it is nothing but a Dwarf's burp.

...

27th of Mitoren, 2 MDW
A perilous encounter marred our morning practice. As I accidentally brushed against a thorny branch, blood flowed, and her eyes glowed red. She pounced, intent on draining me dry. I suspect she is a Vaermiraiit, a creature I've never encountered before. Her fascination with Vaonical magic now makes sense. I repelled her with ice magic, but not before she revealed the location of her cult – surprisingly, in Euphata, my homeland. I shall depart for The Order at dawn. I'm getting closer, Thaxiobos.

...

30th of Mitoren, 2 MDW
Upon reaching the altar, I was transported to the grand headquarters of this esteemed organization. There, I beheld a multitude of scholars, students, and professors – all mages. I foresee a most enriching tenure here

...

I sought out one of the learned professors and laid my circumstances before him. His curiosity was piqued, and he proposed a test of my knowledge and prowess. I acquitted myself well enough to earn an audience with the high-ranking officials of The Order, which shall take place in two days' time. May fortune smile upon me.

...

I have encountered women unlike any I have known. Powerful, zealous, and intelligent, they are a marvel. Among them, I met Alessia Alteiri, a woman of captivating presence. She guided me through the premises and then we sat beneath the open sky to converse. I find myself drawn to her.

...

Don't be angry with me, Thaxiobos, I beg of you. You know it's difficult for me to control myself...

...

1st of Jien, 2 MDW
Upon the eve of the New Year, Alessia and I strolled through the nearby villages, where her dancing proved a wondrous sight. I wonder what she would think of my advances.

By a lake's tranquil shore, she shared with me

the tale of her past — her introduction to the mystical arts and her time as a slave.

Her story, though fraught with hardship, held a certain allure. Her fair countenance seems ill-suited to the trials she endured. She showed me the scars that mar her skin, a great gash upon her back among them.

Who would dare to bruise such an attractive figure?

...

The festivities here differ greatly from our customs. Though they imbibe heartily, none know of Yasa. I yearn for its silken texture and fragrance. Thaxiobos, I recall your disdain for it, yet now it serves only to evoke your memory. Alessia, too, knows not of Yasa. I must acquaint her with it. Despite its absence, I found myself thoroughly intoxicated and merry.

Curiously, Alessia insisted on procuring my liba-tions. Perhaps it is a sign of her favor? The sum she spent—over eighty Samarices—rivals the cost of two cows and three fowl in most markets. I dare hope this gesture bears meaning.

...

2nd of Jien, 2 MDW
Alessia rejected my advances today. Our shared

moments were naught but friendly gestures. We embraced, and I departed for my meeting with the Order's leaders.

...

The council received me well, impressed by my knowledge of the magical arts. I even met my ancestor, Rui. He shook my hand and called me "One of great potential". I am to study under the masters of each school, a most fortuitous opportunity. Teleportation shrines shall ease my travels betwixt academies.

I commence with the school of "Provision"—healing, enchantment, and runic lore. It is the art of bestowing Olons upon oneself or others.

...

4th of Jien, 2 MDW

On this day, I encountered Ms. Eliana Vundrael, head of the School of Provision and a High Elf. I have never met her kind, as they don't allow foreigners in their cities. We converse in Elvish. Her speech was melodious, with peculiar pronunciations and unfamiliar idioms.

Nevertheless, we understand each other. She gave me a tour of the school and showed me to my dormitories. Did I try to flirt? Of course... I failed, however, as she is a married woman. I shan't try again, for I need her. Maybe this will be the one that could get him back.

...

5th of Jien, 2 MDW

Eliana declared the coming week shall be devoted to assessing my prowess. I must excel to advance my studies. Failure would condemn me to learn among novices, or worse, be instructed by one. Such a fate I cannot abide.

...

13th of Jien, 2 MDW

I neglected my quill yesterday, consumed by training with Eliana. She deems me proficient in expert-tier spells, with but thirty more to master. This task shall span centuries. I must now seek acquaintance with fellow experts, for companionship is crucial in these hallowed halls of learning. Who knows, perhaps I'll manage to bed a few of them. Healer mages are insanely attractive after all.

...

6th of Ruyen, 249 MDW

On this day, I graduated from the Provision School with Eliana's blessing. A grand ceremony marked the occasion. Tomorrow, I journey to the School of "Alteration".

My reputation at the academy grew formidable.

Students, particularly the ladies, knew well the name "Ley Faëli". I became known as an oddity—often inebriated yet capable and wise. Such renown pleases me greatly. Perhaps I shall take disciples.

Of all spells learned, "Rehabilitation" intrigues me most. It fully regrows limbs at a great cost of Olons. I mastered weapon enchantment as well, imagine the possibilities. A sword that heals that which it cuts. It's so ridiculous that it might just be glorious!

Unfortunately, this school offered no knowledge to retrieve him. I shan't give up.

...

7th of Ruyen, 249 MDW

I journeyed to the distant continent where Thaxiobos and I first met, now home to the "Alteration" School. Rodnar Keffes, a giant, leads this academy. While Provision bestows Olons, Alteration reshapes their structure and purpose.

This art encompasses Conjuration, Enhancement, and Transmutation. I eagerly await the master-tier spells unique to this discipline. The school's breadth intrigues me, spanning from bodily augmentation to alchemical transmutation.

Memories of Thaxiobos linger in these familiar lands, stirring both joy and sorrow. Yet I press on, for knowledge may yet lead me to him.

...

18th of Naruyen, 346 MDW

Of all the Alteration School's arts, conjuration alone captivates me. The craft of replicating subjects using existing Olons—be they mortals or objects—demands profound concentration. How does one fathom the intricate structure of a humanoid to replicate it?

I confessed my disinterest in other sub-schools to Rodnar. He directed me to a figure of legend, whom I shall meet on the morrow. Perhaps the solution lies in summoning a copy of him?

...

19th of Naruyen, 346 MDW

I met him – a peculiar, bearded man named Martin Segra. He was thin and wore long dark blue robes that covered his entire body. Unversed in this art, I must heed his words with great attention.

...

7th of Luyaren, 367 MDW

Martin Segra unveiled the true nature of Conjuration, dispelling my misconceptions. The art lies not in summoning, but in transformation. One employs spare Olons, altering their structure and activation to mimic a desired subject. To conjure a sword, for instance, one must replicate its entire "Olon code". Nothing is added; all is merely changed. This revelation illuminates conjuration's place within the alteration school. My understanding grows, yet the path to mastery remains long.

...

28th of Yaruven, 380 MDW

Today, I gained insight into the mysteries of Olons. Each bears signs that form a sort of rune, comprising layers known as activations: Physical, Life, Spirit, and Mind. All things possess the physical layer, while inanimate objects are bound solely to it. Beasts, in turn, have both physical and life activations. Those with consciousness add the mind layer, and mortals possess all four.

One who lacks a particular activation cannot perceive or touch entities that possess only that activation. The more skilled one becomes in conjuration and magic, the stronger and more precise the summons.

I chanced upon the tale of Xiong Yang, a former head of Alteration, whose disappearance occurred many years ago. Rumors speak of kidnapping and assassination. How could such a powerful figure be overthrown? He was seen attending his duties one day, only to vanish the next. This enigma has piqued my interest. Perhaps I should try to find him.

...

30th of Yaruven, 380 MDW

On this day, I gained knowledge of conjuration's workings. Upon the caster's demise, summoned objects vanish forthwith. This revelation stirred my curiosity about "Blood Conjuration", a Vaonical art beyond the reach of common folk.

Martin spoke of this school's power to sever summoned objects from their creator, birthing independent entities with minds of their own. Such practice defies the first law of Alchemy — equivalent exchange. It challenges the very notion that naught can be truly created, only transformed.

Does our world truly permit the creation of the new through magic? A wondrous yet terrifying prospect! I shall reserve this knowledge as a final recourse, should all else fail in my quest.

The implications of such power weigh heavily upon my mind. To create life, to play at godhood — these are dangerous waters indeed. Yet the allure of such knowledge proves difficult to resist.

...

15th of Naruyen, 673 MDW

Today, I completed my studies at the School of Manipulation, mastering the arts of Telekinesis, Illusion, and Telepathy. I was granted the rare privilege of learning from Theseus, son of Cyrus, the most ancient of our ancestors. My knowledge of Snow Elf magic has grown vastly, and I now possess the power to meld Pyromancy with Cryomancy.

In my pursuit of this arcane fusion, I birthed a new spell: "Whitefire". This enchantment combines flame and snow, inflicting both frostbite and burns upon its target. The potency of such magic fills me with wonder and trepidation. Simply astonishing.

...

2nd of Inoren, 1181 MDW

On this day, I have completed my studies at the School of Exploitation. Though brief, the experience was most enlightening. Time and gravity control fascinate me greatly, yet even the school's head lacks true mastery. The school, being newly established, offers naught but theoretical knowledge.

Some claim this art exploits the realm's physics, digging through loopholes in its logic – a notion I find blasphemous. Our gods, in their perfection, surely created no imperfect realm. I prefer to view it as using the world to one's advantage.

I have now graduated from all six schools of magic: Provision, Alteration, Manipulation, Extraction, and Exploitation. My favoured arts include the Rehabilitation spell, Conjuration, the Whitefire spell, passive Olon absorption, and Exploitation.

My renown surely spreads across the land. I imagine my brother, that prideful fool, consumed with envy. He knows nothing of the world beyond our village. I shall make him rue his lack of curiosity.

...

Yet I must not let fame cloud my purpose. Forgive me, Thaxiobos. I shall return to my true quest, assessing my new powers and crafting spells that may bring you back.

...

2nd of Sakuyen, 1185 MDW

Munesa! My efforts prove fruitless. The Order's teachings have yielded naught but disappointment. Conjuration summons only grotesque facsimiles or abominations. Navigation magic fails to locate or transport his mortal remains. It is as if he were struck from this realm entirely.

No other school of magic shows promise. Exploitation magic, though poorly understood, remains my sole hope. Time grows short. I shall attempt a few more arcane tricks, yet I must soon acknowledge defeat and seek aid elsewhere.

My heart grows heavy with each failed endeavour. The path to reunite with him grows ever more treacherous. Yet I must persevere, lest all be for nothing.

...

22nd of Kabuyen, 1187 MDW

Out of deep desperation I decided to try Vaonical magic. How bad could it be? I am certain the restrictions Lul told me about were nothing but bluffs, told to her by the Vampire grandmasters. I will read every book in my possession to come up with an idea for a spell. I will get you back in no time!

...

1st of Inoren, 1187 MDW

Today, I will test my luck in summoning a "Pure Clone". Allegedly, it is the art of combining clone magic with Blood Conjuration.

...

2nd of Mitoren, 1187 MDW

Yesterday was a complete disaster! Not only did I fail to summon a clone, but I also lost both my hands and legs in the process. Here I was, only a torso and a head, bleeding out gallons and gallons of blood into the ground. I was about to die. With no other choice I risked it all with the master spell of Abjuration – Rehabilitation, to regrow my limbs. It worked well, though my body feels incredibly heavy for some reason.

...

14th of Jien, 1188 MDW

I am growing more and more tired by the days. I find it difficult to sleep sufficiently.

...

10th of Severen, 1189 MDW

My condition worsens and I find it incredibly hard to stand up, let alone run. Also, I found a lot of hair on my pillow. Am I balding?

...

18th of Sakuyen, 1191 MDW

I am now completely bald! Not a single strand of hair is left on my body, including my head. I don't know what to do. People tell me I look pale. Am I ill? What is happening to me? I must visit my family in the village tomorrow. How do I hide my condition?

...

5th of Aven, 1194 MDW

I feel like I am dying. I don't want my life to end. I cannot sleep. I cannot eat. I cannot walk normally. This is no life... My condition prevents me from using magic, thus rendering my time with The Order obsolete. What should I do? I don't think my brother is suspicious, but suspicion will surely arise eventually. What should I do? What shou– [turned into gibberish]

...

28th of Aven, 1197 MDW

I am starting to consider asking Lul for help. Maybe Vaonical cults have special healing methods? Oh, who am I kidding? They will probably demand me to join them. This will not fly! Or will it? It is not a question of risking my mortality anymore, for I will surely die soon.

Maybe I am supposed to join them? Maybe that is part of my destiny? To live more? See more? What would I lose in exchange? My emotions? My pride? My values? I fear I will never get the answers I seek without bearing the consequences. Either I die, and my journey ends, or I ask them for assistance. But... what value does anything I've ever achieved have if I perish this way?

What would my family think of me? What would the village think of me? Probably that I really am that "rogue" who decided to ditch his father's role to explore the world like a spoilt child. Veridia will probably tell her brother, "I told you so." Why do I deserve this? I worked so hard to experience and see as much as I could.

I forewent my claim to the throne in favor of my brother, so that I might pursue my dreams. Was that so bad? So bad that I am now forced to choose between physical death and potential mental death? To choose between losing all I've had and joining the forces of evil?

This decision is tough to bear. It is an ultimatum given to me by the gods. An adventurer, dying because of greed and selfish lust. What a cliche. So terribly pathetic. Why is this happening? I don't want to do this. I really don't. I detest this idea. I resent that it is my only one. I loathe that my incompetence in magic has resulted in this situation.

What pains me the most is that I will never see my beloved again, even on my deathbed. It all came to place. The coward pays the price for his cowardice, how fitting. Love did not win.

...

30th of Aven, 1197 MDW

I have no other choice. I will head to Lul's clan and ask for assistance. Perhaps they would help me without expecting anything in return? Is that possible?

...

12th of Ruyen, 1197 MDW

The Vampires agreed to heal me but only in exchange for information. The healing demands my transformation into a Vaermiraiit. This path seems my sole recourse. Without it, I fear I shall not live to see Yaruven. Yet I ponder, what knowledge do they seek in exchange? I must tread carefully, lest I lose myself in pursuit of survival.

...

15th of Ruyen, 1198 MDW

I have uncovered knowledge that Lysander, the Vampire leader, seeks – the precise location, date, and hour of the Hekket Trials. My younger brother is to host this event. I ponder the vampires' intent as they are surely vile. Maybe they plan to raid and slaughter all present, my kin included.

My heart grows heavy with this burden. To betray my blood or withhold this information from Lysander – both paths lead to peril. I must choose wisely, for the consequences shall be dire. May the gods grant me wisdom in this hour of need.

...

20th of Ruyen, 1198 MDW

I fear there is no other choice. I must tell Lysander the details of the trials. I apologize, Aeden. I am sorry, Elyis, Veridia. Forgive me, Alduin. Forgive me.

...

21st of Ruyen, 1198 MDW

On this day, I have struck a bargain most foul with Lysander. In two years' time, ere the Hekket Trials commence, I shall be turned into a creature of the night. Though I beseeched him to spare my kin, he refused all but my nephews. Their lives hang upon a test called "Vaonie's Necklace", which I swore they would pass.

The vampire general Gozo shall orchestrate this grim affair, disguising it as mere happenstance. My heart weighs heavy, yet I cling to the hope that my nephews shall live.

Lysander spoke of "Royal Vaermiraiit Blood", a draught that shall elevate me to a high-tier vampire. The price of power is steep indeed, paid in the blood of my own flesh and blood.

May the gods forgive me for what I have wrought

...

27th of Ruyen, 1220 MDW
Tomorrow my nephew will finally attend the Hekket trials, ignorant of the upcoming tragedy. I am so sorry. I love you.

...

29th of Ruyen, 1220 MDW
This day marks the end of all I once knew. My village lies in ruin, and with it, the nearby Snow Elf settlements that once thrived. I fear I have brought about the extinction of my own kind.

Yesterday, I drew my final mortal breath, only to rise anew as a Vaermiraiit. The vampires now claim me as their own, promising to instruct me in their dark arts and Blood Magic.

My body, once frail and dependent on a cane, now pulses with unnatural vigour. Yet this newfound health comes at a terrible cost.

I had no choice. Death's cold embrace loomed ever near, and I recoiled from it. May those who come after understand the desperation that drove me to this. I beg forgiveness, though I know I deserve none.

The weight of my deeds shall haunt me for all eternity.

...

3rd of Luyaren, 1220 MDW

It appears I was lied to, as Lysander told me no one had survived the attack. I... What have I done? An end to my family because of a single love story. Really, Ley? Are you serious? How fucking childish can you be?!

Also, there is no such thing as "Royal Vaermiraiit Blood". I am the exact same as the rest of them. They will pay for this. I have already defeated Gozo in a duel; how hard could killing Lysander be? I will rise through the ranks and rule them all!

...

30th of Severen, 1238 MDW

I heard Vaonie found a new Lodus, a new

Araqhaiit, to replace the one who fell. The new cham-
pion was allegedly chosen from the vampires of this
very clan, I wonder who they might be... Will I ever
meet them?

...

11th of Sakuyen, 1264 MDW
I killed that fucking liar, Lysander, and it took
everything I had! Blood Conjuration, Pure Clones,
Blood Telekinesis, everything there was to know. I
have mastered every single type of magic there is. I
am the most powerful, the strongest being. ALL
SHALL FEAR ME. ALL SHALL OBEY ME. I WILL
GET THAXIOBOS BACK. THOSE FUCKING
BASTARDS WILL PAY.

...

'

Alduin threw it on the ground and stomped on it
angrily. Suddenly, he folded up his right sleeve to reveal a
silver bracelet. He took it off and threw it on Ley's body.
'You fucking bastard, I loved you! How could... How
could...' He spat on his corpse and turned around.

He stared at Hanali, frowning. She said nothing. He
showed her the way out of the cave while she was telling
him about the origin of Olana[ii], its purpose, and its restric-

---

[ii] (Omnitongue) Justice, the Void Realm.

tions. Only pure divines could exit it, and only The Originals possessed the power to pull someone out. He suddenly realized convincing Vaonie to bring him back must have taken a lot of effort, so he thanked her once again. They finally reached the exit

'Hanali,' he muttered.

'Yes?'

'I met a powerful person in Olana, a man my uncle had met long ago. He shares my ambition for justice. I would like Vaonie to bring him back.'

'Why?'

'He is the only Merarian left in Vanthea, perhaps he could undo the extinction of his kind. And he is talented, I believe his research could improve the life of mortals.'

'Well, Alduin, with all due respect... Why should I care about all that? Humans were made to figure things out by themselves. They may appreciate his help but certainly not need it... It would take them a lot more time, sure. But it simply isn't a must. I'm sorry, I won't be bringing this up to my creator. You can do it yourself if you so wish...'

'I see, alright, I'll see what I can do. Thank you nonetheless.'

'Gladly.'

'I'll see you later,' Alduin smiled.

"Alligator."

'What? Where are you going?' Hanali asked, her mouth turning into a frown.

'To Tyronah[iii].'

---

iii (Omnitongue) Hell.

'What for?'

'To take care of what we've just talked about.'

'So soon? You just came back. In addition, the concept of time doesn't exist in Olana, it would technically never be too late…'

'I want to get it done. I'm sorry.'

She scoffed, 'pfft… Fine, good luck convincing Vaonie.'

He waved her goodbye and put on the ring Lysander had given him.

'Farewell,' she sulked and sighed.

'Los ant di Tyronah[iv],' he chanted and was transported to Vaonie's court. He bowed immediately.

'Look what we have here… How can one man cause me so much trouble, huh?'

'I am sorry to disappoint you, lord.'

'Honestly, it baffles me how pathetic you can be.'

'I deserve that.'

'Give me one reason why I shouldn't just kill you right here and look for a more suitable replacement…'

'Frankly, I have none. You have saved my life many times already and have spared me even more times than that.'

'Exactly.'

'But still.'

'Still what?'

'I am already trained, and your daughter trusts me. She joined your side because of me. I deserve your support.'

Vaonie growled dismissively.

---

iv (Omnitongue) (To) take me to Hell.

'Nevertheless, I come to you with a request.'

'Another one?'

'Yes, lord.'

'The audacity! How dare you ask for more favours, especially after all that my daughter had given for your foolishness?'

'I merely ask for a favor that would be in your great benefit,' Alduin bowed again.

'What could you possibly give me? You couldn't even defeat a lowly vampire,' Vaonie bellowed.

'I...' He recalled his encounter with Ley and his face turned sour.

'You what? Want me to save that friend of yours, from Olana?'

'Y-Yes, lord,' he stuttered.

'Why would I do that exactly?'

'Because I believe his body has intertwined with one of your artifacts, one your demons could not find.'

'How so?'

'Apparently, he found one of them on planet Memrin. When I fought him, I felt an odd resemblance in his aura to yours... That alone should suffice as a reason. Also, I plan to persuade him to fight in your name, alongside me. He could be of great asset to you.'

'And why is that?'

'He can move incredibly fast.'

'What use do I have with a swift sprinter? You insult me.'

'He isn't just *fast*, he is much more than that. I was not able to defeat him, not even with my flames.'

'That shouldn't be possible.'

'He was so quick my eyes couldn't trace him. Think of the possibilities…'

Vaonie tapped the arms of their throne with two fingers, pondering. 'What if he refuses to follow me? I do not desire another project like you.'

'Kill him if he refuses.'

'Alright. Don't fail me, Alduin. Your life is on the line; don't forget it. Also, I have another condition that he must accept.'

'What is it?'

'When I finally recover of all the artifacts, he must sacrifice himself so I can escape this prison.'

'Agreed.'

Vaonie summoned Han with a nod and sigh. Alduin beheld him in color for the first time: tanned and bearded, with short brown hair. His royal attire consisted of a silver-adorned blue shirt, dark-brown leather, and a gleaming blue gem set in his belt. Navy-blue leather pants and sandals completed the ensemble, topped with a magnificent silver amulet, arm bracelets, and rings.

Han's eyes shifted hues with his movements: green when hastening, red when slowing, and ocean blue when still. The colours shifted and flickered, ever-changing, never the same – except for when he didn't move for more than a second. As if his body were glitching – a living bug in the system.

Initially refusing to join the 'evil' forces, Han relented after hours of Alduin's persuasion. Exhausted, Vaonie transported them back to Vanthea.

Stranded on a Syluetta island, they conversed at length. Han rejected murdering innocents or inventing diseases. Alduin proposed destruction through noble means: toppling oppressive empires and leaders, dismantling concepts mortals deemed necessary despite their detrimental effects.

They clasped hands, uniting to overthrow mankind's tyranny and the commonplace evil. Thus, 'Forespoken Judgement' was born – the name they gave themselves.

EPILOGUE

A few months passed, and Alduin turned eighteen. He and Han grew close, exchanging knowledge—technology and culture from Han's time with Ley, and in return, Alduin tutored him in magic. Though despite their bond they rarely saw eye to eye, debating worldviews, philosophies, and stories.

Once released back into Vanthea they each returned to planet Syluetta – Han to the deserted oceanic kingdom of Xierēnia, where he published his book – 'The Mystery of Olana[i], and Alduin to Euphata.

He took Hanali to his village – what little remained of it. Ruins stretched before them; the earth stained with old, dry blood. Nothing resembled what it once was. He sat among the wreckage, lost in memory, the ghosts of his family lingering in the silence.

---

i   (Omnitongue) Justice, the Void Realm.

He built a small bonfire, the flames crackling softly, and stared into them, finding solace in their dance. If only for a moment.

'Alduin, I need to talk to you about something...' Hanali said.

He turned to face her. 'Sure. What is it?'

'I-I wanted to talk to you about your return from Olana,' she sat in front of him.

'What do you mean?'

'My leg and arm weren't the only things I sacrificed for Vaonie's forgiveness. I also made them a promise.'

'What?' he raised his eyebrows in shock, 'that wasn't enough for them?'

'Let me finish!' She kicked the ground.

He nodded, setting a kettle of water and leaves over the fire. Once ready, he poured himself a cup and offered her one. She refused.

'It's not that I sacrificed something else. Well... Please don't get mad ...'

'I will not.'

'Promise me you won't. I'd never have done this if it weren't my last resort. I swear it.'

'Relax... I promise.'

'Well... Uhm... I...'

'Yes?'

'I vowed we'd bring new divines to Vaonie's side. There, I said it.' She let out a shaky breath, shoulders sagging as if a weight had been lifted. 'Gods, that was hard to admit.'

'What do you mean? I don't understand.'

'You know...'

'I really don't.'

'Come on...' She hesitated, too embarrassed to say it, then gave him a playful but awkward punch on the shoulder, her gaze flickering away.

'Ouch, that actually hurt!' he teased, clutching his shoulder with an exaggerated wince before letting out a mock sob.

She rolled her eyes with a smirk. 'Pfft.'

He chuckled. 'Come on, tell me. I'm curious.'

'Pfft... Silly mortal.' She waved a hand dismissively. 'Right, okay. It means we are to breed.'

Alduin choked mid-sip, spraying his drink as he coughed violently. 'We are to WHAT?!' he sputtered, eyes wide in disbelief.

'Make offspring together.'

'How? What? Why? When? You,' he pointed at her, 'and me?' he pointed at himself.

'Yes. Are you that against the idea?' she frowned.

'No, no, it's not that,' he said. 'I just didn't know divines could procreate.'

'They can't.'

'You lost me there,' he said, scratching his head, his eyes narrowing as he looked at her, trying to piece together what she meant.

'*You* are not divine...'

'Oh. Right... But *you* are...'

'Yes.'

'So?'

'I am different from my siblings.'

'How so?'

'I was the first divine child, a prototype for the others. When Austomia created the mortals, they borrowed traits from my design...'

'Like which?'

'Apparently, emotion, insecurity, depression... I never realized I had any of that before meeting *you*. A mortal. Before, I just ignored my feelings, brushing them off as nuisances. But you made me see them differently. You taught me how to deal with them.' She looked away briefly, fidgeting with her fingers.

'Is that a good thing?'

'It's a wonderful thing!'

'Are there any other similarities between the mortals and you?'

'The ability to procreate.'

'You... can give birth?'

'Kind of, yes. Though it's not as painful for me, and it takes much less time—only a day or so.'

'I see.'

'Well? I'm sorry for telling you this now. I was too embarrassed before... I regret putting you in this position. I vowed it to Vaonie, and I can't take it back. I'm sorry.' She lowered her head, avoiding his gaze, her shoulders slumped in apology.

He looked away, hesitant. 'Should I?' he asked himself, tapping his knees with the palms of his hands.

He turned back to face her. He tilted his head forward as he brushed his fingers across the curve of her jaw, bringing her face closer to his. His pulse raced as his mouth covered her. Their lips melded together in a deep embrace.

He slowly eased his lips and fingers from her. Hanali's breath caught in her throat. A true kiss this time. Her cheeks turned pink. She was both confused and intrigued as she felt a warm flutter in her chest and her heart hammered, 'w-what? What did you just do?'

'Something I should have done a long time ago. And, I have something to tell you as well.'

'What is it?' her lashes lowered slightly as she locked her gaze with his.

Alduin's voice cracked as he pushed the massive words through his throat. 'I love you.'

'Y-You do? Since when?'

'For a long time already. Almost a year.'

'Really?' she whispered, her eyes set on the hollow of his throat where his pulse fluttered. A hot shiver ran through her. "Why?" she breathed.

'When I am with you, I feel like I am healing. I no longer feel like broken merchandise; too damaged to be of value. You treat me well despite how complicated I am. You didn't give up on me. Without you, I would have surely sunk into the void of my own subconscious. Of my own trauma.'

'I-... I don't know what to say.'

'It's okay. You don't have to say it back.' Alduin released a shaky breath.

'No, listen! It's not like that, I swear.' Her face flushed bright pink as she inhaled. 'I just don't know what love feels like, or how to identify it. The only thing I can say for sure is that when I'm with you, or when I hear you speak, I feel strange things. Things that I have never felt before. ' She clasped her hand over her heart. 'I feel peaceful.'

'I have an offer for you then.' His tone softened and his eyes widened in a love-struck gaze.

'What is it?' reflexively, she wet her lip in anticipation.

'How about we discover what those strange feelings of yours mean, together?'

'Whatever do you mean by that?' she rubbed the tingling goosebumps on her arms.

'We are to breed, right? What do you feel about changing the word *breed* to *starting a family*?'

'Like marriage?'

'No, that would require way too much bureaucracy and a silly religious ceremony.' Alduin clasped both of his hands to his chest. 'We could simply start a family together without it.'

'I see.' Hanali leaned closer to him.

'What do you say?'

'It wouldn't hurt to try.'

'It wouldn't.'

'So... Do we just do it?' Hanali asked.

'Do what?'

'Have sex, I mean...' She said and shyly played with her hair.

'Not yet,' he said.

'Hmm?' her brows furrowed.

'I wish to rebuild my village first, create a home for us— one where our first child can grow up.'

'Alright.'

They wrapped their arms around each other, clinging tightly, savouring the promise of togetherness. Slowly, they pulled back, standing with relaxed arms at their sides, smiles wide enough to crinkle their eyes. Their cheeks flushed with warmth, their eyes soft and sparkling—an expression foreign to them both.

With the first matter settled, Alduin finished the last of his tea, set the cup down, and stood.

'Can I help?' Hanali clasped her hands together in supressed excitement.

'How?'

'I can travel back in time to see how it once looked, then return and restore it with my magic.'

'Oh, alright then.' Alduin flashed a grin and a brisk nod. 'I will be in charge of repopulating the village.' He watched as she tilted her head slightly, her gaze narrowing as if failing to comprehend. 'You will see,' he said with a mischievous glint in his eyes.

'Okay.'

They leaned in, lips meeting in a soft pop as their warmth mingled. He inhaled deeply, savouring her scent, the familiar comfort of vanilla and that he adored. As their kiss deepened, his own fragrance—the crisp mint and grounding cedarwood that clung to his skin—wove into hers, creating a new, intoxicating accord.

Hanali parted her lips from his and smiled. 'I'll be back soon,' she whispered as she vanished in a shimmer.

Even though she left the air still thrummed with her presence, a ghostly caress of scent that lingered on his lips, a promise of her return.

Alduin blinked, his jaw slackening and his brows arched. Then, the tension eased from his face, turning into a serene smile. He focused, activating his aura-sensing ability.

Within minutes, Edward's presence pulsed in his mind. Without hesitation, Alduin teleported to him, appearing suddenly before the startled vampire.

'What are you doing here? Did you change your mind? Are you here to kill me?' Edward's voice shook, his body tense, hands instinctively raising as if to shield himself. His wide, panicked eyes darted around, searching for escape.

'Don't worry, I will not harm you,' Alduin replied, his voice calm but firm. 'I am here to offer you a chance – a chance for a new life. Join me.'

'Excuse me?'

'I am rebuilding my village and wish to bring in all the orphans from the city. I want you to be their mentor, their godfather. To train them to fight for me as their lord.'

'You wish to become a vampire clan chief?'

'Not a *vampire* clan chief, a regular one. A leader of an army in Vanthea. It just so happens that the entirety of the clan would be vampires,' Alduin said and winked.

'Uh-huh.'

'What say you?'

'Sure, I'll do it. Where will we live, though? Vampires are weak to the cold.'

'The Euphatan weather would help to restrain their chaotic nature. No longer will vampires raid, pillage and torture the innocent.' Alduin's eyes sparkled.

'Huh? What would you have them do instead?'

'Raiding, pillaging and torturing the *guilty*, of course.' He chuckled, 'killing, slaughtering and feeding on mortals that simply shouldn't exist. The bad ones, evil ones. Rapists, thieves, murderers, liars, and the like.'

'A bit drastic, don't you think? You're talking about a lot of mortals,' Edward said, his voice unsteady, his eyes flicking nervously around the room as he took a small step back.

'More than I could count, yes. I deem it necessary. Ridding Vanthea of evil *is* necessary.' Alduin put a reassuring hand on Edward's shoulder, 'We'll do it together, as a team.'

Edward hesitated for a moment, his eyes darting as he weighed the situation. Finally, he nodded, though his voice was uncertain. 'Fine then. I'll pack my things... and see you there.'

'Right on.' Alduin's voice was steady, and with a firm grip, he clasped Edward's forearm in a warrior's embrace, his gaze steady and filled with respect. 'Farewell, my friend.' He released him, their brief connection lingering in the silence that followed.

Alduin vanished into thin air, leaving Edward standing, fazed but intrigued. The idea of a vampire clan fighting evil excited him. After all, no evil can be condemned without another evil, and only evil can recognize evil's true capabilities.

'"You can't fight fire with fire, my ass.' I, the writer, said in my mind as I wrote this."

Alduin reappeared in the city, running through each building, seeking out the children. He barely recognized them, as they were already feasting on their families. Such cannibalism could only be driven by extreme hunger. Alduin spoke to them, explaining his intentions. Most accepted his offer—food, shelter, and water. Survival, after all, was instinct. Those who refused were likely dead by now.

Once the orphans were settled and given directions to their new homes, Alduin teleported back to the village.

'Oh my god! Evis tesferti[ii].' His voice cracked with joy.

Before him stood the completely rebuilt village of Aldu, just as he remembered it. Every detail flooded back: the familiar smells, the sounds, the tastes, the way everything looked. A single tear escaped, trailing down his cheek, dripping onto the earth below.

Hanali stood by the gate, her gaze proud, waiting for his reaction. 'Well?' she asked, a soft smile tugging at her lips.

'I love it! I love it, evisi[iii]!' His eyes sparkled, his whole face lighting up as he took in the sight. He rushed to her, his heart pounding.

Hanali's smile deepened, her warmth radiating through her. 'I'm glad,' she said, her voice soft and tender.

In a blur of motion, he cupped her face, pulling her close. 'Evisi.' He kissed her deeply, his lips trembling with the weight of his feelings.

She melted into him, her arms wrapping around his neck, pulling him tighter as if she could never let go. They held each other, their embrace a wordless promise, a shared joy in their love and the life they were building.

'What do you think of my beard, by the way? I decided to grow it,' Alduin said.

'It gives you an air of maturity. I like it.'

[ii] (Elvish) Thank god.
[iii] (Elvish) Thanks.

'Thank you. I always had such a baby face. Finally, I found a way to look my age,' he laughed.

'You were handsome even before,' she said, her voice soft and warm, her eyes lingering on him as if she were seeing him for the first time all over again.

'Thank you,' he smiled and caressed her right cheek.

Over the next few days, more orphaned children arrived at the village. Hanali welcomed each one, guiding them through their new home. Edward joined them after a week, settling in quickly. His role wasn't just to teach the children to fight and survive, but also to protect the village and enforce Alduin's laws within its walls.

The children grew quickly, transitioning to skilled fighters, mages, and scholars. They became cooks, tutors, guards, farmers, and shopkeepers. The village flourished, still known as 'Vel Tissia Ke Aldu[iv]', but its clan now bore a new name: 'Vel Vestinde Aqat[v]'. The banner featured the image of Acaroth – Alduin's mount.

Alduin earned a nickname from passing travellers and rumors – 'Whitefire.' With his Snow Elf heritage and piercing red eyes, people mistook him for a vampire, and he preferred it that way. Hanali had insisted that his true identity remain a secret to the mortals.

The village was alive with the sounds of laughter, the smells of fresh food, and the bustling energy of its people. It was everything he had dreamed of, except for one last

---

[iv] (Elvish) The Tree of Hope.
[v]   (Elvish) The Silver Fox.

thing. Though a few days later, it had finally come. And its name was...

'Cylie[vi]', as Alduin was given back the time he had lost in the cellar. She would be his continuation, protected from the evils of this world.

Cylie Faëli.

TO BE CONTINUED.

'So... What do you think?' Tal said and leaned back in his chair, before checking his phone for new messages.

'Hmm... I like it, but do you reckon it'd be interesting enough for a book?' Mordechai asked.

'I have absolutely no idea.'

They both laughed.

'Tal, Mordechai, Leshem, Shoham, Yaara, it's time for Kiddush!' the voice of Tal's mother suddenly echoed from downstairs.

'Coming,' Tal replied, locking eyes with his cousin. Without a word, they exchanged a shared understanding, their eyes lighting up with excitement. 'It's time for Grandma's Couscous!' their hearts rejoiced.

[vi] (Elvish) Time.

Elvish Dictionary

Elvish	English
Acaroth	Revenge
Aldu	Peace
Alis	Light
Alit	Rainbow
Anot	Invisible
Aqat	Fox
Cylie	Time
Dunbar	Asshole
Evisi	Thanks
Fa	Forest
Heel	Water
Heelisa	Tsunami
Hekket	Special Forces (Snow Elf)
Henna	Heaven
Hetla	Universe
Joog	Great
Kaban	Blood
Ke	Of
Lune	Goddess of the night
Madaran	Mountain
Mer	Coffee
Merissa	Goddess of the sun
M'falnar	God of death
Munesa	Hell
Neyla	Solar System
O	And
Odrum	God of nature
Resnem	Horizon
Sala	Galaxy
Srynaia	Goodbye
Tanla	Planet
Tesferti	God
Tissia	Tree
Vel	The
Veridia	Hope
Vestinde	Silver
Vo	My
Yasa	Beer
Zaffai	Deceit
Zul	Good
Zuuvi	Dear

Omnitongue Dictionary

Omnitongue	English	Omnitongue	English
An	I	Ophiin	Honesty
Anor	Leadership	Pavette	Path
Ant	Me	Pheolet	Fox
Araqhaiit	Impure Divine	Pholexu	Humility
Astrugiel	Peace	Platir	Spear
Ayurë	Curiosity	Pol	White
Balerisa	Blade	Qulteba	Family
Benejil	(To) heal	Sal	Silver
Cent	Castle	Samarice	Gold
Cillie	Time	Sarathiin	Pure divine
Deovhaiit	Demon	Sav'ul	Army
Di	To	Senkel	Ball
Din	The	Sent	(To) be
Dreem	(To) disappear	Serandi	Spike
Fema	Equality	Set	Around
Feni	(To) form	Sner	Forest
Fennen	Follower	Talismirit	Name of the first element
Gonuiel	Gratitude	Te	In
Hanali	Loyalty	Temas	(To) come
Heonmeyu	Heaven	To	a (something)
Jaone	Generosity	Tubiri	(To) go
Jerda	Amulet	Tvek	Body
Jul	Sky	Tyl	New
Kans	Empathy	Tyrewhiin	Angel
Ke'ev	Thanks	Tyronah	Hell
Kentri	(To) detect	U	Of
Kyyn	Courage	Ulat	Fast
La	Lord	Uli	Ice
Leil	Light (weight)	Vaermiraiit	Vampire
Lodus	Honor	Veridia	Earth
Los	(To) take	Vetir	(To) call
Nasyryl	Magical bear native to Heonmeyu	Yorda	Wave
Nir	Up	Yul	You
Nor	(To) release	Yur	Mark
Nye	Mount		
Obliryne	Flame		
Olana	Justice		
Olon	Particle		
Oniya	Blood		

After You Read

This story is something I started working on at the age of eight with my cousin (Mordechai Hadad), who has become my greatest friend. It all started with us buying LEGOs and making up backstories, powers, family trees, etc., for each character and then expanding the lore as we bought more and more LEGO sets.

When we both reached the age of eighteen, we decided to work on our lore more professionally and maybe even produce it in some artistic way, like a video game or a TV show. I hope you've enjoyed this product of my imagination!

SPECIAL THANKS

I would like to convey my gratitude to the following people:

Mordechai Hadad, for being my best friend, and also for helping me come up with the nearly infinite wonders of Vanthea.

Maor Yosef, for reading my book thoroughly to try and find typos, grammar mistakes, loopholes or just things that made no sense.

Cornelia Amiri, for being an incredible editor and helping me hone my writing skills.

My parents, for always being there for me and pushing me to make a name for myself.

You, for having read this :)

www.ingramcontent.com/pod-product-compliance
Lightning Source LLC
Chambersburg PA
CBHW070742160726
48004CB00001B/14